MEET KIDDIE. . .

The next morning Kiddie sighed heavily as she gingerly rolled over in bed, fluffing her pillow to prop her head up more. Her head was throbbing, but Kiddie regretted nothing. Her headache would move on, but her memories created yesterday would last forever. She wasn't a teenager anymore and would stoically take responsibility for her actions, particularly when it involved champagne, among other things. Kiddie smiled to herself as she closed her eyes to relish in the other things.

MEET THE MAJOR. . .

Another thought crossed the Major's mind as the cab drove him into Manhattan. It was time for his mother to meet Kiddie. Commencement would take care of that, but what would his mother think of Kiddie? He knew his mother expected him to come home to Missouri, even if he lived in St. Louis like Uncle Crutch, but he wasn't headed home anytime soon. He loved the energy of New York. His job with the *New York Times* was the tip of the iceberg for him, knowing soon enough he would be writing his own sports stories. New York was his home now, and he frowned slightly at the possibility his mother would blame Kiddie for him staying in New York. He would see to it that she didn't. His mother was important to him, but he loved Kiddie. It might be awhile, but he was going to marry Miss Kiddie Kolle.

Des-
The author of this book was
a first grade teacher with me at
Derby Ridge. She retired and is
following her dreams— Just like
you. Congrats on your RN!
Wishing you all the best for
future dream chasing. ♡ -Rebecca

Kiddie & the Major

Elaine Corum Strawn

Always wishing you the best in
your pursuit of happiness!
Happy reading!
♡ Elaine

Kiddie & the Major
© 2021 Off & Running Publications

While this is a work of fiction, this story includes actual people and real events. I've worked to make it as authentic as possible by drawing from a number of sources including, but not limited to Bill Corum's book "Off and Running" published in 1959. I have given some characters in the story nicknames to respect their privacy. Although I worked hard to keep this book as authentic as possible, please know I've woven fiction into every detail to create this remarkable story of Kiddie and the Major. Enjoy.

Paperback ISBN: 978-1-7343673-2-4

Cover design by Alexandria Rogers
Interior design by Liz Schreiter

Join our conversation on social media as we share photos, recipes, and the truths and wishful thinking from *Kiddie & the Major*.

@off.and.running

@offandrunningpublications

@offandrunning_

OffandRunningPublications.com

Contact the author at strawnelaine@gmail.com

THIS BOOK IS DEDICATED TO MY HUSBAND JOE, FOR
ALL HE HAS BEEN AND TO OUR DAUGHTERS, HANNAH
AND GRACIE, FOR ALL THEY WILL BE.

LAST TO MY GRANDPARENTS, ELAINE, BILL, AUDREY, AND
GEORGE. ALL BECAUSE TWO PEOPLE FELL IN LOVE.

PROLOGUE

— APRIL 1953 —

I t was time to go. It was still very early in the morning, but now it was time. He had left her hundreds of times over the years. It was his job to show up front and center whether it was ringside or at the track or in a baseball stadium. As usual, he had a train to catch, people waiting, another story to write.

Of all the times he had to leave her, this was by far the hardest. He was afraid of what would happen when he was gone. He wanted to believe that as long as he was by her side, he could keep the inevitable away. It broke his heart that his head told him he could not. He needed more time, more time to make up for the missed birthdays, anniversaries, and all the little things in between. He had missed so much. She rarely seemed to hold it against him, and he knew she continued to share stories about her "Major," even if it had been weeks since they saw each other. He was grateful they wrote letters over the years, and knew that would be his saving grace in the weeks ahead—a part of her he would always have.

He lifted her pale, thin hand and kissed her palm, looking deep into her face. Despite time and sickness, hers was still the most beautiful face he had ever known. Throughout his career, he came to know many famous faces from the sports world to Hollywood. Those faces blurred in his memory now as he gazed into hers. He loved her laugh lines. He liked to think he was responsible for some of them, albeit not so many recently. Her laughter in a room could draw anyone's attention.

Her gorgeous brown eyes had caused him to pause on more than one occasion. She used them in a variety of ways without even realizing it. When she had to be on good behavior for formal events, she sometimes seemed to share a private joke on the speaker, laughing with him through her eyes. After a long night of dinner and dancing, she would beckon him to come closer with her eyes. A night of too many cocktails could lead to anger flashing in her eyes. But that stoic, lonely look in her eyes when he would kiss her farewell, off to write his next story, often caused him a painful pause.

He was grateful to not see his sadness reflected in her eyes now. She lay sleeping peacefully, aided by a morphine drip. He wanted to believe she knew he was there. He had come in the middle of the night, long after visiting hours were over. He wanted to be certain no one else would be there, not wanting to make small talk, share his sadness, or to be judged. He gently kissed her forehead, cheek, and lips. For the last time he whispered, "until next time my love." He had no choice, it was time to go.

After catching the train on it's final call, he settled into his seat and laid his head back to rest his eyes. He knew it was time to wrap his head around baseball's spring season, but struggled to shake her from his thoughts. He didn't resist as his thoughts carried him back through the years. With no effort at all he remembered the first time he met her, the first time he said hello to Kiddie.

CHAPTER ONE
=1920=

K iddie stood up to stretch and let her skirt fall back to her knees. She had been sitting at the table in the library working on her essay for over an hour. Her professor had given her class the task of comparing the work of two favorite artists. An elementary assignment, Kiddie mentally scolded herself for spending so much time on the three page essay. But still, she needed perfection.

She smiled as she reread what she had written. Her professor would not be expecting her two choices. Her first choice was Edgar Degas— somewhat cliche—but Kiddie had always loved his work. As a little girl, she grew up with two Degas ballerina paintings hanging in her room. She knew Degas was regarded as one of the founders of Impressionism, although he rejected the title. Like so many other artists, she had learned that Degas led a life full of drama and turmoil. She loved how Degas had not limited his talent to a mere paintbrush, but was also known for his sculptures and even photography in his later years. Degas's quote "Art is not what you see, but what you make others see" rang true for Kiddie, especially as it related to one sculpture in particular. *Little Dancer* spoke to her and where she was in her own life. Kiddie had an eagerness to learn and share her passions with the world, but feared rejection and judgement from others. Kiddie had left her connection out of her essay—too personal for her to admit on a piece of paper.

Degas's multifaceted talent brought Kiddie to her other favorite artist, an amatuer, her father. While her father's passion revolved around medicine, he occasionally loved to explore his creative side. Her father was a painter as well as an inventor, an author, and occasionally a different character altogether when he had performed on stage at Prospect Hall. Kiddie loved that he knew no boundaries and simply lived life to the fullest. She couldn't wait to embrace the opportunities life had in store for her.

Kiddie glanced at the clock, fearful she was about to miss one such opportunity. She quickly stacked the books she was using into a neat pile and slid her papers into her bag. She left the table just as she had found it, ready for the next student to embrace whatever assignment brought them to the library.

She raced down the stairs, and headed for the doors. Just as she reached for the door, a voice said, "Allow me, mademoiselle." The man politely opened the door, holding it for her as she rushed through.

Not wanting to be late, she quickly replied over her shoulder, "Merci, Monsieur." She was so intent on getting down Morningside quickly, she did not even notice the man seemed to be following her.

She heard the cheering before seeing the cause of it, knowing she was not too late and most likely had only missed Presidential Candidate James Cox's introduction. She was pleased to see nearly as many women as men present at the rally. Like her, they were here because women had finally won the right to vote. Kiddie was excited her first opportunity to vote would be such a historical occasion, as the country elected a new president in a few short months. She was realistic in that Cox would have a hard time getting elected on his democratic platform, keeping him tied to President Wilson. She was happy Wilson was out, even if he liked to think it was due to his stroke. He did not support the 19th Amendment and for Kiddie, that was reason enough for him to be done.

She tried to focus on what Mr. Cox was saying. She didn't take her right to vote lightly and wanted to be an informed citizen. Kiddie appreciated that Cox was addressing women in his campaign, believing they should be interested in the election of Cox and Roosevelt. Not everyone recognized womens' value as citizens just yet. She watched as his running mate, Franklin D. Roosevelt stood stoically nodding in agreement with Mr. Cox's comments here and there. His plea for peace, combined with his promise for progress and prosperity seemed to be just what this group needed to hear. They cheered him on loudly as a strong breeze made the shadows dance among the tree lined sidewalk.

Although Kiddie would be a young voter, she often read the paper to be familiar with both candidates' platforms. She knew Harding preached a return to normalcy campaign from his front porch. She didn't care for the fact that he made voters come to him. Kiddie and her father would occasionally talk politics at the dinner table. She knew her father appreciated she cared enough to be educated, but also knew he believed she lacked life experience to give her a true picture of the world. Kiddie was indifferent to her sister Iris' eye rolling and long sighs as they bored her with their political conversations. Her father liked to play devil's advocate to the point that Kiddie was unsure who he would vote for. She wondered if it was to make sure she made her own choice or because he believed it wasn't really anyone's business to know.

Suddenly someone was speaking to her, handing her a scarf. "I believe this is yours," he said with a smile.

Kiddie immediately recognized him from the library doors. She took the scarf graciously, finding herself once again thanking him. Iris had given her the scarf for her birthday last summer and she would have been sad to have lost it. For some reason she found herself sharing this with the stranger.

She ended her story, then introduced herself. "I must have dropped it in my rush to be here. My name is Elaine. And you are?"

Cheerfully he introduced himself as "Major Martene Windsor Corum, here to be of service mademoiselle." He was somewhat short and stocky, but dressed handsomely in a suit and tie. She suddenly felt thankful she had put on her pink chiffon dress this morning. Pink was her favorite color and always brought out her stunning dark hair and rich brown eyes.

They both turned to look back at the stage as the crowd exploded with appreciation for Cox's final remarks. They maintained their position on the outskirts of the crowd as people dispersed, seemingly happy with what they had heard. Kiddie turned back to look into the man's face. "That's quite a name you have there. And you speak French?"

The Major smiled, "My friends call me Major. I learned enough French to get me by when I was stationed in France during World War I."

Kiddie smiled back, "My friends call me Kiddie. I'm taking a French class at Columbia this fall. You seem so young to already be a major. Or is that just what your friends call you?"

"Both," he said matter of factly. "I'm in the School of Journalism at Columbia. I left my books to do some real life learning and hear for myself what Mr. Cox is all about. I assume you plan to vote in November?"

"I do," Kiddie said matter of factly. "One can never be too informed when making such decisions as who will be our next president." Even as she said it, Kiddie regretted how prim and proper she sounded.

The Major smiled at her and merely said, "Touche.' Are you headed back to class?" When she nodded yes, he asked, " May I walk with you?"

While they walked along the campus, she asked him about his time in France. He shared with her about Nice, kind enough to leave the war details out. She dreamed of going to France someday, although certainly not during a war time. He said "au revoir," to her when they reached her French class. With a smile she waved so long, hoping it wasn't good-bye.

He signaled the bartender for another drink. After his last class he ventured to one of his favorite speakeasies for a steak dinner and a stiff drink. He could not shake Kiddie from his thoughts. He had first noticed her at the library a few weeks ago. He was surprised and delighted when fate had brought them together over a scarf. She seemed young compared to his twenty-seven years. But not too young. He was a long way from home, but she seemed right at home walking down

Morningside and along campus to class. He was a year out of the army since the war, focused on a degree in journalism. For him, it wasn't that hard. After fighting in a war, nothing is that hard. He was certain he was the oldest student living on campus. Sports events were one of his favorite perks of college life & he was happy to go any chance he got. He also always had time for good food, and a drink. Despite prohibition, there were plenty of drinks to be had in plenty of places in Manhattan.

She had said her name was Elaine, but her friends called her Kiddie. He liked how she had politely challenged him on being called Major. Coming from her, he didn't mind. It was true, at age twenty-three he was the youngest major to come out of WWI. He had worked hard in France to stay alive while getting the job done and get back to living the good life here in the states. Although in the end, he had found ways to enjoy France too.

He knew he must see Kiddie again. He assumed her class met every other day, he just had to show up where he had left her. But what to say to her when he saw her again? "Decided on who you're voting for yet?" No good. Even though she seemed young, she had confidence and poise too. She was clearly educated, and dressed from head to toe. He found every bit of her stunning. He had known plenty of girls in his time. He knew he was somewhat stout, but handsome enough. His charm made him popular with the ladies, but his cheerful and confident manner made him a friend to pretty much everyone he met. His deep, gravelly voice could turn heads in almost any room.

He didn't have a lot of dating experience, but it seemed forward to ask her out when he only knew her name. He needed a reason to get to know her better in a proper, socially acceptable way. It was 1920—a new era—but he remained old fashioned at heart. He also didn't want to scare her off. They were both college students, although he was far from fitting the norm. Somehow he felt that was true for her as well. It occurred to him who wouldn't love a football game on a beautiful fall day? Columbia's football team wasn't anything to write home about, but it was your typical collegiate activity boasting large, enthusiastic crowds. Confident in his plan, he finished his drink and tucked cash under his glass to pay the bill. He knew it wasn't the whiskey, but the anticipation of seeing Kiddie again that put a pep in his step as he started home.

I t was a beautiful October day, the kind where you're not sure if summer is coming or going. The sky was so blue, the sun warming him as he walked along the campus. He could see her sitting on the steps as he approached the building where she improved on her French. She was busy reading something, or pretending to be he hoped, waiting for him to show.

"Good afternoon, mademoiselle." he greeted her as she looked up.

She smiled and replied with, "Good afternoon, Monsieur." She stood up tucking her dark, short curls behind one ear.

"I hope I'm not too forward just showing up like this, but I wanted to see you again." He was sure of himself, but cautious of being rejected.

"I'm happy to see you. I forgot to properly thank you for returning my scarf." She hurriedly added, "So thank you."

He decided to jump in knowing she would need to be getting to class. "I wondered if you enjoy football by any chance? The Lions play Wesleyan on Saturday and I would like your company. If you're interested in that sort of thing." he added hastily.

"I've never been to a football game, but I would love to join you. You'll have to teach me about the sport. What time is the game? I can meet you at the South Field." She wasn't sure if he had a car and she didn't want to assume he would pick her up. Besides, getting picked up made it seem more like a date. She didn't know him well enough to go on such a date, but the game would be the perfect opportunity to get to know him better.

"Game time is 1:30. I can meet you at the library and we can walk over together?" He smiled, as she nodded yes.

"Perfect! I'll see you then," she said. He watched as she and her dark curls bounced up the rest of the stairs. She needed to get to class, but she stopped and turned to wave and give him a big smile before the door closed behind her. She was gone, but he was still smiling. There was something about that girl and he was happy to have a chance to find out what it was.

Iris sat on the end of the bed, dresses strewn all around her. Kiddie was trying to get ready for the football game, but never having been to one, was completely unsure of what to wear. She wanted to look pretty, but not like she was trying too hard. Columbia's school colors were blue and white so she had laid out every blue dress she owned. Iris was enjoying the show, although she was a bit surprised to see Kiddie a little undone by what to wear. It was only a football game after all and guys were always interested in Kiddie, regardless of what dress she wore. Iris decided to be helpful.

"This blue dress seems more like spring and the organza ruffles on this dress are too girly for a football game. And the low back on this dress will make it hard for the Major to focus on the game."

"It's silly I'm wearing a dress to a football game to begin with!" Kiddie exclaimed in frustration. "When will Coco Chanel start designing pants for women? I'll be first in line to buy them when she does!"

"That's just like you, ever the trendsetter." Iris said sweetly. Then in a more demanding tone, "Now choose already! You need to be leaving soon so you don't keep him waiting." Iris had to admit she was curious about this Major, who somehow had her sister more than a little out of sorts. "If you need me to go with you, I know exactly what I would wear!"

Kiddie paused for a moment from taking the dress off the hanger. Should she have Iris go with her? No, she wasn't a child who needed babysitting, especially by her younger sister. Ignoring Iris, she finished taking the dress off the hanger and pulled it over her head. She checked herself in the mirror, put on her favorite cloche hat and gave herself a nod of approval. Who wouldn't love her dark hair and brown eyes in this dress? It would have to do, for it was time to go.

S he saw him standing by the library stairs, waiting for her. She noticed he was dressed in a suit once again, but this time wearing a hat as well. She felt better about her dress choice, but wondered if he always wore a suit. Why not? she thought. She always seemed to be wearing a dress. It was another beautiful fall day and she was happy to have an excuse to be out and about on campus, especially with a well dressed, handsome man. Kiddie loved a new adventure.

He turned to greet her with a smile and a slight bow. Without even thinking about it, she put her arm in his, and asked, "Shall we go kick some Wesleyan butt?"

The Major roared with laughter, causing her to pause, but she relaxed when he said with gusto, "Absolutely!"

Kiddie's father had explained the basics of football to her at the dinner table the night before. She was happy to be at the game, learning for herself the details of when and why to cheer. Kiddie quickly learned real fans took the third down seriously, standing and making a racket to distract the other team. It was exciting to watch Wesleyan offense have to punt over and over again without a touchdown. It was slow going, but the Columbia Lions pulled off a win with two touchdowns, and held Wesleyan to only three points. Kiddie loved the competitive, loud cheering and had even hugged the Major in her excitement during the Lion's first touchdown.She was confident he didn't seem to mind.

"So who do the Lions play next week?" Kiddie asked as they were walking out of the stands. "New York University." the Major answered. "Care to join me next Saturday?" Kiddie didn't hesitate to think about it. "Of course!" For a moment their eyes locked.

Distracted by laughter, the Major turned to look back over his shoulder at his roommate Bob and his date catching up to them. Kiddie had learned that the Major and Bob lived in Livingston Hall and Bob was the graduate manager of athletics at Columbia. It was no wonder they had prime seating for the game! Turned out they were both avid sports fans. Kiddie was good with that. She didn't know a lot about sports, but she did occasionally join her father for a Giant's game and loved to swing a tennis racquet when she could.

"So where to now?" Bob asked. The Major turned to look at Kiddie, using his hands to ask if she wanted to join them.

"I'm starving!" said Kiddie. She had been so occupied with getting dressed she never really had lunch. It was too early for dinner, but still Kiddie thought food seemed like a safe next step for this "not on a date" afternoon. And she really was starving.

"I can always eat," the Major answered.

"Great!" said Bob. "Let's head out for some eats." The foursome headed down Morningside, easy enough to be in midtown Manhattan, close to campus. Kiddie was having the best day ever, feeling completely at home with the Major, safe in his presence, and excited to see where the rest of the afternoon would take them.

Soon enough the four of them were settled into a nice booth looking over their menus. The staff seemed to already know the Major, if not both boys, when they had walked in the place. Kiddie mentally checked the "boys" reference. Clearly she and the other girl were with men. A little shiver ran up Kiddie's young spine. She may still be a teenager, but she was happy to finally be out in the world, enjoying the good life. What would her mother say if she saw her sitting here?

The Major smiled at her over his menu. "Kiddie, everything they serve here is good. What will you have?"

Having given their orders to the server and taking care of formalities, they all settled back, sipping their drinks.

"Now that you can hear me, I'm Grace by the way." The girl looked directly at Kiddie, a warm smile on her face. "Are you a student at Columbia too?"

"I am. I mostly take art classes and a class in French." said Kiddie, smiling sideways at the Major, remembering that was how he found her after their chance encounter at Columbia's library.

"What hall do you live in? I've probably seen you before."

"I'm living at home this year. I'm from New York, well Brooklyn actually." said Kiddie.

The Major was all ears. He was fascinated to learn more about Kiddie, as he realized he didn't even know her last name.

"Ahhh," said Grace. "Lucky you. This town has so much energy it's drab to spend time on campus anyway. Unless it's for a good football game!" she added with a laugh.

Kiddie smiled, but scrambled for a way to turn the conversation. She looked at Bob and the Major. "So besides football, what other sports are you two fans of?"

"Baseball!" they said in unison.

Kiddie was on safe ground here. She nodded in agreement. "I sometimes go to Giants games with my father at the Polo Grounds."

Now it was the Major's turn to nod. "Great team! The fans love to come out for the Giants as well as the Yankees. I'm thinking Babe Ruth could be just the player to take the Yankees to a World Series. If I can't watch my hometown team, the St. Louis Cardinals, I enjoy cheering on the Yankees."

"Here it comes!" said Bob with a grin and an eyeroll. "The Major loves to tell stories about growing up in Missouri!"

The Major let out a hearty laugh. "What's not to love about pet pigs and enough fried chicken to feed a small army on a Sunday afternoon?"

"Ahh, your favorite points to make. Tell them about going to the World's Fair in St. Louis with your Uncle Crutch." Clearly Bob was quite fond of the Major.

"Hold up, I don't want these young ladies to think I'm old. I was only nine at the time. It was also the first time I got to see my Cardinals play ball. My Uncle Crutch took me. That trip was quite an adventure."

Listening to the Major talk, seeing that twinkle in his eye, Kiddie knew her instincts were right. He was a decent man who had already done a lot of living, somehow reminding her of her father. Their conversation paused as the server set down plates of hot food in front of them. They sat eating comfortably, each of them lost in their own thoughts.

With a full heart and heavy eyes, Kiddie snuck into her parents' house. She shut the heavy front door as quietly as she could and headed up the stairs, careful not to step on the creaky planks. The house was completely quiet until she gave a little yelp sitting down on her bed.

Iris was laying there waiting for her to come home and gave her quite the fright.

"Where have you been?" Iris demanded, greeting her older sister.

Kiddie recovered quickly and Iris could see her smile even in the dark. "I've been out. We went to dinner after the game. It's been the best day ever!"

Iris snorted, jealous and annoyed at the same time. "Do you know how much trouble you're in?"

"Oh poo. I called and talked to Mother. The Major insisted she know where I was. Such a gentleman." It had been annoying at the time, feeling like he was treating her like a child, but now that she was home so late, she was happy she could be open about her adventure. And an adventure it had been, the Major seeing to that.

"Move over," she told Iris with a yawn. She was happy to finally be out of the dress she had agonized over so long ago. She pulled the covers up around her chin and was asleep within seconds. Iris lay beside her, listening to her even breathing, happy to have her sister home.

I t was finally here. Today was the day. November 2, 1920, the day Kiddie would cast her vote for the next President. She thought of Elizabeth Cady Stanton and Susan B. Anthony. She thought of all the women who had stood up to men and the political system to say women were citizens too, with just as much right to vote as any man. She also thought of the men in office who had supported those fearless women and had passed the 19th Amendment into law.

Kiddie was hardly able to sleep the night before from all her anticipation. She knew the Major had wanted to go with her, but there were only two people she wanted to join her today. First and foremost her mother, Loretto. Her mother wasn't your typical housewife and yet she was fine letting "others" vote today. Kiddie wanted her to know this was her right, her duty, her voice to use today. Kiddie also wanted Iris to go, even if she wasn't yet old enough to vote. At eighteen, Kiddie barely was, but she wanted Iris to know, thanks to these women pioneers, she and Iris have a voice in their future. They could dare to chase their passions and dreams. Their future didn't have to be only about raising children and keeping house. They were paving the way for women a hundred years from now, to know that they deserved equal rights, that they had a voice, and that women could be movers and shakers in the world too.

Kiddie wore a navy dress made of silk with a pleated skirt and coordinating cardigan for the occasion. Both her mother and Iris had resisted her request for them to go with her, but in the end, Kiddie had won. Now they walked together to their polling station to vote. It was a big day for the Kolle women, and even the men who loved them.

A s the weeks flew by, it was hard for Kiddie to focus on class, although she knew the Major took his schooling very seriously. On Saturdays they continued to go to football games and then dinner. During the week they would often picnic on campus in between classes. When the weather was really nice they would even venture down to Central Park, and sit under the trees, talking for hours. Slowly but surely they were getting to know each other. Kiddie had never felt happier or more alive. Love was a strong word to use, but Kiddie often wondered if this was what she felt.

She learned the Major was a small town boy who enjoyed living the big city life in New York. Kiddie could see that the Major's zeal for life came from deep down inside him. His childhood seemed mostly perfect, a solid family foundation. His grandmother America had been a big influence in his life until her death. His father was a postmaster and his mother a force to be reckoned with. The Major had fond memories of calling pigs, playing baseball, fishing on the Missouri river, and Sunday family dinners so big that double portions sat on the tables. The seven to eight chickens his grandmother would catch, kill, clean, and fry were the jewels on the menu. He was truly a slice of Americana.

He told her about attending school at the University of Missouri, working on his first degree in journalism. He had worked as an usher at the local movie theater to help pay his way. He belonged to the fraternity Sigma Nu and was proud of the fact that Homecoming traditions had started at the University of Missouri. Shortly after graduation, the war came calling.

In a more serious conversation he shared a little bit about the war. The Major shared only some of the horrors he had witnessed, his fellow soldiers dying before his very eyes. He was appointed Major with good reason, after receiving citations for heroic efforts three times during the war. He was awarded a purple heart, but purposefully refrained from sharing why. Kiddie knew enough to know war had changed Martene Windsor, but that he tried his best to keep moving forward, even on his hardest days. After the war, the Major came to Columbia University to pursue a degree in journalism, paid in full by Uncle Sam. Knowing he was due to graduate in the spring, Kiddie pushed away her worry of what would happen when he left Columbia.

The Major was in love, or at least he assumed that's what his infatuation with one Miss Kiddie Kolle could be called. He thought about her nonstop. It was challenging to stay focused on school and yet at the same time he couldn't wait to graduate and ask her to marry him. The Lions weren't having the best season in football, but he and Kiddie were happy to be at the games, win or lose.

During the week they would have picnics in between classes. She would bring baskets full of sandwiches, pickles, deviled eggs, and potato salad. Sometimes she would keep it simple with just cheese and bread, fruit and vegetables. He knew she didn't prepare the food, it was her family's cook. He thought that it was kind of both of them. He could tell Kiddie wasn't going to be the kind of wife that stayed home with the kids and cooked and kept house. Kiddie had mentioned that one of her uncles had teased her that she was at Columbia to get her Mrs. degree, but he knew that wasn't the case. Kiddie was an independent force to be reckoned with. She talked of having a job, paying her own way, and making her own choices, which was a lot for a woman to take on in 1920. He had no doubt that she would do it all and he would love nothing more than to be the one to stand beside her and support her.

It was easy for the Major to see where Kiddie got her drive from. Her father was a brilliant surgeon making many contributions in the field of medicine, as well as on staff at several New York hospitals. Kiddie's mother was a published author. The Major knew Kiddie had two siblings and was the middle child of three. She often talked about her sister Iris, who had joined them one Saturday for a football game. He looked forward to meeting the rest of her family, which would be soon, on Thanksgiving Day.

K iddie was full of nervous energy as she set the table for Thanksgiving dinner. Today the Major would meet her family. It was time and she couldn't see their relationship moving forward until he did meet her family. After much begging and bargaining, Iris had met him at one of the football games they took her too. She knew Iris was a fan, but nervously wondered what her father would think. Not only did she love her parents, she deeply respected their opinion.

The Kolles were not your typical American family. Her father was born in Germany and came to America as a young man. After medical school, he not only practiced medicine, but contributed to the invention of the x-ray machine. He wrote often for medical journals and practiced reconstructive surgery as soldiers had come home from WWI. Her mother was a Brooklyn native and not your typical housewife herself, having published her first successful novel when Kiddie was a young child.

Kiddie grew up knowing she had the freedom to choose where life would take her. She wouldn't let society keep her dependent on a man for the rest of her life. She liked that the Major didn't dismiss her when she shared about her ambitions, seeming to be fully supportive of her desire for independence. She couldn't help but wonder if that was what he wanted in a marriage or what worked for now? Again she pushed her worry to the back of her mind.

She took a last look at the long table, her mother's china and glassware gleaming in the candlelight. She loved the smell of Cook's turkey and fresh baked pies. As her mother finished up the side dishes, her father busied himself with opening the wine. Kiddie's family was a lively bunch and she looked forward to having extra guests join them today. It was bound to be a memorable holiday. Hearing the doorbell, she smoothed down her burgundy dress and went to welcome the Major into her family's home. She opened the door with a happy smile, knowing there was much to be thankful for.

In a few hours Kiddie and the Major would ring in the new year together. It had been torture having him gone for so long, back in Missouri for Christmas with his family. Tonight they were in her parents' home, snuggled on the couch in front of the fireplace, glasses of red wine in their hands. Her parents invited over the usual family and friends to ring in 1921 with them. Kiddie's eyes danced as she listened to the lively conversation focused on current events. The Major sat beside her, interjecting here and there, but cautious about getting himself in too deep. The Major loved how Kiddie didn't hesitate to share her opinions when her thoughts provoked her to do so.

Kiddie was a girl who loved to go out on the town, but she also loved being home with her family and friends, embracing their ideas, opinions, and spirits. Noticing the empty wine bottles sitting around, Kiddie offered for her and the Major to go to the kitchen to open more, assuming he knew his way around a corkscrew. Although prohibition was a continuous topic in the papers, the Kolles most likely had plenty of wine in their cellar to survive it comfortably. Her father considered himself a connoisseur before prohibition started, even dabbling in making wine from grapes in their backyard. More importantly, he had stockpiled several cases before the 18th Amendment went into effect almost a year ago.

As the kitchen door swung shut behind them, the Major took Kiddie's arm and pulled her to him. At first he just hugged her tightly, taking in her perfume, her softness, and her hair. She loved how warm and manly he felt as she embraced his hug.

"Kiddie, I missed you," the Major said in her ear. Kiddie smiled with delight, happy to know she wasn't the only one. When he arrived earlier there had been too many family members around for a proper welcome home. Kiddie pulled back, lifting her face to his, obvious in her expectation of being kissed. He happily complied.

Catching her breath, Kiddie pulled back. "I guess we should open more wine?" she said shakily. Kiddie wasn't sure if it was the wine or if absence really did make the heart grow fonder, that led to the long, deep kiss they shared.

"Too much?" he asked her, amused.

Her face flushed, she didn't hesitate, "Not for me, you?"

He growled in her ear, "Not enough for me."

She touched the lipstick she left on his lips, knowing it would not escape Iris's attention. As if reading her mind, he kissed the palm of her hand and said, "I guess we better get this wine opened before Iris sends out a search party." Kiddie laughed, knowing he had a point.

Iris eyed them both with a smirk as they returned to the others, opened bottles in hand. Kiddie ignored her, refilling empty glasses for her family. She gave herself only a little, confident it was safer to not drink much more. Kiddie was steadfast in her boundaries with the Major, but she was also a girl in love, and quite likely to cave under his warm, deep kisses.

"Enough with this serious talk." Iris suddenly demanded. "Mother, please play us a song on the piano. We have less than an hour until that new ball drops at the Times building. It's now or never to live it up in 1920!"

"Well, alright darling," said Mrs. Kolle with a smile. Iris and Kiddie gathered around the piano with some of their family and friends.

The Major chose to stay seated, taking in Kiddie as she enjoyed the music and her family. For a moment, he thought of his own family, much more reserved and peaceful in their celebrations. Missouri was far away, but he felt right at home sitting in the Kolle's living room. As he checked his watch, he went to stand by Kiddie, confident a kiss at midnight was expected. He smiled from ear to ear as they all boisterously counted down to midnight. Amid clinking glasses and hearty handshakes, the Major could still feel Kiddie's kiss on his lips. It was not lost on Kiddie how comfortable the Major was here, in her family's home. His kiss at midnight, in front of her family, seemed to make a statement. They all gathered around the piano to sing *Auld Lang Syne*, Kiddie swaying in his arms as she sang. He didn't have to ask, he knew they were both excited to welcome 1921, confident it would be an exciting year for the two of them.

CHAPTER TWO

= 1921 =

*"I LOVE HER AND THAT IS THE BEGINNING
AND END OF EVERYTHING."*
—F. SCOTT FITZGERALD

It was a beautiful spring day and Kiddie was happy to feel the warmth of the sun on her face as she sat waiting for the Major to join her. New York winters could be brutal, but at least this one wasn't as bad as last year's crippling cold and snow. Still, it had been challenging to find places and ways to meet other than their dinner dates on Saturday nights. Kiddie was not a fan of winter and was happy to enjoy the unseasonably warm day in March. She knew their afternoon rendezvous were numbered as the Major was soon to graduate from Columbia.

Suddenly the Major plopped down beside her, greeting her with a quick kiss and a big smile. He tossed two tickets down on the blanket beside her.

"What's this?" Kiddie asked, delighted at the prospect of a new adventure. She checked the tickets as the Major sat and watched, his eyes dancing.

"We're going to see the Ziegfeld Follies?" Kiddie squealed in disbelief. When the Major nodded, she said it again excitedly, "We're going to see the Ziegfeld Follies! At Amsterdam Theater?" She threw her arms around him. "Oh thank you, Major! What a wonderful surprise!"

"Really? Is that the best you can do? A little excitement and a hug?" he asked her mischievously.

Kiddie smiled as she crawled into his lap, took his face in both her hands, and kissed him. "Oh thank you, Major," she said with a more deliberate tone. She laughed as she rolled back onto the picnic blanket they were sharing. Laying her head in his lap she asked dreamily, "Now what should I wear?"

He pulled her back up to him and kissed her again. "Whatever it is, I know you'll look stunning. Those Ziegfeld girls got nothin' on you, Miss Kiddie Kolle." She smiled into his face. It really was a beautiful day.

Iris was not happy with this new pattern on Saturday nights she and Kiddie had established since she met the Major. Once again she sat on Kiddie's bed in the midst of layers of tulle and silk as Kiddie decided which of her new dresses to wear tonight. She was lucky to be out of high school, being wooed by a man, especially when it was the Major. He was handsome enough, but his charm and wit had both the Kolle girl's attention. Kiddie was looking at her expectantly.

"Well? Does this one look better on me than the last?" she questioned Iris.

"What does it matter, the Major will think you're stunning in whatever dress you wear!" Iris could not wait for it to be her turn to live the good life in the big city.

Kiddie smiled impishly, "You do have a point. So that leaves it up to you to decide! This flamingo pink dress with the fringe skirt or the blush pink silk dress with flutter sleeves?" she said, pointing first to the dress she was wearing, and then to the one lying on the bed.

When Iris didn't respond, Kiddie said, "I love them both, it's too hard to decide! I have an idea. You choose which one you like best on you and I'll talk mother into hanging it in your closet rather than back on the rack at Nordstrom. That way I'll know just where to find it when I want to borrow it." Kiddie smiled at Iris expectantly.

"Really? You would do that for me?" asked Iris, her face finally brightening.

"Of course." Kiddie answered. "We can call it your consultant fee for helping me through all my fashion decisions. Besides, it's spring, and everyone needs a new dress for spring!"

Iris looked up from the pink dress she was holding, pausing for a second before she put it on over her head. "So that's how you got mother to buy you new dresses! You didn't tell her you're going to the show, did you? Is this my bribe to keep it a secret?"

Kiddie smiled at her sister mischievously. "Since when have I had to bribe you to keep my secrets? I know mother can be open minded, but I'm not sure what she knows about the show. For all I know, she thinks the Ziegfeld girls all dance around practically naked!"

Iris smirked. "Well don't they?"

"No! Of course not! There's going to be music, and dancing, and glamour, and romance. It's going to be a magical night." Kiddie sighed with a smile.

"You know the Major would never take me to see something vile and in poor taste."

"Fine. Tell mother you're going then. You're almost nineteen you know. Plenty old enough to be out and about on a Saturday night. Besides, I hear some of the Ziegfeld girls are barely eighteen themselves."

Together they stood in their pink dresses, admiring themselves in the mirror, oblivious to the price tags dangling down their backs. Kiddie gave Iris a hug. "Don't worry, you'll be out in the big city soon enough."

K iddie was finally dressed and ready to go as the Major pulled up in a cab. She had come clean and told her mother where they were going. Although she protested somewhat, Kiddie convinced her it would all be in good taste, fingers crossed. Besides, the well known Victor Herbert was the composer tonight. Born Irish, he studied music in Germany before coming to the states. Her family was familiar with his music and occasionally played his records on their Victrola and she was excited to hear him sing.

Kiddie snuggled up to the Major as the cab whisked them away to Manhattan.She felt fancy in her blush silk evening dress. Her mother even let her borrow her pearls for the night. The Major looked dashing in his black suit, sporting a bow tie for the evening. Kiddie kissed him on the cheek.

"Thank you again for taking me to the show tonight. I can't wait to see it!"

He squeezed her hand tightly, feeling her excitement run through him as well. "You're welcome, Kiddie. It makes me happy to make you happy."

The Major wasn't sure if Kiddie became more beautiful as his feelings for her deepened, or if he was watching her grow into a beautiful young woman. The Major had a job at the *New York Times* as a copy editor and was busy saving money. He was ready to find a beautiful diamond ring to put on Kiddie's finger, even though he knew she was young to his twenty seven years and she had plans for her own future. He would have to be patient, but knew the wait would be worth it. Besides, there was plenty of fun to have before then, like tonight. Tonight he was going to tell Kiddie he loved her, the thought making his palms sweat and hoping it wasn't too soon. He thought she loved him too, but couldn't be sure until he heard her say those three little words. Still, he was looking forward to an extravagant night.

Kiddie craned her neck to see where the cab was taking them. She thought they were on Fifth Avenue, but they had never been to dinner in this area before. The cab came to a stop and the Major paid the driver as he exited, then held out his hand to help Kiddie out of the cab. With his hand on her waist, the Major steered her in a particular direction as she asked him where they were. They were standing across the street from the Plaza Hotel. Kiddie's eyes shone with delight as she took in the spectacular view of the sun setting, creating a beautiful pink glow around them. The nineteen story chateau-style building was breathtaking. The row of flags above the grand entrance snapped crisply in the breeze while the lights showcased the columns rising up to greet each floor.

"Wait until you see the inside." the Major said behind her in her ear.

Kiddie was speechless and could only follow as he led her across the street. He tipped his hat at the doorman as he held the heavy gold door open for them to enter. Kiddie found herself in a large foyer with high ceilings and opulent chandeliers reflected in mirrors everywhere, the plush carpet beneath her stilettos welcoming. It was the most beautiful place she had ever seen. She wasn't sure where to look first, or even where they were going, but Kiddie was cautiously excited to find out.

The Major took her arm, steering them to the left into another beautiful room. A tall bar greeted them immediately when they entered and Kiddie took in every detail from the tables to the red velvet staircase leading to a second level of grandeur. Leather chairs sat around the tables, lit discreetly by a single small votive. He gave her a moment to take it all in, his hand still on her elbow, enjoying her appreciation for the grandeur of the hotel.

They were soon seated at a table near the floor to ceiling windows, allowing them to take in the colorful lights as night took over the city. The chandeliers were gorgeous, giving an elegant glow to the large room. A waitress appeared with menus, but the Major waved them away.

"We'll have two glasses of your best sparkling water," he said discreetly. Can you also add a small plate of cheeses and your seafood platter."

Kiddie and the Major had been out to dinner many times, but she could tell tonight was different. Tonight Kiddie had the distinct feeling she was being "wooed," as Iris liked to call it. The Major turned to look at her, taking in her bright eyes and big smile. Tonight they weren't just living the good life, they were out on the town.

"I hope you don't mind me ordering for both of us. I've heard the oysters here are the best to be had in New York. Not that I'm a connoisseur by any means." Was it her imagination or was the Major rambling just a bit?

She put her hand on his leg as if to reassure him. "I can't wait to try them. Those and their best sparkling water." Kiddie said with one brow raised.

He knew that wouldn't be lost on her, not on his girl. The waitress arrived, setting napkins and glasses down in front of them. The Major handed a glass to Kiddie and raised his own in a slight toast gesture.

"Here's to a night to remember." he said simply.

Kiddie repeated what he said, lightly clinking her glass to his. The sparkling water was the best she ever had as was everything they ate that night. They sat enjoying the food, the ambience, and each other. Before she knew it they were back in a cab headed to the Amsterdam Theater for the show.

It occurred to Kiddie more than once that the Major had to be spending a lot of money tonight. She didn't worry about how, but why. Surely he wasn't going to propose. It wasn't that she hadn't thought about it, but it was too soon and she wasn't ready. Kiddie pushed it to the back of her mind and focused on the present.

As the cab pulled up to the Amsterdam Theater, Kiddie's heart raced with excitement. She stood taking in the lights and glamour of the theater while the Major paid the cab driver. Hand in hand they walked in, the Major pausing long enough to pull out their tickets to hand to the attendant. It took a few moments to find their seats, heading down almost to the front row. Sitting in their seats, Kiddie took in the ornate ceilings, the box seats above them, the velvet stage curtains. Kiddie loved sitting there, amidst all the glamour.

It wasn't long before the show started. The Ziegfeld girls lived up to their name, coming out in the beginning number, even dancing out into the audience. The show continued, a mixture of singing, dancing, and a little comedy here and there. The real show for Kiddie were the girls' costumes, both suggestive and romantic at the same time. They were creatively extravagant with their mix of sequins, fringe, and feathers.

The night stopped for Kiddie when Victor Herbert sang a beautiful ballad, *Princess of My Dreams*. Kiddie instinctively reached for the Major's hand, hanging on every word he sang, accompanied by the beautiful piano music. Kiddie turned to find the Major watching her, his eyes glowing in the darkness. He squeezed her hand tightly and brought it to his lips, gently kissing it, his eyes locked with hers. Kiddie's heart pounded, feeling overwhelmed by it all, her rush of emotions strong.

Too soon the show was over and they stood with the crowd, applauding wildly, hoping for an encore. They walked with the crowd up the carpeted aisle to leave, Kiddie holding her program tightly in her hand, the music still ringing in her ears, the Major's kiss still on her mind. They sat close in the cab, headed back to Brooklyn and her family home. For just a moment Kiddie fantasized about them going to their own home on some quiet tree lined street, just a short cab ride away from the heart of the city. They were both quiet, lost in their own thoughts.

It was very late as they pulled up to her house, the windows dark, only the street lights to illuminate her front door. It was a warm spring evening and Kiddie was reluctant to go in and bring their evening to a close. The Major pulled her to him.

"Kiddie, that song tonight. I felt like Victor Herbert was stealing my thoughts and putting them into his song. Do you remember it?"

"I do." Kiddie said softly. "You kissed my hand." She could see the Major smile in the lamp light.

"Kiddie, you are the princess of my dreams and I love you."

Kiddie didn't even realize she was holding her breath, or that she had been waiting for him to say those three magic words. She reached up to kiss him, not on the cheek this time. Pulling back from him she said, "I love you too Major."

"You're all I crave Kiddie. My life and love are yours alone." She knew he was quoting the song. "I've been wanting to tell you for so long, I really wanted it to be a perfect night when I did."

Kiddie blinked back her tears, pulling her to him, laying her head on his shoulder so he wouldn't see. She was crazy about him and once again overwhelmed with emotion. He lifted her face to him, kissing her deeply.

"I can't think of any place better than being yours and yours alone." she said softly.

They both jumped as the cab suddenly inched up the street just enough for them to notice. The Major had kept it running, needing to take it back to the city.

"I guess I'll be walking back across that bridge if I don't go now." he said regretfully. He hated to see the night end.

"Thank you Major, for the most perfect night a girl could ask for. I had the best time ever." She kissed him one last time before heading in.

She stood at the window watching him get into the cab, smiling as he turned to the window, seeming to know she was there. She could still hear the song, *Princess of my Dreams* as she waltzed around the living room to the stairs. How lucky could one girl be, she asked herself.

As expected, Iris was in her bed, wide awake and waiting for details. For once Kiddie regretted that the sound of a cab door was enough to wake her. "Well?" Iris demanded. "Tell me everything! How was it? Were they only half dressed? Did you see anyone famous?"

Kiddie discarded her silk evening dress for her comfy cotton night-gown and crawled into bed. She could see Iris sitting in the darkness, waiting for answers. Fluffing her pillow, she turned to Iris and simply said, "He loves me."

Pulling the covers up to her chin, she turned away from Iris and closed her eyes. She didn't want to talk tonight. Tonight she wanted to play back every second of her evening in her dreams. Tonight her prince had told her he loved her. Iris didn't pry, but lay down beside her, happy to have her sister home.

The Major laid his head back against the cab seat, tired, but energized at the same time. She loved him, making it the most perfect night. He couldn't have asked for a better night if he had written it himself. Victor Herbert's song left him frozen in his seat when he first started to sing. Kiddie reached for his hand and he knew she felt it too. As long as he lived, he would never forget this night. She truly was the princess of his dreams and she loved him.

Another thought crossed his mind as his cab drove him into Manhattan. It was time for his mother to meet Kiddie. Commencement would take care of that, but what would his mother think of Kiddie? He knew his mother expected him to come home to Missouri, even if he lived in St. Louis like Uncle Crutch, but he wasn't headed home anytime soon. He loved the energy of New York. His job with the *New York Times* was the tip of the iceberg for him, knowing soon enough he would be writing his own sports stories. New York was his home now, and he frowned slightly at the possibility his mother would blame Kiddie for him staying in New York. He would see to it that she didn't. His mother was important to him, but he loved Kiddie. It might be awhile, but he was going to marry Miss Kiddie Kolle.

K iddie was rushing to turn in a final paper when she practically ran over Grace, Bob's girlfriend. Since that first football game last fall, the four of them had become good friends, usually hanging out on Saturday nights. Occasionally Grace and Kiddie would have lunch somewhere close to campus for some girl talk.

"Hey Kiddie! Late for a final?" quizzed Grace.

"Grace, I'm so sorry! No, just rushing to turn in my last paper and then my semester is finished!", Kiddie answered dramatically.

"I just finished myself. Want to grab lunch somewhere and celebrate?"

"Sure," answered Kiddie. "I'll be right out."

The girls were soon seated and busy ordering sandwiches and drinks at one of their favorite eats. Kiddie knew Grace was older than her, but wasn't sure if she was graduating this year or next.

"So, how was your first year at Columbia? Will you have sophomore blues to look forward too in the fall?" asked Grace.

"It was good and I do plan to return." said Kiddie, smiling at the thought of sophomore blues. "How about you?" she asked Grace.

"I have a year left before I get my teaching certificate and graduate." Grace answered.

"You're so lucky to know exactly what you want to do with your life," Kiddie said wistfully.

Kiddie did plan to return in the fall, but she wasn't sure where her art classes were taking her. It was hard to be a modern woman. Kiddie was grateful to be in a serious relationship with the Major, yet at the same time she was in no hurry to keep house and have children. Kiddie also enjoyed the academics of being a Columbia student, but what was her plan after she graduated? Kiddie didn't have the talent to be an actual artist. She enjoyed what she was learning and occasionally fantasized about working at the Metropolitan Museum of Art someday.

"Kiddie you have plenty of time to figure out what you want to do. Your passion for art is just as important as my passion for education. The world needs people like you to educate heathens like Bob and I. Art is part of our culture, our history." Kiddie knew Grace wasn't patronizing her, but genuinely trying to make her feel better.

Kiddie smiled. "Thank you Grace. I do enjoy my classes and I know I'll figure it out. It's hard not to think ahead and have a plan. One thing I do know though," she paused dramatically, "is the Major loves me." Kiddie could feel herself blushing as she said it. She wanted to tell Grace since their magical night and now seemed as good a time as any.

"What? The Major said that to you? Oh Kiddie that's wonderful! When did it happen? Do you love him?" Grace wanted details. Kiddie happily shared the details of their night out on the town—first to the Plaza Hotel and then to Amsterdam Theater to see the Ziegfeld Follies.

"I'm so happy for you both! The Major is as good a fellow as you can find." Kiddie nodded in agreement. She couldn't have said it better herself.

It was a warm day for commencement as the Major sat in his blue gown waiting for speeches to be done and diplomas handed out. Per usual, the event was held outdoors on the Morningside campus. He knew Kiddie and Iris sat in the crowd behind him, as well as his Mother. It was hard to get his father out of Missouri as the postmaster of their hometown. The Major was used to it by now and understood his father's strong work ethic.

It was finally the School of Journalism's turn to call names and he waited expectantly to hear his own. He was proud of his hard work and his degree that he was soon to be the recipient of. The University of

Missouri taught him the mechanics of news production and plant operations, but this degree taught him how to write and edit stories—exactly what he wanted to be doing in the future.

Thanks to his roommate Bob, the Major was graduating already employed. He was proud to be working at the *New York Times,* one of the biggest papers in the city. He might only be reading copy for now, but he knew his time would come when someone would be editing his own stories. The Major was happy to read copy, and found it to be a breeze. He was also making good money, saving for the future Mrs. Major's ring.

Ceremonies were over and the Major stood in the grass with his mother at his side, Kiddie and Iris on the other. Formal introductions were made after searching through the crowds and finding their familiar faces. Iris offered to take their picture, so they stood posing while the warm sun beat down on them. It was time to move this celebration indoors, to the Kolle's home as they had graciously invited the Major and his mother to dinner. It was a big day for all of them.

Hailing a cab, the Major let the women sit together in the back. He could tell Kiddie felt awkward, while Iris chatted away, making small talk. Iris asked about his mother's train ride, their family farm, and shared about her own graduation from high school coming up in a few weeks. Kiddie sat quietly while his mother answered Iris's questions with indifferent patience. The Major realized it could be a long night. He didn't worry about it too much, as in his mind, they would all be family someday. He checked the time on the new watch Kiddie gave him for graduation. He assumed there would be wine with dinner, knowing he would need at least a glass.

As the Major and his mother settled into their cab back to the city, he realized they were finally alone. He sat waiting for her comments—bound to be forthcoming. The Kolles hosted a lovely dinner of tender pork chops, creamy mashed potatoes with gravy, green beans dripping with bacon and onions, and dinner rolls the size of Texas. In the Major's honor, there was carrot cake for dessert—his favorite. Thankfully there was plenty of wine too.

The two families shared similar values, but clearly came from very different backgrounds. It was the latter he knew his mother would focus on. Both of their mothers were intelligent women, but grew up under very different circumstances. Kiddie's mother was a Brooklyn native and the Major's a small town girl from Missouri. Conversation flowed easier than he anticipated, as they navigated social graces successfully. He knew the ease he shared with Kiddie's family was not lost on his mother.

His mother was the first to break the silence. "Kiddie is a lovely girl. I can see why you feel so at home with her family." his mother said. "Clearly you've spent a lot of time there."

The Major ignored the last remark, knowing his mother missed him being at home with his own family. He dreaded where their conversation was bound to take them, but it was time to break the news to his mother.

"Kiddie is a lovely girl, a girl I plan to marry, Mother. I assume her father will say yes, when I ask his permission." There, he had thrown it out there.

"Marry? Marry! Really Martene I don't see her moving so far away from her family let alone being happy in Missouri. I'm not sure, she's a good choice for you!" As he knew she would, she threw it back to him.

"Sorry Mother, but New York is my home now. I'm already working for one of the biggest papers in the city. With or without Kiddie, I will be staying in New York City."

He glanced cautiously at his mother, not surprised to see her jaw set tight, her eyes hard. She would not be emotional, but he could feel her disappointment as it settled like a weight on his shoulders. He truly was sorry to disappoint her, as she was his mother and he cared a great deal about her feelings.

"But Martene, she's so young! And listening to her talk, I'm not sure she will be the kind of wife who will make a home for you and give me the grandchildren I deserve."

"You're right, Kiddie is a modern day woman. All I need to make a home is Kiddie and we will figure it out as we go Mother. We don't know where life will take us, but we know we want to go on this adventure together."

"I see. How soon do you plan to start this adventure? The girl is still a teenager for heaven sakes."

He ignored the brittleness in her tone and put his arm around her before he answered, "Don't worry Mother. Not anytime too soon."

He knew that would make her feel better, giving her a false sense that there was time for him to change his mind. She might have to see if there was anything she could do to help with that.

"Are we almost to my hotel?" she asked pleasantly. "I guess I better get used to staying in hotels if you're going to be living in this big city. I'm sure it will be easier for me to come see you, rather than you coming home to Missouri." She patted her son's leg, feeling a little better there could be a silver lining. Kiddie might be important to her son, but to her, her son was the most important thing. He would not be walking away that easily.

He smiled at her, "You're going to love The Plaza Mother."

Summer fell into a routine of somewhat boring quiet family nights out on the porch, and rowdy Saturday nights out on the town. The Major was busy working hard at his new job, while Kiddie worked to find ways to amuse herself without the routine of college classes. If she was lucky. Iris would grace her with an aggressive game of tennis on nearby courts. It wasn't lost on Kiddie that Iris seemed either aloof or annoyed around her these days, but she knew Iris was struggling to find her own way since graduating high school in May and Kiddie didn't worry about it too much.

The big excitement for the summer was their father buying a new Ford for the family. Kiddie had convinced her father that buying the car would eventually be cheaper than all the cab fare the family spent going back and forth over the Brooklyn Bridge to the city. Occasionally she and her brother Freddy would go into the city to see a movie, a pastime they both enjoyed. The big hit for the year had become *The Kid* starring Charlie Chaplin, a favorite actor for both of them on the big screen.

Kiddie's birthday landed on a Saturday in June and the whole family packed up and took the train to the Jersey shore to enjoy Asbury Park for the weekend. Kiddie's family had a love for the beach, vacillating between the crowded boardwalk of Asbury Park to the more relaxed Daytona Beach in Florida. They pampered themselves with hotels right on the beach to enjoy the ocean views. There were long walks on the beach, bonfires at night, and all the fresh seafood they could eat. Although not the most exciting weekend of the summer, it was a nice break from the city, with or without the Major being there.

Kiddie loved the rhythmic sound of the waves mixed with the busyness of families playing on the beach. Kiddie's family was a lively bunch, wherever they were and there was rarely a dull moment when the five of them were together. Kiddie enjoyed the company of her family, but she was most happy to spend time with Iris. As her relationship with the Major became more serious, her relationship with Iris had shifted ever so much and Kiddie realized she missed feeling close with her sister.

As the middle child, Kiddie was always striving for her fair share of the quips and the ensuing laughter. Her older brother was a combination of both her mother and father's creative genius and it was anyone's guess where life would take him. Her sister was the youngest and found ways to get attention without even trying. She had definitely inherited the good looks of the family as well as established a "cute" repertoire that got her out of as many things as into other things. Kiddie was rarely jealous of Iris, but she did enjoy when she was the one to have the opportunity to fuel a lively conversation with her sharp wit. Kiddie would toss her short dark curls in a challenge to anyone to make a better comeback.

Having a doctor for a father left plenty of times he was not available, but Kiddie and her siblings never complained, knowing their father's work was important. When they had the chance, Kiddie's favorite way to spend time with him was when he catered to his creative side and they would paint together. Kiddie knew their shared love for art was primarily what lured her to Columbia to take art classes. Just like their politically driven conversations, Kiddie enjoyed being the family's second expert in the art world, requiring their family to let the two of them monopolize those conversations at the dinner table. She enjoyed Iris's eyerolls and her mother and brother's patient occasional questions and generic comments.

Kiddie's mother was another story. She was a nurturing enough sort and always ready with the pep talk you might need, but you were never allowed to whine or complain about anything. Her children always knew they were loved, but it was important Kiddie and her siblings also know how easy life was for them all. Her mother was independent and creative as well, and it was not unusual for her to disappear into her own study in the house, writing for hours, until Kiddie or Iris would go and retrieve her for dinner.

As a published author, with several books in print, her mother's first book covered a controversial topic and as such had catapulted her into an instant sort of fame of her own. Kiddie sometimes wondered if her mother was trying to keep pace with her father and all his achievements. Kiddie was smart enough to realize it was much harder for a woman to gain a sense of contributing to society, than it was for a man. She recognized her parent's marriage worked because they both lived their lives in an unconventional way, owing nothing to society, but only to themselves and their family. Sometimes it seemed more of a business partnership than a romantic relationship, but Kiddie appreciated that she always felt safe and secure in their home. As Kiddie thought about starting her own home with the Major, she knew she too wanted to have it both ways, embracing the romance as well as the unconventional roles in her marriage.

Kiddie and her siblings often found themselves with free time, answering to no one but to Cook, who came to be part of their family after Kiddie was born. Her given name was Clara, but the young Kolle children failed to master it before they morphed it into Cook. She carried out multiple tasks daily—their beloved Jill of all trades—but her primary responsibility was to keep the kitchen well stocked and have dinner on the table. She worked hard in the kitchen and expected people to show up and eat the hot food she put on the table. Cook also quickly became who Kiddie and her siblings ran too with a squabble or scraped knee when their parents seemed unavailable. She would always take a hard line with them, but they knew she loved them too.

Given this freedom, Kiddie's brother was often out doing boy things, although Kiddie wasn't sure what that entailed. Her favorite thing about having a brother turned out to be the boys that occasionally showed up, some of them falling victim to her sharp wit and others leaving her hunting through her closet for the perfect dress to wear.

This also left Kiddie and Iris lots of time to be off somewhere together. Kiddie and Iris grew up close as sisters for many reasons. Their birthdays were not even a year apart, as Iris was born prematurely and established her family's sense of urgency to protect her from the very start. They grew up as each other's playmates, partners in crime, and best friends. The girls were successful in school with their fair share of gal pals and boyfriends, but at the end of the day, it was their bond that mattered most. No matter how busy their parents were, the girls always had each other. As the older sister, Kiddie was fiercely protective of her little sister although she had to admit, she got Iris into as many adventures as she got her out of. Although they each had their own rooms, they would often lay in one of their beds at night, talking and dreaming for hours about boys and the things they would do when they grew up. It was not lost on either of them that their parents left big shoes to fill, even though they never felt pressured to be anything more than true to themselves. Besides knowing they were loved, the girls knew they needed to stay out of trouble, be good human beings, and when possible, find a way to contribute to society. This seemed reasonable to Kiddie and made her wonder if they were actually more conventional parents than she thought.

The night of Kiddie's birthday, she and Iris had their first heart-to-heart in quite some time. The family built a big bonfire on the beach, wine discreetly stowed away in a big beach bag, Iris and Kiddie the last to call it a night. Kiddie couldn't help but feel that Iris was snubbing her hard all weekend, and decided to get to the bottom of it. Kiddie hoped her sister had drank enough wine to be liberal with her words, but not so much as to turn their conversation ugly. Feeling generous, Kiddie walked over to lay right beside Iris on the blanket. She lay on her back, admiring the stars, which were harder to come by in the city.

"Iris are you annoyed with me?" Kiddie asked lightly.

"I'm sorry Kiddie, why do you ask? Are you not getting enough attention on your birthday without your precious Major here?"

Kiddie froze for a moment, choosing her reaction carefully. Was this about the Major?

"So you are annoyed with me. Because of the Major?" Kiddie asked.

"What could possibly give you that idea? I've done my best to be pleasant since you've been so kind to grace us with your presence this weekend, especially on your birthday." Iris's words were short and biting.

Iris lay on her stomach, chin resting on her crossed arms, her angry gaze focused on the waves crashing to the shore. Turning to lay on her side, Kiddie pulled Iris's stray curls back from her face, but resisted rubbing her back. Since they were little, this had always been their routine when Iris was sad, mad, or even just tired.

"Talk to me Iris. How can I fix this? Are you jealous of the Major?" Kiddie asked.

"Why would I be jealous just because he's all you talk about and care about now? I get it, you love him, you want to marry him, you're going to leave me. . .leave the family!" Iris swiped a tear angrily as she realized she had given herself away.

Kiddie pulled them both up to a sitting position, trying to get Iris to look her in the eyes. It suddenly dawned on her, exactly where Iris was coming from. For years it had been the two of them in cahoots together, and now the Major had changed that.

Kiddie knew Iris was fond of the Major and appreciated how he was able to keep up with them during dinner, adding his own witty comments here and there. Being a freshman in college and Iris still in high school had changed their routines and rhythms as sisters. Since Kiddie started dating the Major, Iris was always a good sport, giving Kiddie the attention she asked for when she was getting ready for dates and staying up late, waiting to hear all Kiddie's details when she got home. Iris knew Kiddie was in love and she worried about just how soon the Major planned to ask Kiddie for her hand in marriage. Iris knew she would miss her sister terribly when she moved out of their family home.

"Iris I am so sorry, I've been so selfish! I'm sure it does seem like all I care about is the Major, but you're my sister and I love you more than anything! You're right, I do love the Major and I do think he will ask me to marry him someday, but I'm in no hurry to get married. You know I want to do some living first, I'm just waiting for you!" Finally Iris looked Kiddie in the face, searching to see if her words rang true.

Kiddie pulled Iris closer, giving her a fierce hug. "You know you're my little sister and I will have always loved you first! Can you forgive me for neglecting you so?"

"It's not that I don't want you to marry the Major—you know I adore him!" Iris said defensively. "He's perfect for you in so many ways. But I worry you're going to get all grown up and I'm going to be stuck at home with mother and father! That's just the worst!"

Kiddie smiled at Iris, thinking her overdramatic, but seeing her point at the same time. Maybe it was as hard to be the little sister as the big sister.

"Don't worry, when it gets too horrid you will come and stay with us in the city. I could never leave you, you can't really believe that?" Kiddie said.

Iris shuddered a big sigh as she sat beside Kiddie on the blanket, Kiddie's arm still around her. It felt good to be honest with her big sister. Iris knew her family loved her, but Kiddie was her rock, her best friend, her soul mate and she was happy to have her back.

K iddie and Iris once again became almost inseparable after that night on the beach. They spent their days together looking through magazines or playing tennis. Occasionally they would go to the city, walking around the Columbia campus or Central Park, or shopping on Fifth Avenue. Kiddie and the Major continued going out too, although he was just as likely to join the family for dinner when he could. He seemed quite focused on his job reading copy and quite often worked late into the night.

As July came to a close, they spent time celebrating the Major's birthday, out drinking until all hours of the morning one night. Kiddie's mother insisted on him joining them for dinner the next night, a celebratory family dinner which included several bottles of wine and carrot cake for dessert. Iris surprised everyone by inviting a date. Kiddie remembered him from the night before, showing up somewhere along the way. She vaguely remembered Iris mentioning he was her friend's cousin. It wasn't hard for Kiddie to see Iris was smitten and she politely asked him questions at dinner trying to get to know him better.

That night, as he sometimes did, the Major occupied one of the guest bedrooms for the night, saving him the trip back into the city. Knowing that her parents trusted both of them to be respectable, only fueled Kiddie's desire to sneak into the Major's room and wish him a real happy birthday. The Major had watched Kiddie enjoy her fair share of the wine, which only fueled the Major to limit Kiddie's birthday present to some heavy petting and kissing before he sent her back to her own bedroom. Early the next morning Kiddie felt a little deflated as she said good-bye to the Major, knowing he would catch the train to Missouri after work, his mother wanting him home for a visit. For once the girls were thankful both their parents seemed to be busy, her mother writing in her study, her father doing rounds at the hospital. The girls were lazy and happy to lay about, recovering from their busy birthday shenanigans.

Today the girls sat on the porch trying to find a breeze to cool them off from their morning on the tennis courts. They were both becoming quite good now that Iris wasn't hitting her balls with so much hostility. They were bored, but knew better than to go into the house and mope around for fear that their mother or worse, Cook would put them to work in some way.

"Kiddie, we need a project, to plan something, to create an event." Iris said thoughtfully sipping her lemonade.

"I've been thinking about that too." said Kiddie, equally thoughtful.

"Father turns 50 on his birthday this year. What if we planned a big gala for him and his birthday? We could invite all of our friends and family, his doctor friends, have Cook bake a cake, and have an excuse for Mother to buy us a new dress. What do you think?" Iris asked hopefully.

Kiddie was smiling, but not convinced. "Do you think Mother, let alone Father would agree to that? And where would said event take place?"

Iris came back excitedly, "We won't tell him. It will be a surprise birthday party! And how could mother say no? We can have it at Prospect Hall. I believe we know people there." Iris added dryly.

Now it was Kiddie's turn to look excited. "Iris, I think that's a lovely idea! With all the family it would make sense to have it at the Hall and easier to keep father in the dark that way!" Kiddie sipped on her lemonade, looking at Iris expectantly.

"The first thing you'll need to do is to set a date with Mother. After you ask her of course." Kiddie said with a smirk, before she looked away.

"Me? Why does it have to be me? I think it should be us!" Iris said loudly.

"What should be us?" asked their mother as she joined them on the porch, pouring herself a glass of lemonade as well.

Seizing the moment and hoping it was an opportune time, Iris rushed out, "Kiddie and I want to give Father a surprise party for his birthday!"

"Really?" said Mother, somewhat surprised. Like Kiddie, she asked the same question. "Where would this party take place? You know we have to invite all the family and friends. And probably his doctor friends too."

"Oh Mother, Prospect Hall is the perfect place to have it. That will give Kiddie and I time to set everything up. Plenty of room for all the family and friends. We can ask Cook to make a cake. Father will love it!" Iris gushed.

"Hmm, *love* seems a strong word to use, but I think in the end he would enjoy a party in his honor. He works so hard. And when should we have this party? I suppose we should check the closest date with the hall first."

Iris and Kiddie could see their mother thinking about all the logistics.

Kiddie jumped in, "Mother we'll take care of everything. We can plan the food, drinks, and the cake. We'll invite all of our family and friends and make sure everyone knows, even his doctor friends!"

Their mother smiled, happy to see her two girls finally on the same page again. Besides, they were old enough to plan such an event for their father. It would mean more coming from them and harder for him to protest, of that she was sure.

"Ok, go ahead and plan his party. I'll talk to his doctor friends. You might as well have Freddy help with this and he can invite our family and friends. But, first we need to find a date that works."

The girls jumped up to hug their mother, delighted to have her blessing. It would be their first event and they wanted it to be special for everyone, but especially for their father. He did work hard for his patients, but they knew he was working hard for them and to provide a good life for his family. He most definitely deserved this party. The girls went to sit back down and picked up their lemonades. Kiddie was hopeful the Major would be back by then, while Iris wondered if this would be too much of a family event to invite her new friend Bernie.

The Major sat on the train, head back resting his eyes. He had made a quick trip home—per his mother's insistent request—his birthday just the excuse she needed. She let him know in no uncertain terms he could come home, or she could come to New York, either way worked fine for her. The Major took a long weekend, knowing his father and brother would never make the long trip. His mother pulled out all the stops, creating a dinner that felt like most of the town had attended. She neglected to let people know he was in a serious relationship in New York and as such he appeared to be quite the eligible bachelor. Against his better judgement he had been talked into taking a walk with one of the girls he'd known since primary, her motives becoming obvious a little too late for him to save himself. Awkward for both of them, the Major was annoyed with his mother as well as himself.

The Major was thankful to have some time with his father as he drove him to St. Louis to catch the train. The small talk ran out quickly, but the Major didn't mind the ride in silence. He also left time to see his Uncle Crutch, joining him for lunch and catching up on all the latest news around St. Louis and their beloved Cardinal's baseball team. After a rough spring, the Cardinal's finally had a series of wins in June, only to be currently back in a series of losses. Ironically the Cardinals spent the past few weeks playing either the New York Giants or the Brooklyn Robins, losing most of those games much to the Major's disappointment. If Uncle Crutch taught him anything, it was to know that the baseball season is long and you will do better to be patient with the Cardinal's, whether they're winning or losing.

Sitting on the train now, heading back to New York City, the Major was happy he took the time to be home and catch up with his family. His last visit at Christmas was a while ago, although he saw his mother in May for his graduation. The Major was becoming a true New Yorker, and loved spending time with Kiddie's family, but he would always be grateful for his roots and the ties that came with them. As he closed his eyes, he pictured Kiddie that night they had celebrated his birthday, sneaking into his room. She was lucky he was a gentleman and he wondered how much longer he could keep that up. Thinking of Kiddie made him smile, wondering what she was up to while he was gone.

The party was a day away and the girls were doing their best to hide their excitement from their father. Cook had been most gracious in helping them plan the food and make sure it was all prepared and ready in a timely manner. In the end though, she made them bake his cake, teaching them and encouraging them along the way. It wasn't the prettiest cake to be seen, but they trusted Cook to not lead them astray and knew that it would taste delicious. Like the Major, Kiddie's father loved Cook's carrot cake.

Everyone was excited to attend the party. The girls knew a party at Prospect Hall was an event not to be missed, and the fact that it was in honor of their father made it even more special to their invited guests. The girls collected pictures of their father over his fifty years and made a little book for him as their present. They left room at the back for guests to sign as they arrived. Everything was in place and ready to go.

It was finally the day of the party. Kiddie wore a pale blue silk dress while Iris wore a similar dress in a pale lilac hue. Both girls looked gorgeous and their eyes danced with excitement. Kiddie and Iris were pleased to see their guests dressed to the nines, including their mother who looked devine in a jade green silk dress with a gold metallic lace overlay. Noticing their father couldn't take his eyes off their mother made them smile, as he kept her hand tucked into his elbow, greeting guests with the other hand.

The ballroom at Grand Prospect Hall looked splendid, the chandeliers sparkling much like the champagne that would be flowing throughout the night. Long tables were piled high with light finger foods, knowing appetites could be hard to come by in the late summer heat. Somehow the cake Kiddie and Iris worked so hard on, stood tall and inviting in the middle of the tables. The house orchestra played, the dance floor beckoning guests to work up a thirst for champagne and life itself. Both Iris and Kiddie held glasses in their hand, thankful for the distraction from all the small talk, sometimes with people they did not really know well.

As the latest collection of people wandered off to the dance floor, Kiddie was delighted to hear a deep gravelly voice in her ear, a hand on her elbow. "I see you're the belle of the ball as usual. But how is it you're not on the dance floor yourself?"

"Oh I've had offers, but it seems the prince of my dreams is late in his arrival, forcing me to stand around and make small talk in the most dreary of ways!" Kiddie answered back with a playful pout.

Kiddie was so distracted with the voice in her ear, she forgot Iris stood beside her, until Iris let out a snicker. "Tsk, tsk, such a bore you two are. Get a room already! There are plenty of them to be had here at the Hall." And with that, Iris flounced off, going to find Bernie to dance with.

Kiddie turned to look into the Major's face with a big smile and a quick kiss. "Welcome home, Major! Tell me how much you missed me!"

The Major let his lips linger a little longer for a second kiss, as he said in her ear, "So much, I missed you! Don't let me drink too much of your go go juice or I may have to show you just how much later when we're alone." Kiddie shivered with anticipation, her cheeks flushed ever so slightly. Not knowing what to say, she took the Major's hand and dragged him to the dance floor.

Too quickly the party was over, and the beautiful night celebrating the doctor's birthday. The girls enjoyed seeing all the cousins, aunts and uncles, and family friends celebrate their father. There had been toasts, cheers, dancing, and champagne, so much champagne. Iris and Kiddie were both relieved and proud their cake met with everyone's hearty approval, particularly their fathers. While Kiddie stuck close to the Major for the night, it had not escaped her attention Iris was sticking close to her handsome date as well. Kiddie knew this was the same man Iris invited to dinner the last couple of weeks and she wondered how serious the two were about each other.

As the last guests departed, Kiddie's brother Freddie brought the Ford around to take their parents home. Their mother insisted she help clean up, but the girls refused to let her stay. They noticed their father, persuasively urging her to get in the car, leaving the girls to take care of cleaning up.

As Kiddie, Iris, and the Major surveyed the damages, Bernie suddenly appeared with a new bottle of champagne and four glasses. "I hear the garden here is almost as lovely as the two of you! Seems it would be a waste not to go enjoy it in the moonlight on such a fine night."

Somehow he managed to look both smug and sheepish at the same time, waiting for them to join him. Without hesitation, Iris hurried to his side, turning to beckon Kiddie and the Major. Kiddie grabbed the Major's hand and another nearly full bottle of champagne from a nearby table and followed Iris and her date out to the garden.

It was a beautiful night and the girls were high on the success of a memorable party. Together the four of them sat, sharing stories, laughs, and more champagne under a full moon and a sky that seemed to twinkle with diamonds just for them. The air was fragrant with jasmine and roses from the garden beds. In no time at all the bottles were empty and the Major was offering to call Bernie a cab back to the city. Iris took hold of his arm and said cheerfully, "No need. Bernie is a Brooklyn boy and lives not too far away. He can drive us all home if we're ready."

The Major stood up, turning to offer Kiddie his arm, and said, "I think it's such a beautiful night, why don't we walk? It's not that far." As the two couples found their way to the street from the garden, Kiddie paused one last time to take in the grandeur of Prospect Hall.

The opulence of the building was not lost on either of the men, but it was Bernie who said, "Your father was lucky to have such a grand place to celebrate his birthday."

Iris turned to him and said, "Luck has nothing to do with anything my father does. His father is the one that built Prospect Hall, and it was his childhood home for a while. Can you imagine?" Linking her arms between Bernie and Kiddie, Iris resumed walking, headed in the direction of her own home, her eyes drunk with happiness, pride, and most certainly champagne.

It was August and summer was starting to wind down. The Major was most excited to share some news as he whisked Kiddie away in a cab to go to dinner. After only a few months of working as a copy reader, the Major had unexpectedly received his first writing assignment. He wasn't surprised to learn his connection to this particular athlete had been the deciding factor in him acquiring the assignment.

To celebrate, the Major was taking Kiddie somewhere new for dinner, the cab dropping them off at the Biltmore Hotel. Seeing Kiddie's confusion, he steered her through the open doors to the elevators. Tonight they were dining on the twenty-sixth floor, under the stars at the Cascades, the hotel's rooftop restaurant. The Major told Kiddie he had a surprise for her and she was thankful she had dressed up. She looked stunning as usual, tonight dressed in a light yellow strapless gown, the dress hitting just below her knees for all to see her fancy satin kitten heels as well.

Kiddie wondered how the Major could afford such an extravagant place for dinner and her heart started to race at the thought that maybe tonight he was going to propose! Kiddie remembered warmly the last time they had a big night and the Major had told her he loved her for the first time. As they looked over their pricey menus, Kiddie generously offered to share a plate with the Major, adding that she wasn't really that hungry. Smiling gratefully, he asked her if a plate of pasta would suit her for dinner.

"Now that I'm going to be a big writer for the *New York Times*, I plan to take my best girl out on the town more often." He was casual, but hopeful Kiddie would share his excitement.

Kiddie's face lit up and she exclaimed, "A writer? You've been promoted? That's wonderful news, Major! What are you writing first?"

"It turns out Mademoiselle Suzanne Lenglen will be arriving in New York tomorrow on a steamship to compete in the Women's National Tennis Championships. The tennis courts at Forest Hills will be graced with her flamboyant footwork and I will have a front row seat to her adventuresome matches! Apparently my friendship with her has warranted my assignment." The Major didn't mean to boast, but he was still a little beside himself over this latest turn of events.

Kiddie was stunned. As a tennis player in her own small world, Kiddie was a huge fan of the famed french tennis player, a winner in the Olympics just last year. And now, the Major was not only going to write about her in the *New York Times*, he was actually a friend of hers! Knowing how much Kiddie loved to play tennis, the Major was right to assume Kiddie would be familiar with the French tennis star.

The Major shared with Kiddie how this opportunity had come his way as they sipped their drinks. He met Suzanne years ago at a cocktail party while he was stationed in France, just after the war ended. They spent time together, establishing an easy relationship more about tennis than any attraction to each other. When the Major's boss heard this, he summoned the Major to his office, bestowing the assignment upon him, hopeful he would be more than capable. The Major was confident that knowing Mademoiselle Lenglen personally would be a tremendous asset in writing his first story. If truth be told, he was a bit more hopeful than confident.

Now he took Kiddie's hand and asked, "Do you want to go with me tomorrow to meet her ship?"

Kiddie exclaimed, "Oh yes, you know I do!"

They had ordered a plate of pasta to share, ignoring the waiter's withering look and now Kiddie waited for him to put down the plate of hot, steaming noodles on the table between them. She turned to the Major excitedly. "Are you sure it's ok for me to go with you to meet her?"

The Major paused mid-air with a fork full of pasta. "Actually I will have to meet you down there, as the *Times* is sending a fleet of writers to meet and greet her. Iris can join you and then I will be most happy to introduce you both to one Mademoiselle Lenglen."

Kiddie was temporarily disappointed, but quickly recovered wondering what she should wear to meet and greet a French tennis celebrity. She was confident Iris would want to join her. Smiling proudly Kiddie raised her glass to the Major. He was happy to comply, relishing in Kiddie's simple toast.

"To you Major, your first story in the *New York Times*, and to one Mademoiselle Lenglen."

"There! There's the ship Paris!" Iris exclaimed excitedly to their taxi driver.

Kiddie quickly paid him and both girls dashed to the rail, worried that they had missed Mademoiselle Lenglen disembark from the ship. It was late in the afternoon, but the sun still beat down on them as they stood taking in the big ship. Out in the ocean the water sparkled and graced them with a breeze to fan their excited faces. There was a small crowd gathered, but Kiddie wondered how many of them were actually reporters. She scanned the crowd, searching to find the Major's handsome stocky frame. As if sensing her presence he glanced down the rail, returning her excited wave. Noticing the exchange, Iris clutched her hand, pushing them both through the people until they were as close to the Major as they dared to be.

Reporters and tennis fans alike were soon rewarded with Mademoiselle Lenglen's appearance at the top of the gangplank. The girls knew she was known for her style both on and off the court, and were pleased to see her in a big red hat and matching red heels. For a minute everyone held their breath as she seemed to almost trip coming down the plank. The crowd clapped and whistled appreciatively as she quickly recovered, a big smile sparkling under her hat. Kiddie and Iris watched as the Major greeted her, his extended hand tossed aside with a big hug thrown around him. They waited patiently for him to motion to them to join him, but to no avail. Disappointed they watched as she was swept into a car which smoothly carried her away from the ship.

Only then did the Major walk over to them. Placing a hand on each of the girls shoulders, he smiled broadly at them. "No worries, ladies. I have just recommended Mademoiselle's dinner destination and she has insisted I join her. I told her only if I could bring my best girl and her sister, two of her biggest American fans. She is more than happy to have us join her."

It was the girls' turn to smile broadly at the Major, both of them giving him their own big hug and an "Oh thank you, Major!"

They hurried to find a taxi and head back into the city. The Major had recommended Shanley's, a popular lobster palace on the east side of Broadway and 43rd street. The Major knew Suzanne would love the ornate chandeliers and elegance that made it a popular place to eat. There was a full menu of steaks, chops, and what they were most famous for, lobster.

The Major had arranged for a discreet table in the Empire Room to give their French celebrity some privacy, but she seemed happy to welcome her occasional fan to the table. The night proved to be quite memorable as their group feasted on lobster and sipped champagne while listening to stories shared between Mademoiselle Lenglen and the Major. They shared stories about the war and she told of the devastation left in France. Mademoiselle Lenglen was primarily in the states to play exhibition games and raise funds for rebuilding the worst hit areas in France. Upon hearing of her visit to the states, she had somehow found herself dragged into the US Championship at the last minute. She shared stories about her most challenging matches she had won, including playing at Wimbledon a few years ago while King George V and Queen Mary watched on. Kiddie and Iris were quite taken with her and were dying to ask her if she really drank brandy between her sets. They not only admired her fashion style, but also her ability to command everyone's attention at the table with her lively stories.

In no time at all the Major was putting Mademoiselle Lenglen into a cab, sending her to her hotel for the night. The girls were aware she would have her first match tomorrow, having not even a day to recover from her long voyage, most of which she had been ill. Soon to follow came a second cab to send Kiddie and Iris back to Brooklyn and home for the night. Kiddie was reluctant to bring the evening to a close, but she knew the Major had work to do as he headed to his office to write his very first story. Besides, they were invited to Forest Hills to watch Mademoiselle Lenglen compete on the courts tomorrow, making today just the beginning of their tennis adventure.

K iddie bounced down the stairs to get the door, yelling at Iris to hurry up at the same time. She opened the door to the Major who stood proudly holding the Sunday paper.

"Kiddie I did it! My story is right smack in the center of page one! Quite naturally it's the greatest story ever printed I might add!" The Major was beaming as he handed it to Kiddie to read for herself.

Iris came bouncing down the stairs, ready to spend the day watching tennis in her big hat and a crisp white cotton dress with a pleated skirt. Kiddie was dressed similarly in a light blue dress. Kiddie took the paper with a big smile under her hat, even as the Major was ushering them out to the cab. It would be at least a thirty minute drive from Brooklyn to Queens where Forest Hills sat ready for a full day of tennis. The Major did not want to be late as he liked to consider himself the lead reporter for the Championship. The girls did not want to be late as they wanted the best seats complimentary tickets could buy. They learned that Mademoiselle Lenglen had been given a day to recover from her voyage, requiring Kiddie and Iris to wait another day to see the sparkle of France in action.

The girls fanned themselves thankful their dresses were light enough for a hot summer's day, more so than the suit and tie the Major was wearing. As it turned out Mademoiselle Lenglen was scheduled to play Eleanor Goss first, a leading American player, but Goss had quickly defaulted. This left Suzanne Lenglen to compete against Molla Mallory in the second round. As she came courtside, Kiddie and Iris clapped, politely excited, trying to remember they should also support their American champion. Being that Mallory was Norwegian-born, the girls didn't feel too bad cheering for both. The girls admired Mademoiselle Lenglen's crimson bandeau on her short cropped hair, paired with a sleeveless one-piece crepe de chine pleated dress and white stockings that even *Vogue* would approve of. The girls bantered with each other if she would show up in her fur coat after the match, knowing very well it was way too warm for that.

Sitting in the stands, the girls flinched as Mademoiselle Lenglen missed yet another ball Molla Mallory served swiftly over the net. The girls were disappointed to watch her lose her first match 6-2 to Mallory, but were confident in her comeback in the second match. Mademoiselle Lenglen was poetry in motion, moving like a gazelle as she swerved and lept around the court to return balls with power and grace. But still, Mallory was an equally strong competitor and the girls knew the match was not going well. Suddenly Mademoiselle Lenglen went to her chair, leaning over in a coughing fit unable to stop. As someone handed her water to drink, she burst into tears. For a moment the crowd sat in silence, stunned by this unexpected turn of events. Taking the water, Lenglen got up and walked off the court, her coughing fit following her out. The crowd came back to life, finding their voice, jeering and booing her as she walked out. Kiddie was watching the Major and when he turned to look at her, they both shared a look of concerned disbelief.

The girls were devastated as the match was called and Mallory won by default. Kiddie wondered how in the world the Major would write this story without criticising his long time friend.

A few days later it was announced Mademoiselle Lenglen had contracted whooping cough. Kiddie and Iris were privy to this information before it was announced in the paper, thanks to the Major's inside scoop. The press had a heyday with Suzanne Lenglen, their articles somewhat rude and not the least bit understanding. Eventually she decided to cancel her exhibition tour and head home to France to recover. The girls were severely disappointed for both Mademoiselle Lenglen and themselves.

The Major had his own thoughts about the tennis fiasco. He had been assigned to follow Mademoiselle Lenglen around during her stay, writing stories as she played matches and socialized around New York City. While the Major waited for Mademoiselle Lenglen to recover and participate in her exhibition tour, he had been assigned a few other tennis matches around New York. The Major enjoyed tennis and seeing Suzanne, but he wasn't sure he wanted to be known as the *New York Times* leading tennis reporter his whole career. Although this writing assignment had come to a somewhat abrupt halt, the Major was confident the caliber of his stories would lead to more opportunities in the near future. He would just have to wait to see.

K iddie tried not to slouch on the park bench as she continued to watch for Iris to arrive at Central Park for their picnic lunch. She checked her watch and sighed, not that surprised she was running late. Kiddie knew Iris well, building in plenty of time for lunch before their big afternoon. Finally the yellow cab came to a smooth stop in front of Kiddie, as Iris bounced out with a picnic basket in tow. She saw Kiddie immediately and the two girls waved to each other before closing the short distance between them. Together they spread out the checkered blanket and laid out sandwiches, deviled eggs, watermelon, and sliced cucumbers. It reminded Kiddie of all the picnics she and the Major had shared that first fall they had dated, the Major always happy to enjoy Cook's home cooking.

The girls made light small talk while they enjoyed their lunch. Eventually they stretched out with full bellies on the blanket under the tree, kicking their shoes off and enjoying the slight breeze ruffling their hair. Although Kiddie was trying to appear nonchalant, she was keeping an eye on the time, committed to Iris joining her to attend an event on campus.

Hearing Iris' big sigh, Kiddie rolled over on to her stomach to look at her asking, "What's that about?"

"It's such a beautiful day and we have all this food left, it's a shame the boys aren't here to enjoy this with us."

Kiddie rolled her eyes at Iris' statement and quickly threw back to her, "Iris, you don't need to spend all your time with Bernie!"

Iris sat up on one elbow and looked at Kiddie, a little surprised by her comeback. Retreating back to the blanket she responded mildly, "Well since Bernie works all day, just like the Major, I don't spend all my time with him, now do I?" Kiddie smiled at her sister's practical answer and decided to start at the beginning, but get right to the point.

"Iris, I just wonder what you plan to do with yourself now that you've graduated from Erasmus Hall?" Kiddie said expectantly.

"Why do I need a plan?" Iris responded. "I like taking it a day at a time and see what the day brings."

Kiddie looked at her skeptically. "Iris, are you just waiting for a ring on your finger? Is Bernie the one for you?"

Iris blushed and beamed all at the same time. "Oh Kiddie he is quite the catch, wouldn't you say? He's devilishly handsome, comes from a good family, works hard, and we both love to hit the town when the sun goes down. What more does a girl need?"

"All I hear in there is about Bernie. What about you? What do you want out of life?" Kiddie was being earnest, worried about her little sister.

"Me?" Iris looked at Kiddie a little confused. "Aren't you listening? All I want is a good man who will take care of me and wants to make me happy. I want to have fun and live a good life!" When Kiddie didn't say anything, Iris took her hand. "Kiddie I don't have to be like you and Mother. I'm not thinking about a career. That's why I'm not wasting father's money on college just so I can pretend like I'm doing something important."

Iris immediately regretted her choice of words as Kiddie snatched her hand away. "Is that what you think I'm doing Iris? Wasting father's money just so I can feel important and like I'm going somewhere?"

It was Iris's turn to look concerned. "I didn't say that Kiddie. But maybe the better question is "what do you want out of life?""

Seeing Iris' sincerity in her face, Kiddie relaxed and unexpectedly switched gears. "Actually I'm glad you asked! I have a surprise for you! Earlier this week we had a guest artist in one of my classes. Her name is Edna Crompton and she paints mostly portraits of today's young women. She's getting a lot of attention and has an art show on campus this afternoon. I thought we could go together!"

Iris looked at Kiddie, mildly entertained with Kiddie's announcement. So this was why she insisted on a picnic lunch in Central Park today. Iris shrugged. It was a beautiful day and why not spend it with her big sister enjoying good food and a new artist.

"Of course I'll go with you Kiddie. You know I enjoy art as much as most people, even if it's not as much as you and father."

It was Kiddie's turn to beam as she jumped up, quickly closing the glass containers of food and putting them back in the picnic basket. Together she and Iris folded the blanket and laid it on top of the food. They walked along Morningside on the edge of campus where Kiddie parked the family's Ford. Heading to the exhibit, Kiddie was keeping the biggest surprise of all from Iris. She was curious to see what Iris would say once she heard the news, particularly given their conversation this afternoon.

The girls were handed a program as they walked into the exhibit, detailing the pictures presented in today's exhibit. Ms. Crompton titled her exhibit "Girls of America." There was a brief history of Ms. Crompton's credentials, which included her studies in three different schools in both Boston and Chicago. She appeared to currently reside in New York City. Working magic with her oil paint on her canvas, her focus was on interpreting the women of this new flapper era. Walking around the exhibit, Iris and Kiddie were taken in by her ability to capture the girls vulnerability and sassy personalities at the same time. The women were beautiful, but not in an overly abundant manner, making them seem relatable to Kiddie and Iris. As Kiddie gazed into their beautiful faces, she longed to see her own face on a canvas.

Suddenly a small crowd gathering distracted Kiddie from the artwork. She clutched Iris' arm. "There she is!" she exclaimed urgently.

"Who?" asked Iris as she looked in the direction Kiddie was focused on.

"It's her! Edna Crompton, the artist. Let's go meet her!" Kiddie said excitedly. Not giving Iris a chance to decline, Kiddie hustled them both over, standing on the outskirts of the small group of women gathered around her.

Kiddie tried to focus on the conversation as Ms. Crompton was explaining her brush stroke technique to an avid group of listeners. Kiddie patiently waited until there was a lull in the conversation before she presented her own question and mostly her sole purpose for being there that afternoon.

"Ms. Crompton, is it true that your American girl paintings are being featured on the covers of magazines such as *RedBook* and *Modern Priscillla*?" Kiddie tried her best to sound nonchalantly interested.

She could feel Iris staring at her somewhat stunned, but chose to focus on Ms. Crompton's full attention to her question. These were magazines the girls read regularly.

"Why yes, that is true, and *The Saturday Evening Post*." It seemed to Kiddie that Ms. Crompton was pleased and reluctant to toot her own horn.

"As an art student, I try to keep up on the latest trends, especially when women are sharing their talents. That must have been quite the challenge to get your first cover?"

It was Kiddie's turn to look pleased as she had the entire group's attention. Clearly it was not a well known fact that her paintings were being turned into magazine covers.

"Are you an artist? A painter umm. .. Miss?" Edna Crompton asked.

Kiddie paused for only a moment before she threw it out to the universe for all to hear. "I'm Kiddie Kolle and this is my sister Iris. I dabble in painting, but more as a hobby. I do appreciate good art, particularly when it serves the dual purpose of both defining and celebrating young women of today. What I'm most interested in is how I can model for an artist and become art itself?" Kiddie could feel her cheeks warming and hoped she had not been too outspoken. Intrigued, the group of girls turned to the artist.

Edna Crompton smiled generously at Kiddie, including Iris in her sweeping glance. "I'm confused, Miss Kolle. Are you wanting to know how I got my first magazine cover or how you can get your first cover?"

Kiddie was not daunted and answered respectfully. "Both actually. Ms. Crompton your story is the inspiration for my story. You've achieved what so many of us here hope to accomplish. You've taken what you're passionate about and found a way to share it with the world, a man's world I might add. At the same time you're making a name for yourself and getting paid to do so. Please, teach me your ways."

There it was. Iris had asked Kiddie earlier this afternoon what she wanted and now, Kiddie had been handed the perfect opportunity to share exactly what she wanted. Kiddie had been so earnest in her request, she felt certain Ms. Crompton could not refuse her. She could feel the stares of the other girls, even her sister, but she kept her gaze focused on Ms. Crompton.

Suddenly Kiddie's professor walked up to the group, intent on moving them along. "Girls, we mustn't keep Ms. Crompton to ourselves. She has many guests waiting to talk with her. I'm sure she appreciates your questions and appreciation for her work." With that, her professor whisked Ms. Crompton away to meet the dean of the department.

As the girls dispersed in different directions, Kiddie worked to hide her disappointment. She was crushed, having gotten so close to an answer only to have it literally swept away by her professor. She was vaguely aware that Iris had her by the arm and was trying to guide her to a more private spot to collect herself. Kiddie and Iris had poured over and obsessed about magazines for years together, but until now, Iris never knew Kiddie had set her sights on being on the cover of a magazine. She felt proud of her sister for laying it all out there, even if it had been somewhat of a fail.

Suddenly someone was tapping Kiddie on the shoulder. It was Ms. Crompton and she was handing Kiddie a piece of paper.

"Miss Kolle, I believe. I wanted to thank you for your comments. You can reach me at that address and we can talk more about how to get you on your first cover." She smiled at Kiddie and Iris and then was gone as quickly as she had appeared.

Kiddie opened the piece of paper she had been handed to see an address scrawled across it. She looked at Iris in disbelief. Iris squealed with delight and quickly they exited the exhibit before Ms. Crompton could change her mind. Only when they were safe inside the family Ford, did they let it go. They were both talking at once, Kiddie a mix of tears and laughter.

"Kiddie, why didn't you tell me about this before now? I never realized you wanted to be on the cover of magazines!" Iris exclaimed.

Kiddie could still feel her flushed cheeks. Putting her hands to her face she answered sheepishly. "Iris it's such a lofty goal and who am I to think I'm special enough to be that girl?"

Iris was surprised to hear this. "YOU are one Miss Kiddie Kolle and come from a long line of people setting lofty goals and being special enough to reach them. What if Mother had focused on keeping house and never wrote a book? What if father never envisioned the X-ray thingamijiggy? What if grandfather never built Grand Prospect Hall? Of course you can do this!"

Kiddie's hands were still shaking as she searched in her purse for the car keys. Taking a deep breath, she smiled at Iris. "Thank you Iris. It feels so good to finally share this with you and know you don't think I'm crazy."

Iris laughed at Kiddie and said slyly, "Crazy? I didn't say you're not crazy. I said it's possible to be on the cover of magazines. For sure you're crazy!"

Kiddie was smiling too as she pulled the Ford away from the curb and headed home to Brooklyn. It was time to let her mother in on her plan and then time to celebrate. Kiddie was both relieved and excited to finally have her plan out there in the universe, ready for her dream to be snatched up and turned into a reality. As if reading her mind, Iris asked, "When are you going to tell Mother and Father? And what about the Major? What will he think of your grandiose plan?"

As they crossed over the bridge that led into Brooklyn Kiddie turned to Iris. "Oh the Major already knows. We both have grandiose plans for the future and one hundred percent support each other. Turns out we both want to be recognizable in print!" Kiddie said happily.

Iris turned to look out the window, somewhat surprised by this news. She thought Kiddie always confided all her hopes and fears in her and felt a little disappointed to find out the Major was on the front lines now. Iris acknowledged she was spending a lot of time with Bernie, and it was hard to get one-on-one time with Kiddie these days. That's why she had been so happy when Kiddie had asked her to picnic with her today.

Iris thought back to earlier when Kiddie had asked her what she wanted out of life. Given the afternoon's events, she better understood what Kiddie was getting at. Iris wondered if she really were ready for a ring on her finger or if there needed to be more for her too. The Kolle family did present big shoes to fill and yet their mother and father had never pressured any of them into making something of themselves. Maybe they assumed it was ingrained in them, somewhere deep in their genetics, waiting to surface sooner or later.

Iris realized Kiddie was speaking to her. "Iris let's go to Grand Prospect Hall to celebrate tonight and stick close to home. I feel champagne is called for and lots of it!"

Iris nodded adding lightly, "Of course." She definitely was going to need lots of spirits to lift her own.

For once Iris stood at the bottom of the stairs waiting for Kiddie to come down. Kiddie had put off getting ready to go out while she and their mother talked after dinner. Then she had hung around waiting for the Major to call only to give up and rush upstairs to freshen up and accessorize for evening wear. Now Kiddie was finally ready, headed down in the same dress, but with her wrap and new pumps. It was late September and the warm days often gave way to cooler nights. Iris watched Kiddie come down the stairs with a new appreciation for just how beautiful her big sister really was. Her glass of wine at dinner had created just the buffer she needed to boost her spirits and she happily put her arm through Kiddie's as they headed out the door ready to embrace the evening.

Freddy offered to drive them to the Hall, joining them for the first round of drinks. Whether warranted or not, the girls always sashayed into Grand Prospect Hall like they owned the place. Like so many places across the bridge, the Hall had its own speakeasy and was quite popular with the locals and New York celebrities alike. They were delighted to learn Freddy had called ahead and reserved their usual table for the night. Iris was happy to see Bernie already there, champagne and glasses ready and waiting. She snuggled up to him, feeling more secure in the thought he really was her dream come true for a happy life. As the group started on their second bottle of champagne, Freddy raised his glass in a toast. "To having dreams and finding the way to make them all come true."

Just as they clinked their glasses, the Major walked in, his hat in his hands. Freddy downed his champagne and jumped up. "Perfect timing Major, as I'm headed home. Tag you're it and she's all yours!" his arm sweeping across to Kiddie.

Kiddie scowled at Freddy. "I am plenty capable of taking care of myself big brother, thank you very much!" she said testily, finishing her own glass of champagne.

Freddy kissed the top of Kiddie's head and added smoothly, "Of course you are Kiddie, but it's nice when someone else wants to do so. Enjoy."

As the Major sat down beside Kiddie he noticed the empty champagne bottle on the table. He knew he was late and regretted it knowing today had been a big day for Kiddie. As he met Iris' gaze across the table, he was grateful to her as she grabbed Bernie's hand and jumped up. "C'mon Bernie let's go see about getting more champagne for the table."

Turning to Kiddie and taking her hand, the Major acknowledged he was late. "Kiddie I'm sorry I'm running late, but it couldn't be helped! We had a big meeting about the Giants and Yankees are most likely to be in the world series. It's a big deal and I had to be there. How was your day? Did you meet Edna Crompton as you hoped for? Kiddie?"

When Kiddie sat without saying anything the Major let go of her hand. Taking his hat, he stood up, and added, "Miss Kiddie I've had a long day, but I would love to hear about why empty champagne bottles are lining up, and celebrate with you. However, I won't sit here and be ignored by some gorgeous, pouty brunette."

Kiddie grabbed his hand as he turned to leave. "Wait! I'm sorry Major! Do you really think the Yankees and the Giants will both be in the World Series?" The Major cautiously relaxed as he sat back down beside Kiddie.

"I do and it will be a sportswriter's dream! But tell me about your day. I take it all went well?" The Major leaned into Kiddie, squeezing her hand and kissing her on the cheek.

As Kiddie finished sharing with the Major about her afternoon, Iris and Bernie returned to the table with two more bottles of champagne.

"Guess who we saw at the bar?" Iris asked excitedly. Looking up, Kiddie and the Major asked "who" at the same time.

"Al Capone!" Kiddie felt the Major stiffen just ever so slightly, looking at Bernie for confirmation. "Yeah we both grew up in Brooklyn. I recognized him, but I don't know him, more like I know of him. We kept the conversation short."

The Major nodded as he uncorked a new bottle. He had heard the rumors of Capone taking advantage of the prohibition laws to encourage bootlegging and other illegal activities. As a man who enjoyed a strong drink at the end of the day, the Major wasn't there to judge.

But still he didn't want to be around for any trouble that might follow Capone in from the streets. He had heard Capone had relocated himself to Chicago, but guessed every man has to come home sometimes.

As they started to uncork the last bottle, the Major suggested heading home to enjoy it in the backyard. It was a beautiful night and the Major was itching to get moving. The girls agreed and they all piled into Bernie's car to drive the few blocks to the Kolle's home. As Kiddie and the Major got out of the backseat, Bernie rolled down the window to hand them the bottle and let them know they would be along soon. Taking the bottle the Major shrugged and followed Kiddie up the front porch. As they snuck in quietly, the Major took Kiddie's hand and steered her toward the kitchen. Kiddie watched in amusement as the Major pulled food from the fridge and helped himself to leftovers. Grabbing his plate of food and the bottle of champagne, they headed out to the backyard.

It was a beautiful night and they sat together silently enjoying it while the Major finally had some dinner. Kiddie nibbled here and there, content to hold her glass and sit close to the Major, the warmth of his body and the buzz of her champagne coaxing her to feel content in the cool evening air. She released a big sigh and laid her head on the Major's shoulder.

"Major, I'm sorry I acted like a child when you got there." Kiddie said quietly.

The Major paused, then finished his mouthful and sat the plate down. He wrapped his arms around Kiddie and said equally quietly, "There are going to be times Kiddie when I have to put work first. I hope you're going to be okay with that. We both have goals and dreams we want to reach for and that's not always going to be convenient for either one of us."

Kiddie nodded her agreement and then stood up. "I know. It's been a long day. I think it's time to call it a night."

As the Major went to put his empty plate in the kitchen sink and say his goodnites, it turned out Iris had just gone to bed and Bernie stood by his car lighting up a cigarette. The Major kissed Kiddie on the top of her head, telling her goodnight before he went to bum a ride back to the city with him.

As Kiddie crawled into bed she was surprised to find Iris there, all snuggled up in the blankets and softly snoring. Kiddie found it comforting to have her there, taking in the rhythm of her snores, while trying to find her own sweet dreams. The Major's comment about not being convenient for either of them rang in her ears. She was disappointed in herself for acting childish, but shrugged it off best she could. Kiddie didn't know much about a sports writer's life, but that it seemed like an exciting job to have. For just a moment Kiddie wondered if Iris had the right idea of letting a man give her the good life? Kiddie let out a big sigh, pulled her covers up tight and closed her eyes with a big yawn. It was way late and too much champagne to figure out things like that now, but something told Kiddie she would find out sooner or later.

For some, baseball is a bore with little reason to partake in other than a way to make small talk given that the weather isn't that interesting either. For others, baseball is a way of life, particularly in the month of September, and if you're really lucky, even into October. In the fall of 1921, baseball took center stage as New York celebrated its first "subway" series between the Yankees and the Giants. That fall all of New York became a fan of baseball as people from around the states traveled to their city, bringing with them stacks of cash to pour into hotels, restaurants, cab's, and the Polo Grounds. For the Major, there were stories to be written and quite possibly, a name to be made. For Kiddie and her father, it was an opportunity to spend time together, cheering on their home team, the Giants.

The Giants weren't new to winning National League titles having been here eight times prior. Their only win as World Series Champions happened in 1905, way before Kiddie was old enough to appreciate baseball. Kiddie enjoyed the opportunity to spend a Sunday afternoon at the Polo Grounds, just her and her father, enjoying hot dogs while they watched and waited for the big hit that would score runs.

For Kiddie's father, baseball was one of the few distractions he allowed himself as his professional life consumed most of his time. When his children were young, Dr. Kolle would occasionally indulge his family and take them out to the ballpark on a sunny afternoon during the summer. Over the years they all begged off for one reason or another, until it was only Kiddie who would get excited to see baseball tickets on the dining room table. Kiddie would never turn down an opportunity to go into the city, especially in style the way her father moved.

While Kiddie had never worn a baseball mitt to catch a ball, much less swung a bat to hit one, there were plenty of things she enjoyed about baseball. Besides the legendary hotdogs, Kiddie loved to watch people at the ballpark, observing what they wore and interactions between people. She also loved the anticipation of waiting for the crack of wood hitting leather causing the sleepy crowd to come to life to see the runners round to home plate. The Polo Grounds sat in Manhattan, just off the Harlem River at the bottom of Coogan's Bluff. It had quite the sense of history after more than one location and a devastating fire. The Polo Grounds sat with two decks of Giants fans as well as fans seated deep in the outfield and even on the hill affectionately known as Coogan's Bluff. There was nothing better than the ballpark on a summer day, the anticipation for an eventful game palatable.

Giants fans mixed their anticipation with a healthy dose of anxious bravado as they prepared for game three of the Subway Series, confident it was time for their first win. People started their weekend early to fill the Polo Grounds to a record number of fans. Giants fans weren't sure what went wrong in the first two games and dismissed losing both games 3-0. Babe Ruth was definitely a deciding factor in the games, and the Giants pitcher had wisely walked him three times in game two. But still, with the Yankees two wins, the Giants were more than ready to get game three underway.

Kiddie was surprised her father had participated in the first two games from home, choosing to listen to the games on their family radio. It was the first time the World Series was broadcast live and given the Giants losses, Kiddie was thankful not to have to endure that in person at the Polo Grounds with her father. At least at home they had the usual household distractions and places to sneak off to as her father became more and more frustrated with the game. Nevertheless, like lots of other fans, Kiddie's father had tickets for the two of them for today's game. He was dressed to the nines and clearly expecting a victory.

The sun shone bright on a beautiful October afternoon, doing it's part to support the home team. There inlay the rub, as both teams were the home team and had the fans there to show it. Technically, since the Polo Grounds was the Giants home stadium, the Yankees remained guests. New Yorkers are passionate people, especially about baseball and the Major warned Kiddie to stay close to her father just in case some fans got out of hand. Kiddie and her father had seats behind home plate, while the Major sat in the press box with other journalists ready to write their own spin on the game. Kiddie searched to find the Major and see him in action. The Major loved baseball, and although a Cardinal's fan through and through, Kiddie also knew he was a Babe Ruth fan. Like any good reporter, the Major kept his biases to himself in his writing, and Kiddie was relieved for that as she knew her father read the *New York Times* from front to back everyday, including the sports page.

Like the other games, it was a slow start. The game took on a new sense of urgency in the third inning though, when both teams managed to score four runs. Giants fans were relieved to finally be on the board, and the stadium roared as fans on both sides demanded more from their teams. Despite an injury, Babe Ruth had managed to score a run, forcing the Giants to try their best to shut him down once more. In the seventh inning the game rose to a new noise level as the Giants magically brought home eight runs. Kiddie hugged her father with excitement, happy to see even him full of baseball joy. Despite the long afternoon and a massive crowd of fans to push through, it was an animated cab ride home as the two of them replayed highlights from the Giants victorious game.

The series gave Saturday as a day of rest for the players as well as the fans. New York bustled between the out-of-towners playing tourists and the New Yorkers pouring their nervous energy into drinks in their favorite speakeasies. Early Sunday afternoon, Kiddie and her whole family joined the other fans as they stood in long lines waiting to hand over tickets and hurry to their seats and start game four. Newspapers reported that Babe Ruth's doctor had urged him to sit out the rest of the series due to an injury. The Major had casually mentioned "we'll see" when they talked about it over the phone. The Yankee fans were beside themselves when Babe Ruth squeaked out a home run in the ninth inning. Despite being tied at some point in the game, the Giants pulled off a 4-2 win. With the series now tied at 2-2 wins, the players and fans alike could only eat, sleep, and talk about baseball. It was a great time to love baseball in New York City.

Game five of the series played on a Monday afternoon, and once again Kiddie's father chose to stay home and listen on the radio. It was a slow scoring game and despite having ten hits, the Giants could only score one run. The Giants fans frustration grew as Babe Ruth uncharacteristically bunted the ball, but made it across home plate on the next hit. The Yakees took their third win with a score of 3-1. Kiddie's father became quite grumpy and said the Giants would have to win the next game for him to ever set foot at the Polo Grounds again.

Other fans must have shared his sentiment as the crowd size ebbed for game six of the series. It was a hot Tuesday afternoon and Kiddie's father decided to listen to the game at a local pub, needing the distraction to soothe his nerves. Freddy joked it was because father thought he jinxed the games when he listened to them at home. Freddy decided to join his father and to his delight, they shared a memorable, but emotionally exhausting game together. Both teams started the game off strong, turning their hits into runs. Eventually though the lack of follow through on the hits became increasingly frustrating to the fans. For the Giants fans, they waited anxiously for the bottom of the last inning, maintaining their lead of 8-5 over the Yankees. Once again the series was tied up.

As game seven got underway on a beautiful Wednesday afternoon, the massive crowd surged into the Polo Grounds, fans on both sides anxious for a win. Giants fans were relieved to see Babe Ruth would not be playing today. The Yankees caused the Giants fans much anxiety as their batters made hit after hit, while the Giants were held to only two hits the whole game. Kiddie, her father, and Freddy were ecstatic when the Giants pulled off the win, their two hits turned into runs, which was enough to win the game 2-1.

On Thursday afternoon the sun shone bright from a crisp blue sky, as both teams prepared for the eighth and final game of the series. What a difference a week made in the lives of New York baseball players and fans alike. Kiddie and her whole family sat behind home plate anxious for a win. Kiddie noticed the Polo Grounds didn't bustle with nearly as many fans and assumed the Yankees fans were expecting a Giants win as well. The game turned out to be uneventful after the first inning with a 1-0 win for the Giants.

Father was so pleased the Giants won the World Series, he took the family out to dinner at Shanley's restaurant. Sitting at the table with her family, Kiddie took in the celebratory chatter, the restaurant buzzing with lots of happy Giants fans. She jumped to her feet when she noticed the Major making his way to their table. The Major had popped in to say hello, much to Kiddie's dismay, declining to stay for dinner as he had one more story to write before the paper printed. Kiddie sipped her drink trying to stay focused on the Giant's win, and trying not to wonder if she would always play second fiddle to whatever story the Major was needing to write.

For the Major it had been quite a week of baseball, deadlines, and drinking into the wee hours of the morning. Much like his writing about Suzanne Lenglen, the Major had lucked into a historical sports opportunity with the subway series landing in his lap. He had enjoyed wearing his press "pass" into all eight games, feeling a trifle important and most definitely happy to have free access to the series. The other writers he competed with for a front page storyline were a likable enough lot, and he had made the most of the nine days of baseball. Like most people he had bet on the Giants to win, but also rooted for the Yankee underdogs. He was taken with Babe Ruth and the power he brought to a bat, let alone the physical largeness he brought to home plate. He mostly appreciated that the Yankees had played hard and managed to stretch the series out to eight games. That was good for lots of New Yorkers for lots of reasons.

As the Major sent his last story off to copy, he wondered if Kiddie had read his stories. He didn't want his stories to just be about the numbers, but more about the people. Anyone could report a win or a loss, but could they make it interesting to any reader? The Major wanted his readers to feel connected to the people who won and lost. The Major was grateful for the opportunity to hone his craft, acknowledging the need for edits, but always keeping the Corum in his story. Walking into his apartment, the exhaustion started to settle in. His last thought as he fell into a deep sleep was of Kiddie and how pretty she had looked at dinner tonight. He missed his girl and wondered if she missed him.

K iddie flipped through the mail one more time, more than annoyed. Was she ever going to hear from Edna Crompton? Had her patient, but aching muscles been in vain? After that eventful afternoon when Kiddie and Iris had met Ms. Crompton at her art show, Kiddie had wasted no time reaching out to her. She had done her best to be professional, sending a formal letter of inquiry as well as her resume. She had debated on sending her resume at all being that she was still a college student and it lacked much umph. Her mother had encouraged her to include her highlights from Erasmus Hall as well as list her art classes from Columbia University. Kiddie wanted Ms. Crompton to know that she was serious about art, even if she did not have the talent and popularity of Ms. Crompton's paintings.

Kiddie was currently taking classes in illustration as well as a traditional painting class. Hoping to work with a variety of artists, Kiddie was fascinated with how it all worked and wanted to understand what they were trying to accomplish. She knew she would never be as good as Edna Crompton or even her father for that matter. Since she was a little girl, her father had encouraged Kiddie to sit at her own easel beside his, and paint what she felt. Kiddie's father focused his painting more on accuracy, just as any scientist would tend to do. However, he saw Kiddie's paintings being better when she painted from the heart, making her work authentic and therefore appealing in its own right. Father had been very pleased when Kiddie had announced she wanted to take art classes at Columbia and did not hesitate to write the checks for her tuition.

After a few anxious weeks Kiddie had been delighted when Ms. Crompton had asked her to come by her studio for a meeting. Kiddie thought of it as an interview and came prepared to answer questions. Knowing that Ms. Crompton's work was an influence for stylish trends, Kiddie had freshened her dark bob and worn one of her most fashionable dresses from Lord & Taylor. Kiddie guessed Ms. Crompton to be twenty years her senior and learned she was married to an artist involved in advertising. Kiddie was fascinated with a tour of Ms. Crompton's studio as she strolled through racks of women's clothing, hats, shoes, and props, oblivious to her art supplies. Kiddie left that day excited for an appointment for her first sitting, a simple black dress chosen for her to wear.

Edna, as Kiddie had been instructed to call her, had patiently explained what sitting as a model would entail. The long detailed process would require multiple sittings for Kiddie as Edna layered her paint to create the warm, authentic glow that magazines wanted bestowed upon their covers. Although not that important to Kiddie, Edna told her regretfully that Kiddie would not be paid unless a magazine purchased the painting for a cover. Edna finished with a big smile and reassurance that her paintings most always became a cover, sooner or later.

Kiddie hesitated to share with her family this new turn of events and confided only in the Major. The Major quelled her fears and cheered on her efforts to make her mark in the world. Kiddie couldn't bear the thought of disappointing her family, especially her father, if she went to all this effort and then her painting wasn't picked for a magazine cover. Instead Kiddie always created an excuse, mostly school related, when she needed to be at Edna's studio. Kiddie was grateful that Edna had chosen her as one of her models to paint. During the tour, it had not been lost on Kiddie the numerous paintings of girls sitting around the large studio.

While it all seemed glamorous and exciting, Kiddie soon learned the work and patience it took to sit still endlessly, her back straight, the perfect smile frozen on her face. When she was done for the afternoon, her muscles would ache, her body stiff, not used to being inactive in such a way. When the painting of her was finally finished, Kiddie was beside herself with joy and gratitude. Gazing at the finished painting Kiddie took in every stroke. She was fascinated with how Edna had captured her short dark curls, her dark eyes, and narrow smile. It looked like Kiddie and yet it didn't.

As if almost reading her mind, Edna reassured her, "Kiddie you look like every fashionable American girl out there, but people who know you will know it's you. The painting is captivating and what people want to see on their magazine covers." Kiddie could only hope Edna was right and wait for her to let her know. And so she waited and waited, growing more discouraged as the weeks went by.

Tossing the mail back onto the table, Kiddie grabbed her book bag and headed out the door. With Christmas only a few weeks away Kiddie should really be focused on her finals coming up in the next few days. She headed to the library to study and later meet the Major for dinner. He learned weeks ago not to ask, but merely distract her when he could with dinner and a glass of her favorite beverage. Kiddie tried not to think about it too much and let it make her grumpy.

C hristmas was two weeks away and yet Kiddie could not wait for Sunday dinner tonight. After weeks of checking the mail, Santa had come early and delivered a contract to Kiddie regarding her first cover. Kiddie finally knew that her painting had been chosen for a cover with *RedBook* magazine in the upcoming year. Attached to the letter was a contract requiring her signature should she agree to have it released and compensated as stated. Kiddie was thrilled about her big news, deciding to wait to share with her family at Sunday dinner. The Major had spoiled her upon hearing the news with a celebratory dinner at the Plaza Hotel.

Now Kiddie was busy setting the table for dinner. She smiled at how their family of five had grown to seven. The Major had learned months ago about the magic of Sunday dinner, when Cook went all out on the menu and all family members were expected to be present. Even Kiddie's father, barring a medical emergency that absolutely needed his attention, rarely missed family dinner on Sunday evenings. These days Iris often invited Bernie to join them and he was quickly starting to feel like a family member too. Kiddie and Iris often relished in how well their men got along, different as they were.

For Kiddie's mother it was her favorite meal of the week, and she often helped Cook plan the food to be served. Everyone knew it was the love that went into the cooking that could make even a simple pot roast and potatoes taste divine. Besides the food and the wine that inevitably flowed from her father's skilled pours, having everyone around the table made Kiddie's mother's heart full. She occasionally threw out a comment, but mostly sat back and listened to the banter, the laughter, and lively conversations her family shared at the dinner table. At times the conversation would become louder when politics or current events reared it's controversial head, and not everyone could agree to disagree. Eventually Kiddie's mother would intervene and try to channel the conversation elsewhere. Her family usually heeded her soft warning and moved on, but occasionally there would be someone who would stomp off, annoyed beyond reason.

Kiddie wasn't sure what was being served for dinner, but she wanted to make sure the table sparkled and shined when she shared her big news. Feeling satisfied with the way it looked, Kiddie headed upstairs to get dressed. She had thirty minutes until the Major arrived, which would be exactly thirty minutes before dinner was served. Lately her father had taken to inviting Freddy and the Major into his study for a shot of his best bourbon and men talk before dinner. Kiddie wondered when Bernie would catch on, and show up earlier to secure his own shot of bourbon.

Although it was an unspoken expectation to dress nice for Sunday dinner, Kiddie was particularly thoughtful in her dress choice for tonight. She wanted to look stunning and most definitely worthy of a magazine cover. She chose a black dress with long sleeves and a fitted waist that dropped into a soft full skirt. Her eyes danced with excitement and her face glowed in anticipation. She added a touch of lipstick and her mother's pearls and headed downstairs just in time to answer the doorbell.

To her surprise Iris bounced down the stairs announcing airly she would get the door as Kiddie moved aside. Even more surprised Kiddie saw Bernie standing at the door, a rather large poinsettia in his arms. Standing half way down the stairs, Kiddie couldn't help but notice what a handsome couple they made. As Bernie lightly kissed Iris on the cheek, she notice Iris had her own glow about her tonight. Kiddie smiled as she came down the stairs greeting Bernie warmly and taking the poinsettia from him. Both girls smiled as they realized their mother had put a Christmas record on the Victrola. The holiday season was upon them and everyone seemed to sparkle and shine in anticipation of family dinner.

Kiddie was still close to the door when a few minutes later the Major arrived. Kiddie loved how he almost always presented himself in a suit and tie. He was kissing Kiddie on the cheek when her father came down the stairs, beaming at them both. Freddy and the Major headed to the study for their pre-dinner drink, as Kiddie informed her father that Bernie was also there and would be participating. She noticed he seemed not the least bit surprised by this and went to collect him to come to his study before closing the door behind him.

As the food was brought to the table and the candles lit, Iris took it upon herself to open the wine, placing bottles at either end of the table. The large poinsettia had been placed on the buffet, bringing its own holiday cheer to the dining room. As the men emerged from the study, they all took their places at the table. Kiddie's father passed out juicy slices of pot roast while the others passed around steaming bowls of food. Candles sparkled on the table and on the Christmas tree in the corner while *Jingle Bells* played on the Victrola. Kiddie felt a nervous energy as she drank her glass of wine before making her announcement. She had rehearsed how she would say it in her head a hundred times in the three days since she had read the letter. She didn't want to seem boastful, but she was proud of herself.

Wisely Kiddie waited until plates sat mostly empty, a smear of gravy or lone green bean all that was left to tell that food had graced their plates. She felt the Major put his hand on her knee and squeeze it, giving her the nod she needed to get on with it. Picking up her glass as she went to stand up, Kiddie tapped it gently with her fork to get everyone's attention.

As everyone turned to look at her she said, "I have a small announcement to make if everyone can pause for a moment." As Kiddie's family looked at her expectantly she jumped right in.

"As you know, Iris and I met Edna Crompton last fall at her art show at Columbia. Her paintings focus on illustrating young women of today and are becoming magazine covers for some of our favorite magazines Iris and I read. I've been lucky enough to spend most of November in her studio practicing my good posture while she painted my portrait. This week I learned that her painting of me was accepted by *RedBook* to be a cover for an issue in the new year. I wanted you to be the first to know!" As she said it, she had to smile, knowing it was real.

For a moment no one said anything as they processed what she had said.

Suddenly Iris squealed with delight and jumped up to give her a big hug. The table came to life, a buzz of congratulations. Iris went to pick up her own glass and raise it in a toast to Kiddie. "To Kiddie's new adventure and following the family motto to making your dreams come true!"

As Kiddie turned to cheer with Iris, something suddenly caught her eye. She swallowed her wine quickly and then sat her glass down to grab Iris' hand. Iris froze as Kiddie demanded, "What is this?" Suddenly Kiddie could feel the gentle pressure of the Major's hand on her back, a discrete signal to take a minute.

Iris proceeded to jump in with her own announcement and without any hesitation practically shouted, "Bernie asked me to marry him and I said YES!"

For a second time that evening the family paused to process and then came to life, jumping up from the table to give the couple big hugs and handshakes. Kiddie stood to one side taking it all in, her mind working to switch gears and understand what was happening. Iris and Bernie were engaged! Her news was not so big as compared to that! Her baby sister was getting married! After Iris handed her mother a napkin to wipe a tear, she turned to Kiddie, her face expectant and apologetic all at the same time. Kiddie gave Iris a fierce hug, admiring the ring and babbling on about weddings and what a big night it was. Kiddie was ever so thankful when the Major raised his own glass of wine to make a toast.

"To all the women in this family, who keep us men on our toes and how we love them for it!" Kiddie turned gratefully to the Major to clink her glass to his, their eyes meeting, his hand on her knee once again. As everyone turned their glasses up, only Iris noticed as Kiddie quickly downed her half full glass of wine.

"It looks like we're going to need more wine for this family dinner! Kiddie come help me open more wine." Without waiting for her reply Iris grabbed Kiddie's hand and ushered her into the kitchen.

As soon as the doors closed behind them, they both started talking at once. "Kiddie I feel so bad, I didn't mean to steal your spotlight! I'm so proud of you! I knew you could do it! MY sister on the cover of *RedBook*!"

"Iris I'm so happy for you and Bernie, but I didn't expect it so soon! I know you want this though, and I want you to be happy! Did he ask Father for permission? Have you set a date? Let me see your ring again!"

The tearful awkwardness was soon dispelled and they went to rejoin the family, who now sat comfortably around the roaring fire Freddy was busy stoking. As *Adeste Fideles* played on the Victrola, Kiddie realized Santa had come early, giving Iris and herself both what they wished for on their picnic last fall.

Suddenly her father stood beside her mother, his glass raised to make a toast. "Congratulations to all of you. Let's all rejoice in this Christmas and all we have to look forward to in 1922." Everyone agreed, the Major most.

CHAPTER THREE
═1922═

K iddie's subconscious struggled to bring her back, to free her from the pain, the turmoil. Abruptly she sat up, wiping the tears from her face without even realizing she was doing so. Now that she was awake, she searched to go back and find the reason for her struggle, her anguish over the wedding. Wait! Her wedding she wondered as she slowly lay back into her many fluffy pillows. She realized she had been arguing with her mother, over her wedding day. Kiddie was confused, since Iris was the one getting married.

Kiddie closed her eyes, trying to remember her dream. She and her mother had been arguing about canceling her wedding day because of the influenza epidemic ravaging New York City. Her mother was trying to convince her it wasn't safe to bring a large group of people together even if it was for such an important occasion. Kiddie felt heartbroken at the thought of not having her big day, even as her mother reminded her there were people with much bigger problems than hers. Kiddie wondered why she was the one getting married and not Iris, seeing that Iris was the one officially engaged.

Still somewhat rattled by her angst, Kiddie tried to remember what she was doing before bed, wondering how her brain had taken her to this place. Thinking back she remembered she and Iris had been drinking wine and reading about Princess Mary's wedding in the *British Vogue* magazine. The Major had surprised Kiddie with it as a special treat after seeing her excitement over the supplement *The Times* had published to mark England's latest royal wedding a few weeks ago.

Kiddie and Iris both loved anything regarding the royal family, and Princess Mary's wedding had been the first wedding to have so much of a press presence. Her dress had been described as "youthful simplicity with royal splendor." To balance her fancy lacey florals, the Princess had worn a simple strand of pearls. This was Kiddie's favorite accessory to any dress she wore, and most likely the choice she would make someday too. Talk of bridesmaids and wedding gowns had become more prevalent between Kiddie and Iris in recent weeks, ever since Iris's engagement just before Christmas. Even though a couple of months had passed, it still seemed odd to Kiddie that her little sister had a ring on her finger, while she and the Major were content to continue dating. It wasn't that Kiddie needed a ring on her finger just yet, but it seemed surprising her little sister beat her to it.

Kiddie lay back down, snuggling one of her pillows under her chin, embracing the comforting smell of her linens. She wondered why her wine muddled brain brought the pandemic into her dream? Most definitely that had been the hardest time Kiddie had ever gone through. Was her subconscious worried marriage would be that hard too? Still reluctant to close her eyes, Kiddie's mind wandered back to that horrid fall not that long ago. Kiddie and Iris had been teenagers, but old enough to realize the gravity of the situation. The influenza epidemic had been very real as their father had worked day and night in one of the many emergency health centers set up in Brooklyn. Being a doctor, and a well renowned one at that, he had no choice, but to be on the front lines day in and day out.

Health commissioner Copeland worked to educate the public regarding healthier practices, encouraging people to not spit wherever they fancied and to cover their coughs and sneezes. For Kiddie this seemed somewhat appalling that this was not just good common sense for people. City officials staggered business hours to encourage New Yorkers to keep their distance from each other, particularly on the subways and train cars. In a way there was a sense of quarantine expected, but the reality was that it was more voluntary than mandatory.

Theaters and schools stayed open as they became targeted places to educate the public and provide extra medical support. As Kiddie and Iris walked into class each day, their teachers were expected to check them for symptoms and send them on to trained medical staff should they feel it was warranted. Kiddie found this an offensive way to start the day, being poked and prodded, so did not protest when her Father decided his children should be homeschooled for a while.

Although Iris seemed unfazed by most of it, Kiddie didn't like living her life in limbo, waiting for the worst to happen. She loved hanging out with friends and staying busy with tennis and horseback riding. Now father had them stuck at home, forced to study and read the same magazines over and over. As always the *New York Times* was delivered daily, the pandemic always front page news. One day Kiddie wandered into her father's office and started skimming through some of the lead stories. Kiddie felt a sense of despair, reading how people were dying while waiting to be treated, makeshift morgues set up as bodies piled up. Kiddie's mother found her sitting at her father's desk, tears streaming down her face. Taking the paper from her, she let Kidde cry it out on her shoulder, trying to reassure her it would all be okay, sooner or later. Kiddie learned later her Mother put their subscription on hold, deciding no news was good news.

Even the radio was little entertainment as updates on the pandemic often interrupted programming. The girls were not allowed to be on the phone to catch up with friends as their mother kept it open, dreading a call that someone they knew had succumbed to the influenza. Kiddie worried it was a matter of time before it caught up to someone they loved. The hardest part was worrying about her father, and his safety. Although there were long, boring days and even longer sleepless nights, Kiddie understood her father's decision to keep them home from school. He couldn't focus as a doctor if he had to worry about his own family's safety, so they stayed home. Occasionally their mother would send Kiddie and Iris off to the deli to get fresh meat. They hurried through the streets, their masks covering their faces, fearful someone would cough on them, and contaminate them. For the first time, life was hard for Kiddie.

This quarantined time at home also became the first time Kiddie and Iris drank enough wine to wake up regretting it. They had been flipping through magazines before dinner, way past bored and just short of going crazy. Mother had opened a bottle of wine with dinner, but left the table early to go off to do some writing, leaving the opened bottle as fair game. Iris had confiscated it before Cook came and cleared the dinner table. They ran to Kiddie's bedroom with the wine and magazines in tow. It wasn't that they had never been allowed wine before, but it had always been limited to a respectable half glass. The girls downed the bottle quickly, making a game out of taking a drink every time they saw a cigarette or tobacco ad in their magazines. When they came across Prince Albert ads, they had to finish their glass. The girls giggled at how old and unromantic the Prince was in those ads and could only hope to find their own Prince Charming someday, certain he would be quite handsome.

It had never occured to the girls to sneak wine from the cellar before, but tonight seemed to be the right time to do so. A little tipsy, they shushed each other all the way to the cellar, grabbing the closest bottle before they dashed back to Kiddie's room. Feeling elated over having a second bottle, it eventually dawned on them they had no way to open it. This only added to their adventure as they proceeded to sneak into the kitchen, knowing Cook was long gone, and quickly finding the appropriate tool to get the job done. It was Iris who peeled back the foil, using the opener thingy to lift out the snug little cork from it's bottle. Kiddie was convinced such natural talent must come from their father and his surgical expertise. The girls wondered if he had the same sense of immense satisfaction as they did when they triumphantly refilled their glasses. Eventually the second bottle lay empty on the floor, the girls passed out in a tangled heap of magazines, blankets and pillows in the middle of Kiddie's bed.

Kiddie remembered waking up that morning, just before dawn, feeling horrible, at first panicked that she must be experiencing symptoms of the influenza. She had pictured how to go and tell her mother it was her time to get tested, trying to sit up ever so gingerly in bed. Looking around and seeing the magazines and empty wine bottles, the night had flooded back to Kiddie. She sank back into her pillows, realizing with some relief this must be the wine flu she was experiencing. She had heard her older brother bemoan his own experience in an almost bragatory way after a certain social event with his friends.

After that night, the girls were quick to grab the half empty bottles of wine from the dinner table, but never ventured to the wine cellar again. Kiddie and her family passed the time the best they could. Mother kept on them about their school work throughout the mornings and encouraged them to spend their afternoons reading. Before dinner they would play games to find some sweet relief from worry, then be soberly jerked back to the present, feeling guilty they would be so carefree when so many were struggling. When thirty thousand people die in your hometown, you are bound to know at least one of them and it changes you. Although New York City fared better than Boston and Philadelphia, it was tragic and seemed to suck all the joy out of living for a while. Kiddie had seen how fragile life is, and how vulnerable people are. Kiddie's family was fortunate and spared any personal loss, but still you couldn't help feel some of the burden others shouldered at a most difficult time.

Kiddie remembered vividly when their father finally returned home, exhausted, but safe. The girls had run to him, giving him big hugs and loud cheers, their brother Freddy jumping into the fray even if he was a little more reserved. Their mother stood to the side waiting her turn until father had gone to her and scooped her up. Kiddie and her siblings watched quietly as their mother had wept into his shoulder, unable to let go long enough even for him to sit down. It was only then Kiddie realized how strong she had been, keeping their daily routines, answering their questions, never faltering that everything would be okay. Kiddie could feel her mother's worry wash away, replaced with sweet relief and a grateful heart. Eventually life got back to a sense of normal as Kiddie and Iris returned to school, hanging out with friends and being teenagers again.

Now, in the dark, Kiddie focused on a bright path of moonlight at the end of her bed, and wondered what the take away was from her dream. Was she worried Iris was not really ready to take on marriage? Or was Kiddie jealous she wasn't the one engaged already? Was Kiddie trying to protect herself from the Major by prolonging making a serious commitment to him? Kiddie wondered if she was ready to change her name or her address. She finally closed her eyes, letting go of the moonlight, her last thought wondering how she would know when she was ready.

The Major was exhausted, but not even the rhythmic clackity clack of the train wheels on the track could lull his brain to sleep. It had been five days since he got the call from his mother, sharing the tragic news. The Major had been careful to spend his time reacting to what was happening around him, rather than allow himself to process his grief. Now as the rain started to pelt his window, his view began to blur and he couldn't hold on any longer. His beloved Uncle Crutch was dead and buried just like that.

The Major knew it could not be good news when his mother tracked him down on a Saturday at his *New York Times* office. After ringing off he had sat for a moment trying to process that his Uncle Crutch unexpectedly passed away at a hospital in St. Louis. He called Kiddie to let her know he would be going home to Missouri for a few days. She expressed heartfelt sympathy, knowing that Uncle Crutch was one of the Major's favorite people. She offered to go home with him, but he knew he would not be able to handle the additional drama that her appearance would bring.

It was a cold, wet dreadful day in early March, when you wish spring would just get on with it. The Major tied up loose ends at work and then at home before he caught his westbound train late that afternoon. The train ride home seemed even longer than usual, his mind a painful whirlwind of details, memories, and guilt.

While the Major's mother had several sisters, his father had only one brother, one brother named Crutch. The Major too had only one brother and could not imagine how his father must be feeling to lose his only sibling. For years, it had been just the two of them as their parents had died years ago. The Major had few memories of his Grandpa, but had known and loved his Grandma America. The Major had been in college when she died, his first experience with loss. He remembered he felt guilty then for not being home more, the drive not that far from Columbia to Boonville. Now five years later he felt that same sense of guilt, although the trek from New York to Missouri was a much greater effort.

Being home at such a difficult time had been a struggle, all the family dressed in black, dishes of good home cooked food out everywhere, and quiet, solemn conversations throughout the house. It had been years since he had seen his cousin, and he hated that it happened this way. He hugged his aunt fiercely, her sobs into his shoulder a blow to his fragile composure. There had been people from St. Louis to Columbia to Boonville who came to show their respects. His aunt had asked him to stand beside her in the line, and so he stood between her and his father, shaking hands and hearing stories from strangers about the wonderful man Uncle Crutch had been.

The last time he saw Uncle Crutch was during the holidays and late summer before that. Uncle Crutch had always seemed like a hero to him. Just like his uncle, the Major attended the University of Missouri, one graduating with a law degree and the other with a degree in journalism. After practicing in Boonville for a while, Uncle Crutch moved his practice to the big city of St. Louis. Uncle Crutch soon had many big name clients and when he took the Major out, he was bound to be recognized by at least a handful of people. Eventually Uncle Crutch became the attorney for Missouri Pacific Railroad. Now, just like the Major, Uncle Crutch was headed home by train, the railroad considering it a great honor to give Uncle Crutch his last train ride.

The Major's favorite memory with Uncle Crutch would always be the two weeks they spent exploring the World's Fair in St. Louis in 1904. He remembered how his mother had taken him to get a real haircut and a new suit before putting him on the train to St. Louis. For a nine year old boy, it was a magical place with a ferris wheel and a talking horse, not to mention a plethora of newly invented food choices. Uncle Crutch indulged the Major's hearty boyish appetite buying him everything from his first hamburger to cotton candy to peanut butter to his first ice cream cone. The real highlight came though, when Uncle Crutch had taken him to his first Cardinal's baseball game. Like most American boys, the Major considered himself a baseball player and he had reveled in being at the ballpark.

The majority of the Major's fondest memories with Uncle Crutch revolved around Cardinal baseball games. Together they had been avid fans and as a boy, the Major lived for summer days when they would go to cheer on their team together. It was rare that his father took time away from being the postmaster, but he was grateful for those Sunday afternoons they made the trek to St. Louis. The Major now regretted they had not seen very many games since he had taken up residence in New York City. But still, he kept on top of how the Cardinals were doing and called his uncle often to celebrate the victories and dissect the losses. It occurred to the Major now that Uncle Crutch was probably a lot of the reason why he enjoyed sports so much, and why he currently wrote sports stories for the *New York Times*. He knew his Uncle had loved him and been proud of him, and for now he tried to find comfort in that.

The Major stretched his legs best he could from his cramped train seat. He checked his watch, grateful to have only a few hours left before he pulled into Grand Central in New York City. He would have a quick cab ride to his apartment where he couldn't wait to pour a stiff drink and crawl into bed. His thoughts turned to Kiddie, as he debated on calling her tonight or waiting until the morning. Thinking about Kiddie brought some sweet relief to his heavy heart. It was midweek and he knew there were any number of things she could be doing, but he would most likely find her at home. The Major thought about how he was a lucky man to have two families to be a part of.

It had been an easy choice to move to New York after the war. The Major relished in how a man could go out almost anytime day or night in New York City and find a nice juicy steak and a stiff drink. There was always some event to attend from the sports world to the bright lights on Broadway. He loved that Kiddie shared his exuberance for going out on the town and embracing all that New York City had to offer. The Major had settled into a fine routine in the city, writing his stories, stepping out with Kiddie, and retiring to his private space when he occasionally would need to rest. He was comfortable with the fact that most of his friends were college buddies, other sports journalists, and bartenders. He wondered if someday down the road, he would be like his Uncle Crutch and walk into a place, recognized by at least a handful of people. He knew it was about time to take his place officially in Kiddie's family, and put a ring on her finger. Bernie might have beat him to the punch, but the Major had a plan too.

K iddie stretched out lazily thinking about her day ahead of her. It promised to be a hot day, especially for so early in June. For once, Kiddie didn't have to stop and think about what day it was. Kiddie loved the lazy days of summer, but she often used her social life to keep up with what day of the week it was. Today was different because there was a lot going on, even for a Saturday.

Tomorrow was June 4, Kiddie's birthday. Iris had decided they should all go out on the town tonight to check out a new place in the East Village called the RedHead. Kiddie happily agreed and immediately began making plans of her own. The Major and Kiddie had been together for almost two years and Kiddie had decided tonight was the night she was going to give herself to the Major. She vacillated from excited to mortified by the minute, but Kiddie had done her homework, determined her first time would be both romantic and safe.

Kiddie knew she did not want to do it when she was drunk, wanting to be in control and enjoy every minute of her first time. She supposed it could be a little painful, but she trusted the Major implicitly and was not that worried. Kiddie had played this out in her head several times, although she admitted she had never actually seen a man completely naked before. Maybe one little cocktail wouldn't hurt to get them started.

Kiddie rolled over to open the drawer of her little table by her bed. She dug to the bottom to pull out her rather worn out copy of *The Woman Rebel*. Margaret Sanger was on Kiddie's hero list, as she worked with tenacity to bring safe birth control to women. Thanks to the rampant spread of venereal disease during WWI, birth control had finally become a health issue rather than a moral issue. Of course not everyone saw it that way, and Kiddie supposed it was more for those who enjoyed sexual relationships than those who didn't. Kiddie remembered vividly the day her mother had sat her and Iris down to have the talk with them. It had been an awkward conversation to start, but her mother plowed through, enlightening them both as to how the male and female bodies were made to become one, all in the name of love of course. It had been most informative to learn about sponges and condoms, knowing that there were choices to be made. Like most things she did, Kiddie would be taking charge, leaving nothing to chance.

It hadn't been that long since their conversation and Kiddie applauded her mother for realizing her daughters were in love and liked to live life to the fullest. Of course Kiddie's mother advocated for abstinence until marriage, reminding them that was the only sure way to not get pregnant. Kiddie scoffed at society making words such as birth control, sex, and pregnant taboo words, almost to the point of being illegal. Margaret Sanger had been arrested multiple times and even spent thirty days in jail once in her pursuit of helping women protect themselves from disease and unwanted pregnancies. Thanks to reading *The Woman Rebel*, Kiddie already knew most of what her mother had shared. She was nosing around her father's office one day, in search of information, when she came across one of the issues of *The Woman Rebel*. It had been buried at the bottom of a stack of medical periodicals and newspapers and Kiddie was confident her father would never miss it. Of course she shared it with Iris, wanting her little sister to be informed and safe too.

Kiddie was pretty sure the hardest part of having sex was finding your way to procurring condoms or sponges, or both if you wanted to double your protection. Kiddie knew the Major was old-fashioned at heart, and she hoped he would realize this was his cue she was ready to get married. Kiddie couldn't put her finger on what had changed since February, but she knew with certainty the Major was the one for her.

Iris had invited Kiddie and their mother to lunch today in Manhattan and then wedding dress shopping afterwards. Kiddie decided Iris could drop her at the Major's apartment after shopping and they could go to dinner from there, before meeting people at the RedHead. Of course there was one more thing on Kiddie's agenda that was top priority for the day.

Kiddie finally rolled out of bed to go soap and scrub all her female parts thoroughly before slipping into her new dress. The light floral gauzy dress was perfect for a hot summer day. Its drop waist and knee-length hem were nothing special these days, but Kiddie loved how the flutter sleeves delicately showed off her arms and the lace embellished v-neckline showed off her assets in a tasteful way, making her feel like a woman.

T heir afternoon flew by with a lovely lunch followed by visits to Iris's choice of different dress shops. Iris had her heart set on a late fall wedding in November. Having established their guest list, Grand Prospect Hall was secured for both their wedding and reception. As Kiddie watched Iris try on a plethora of wedding dresses, she couldn't help but make mental notes for what she would want in her own dress. She was certain her and the Major's wedding would be a much less formal affair. It would have to be as she didn't want to just repeat what Iris did for her wedding. Kiddie wasn't sure what season she wanted to get married in, but fall seemed like a fitting choice. It would be two years this fall since that day she met the Major at the presidential rally near campus. Thinking about him returning her scarf to her made Kiddie smile, relishing in how much could change in two years.

As Iris came out in yet another gown, Kiddie nearly gasped in awe. Watching Iris turn and twirl and admire herself in the mirror, Kiddie knew this was the one. Seeing their mother with tears in her eyes and her hands clasped, only confirmed what Kiddie thought.

"Iris, this is the dress! You look stunning!" Kiddie told her. Iris stopped her twirling, pausing to really look at herself before searching Kiddie and her mother's faces in the mirror.

"Yes! This is the dress! I'm getting married and I'm going to have my happily ever after!" Kiddie laughed at Iris's drama as they went to give her a big hug. Kiddie and her mother were happy to be done dress shopping, but even more happy to see Iris so happy.

Kiddie's smile broadened as the Major answered the door in his dress pants and a white undershirt. She hadn't been concerned about arriving a little early, but clearly she had caught him off guard. Kiddie rarely saw the Major in anything less than a suit and tie, but when she did, she enjoyed seeing his casual side. It seemed intimate, a side of the Major only Kiddie was privy to.

As she stepped into the apartment she kissed him on the cheek. "I hope you don't mind that I'm a little early, Major."

Closing the door, the Major turned Kiddie around making her dress twirl. "You look gorgeous Kiddie, ready for a night out on the town! Happy early birthday, my love!" he said, sealing it with a kiss on her lips. "Would you like a glass of champagne?" The Major might not keep much food around, but he always had some kind of hooch around. Since he had started dating Kiddie, he had started stashing bottles of champagne as well, even though she didn't come to his apartment very often.

"Why thank you Major, you know I never turn down champagne."

Kiddie watched as the Major deftly opened the bottle and poured champagne into two coupe glasses. Taking both of their glasses, the Major went to sit on the couch. Feeling a nervous excited energy, Kiddie joined him on the couch, wondering what kind of small talk she could come up with, her mind clearly somewhere else. As she took her glass from the Major, she told him about Iris's plan to meet at the RedHead for drinks after dinner.

"It's your night Kiddie, whatever makes you happy." the Major said, looking at her over his coupe glass.

Balancing her champagne, Kiddie moved so that she could straddle the Major. He raised an eyebrow slightly then smiled as she said, "Cheers to you Major, and for making me happy," clinking their glasses together before taking a drink.

Kiddie decided to focus on the Major's chin and jump right into her agenda.

"How does it feel to be dating a woman now?" she asked as coyly as she knew how.

Ahhh, now the Major could see where this was going, but he was curious how far Kiddie was planning to go. "Is that what I'm doing? I had no idea." he teased her.

Sipping her champagne, Kiddie looked at the Major over the top of her own glass. She could see he thought she was playing. She finished her champagne swiftly and sat her glass down on the coffee table. Kiddie put her arms around the Major's neck and leaned into him.

"Major, I'm ready to take our relationship to the next level. It's time and I'm ready." Kiddie said huskily.

At different times in different places Kiddie and the Major often engaged in heavy petting. It was usually the Major who would eventually shut it down, always in control regardless of how much he drank. Kiddie, ever the easy lush, loved to see how far he would go, trusting him to save them both before it went too far. Today was different though, and Kiddie wanted the Major to take her seriously.

The Major took Kiddie's hands out from around his neck, his eyes wandering to her delicious neckline. He held them firmly in front of him. "Kiddie have you already been drinking?"

When Kiddie shook her head no he said, his own voice getting husky. "Are you sure you're ready to see this through all the way." the Major asked, his eyes now focused on her lips.

Pulling her hands free, Kiddie gently took the Major's face in her hands. She knew the Major wasn't asking in just a physical way, but in every way. "I promise I've thought this through and I'm ready. I love you and I'm ready to be yours."

The Major locked eyes with Kiddie and said quietly, "Kiddie I've loved you for so long and if we do this, go all the way, there is no turning back in this relationship. You will be stuck with me forever."

"I know Major, and I'm ready to be stuck with you." Kiddie said softly. She once again put her arms around his neck and started to kiss him ever so lightly on his neck until she came to kiss him on the lips. Their tongues searched hungrily, needing it to be more. When Kiddie pulled back she could see the Major's eyes were dark pools that made her shiver with excitement. His hands were caressing her arms until he came around to her neckline, tracing it's outline with his finger, pausing intentionally where it dipped. Kiddie didn't breathe as he reached around her to partially unzip her dress, then gently pulled it down around her shoulders, exposing her to him. He stood up in one swift move, Kiddie wrapping her arms and legs around him as he walked them to his bedroom. Kiddie could feel how strong and hard he was beneath her and she shivered in anticipation as he nudged the door shut with his foot behind them.

The Major lay beside Kiddie listening to her even breathing while taking in the sight of her in his bed. Her dark curls covered her pillow, her bare shoulder peeking out from under the sheet. Thinking about her nakedness under the sheet made him a little crazy, but he was a very patient man. He had waited a long time for this, always putting what was best for Kiddie ahead of his own basic needs. She was still young and at times he could feel the seven years he had on her. He loved that Kiddie had come to him today, completely sober, and made her declaration. He hoped she realized that he had meant it when he told her there would be no turning back. The Major applauded Kiddie's timing, as it worked beautifully with her birthday.

Since that day he saw her rushing out of the library doors at Columbia, he had known Kiddie was the one. When she had dropped her scarf behind her, he never doubted it was the universe encouraging him to go after her. His arms were wrapped around him as she lay in his bed, her back to his chest. There was just one more thing he needed to do to make sure the world knew Kiddie was finally his. Checking his watch he decided it was time to move this party along.

The Major gently woke Kiddie up, kissing her shoulder, saying her name softly. She opened her eyes, momentarily confused where she was. As he said her name again, Kiddie turned to see the Major, him and his bare chest propped up on his pillows. She turned to face him, smiling sleepily from her own pillow, it all coming back to her now. The Major had taken his time, guiding them both in their first time together. She could feel his controlled urgency, but he had been gentle and giving before they had finished in a sweet relief.

"I believe we missed our dinner opportunity," the Major said casually.

Kiddie noted the dim room and wondered what time it was. "I'm not really hungry," she answered back.

Reaching under the covers, the Major pulled her closer, nibbling on her ear as he said, "Oh but I am." Kiddie laughed as his head disappeared under the covers, thinking herself a very lucky birthday girl this year.

After exiting the cab, Kiddie and the Major crossed the street to enter the RedHead. They weren't surprised to see Iris and Bernie, Freddy and Dot already there, although they weren't that late. Kiddie was delighted to see a few of her friends from Erasmus Hall and relished in introducing them to the Major. They stood together greeting everyone with hearty handshakes and happy hugs. Iris had given Kiddie no clues about the RedHead and as she looked around, she was somewhat surprised to see it was a tearoom, yet most of the customers seemed to be their age. The round tables sat daintily with white tablecloths, decorated casually with small candles and bouquets of tea roses.

Seeing Kiddie take it all in, Iris grabbed Kiddie's arm and said, "Isn't it so pretty here!" She leaned over and added into her ear, "And don't worry, their tea is quite good." Suddenly Iris sniffed Kiddie, turning her to look her in the face. Kiddie was all but blushing, struggling to look Iris in the face. "Well happy birthday to you Kiddie! I will need details later!" Iris said, bouncing away before Kiddie could say anything.

As tables were pulled together for their somewhat large group, a young man came to stand behind Iris. Looking up, Iris exclaimed "Jack!" She jumped up to give him a hug and then turned to introduce him to the group. Having made introductions all around, Iris shared that Jack and his cousin Charlie were the owners of the RedHead.

"Thank you for coming in tonight folks." he said graciously. "Just so you know your "tea" will of course be coming to you in teacups and your first round is on the house in honor of your gorgeous birthday girl! What can I start you with?"

It seemed a stretch to be drinking out of teacups on a Saturday night, but the group understood Jack and Charlie's need to protect their customers, themselves and their business from the constant threat of police raids. Being new on the growing list of speakeasies, they had not yet figured out which cops in the East Village were bribeable and would give them a heads up when a raid was coming their way. Prohibition was annoying, but would not spoil an evening out if you knew how to do it right. As Jack went to collect their drinks, the Major followed him over to the bar. Kiddie watched as he seemed to be explaining something to the bartender and then handed him a tip before returning to their table.

Kiddie turned to him expectantly, but he just smiled and said, "It's a birthday surprise." Impulsively Kiddie kissed the Major on his cheek and squeezed his hand.

Before long their drinks were brought to them and Iris was happy to see at least the teacups were deep. At a dollar an ounce, this night could get expensive fast. Iris too was curious about what the Major had ordered for Kiddie and all eyes were on the Major as he proceeded to tell the story of Kiddie's drink, called a "French 75."

"Kiddie loves champagne so much I thought this drink is perfect for her, a mix of champagne, gin, and lemon juice. The story I know is that her drink was created in France at the New York Bar in Paris. Thanks to WWI, I had time in Paris and the pleasure of drinking more than one of Harry's cocktails. It's named after one of their high powered artillery guns, the Soixante Quinze as the french call it, which as Kiddie knows simply means "seventy-five."

Kiddie smiled and picked up her drink as did everyone else. "To Kiddie, happy birthday my love." said the Major as he picked up her free hand and kissed it. Kiddie felt giddy as glasses clinked in her honor and she sipped her drink. It was divine and Kiddie kissed the Major on the lips to show her appreciation for his thoughtfulness.

Somewhere along the way, Kiddie and the Major ordered food, chicken salad sandwiches that were warm and delicate. The table was a constant ebb and flow of full to empty teacups, and the rowdy group enjoyed themselves immensely. At one point Kiddie feigned embarrassment as the table proceeded to sing her happy birthday. It was a fabulous night and Kiddie knew they would be back to the RedHead for more tea again soon.

The next morning Kiddie sighed heavily as she gingerly rolled over in bed, fluffing her pillow to prop her head up more. Her head was throbbing, but Kiddie regretted nothing. Her headache would move on, but her memories created yesterday would last forever. She wasn't a teenager anymore and would stoically take responsibility for her actions, particularly when it involved champagne, among other things. Kiddie smiled to herself as she closed her eyes to relish in the other things.

Kiddie's eyes flew open as Iris flung her door open with a "Happy birthday Kidde!" She thoughtfully brought Kiddie water, orange juice, and a banana, but Kiddie shushed her enthusiasm just the same. Kiddie gratefully took the water after propping herself up to a sitting position.

"How are you so lively this early in the morning after all our tea so late into the night?" Kiddie asked incredulously.

"Early in the morning!" Iris snorted. "Kiddie you've slept away your birthday breakfast in bed! Father is already home from the hospital and asking for his birthday girl. Rise and shine Kiddie, it's time to celebrate!" With that Iris bounced back off the bed and was gone as quickly as she had swooped in.

Refusing to be rushed, Kiddie sank back into her pillows and closed her eyes, thinking nothing would be able to top yesterday's birthday celebration. Eventually she crawled out of bed, snacking on the banana while finding a dress to put on, knowing family dinner was hours away and not too worried about her appearance just yet. Feeling better after her hydrating and banana, Kiddie headed down the stairs to see her family and embrace their birthday wishes, ready to let part two of her birthday begin.

Now Kiddie sat at the table with her family, a delicious coconut white cake in front of her, the dinner dishes already cleared away. She begged off having "happy birthday" sung to her again as well as another glass of wine, although she happily indulged in a rather large piece of cake. She might be light on the cocktails tonight, but she was enjoying dinner with her family, the Major attentive by her side. As the family finished their cake and adjourned to the sitting room, Iris brought out a beautifully wrapped package for Kiddie. Kiddie had quite honestly forgotten about presents, her heart full enough. But still, who didn't love to open presents on their birthday? As Kiddie moved through her family's gifts, she wondered if the Major had brought something. As if reading her mind, Iris reminded the Major he had come in with his own box to give. The Major waved it off and told the expectant crowd he would give it to Kiddie later, in private.

However, the Major could not persuade Iris otherwise and as Iris went to retrieve it from the hall table, he conceded right now would be fine too. For a split second Kiddie wondered if it was a ring box, but quickly dismissed it when the Major handed her a larger, somewhat heavier gift. She could tell it was store wrapped although their label was not on the paper or the white cardboard box she unwrapped. Balancing it on her knees, Kiddie carefully opened the box to discover a beautiful jewelry box nestled into tissue paper. The box was covered with a light grayish blue satin, embellished with delicate gold trim. It was beautiful, a jewelry box for a woman, no dancing ballerina inside such as her little girl jewelry box had years ago.

Kiddie turned to thank the Major, hoping he did not notice just the slightest disappointment. She scolded herself mentally for thinking it could be a ring box Iris referred too. Turning back to the box, she lifted the clasp to take a look inside the beautiful box. Laying on top of the blue satin lining rested a card in the Major's handwriting. The outside simply had Kiddie's name on it, but when Kiddie read the inside, she froze. The card read "Kiddie my love, will you marry me?"

She read it again before looking to the Major for confirmation. He was smiling from ear to ear as Iris asked impatiently, "What does it say?"

As the Major got down on one knee, Kiddie realized he was taking something else from her jewelry box. It was a ring, which he held up to her as he asked "Kiddie my love, will you marry me?" For just a moment the whole room held their breath as they realized what was happening.

Kiddie recovered first from her surprise, exclaiming, "Yes! Oh yes Major, I will marry you!" The Major wasted no time slipping the beautiful diamond on her finger before standing and scooping her up in his arms. Suddenly her family sprang to life and surrounded them with congratulations and hugs all around. Before they knew it, glasses of champagne were raised, toasting Kiddie and the Major. Kiddie smiled to herself realizing her father now had two weddings to pay for.

Kiddie's summer had been the best, leaving her with much to celebrate. Besides getting engaged to the Major, she had finally graced a magazine cover—the June issue for *RedBook*. She felt like she should be famous, but the busy New Yorkers carried about their business with hardly a glance her way when she was out and about. She wondered if this was how the Major felt, writing his stories for the *New York Times*, but never getting to see his name under his byline. How could anyone know the genius behind the pen?

It was finally the end of August and still hot as blazes in New York City. The summer moved along, a lazy blur of playing tennis on the courts, sitting by the pool reading magazines, and shopping for the latest styles in Manhattan. Iris could spend hours talking about weddings, excited that they were both planning their big day together. Kiddie struggled to commit to much of anything as it all seemed a little too much for her and the Major. Quite by accident one day in Manhattan, Kiddie had found the perfect dress for her big day. Before even trying it on, Kiddie knew it was the one. She was quite taken with the head piece paired with it, buying it as well. Now that Kiddie had found her dress, she supposed it was time to set a date, making it sooner rather than later. The thought of moving out of her family home was daunting, but the thought of being Mrs. Major was exciting and usually overrode any anxiety she might have.

Despite her eventful summer, Kiddie was thankful to finally get back to some routine and her art classes at Columbia. If nothing else it got her into the city and closer to the Major's apartment. Kiddie was discovering that journalists keep crazy hours, writing their stories day or night, as the story dictated, leaving Kiddie happy to see the Major whenever she could. On her way to the Major's apartment now, Kiddie was trying not to sweat as she hustled along, her blouse starting to cling to her back as the sun beat down on her. She knocked on his door realizing she was famished and in need of a nice cool drink. The Major answered the door quickly, expecting her. He kissed her on the cheek as she stepped inside. Putting her book bag down by the door, Kiddie wrapped her arms around the Major and gave him a proper greeting.

"Kiddie are you done with class for the day?" The Major asked.

It was Wednesday afternoon and Kiddie's classes were mostly done for the day, although there was a lecture she should attend later in the afternoon. Kiddie had already checked with a friend to see if she would share her notes, knowing she would most likely miss it.

"I'm free the rest of the day. Why Major? How much time do you have and what did you have in mind?" Kiddie asked.

The Major pulled her closer to him, his arms around her waist, announcing happily, "I'm done for the day too! It seems like it's been forever since we were out for my birthday. I thought we could spend the afternoon together and then go out for dinner and then," he paused dramatically for effect. "then we'll see what happens."

Standing there listening to the Major make plans, Kiddie realized they really hadn't spent that much time together since his birthday at the end of July. Kiddie knew the Major was at the beck and call of the paper, his stories requiring him to attend sporting events and then create bylines creative enough to compete with all the other writers out there. As they headed into September, the Major was usually busy covering baseball and was convinced the Giants and the Yankees were headed to another "Subway Series." Although he never seemed grumpy, Kiddie could imagine the pressure the Major put on himself to be the best.

"Why not Major! What do you want to do first? And can there be food involved because I'm starving and dying of thirst!" Kiddie added.

The Major smiled, answering back slowly as he thought out their plan for the rest of the day. "First, we should go get sandwiches and lemonade and take it to Central Park for a picnic. Then we could walk to the Metropolitan Museum of Art and walk around and pick out works of art we could have in our home someday. Last, I'll take you out for dinner at P.J. Clarke's for a nice juicy burger. I need some time with my girl and time out of the rat race for a little while."

Kiddie happily agreed to his plan, knowing he was choosing all her favorites. It was a hot afternoon, but the tall trees of Central Park would grace them with a shady spot to slow down and enjoy a picnic. Since Kiddie was a little girl, she had always loved to visit the Met and she and the Major had only been there one time before. Thinking about buying artwork for their first home, made Kiddie smile and she was genuinely curious what the Major would want on their walls. She also appreciated the Major had picked a casual destination for dinner so her blouse and skirt would be enough to be dressed appropriately.

They strolled along Morningside close to both campus and Central Park, picking up thick sandwiches wrapped in paper and cold lemonade in glass bottles. Kiddie carried the blanket, happy to spread it out in their favorite spot from back in the day. Kiddie devoured half of her sandwich before passing the rest on to the Major. Their shoes lay in the grass, Kiddie happy and relaxed as she sat leaning against a tree, stroking the Major's dark hair as his head lay in her lap. He seemed to share her sentiment, taking her ring hand and pressing her palm to his lips.

"Kiddie let's get married!" he said randomly.

Kiddie laughed, "Silly, you already asked me and we are getting married!"

The Major sat up and got close to Kiddie's face, looking earnestly into her eyes. "No, I mean now, this week! When I come home from a long day I want to be with you, I need to have you beside me. I'm ready for us to live together, to be man and wife everyday!"

Kiddie sat up straighter, her mind trying to grasp what the Major was saying. She was ready to be man and wife too, but it was already Wednesday afternoon and to do it this week seemed a little crazy, even for the two of them. Her mind whirled with numerous questions.

"Where? When? How Major?" Kiddie asked, wondering if he had really thought this through.

"Kiddie if you don't need the big fancy wedding Iris is planning, then why not? We've made no arrangements to reserve anything, and I can't wait until next fall for you to be my wife. The Giants and the Yankees are both playing out of town this weekend and I can finally have some time off. We could go to the courthouse and get married. There's a chapel there."

Kiddie searched the Major's face and could see he was serious. Even though there were a million details to figure out, Kiddie loved the spontaneity of it all. Doing it like this would make it original and nothing like what Iris was planning. Still, Kiddie would want her family to be on board, starting with Iris as her Maid of Honor and then of course hoping her father would foot the bill. The Major was watching Kiddie's face, looking at her expectantly.

"Why not Major! As long as I have you and fifty of our closest friends and family, I'm good! I already have my dress and I know you have plenty of suits. There's just one catch-how will your mother get here in two days? And what will she say about this rush wedding?" It was Kiddie's turn to look at the Major expectantly. "She will hate me if she's not there!"

The Major admitted to himself he hadn't really thought about his mother in his plan to get married on Friday. He wasn't really expecting a lot of his family to show up for the wedding anyway as the trek to New York was both costly and time consuming. However, he knew Kiddie was right and his mother would want to be there.

"Kiddie she won't hate you, she'll hate me! I guess I need to call her and either she will make it work or she won't."

Kiddie was a little surprised by the Major's nonchalant attitude. "Hmm," Kiddie said, not convinced. "She'll be mad at you, but will assume I'm the reason we rushed and hate me for it!"

The Major pulled Kiddie close and kissed her on the top of her head. "It will be fine Kiddie. I will make her understand it was all my idea and not you. But, should we go talk to your folks about this plan? You're the one with the big family." Kiddie started packing up their picnic, nodding in agreement. She might not be having a traditional wedding, but there was definitely going to be a big party to celebrate their new Mr. and Mrs. status. She needed to make sure her family and particularly her father was on board before she started planning just how big it was going to be.

K iddie was pleased the whole family had been home for dinner so she and the Major could announce their plan to everyone at once. Iris and her mother protested at first, but when they realized it was a done deal, they quickly got on board to help. Kiddie's mother brought out paper to write out the guest list and other details, giving everyone tasks to do. Her mother and Freddy were in charge of inviting family to dinner, but keeping it casual and not telling anyone for what reason. Iris was in charge of flowers and inviting friends from Erasmus. The

Major had made arrangements for his mother to come and was now in charge of inviting his friends to dinner and finding the right suit to wear. Together they would need to go and apply for their marriage license as well, preferably tomorrow. Kiddie was excited to think about seeing everyone's faces when they realized the dinner was actually a reception. Kiddie realized there would be no wedding presents as guests wouldn't know to bring one, but even that made Kiddie smile. What more did they really need?

Kiddie had set up a meeting first thing in the morning with the person in charge of catering at the Biltmore Hotel. Kiddie was relieved they were available and happy to have their glamorous decor set the mood for an elegant dinner. They limited their guest list to fifty people give or take, including the Major's Mother and one of his aunts. Kiddie wanted the guests to sit at tables in a U shape, adding a fourth table at the top for the buffet of food and of course their wedding cake front and center. There would be a dance floor in the middle of the tables and Kiddie was thankful the house orchestra was available. Kiddie wanted crisp white linens with candles and flowers everywhere. It might not be that fancy, but it was going to be romantic, leaving their guests with no doubt that they had been to a wedding reception. Hearing Kiddie's big news, Cook generously offered to bake their wedding cake, adding that her sister could do wonders turning fondant into delicate roses.

Now it was late in the evening, Kiddie's family scattered to different places in the house, while Kiddie and the Major sat outside on the porch swing. Kiddie was tired but happy after the whirlwind of the afternoon they had. Remarkably their wedding plans all came together fairly easily. Kiddie laid her head on the Major's shoulder thinking about his reaction when he saw her in her wedding dress on Friday. Kiddie decided the universe knew this day would come sooner rather than later, guiding her to the perfect dress.

Kiddie thought about how beautiful her dress was and how it fit her like a glove, accentuating her curves in just the right way. The sleeveless dress was made of white satin with a fitted lace bodice. The waistline was low and defined by a band of pearls and sequins before dropping into a long handkerchief hem. Her stunning headband was made of white organza as was the attached veil adorned with lace, pearls, and sequins, leaving Kiddie's dark curls to peek out from underneath. Kiddie planned to borrow her mother's pearls to wear, the same pearls she borrowed the night the Major told her he loved her for the first time. Kiddie could not wait to say "I do" in her dress, only the day after tomorrow!

"Kiddie I realized there's something rather important we've forgotten." the Major announced, looking concerned. Kiddie stopped the rhythmic movement of the swing as she turned to look into his face.

"What is it Major?" Kiddie asked uneasily.

The Major whispered in Kiddie's ear. "Where should I whisk you away to for our honeymoon so I can properly make you my wife?"

Kiddie smiled as she turned to look into the Major's face. In all their rush to figure out wedding details, Kiddie had forgotten about the most important part, the honeymoon! "I'm happy to follow you to the ends of the earth Major."

Now the Major was smiling as he pulled out two boarding passes. "I know it's not Paris or the ends of the earth Kiddie, but how does Bermuda sound to you? We set sail on the ship Victoria on Sunday and will arrive in Hamilton late afternoon on Tuesday. We will have the whole week on the Island to explore and celebrate as Mr. and Mrs. I've heard Bermuda is gorgeous in the fall"

The Major had been hesitant to make plans without Kiddie, but earlier in the day had impulsively decided to purchase the boarding passes. He had planned to use them to motivate Kiddie to say yes, but had not needed to use them after all. Now he waited hopefully for her approval.

Kiddie had read in magazines about royalty making trips to Bermuda as they were ruled by the United Kingdom. It wasn't Paris, that was true, but they had plenty of time for that trip. For the second time that day Kiddie answered with a smile, "Sounds wonderful Major. Why not!"

It had been a full two days of wedding preparations, although easier to do minus the formalities that went with a big fancy wedding.

Kiddie decided she had nothing to wear for the honeymoon so she and Iris hastily made their way through several shops in Manhattan. They searched furiously for a maid of honor dress and outfits appropriate for a week of island living. They finally settled on a soft pink organza dress with a handkerchief hem for Iris that would compliment Kiddie's dress well. Kiddie herself even purchased a few new dresses and a modern white pantsuit from Coco Chanel's latest resort collection. She hoped heads would turn as she and the Major walked about Hamilton, enjoying the sights and each other.

As Kiddie and the Major took their vows in the small chapel at the municipal building, her immediate family and the Major's mother and aunt were the only guests. A close friend of the Major's stood beside him as his best man while Iris stood on the other side of Kiddie. The chapel was small but tasteful, using several candles and white ribbons tied at the end of the few pews as the only decorations. Kiddie barely registered what was said, focused on the "for better or worse" and "I now pronounce you man and wife." She was happy the Major agreed to wear a wedding ring, just as she was expected to, showing the world their commitment to each other. After signing the marriage certificate, Kiddie and the Major took their own cab to the Biltmore Hotel, having time to check in before their dinner guests arrived. Kiddie almost blushed when the desk clerk insisted they take the hotel's one and only bridal suite, a room he promised newlyweds would know how to enjoy to its fullest.

A bottle of chilled champagne greeted them from a table by the bed, a card simply signed *"Congratulations, we are so happy for you both!"* The Major was not easily distracted though and wasted no time carefully getting Kiddie out of her dress, her headpiece resting on the seat of the chair the Major hung his jacket on. At first Kiddie hesitated to mess anything up, but decided that's what her Maid of Honor was for and knew Iris would know if anything needed a touch up. The bed was luxurious with soft linens and pillows galore. Kiddie could feel the Major's sense of urgency and yet he took his time and made her feel like his princess, his wife, the woman he loved. Tonight Kiddie wasn't sure if it was the luxurious bed or the rings on her finger, but it had been special.

As they sat propped among the fluffy pillows in the middle of the bed, they snuggled while they sipped their champagne. The Major sat caressing Kiddie's arm, announcing happily. "It's official my love, we're man and wife, and you're now stuck with me forever, for better or worse. You've made me the happiest man."

Kiddie reached up to kiss his cheek before throwing her covers off to climb out of bed and start to get dressed. He watched her appreciatively as she turned to face him, putting one foot on the bed as she rolled her stocking up over her knee. "Major, I plan to make you happy over and over again, but right now we need to get downstairs to our dinner guests arriving." As she went to roll up her other stocking, she leaned over dramatically, baiting her new husband. She gave a little shriek and then a laugh as he took her bait and dragged her back into the bed, pulling her on top of him.

"The only place we need to be, Mrs. Major, is right here. As long as our guests have cocktails, they won't mind waiting. Besides I've given my best man a story to spread as guests arrive so they won't be expecting us on time."

Kiddie said teasingly, "Well if my husband wrote this so called story, that's good enough for me. I guess we do have time for you to show me what makes you the happiest man." The Major did not disappoint as he pulled the covers up over the two of them.

The Major was one happy man as he stood waiting patiently for Kiddie to come out of the bathroom. For now it made him smile to think this would be his new normal, but believing Kiddie would always make it worth his wait with her stunning good looks. He checked his finger to look again at his wedding band. He wasn't even sure if men today wore them or not, but when Kiddie had asked him to, he didn't mind saying yes. Now he checked his watch and decided it really was time to go. Just as he was about to call her name, Kiddie emerged from the bathroom back in her wedding gown, her head piece like the crown his princess deserved. He zipped up the back of her dress deciding this was something else he would be getting used to. He handed Kiddie her bouquet and then his arm. She seemed to be glowing as she put her hand through his arm, ready to greet their dinner guests.

The Major had let Iris and Bernie know they would join their guests at half past the hour, thirty minutes fashionably late. Her hand still in his arm, they now stood at the top of the stairs admiring the scene below them. Friends and family were standing in small groups, talking and laughing, most of them holding a cocktail in one hand or the other. Iris was the first to see them and nudged Bernie to let the family know they were ready to be announced. The Major's best man took a dinner knife and tapped his glass to get everyone's attention. As the room quieted and they watched him expectantly, people started pointing realizing that Kiddie and the Major were standing at the top of the stairs. Looking over at Kiddie, the Major could see the emotion in her eyes and leaned over to whisper in her ear, "Happy wedding day my love. Shall we?" Giving her the rail to hold onto, the Major slowed his pace to keep up with her high heels and long dress.

The Major's best man proudly announced, "Friends and family, I'm delighted to present to you, Mr. and Mrs. Corum!"

As the crowd grasped what was happening, they suddenly came to life, applauding and cheering as the happy couple finished descending the grand staircase. Kiddie went to hug her family as the Major hugged his and shook his best man's hand. When people started yelling "Speech! Speech," the Major charmingly complied.

"Thank you all for being here tonight. A few days ago the lovely Miss Kiddie humored me by agreeing to marry me with only a few days to plan and this afternoon she became my wife. As you can guess, having my beautiful bride and our friends and family here is all we need to begin our adventure of happily ever after. Without further ado we hope you will join us in celebrating our nuptials by sharing food, drink and dancing tonight. Cheers!" Magically, coupe glasses of champagne had appeared in their hands and in unison Kiddie and the Major raised their glasses to everyone before clinking their own together.

Amidst more cheering and clapping, Kiddie and the Major went to stand behind their chairs at the head of the massive u-shaped tables, signaling everyone it was time to sit down for dinner. Kiddie had arranged for servers to bring plates of hot food to their small wedding party, while other servers moved down the long tables to signal when guests could go and fill their plates. The Major was thankful his best man had wisely decided to sit with their college buddies, giving his mother the seat to his left. Iris and Bernie had followed suit, giving Kiddie's parents the chairs to her right. It had been a full day and Kiddie was famished. She and the Major made quick work of their steaks and fancy potatoes, before getting up to work their way around the tables, greeting each of their dinner guests while they ate. It was awkward at first, but the happy couple soon started to relish in all the attention and well wishes for a long and happy life together.

As the evening wore down to a close Kiddie was still going strong. The cake had been cut, toasts had been made, and Kiddie and the Major had taken their first dance as Mr. and Mrs. Of course there was no other song to play than *"The Princess of My Dreams"* by Victor Herbert. Kiddie felt like a princess that night, the Major staying close to her side, both of them happy to share their celebration with so many people they loved. After most of the guests had departed for the evening, the newlyweds were accompanied by a small group of their friends to the top floor of the Biltmore, to the Cascades, their rooftop restaurant. Despite a room full of guests, it didn't take long for management to find the jubilant group a discreet corner table.

When their evening finally ended, Kiddie was thankful to ride only the elevator down to their honeymoon suite. They were both happy to see silver domed trays of food sitting on a table, including generous slices of wedding cake. Later the Major helped Kiddie out of her dress once more, but exhausted and full of cake and champagne, they were asleep in no time, happy to call it a night as Mr. and Mrs. Major.

K iddie and the Major stood at the rail of the SS Fort Victoria, waving to their families. Kiddie's mother and Iris and Freddy stood beside the Major's mother and his Aunt Maddie. The Major's mother had been a little reserved throughout all the festivities, but his aunt Maddie had been more than happy to be there, her first adventure out of Missouri. Encouraging them to stay until Monday, Kiddie's mother generously offered to show them her favorite sights of New York. The big ship's horn blew, signaling it was time to pull away from the pier. They gave one final wave to their families before heading in to explore the ship.

The newlyweds went to explore the nine decks, happy to find the ship quite luxurious. They noted the grand ballroom where dinner and dancing would be their good fortune later tonight. There was also a lounge with leather couches and velvet chairs placed around to strategically create small intimate groups. Both rooms were anchored with large ornate fireplaces, standing tall in a marble glory and finished off with gold accents. Kiddie and the Major were delighted to find bars in both rooms as well, each bar boasting a plethora of colorful bottles placed on large mirrored shelves. They sat sipping their drinks as the bartender shared how a mere switch in the wall could flip decorative wood shelves to boozy mirrored shelves as soon as they were out on the high seas.

Checking his watch, the Major let Kiddie know that if she needed time to get ready for dinner, they should retire to their quarters for now. Kiddie recognized that look from the Major and quickly finished off her French 75, agreeing she would need some time before dinner. Hand in hand they walked up the glamorous red carpeted stairs to find the deck where their room was waiting for them, their luggage delivered when they arrived. As the Major swung open the door, he stopped Kiddie from entering the room. In one swift move he picked her up and carried her in, before playfully dumping her on the bed. As he closed the door behind them, Kiddie was already coming out of her pumps and bon voyage dress.

The happy couple arrived for dinner promptly at seven o'clock. Kiddie knew people liked to dress to the nines for dinner on the ship and was happy to comply wearing a lovely emerald silk drop waist dress with a black satin sash that tied in a bow just slightly below her hip. The Major looked debonair as always sporting a bow tie and his black suit. Seeing all the fancy dresses made Kiddie wish she had brought the dress Iris had worn as her maid of honor. Pink was her favorite color, but she knew by the head turning as they walked to their table, green worked equally well with her dark hair and pale skin. Kiddie was delighted to find the ship's captain sitting at their table, along with several other guests. The captain stood up to greet them both as Kiddie and the Major took their seats. Hearing the Major introduce themselves as Mr. and Mrs. made Kiddie smile.

"Ah yes, the newlyweds from New York City. Welcome to our ship, the Victoria as I like to call her. I trust your accommodations are to your liking?"

Kiddie and the Major both agreed with the captain their accommodations were perfect, the ship quite lovely. They were thankful when a server poured them first a glass of water, and then a glass of wine.

Suddenly a couple sitting across from them spoke up. "We're newlyweds too, but we took the train down from upstate New York!" They were both glowing with happiness and Kiddie could see he had his hand resting on her knee under the table. "We're the Zimmermanns. I'm John and this beautiful girl is my wife Wiona."

As the Major shook John's hand across the table, Kiddie added it was nice to meet them both. The captain then asked if anyone at the table had ever been to Bermuda. An older couple, the Rooneys, shared they had been before to celebrate their ten year anniversary and this trip was to mark their twentieth anniversary. The captain was delighted with this news, asking them to share what they liked about Bermuda so much as to bring them back ten years later.

The couple told stories of the things they had seen and done in Hamilton. encouraging everyone to visit "The Jungle," where you could see Bermuda's most picturesque and unique scenery. Apparently the Tom Moore Cave on the grounds was not to be missed either. As their dinner was served, the captain ended with a declaration that Bermuda was well known as the enchanted isle of play. Exchanging glances,

Kiddie and the Major smiled in his direction, the Major simply toasting "To Bermuda!" with his glass of wine, the others happy to join him. Dinner was followed with dancing and more wine until finally Kiddie and the Major decided to call it quits and retire to their cabin.

Their two day cruise to Bermuda passed quickly enough and once again Kiddie and the Major found themselves standing at the rail of the Fort Victoria. The colorful triangle banner flapped in the breeze at the front of the ship, a cheery hello as they approached Hamilton. The Major had already pointed out their large white four story hotel, The Princess, as it contrasted dramatically against the green mountains in the distance. He informed Kiddie he knew it was the perfect fit for them because it was advertised as *"the centre of social life."* The hotel boasted every activity from tennis to golf to saddle riding to sun bathing. Kiddie hugged the Major's arm, excited to get started enjoying the quaint oceanside community of Hamilton.

Standing in the midday sun, surrounded by their luggage, Kiddie and the Major were trying to get their bearings. They were surprised to see that horse and carriage seemed to be the most common means of transportation, but weren't sure how to go about flagging one down. The Major was quick to stop someone and inquire politely how one got to their hotel in Bermuda. With a shrill whistle a white horse and carriage appeared before them. The driver jumped down to stow their luggage in the back while the Major helped Kiddie up into the carriage. In no time they were stopped and unloading luggage in front of their hotel. Kiddie was delighted to see hotel staff dressed in white, waving pink handkerchiefs to greet them. Quickly a bellhop was taking charge of their luggage while the Major paid the carriage driver. Kiddie took in the long shady verandas, inviting guests to find a cocktail and come enjoy the view.

Finally they were all checked in and headed to the top floor. When the Major unlocked their door, Kiddie made a beeline for their balcony. She smiled in delight as the double doors revealed the harbor below them. The beautiful turquoise water sparkled like diamonds in the sunshine. Their ship stood out like a giant among all the sailboats bobbing in the water. Kiddie stood at the rail taking in all the people below, some hurrying to their destinations, others moving about leisurely. Kiddie admired the seemingly pink sandy beach below where sunbathers were welcome. Iris had talked her into buying the Jansen swimsuit, a black one piece, the stretchy lycra sure to hug her curves. She had hesitated at first, but Iris had convinced her when she reminded her it was her honeymoon and they wouldn't know anyone there anyway. Now Kiddie was happy she had brought it and wondered what the Major would think.

The Major had come to stand beside her on the balcony, using his hand at the small of her back he turned her to look at him. Kissing her hand where her wedding rings rested he asked, "Kiddie are you happy? Are you ready for the honeymoon of your dreams?"

Kiddie sighed dramatically, wrapping her arms around his neck. "I'm so happy Major. Thank you for bringing me here. The question is, what to do first?" She asked suggestively, sure that the Major's idea would be the same as hers. The Major swept Kiddie up in his arms, holding her tight to his chest. Kiddie laughed, as he once again deposited her in the middle of their bed, ready to get their Bermuda honeymoon started.

I t was late in the afternoon as Kiddie and the Major emerged from their room, ready to go and stretch their sea legs and walk around to get their feel for Hamilton. Hamilton was a quaint coastal town that buzzed with the energy of tourists and natives alike. You could feel a sense of history as told by the shops, well weathered along the waterfront, hopeful that relaxed and happy tourists would share their wealth with them. The landscaping contributed to the relaxed mood, a beautiful blend of swaying palm trees, colorful flowers, and lush green hills for the backdrop. Kiddie and the Major wandered into a small garden patio filled with wrought iron tables and chairs that beckoned them to come and sit. Noticing other couples enjoying food and drinks, they found their own table and waited for service to notice their arrival. Before long they were rewarded with cocktails and fresh grilled fish smothered in a buttery cream sauce. The happy couple relished in their good fortune to have wandered into the garden.

Later they strolled down to the beach and found an empty bench to occupy, watching the sky become a symphony of color as the sun set in the west. Kiddie was resting her head on the Major's shoulder, the crash of the waves all but lulling her to sleep. Kiddie had been to the beach often with her parents and grandparents, but somehow this felt different, more tranquil, more beautiful, more romantic. The Major had never experienced the ocean, let alone the beach like this and he was most grateful one of his buddies had told him about Bermuda. The Major usually ran his clock pretty tight, but tonight, he felt more happy and relaxed than he ever had before. He finally understood why Kiddie was always wanting him to come to the beach with her and knew there would be more trips to the beach in their future. He liked the sound of that, their future a wide open road, welcoming them to their marital adventure.

The click of the door closing jolted Kiddie awake. It took her a minute to get her bearings and remember where she was. She rolled over to see the Major setting down a tray of breakfast pastries and fresh fruit. She hoped there was coffee. Noticing her watching him, the Major smiled and brought Kiddie a cup, greeting her with a kiss on the top of her head and a "good morning my love." He poured a second cup and came to join her, sitting on the edge of the bed. He was dressed the most casual Kiddie had ever seen him, in a short sleeve shirt and linen trousers.

"Thank you Major, you read my mind! You're up bright and early. What's the weather like out?" Kiddie asked with a sleepy smile.

The Major went to open the french doors to their balcony, announcing to Kiddie it was a beautiful day. Hearing the ocean waves crash and seeing the warm sunshine fill the room instantly energized Kiddie. After putting on her robe, she came to stand at the doors and see the beautiful day for herself. The Major watched Kiddie, waiting for her inevitable smile that was sure to come. She wasn't a pushover, but she did enjoy the finer things in life and never hesitated to let him know. "So Mrs. Major, are you ready to rent the bikes or do we play tennis today?"

Kiddie looked at the Major, trying to imagine him doing either of those things. She knew he knew how to ride a horse, and he knew a lot about sports, but she wasn't sure how athletic he was. "Your choice Major, I'm good with either or both." Her eyes twinkled at him over the rim of her coffee cup.

He knew Kiddie was an avid tennis player, but he wasn't sure when she had been on a bike last, if ever. Yesterday they noticed lots of people riding bikes around Hamilton, one young lady even so brave as to ride double with her male companion. They had tentatively added it to their list of things to do while honeymooning, their list growing longer by the minute.

Coming to stand beside her, the Major shared a plan. "Let's play tennis this morning as I've already taken the liberty to reserve courts. Then after lunch we can check out the beach and sunbathe."

This made Kiddie laugh as she turned to the Major to ask, "And did you bring a suit for sunbathing Major? Or should we hit up some of those little shops after lunch and find you something?"

The Major nodded his agreement, "We can add that to the plan, but know that I will mostly be admiring you in your swimsuit."

Kiddie was surprised to find that the Major more than knew his way around a tennis court and was giving her a run for her money. She considered herself quite good, as she and Iris had logged in many hours on the courts. It never occurred to Kiddie the Major had ever even played, as he informed her that he and Suzanne Lenglen hadn't just talked tennis, but that he had learned from the best. The Major was amused to see this competitive side of Kiddie, while she wondered what else there was to learn about the Major.

After tennis they wandered the shops and eateries along the waterfront, finding sandwiches and a bottle of wine to enjoy on their own balcony for lunch. The Major whistled appreciatively when Kiddie emerged from their bathroom in her new Jantzen swimsuit. It wasn't the prettiest thing Kiddie had ever worn, but her curves made it look good.

Grabbing plush white towels, they headed to the beach designated for sunbathers. Kiddie hoped she wouldn't be embarrassed by what she was wearing, but she shouldn't have worried. Bermuda attracted people from all over the world, most of them wealthy and looking for a place to flaunt the latest edgy fashions. While the Major kept an eye on Kiddie, Kiddie enjoyed taking in the latest beach wear trends from Europe, most thankful Iris had talked her into buying the suit afterall. They had a lazy afternoon, taking in the activity on the water, and soaking up the sunshine.

Before they knew it, they were dressed and ready for dinner having set their sights on a place highly recommended to them called Tom Moore's Tavern. As their horse and carriage pulled up to the Tavern, Kiddie and the Major took in the arched doorways, the hurricane windows ajar on the second floor, and the beautiful palm trees surrounding the building. Although it was a little off the beaten path, it was the oldest restaurant in Hamilton and boasted the best contemporary british food money could buy. They had been informed the menu changed often to insure seafood and vegetables were in season. Kiddie and the Major were happy to taste dishes that would not normally be on their plates in New York City. It was a deliciously romantic night and the newlyweds could not be happier.

K iddie and the Major sat on their balcony enjoying a beautiful morning with fresh fruit, eggs and toast, and strong coffee. Kiddie was excited they would be visiting the Royal Bermuda Yacht Club today. Although it was a private yacht club, the Major had somehow elicited an invitation from a member he met one morning in their hotel lobby. Something about them being on their honeymoon had struck a chord and he had insisted that the Major and Kiddie join him on his yacht for the afternoon to enjoy champagne and sailing. Their host shared he had heard rumors there was even to be a match race later in the afternoon, where the winner would claim a substantial wager. Kiddie was dressed in her new white Chanel pantsuit, her hat in tow. The Major was dressed to the nines as well, sporting a tie and his own hat. Kiddie knew somehow they stood out as they walked down the street, their American good looks causing heads to turn.

Captain Bittle's yacht was beautiful with shiny deck floors and mahogany crafted furniture commanding a sense of luxury in the main cabin. After their tour, the Captain took them up on the bow of the ship, handing out tall glasses of champagne as promised. He made a brief, but charming toast to them, congratulating them on their nuptials and wishing them the best of happily ever afters. Although he seemed to have no family of his own on board, there were several guests he welcomed before pulling up anchor and heading the yacht out onto the water.

Captain Bittle's guests had been out enjoying the water for a while, when he announced a race was indeed taking place. The yacht moved out of their way before dropping anchor. The two sailboats were moving much faster than Kiddie would have thought possible, each of them leaning precariously on their sides as they rounded the buoy at the turn around point. Kiddie and the Major smiled at each other as some of the guests started to yell and cheer on the boats, their sails fully stretched out to maximize the wind and move them through the water swiftly. Kiddie and the Major moved to the rail to watch more closely, noting that Captain Bittle was the most animated of all, clearly happy with the way the race was going. The Major wondered to Kiddie if perhaps the Captain had his own wager on the race, motivating him to bring them all out as spectators.

Later as they disembarked, Kiddie and the Major thanked the Captain graciously for their lovely afternoon. After shaking hands with the Major and kissing Kiddie's extended hand, he informed them that they were to be his guests for dinner tonight out on the Club's terrace. He regretted he would be unable to join them, but highly recommended they try the club's specialty cocktail in his honor. Kiddie and the Major didn't hesitate to take the Captain up on his offer, going to the host to give him their names before landing two seats at the bar. The bartender explained the club's specialty drink, a most enjoyable concoction of Bermuda rum, falernum, orange curacao, and lime juice.

Just as the sun was starting to set, the host came and fetched them from the bar, menus under his arm, a beautiful table set up for their dinner on the terrace. Choosing from the menu proved too many choices for Kiddie and she left it up to the Major to decide what would be brought to their table. They feasted on fresh seafood, breads, and cheeses, to soak up their cocktails. Looking across the table at the Major, Kiddie was grateful for how wonderful their day had been.

"You know Major, if I'd known we could get so much attention for being newlyweds, I would have married you sooner!" Kiddie announced impishly.

The Major picked up his glass and pointed it her way with a simple "Touche my love."

Kiddie rolled over, groaning slightly as the movement made her head spin ever so slightly. She could tell the bed was empty on the other side and could only hope the Major would be back soon with coffee and lots of it. Keeping her eyes closed she played back in her mind's eye their newlywed adventures from yesterday. It had been a wonderful day and Kiddie wondered what the Major had on their agenda for today. Hearing the door open Kiddie rolled herself over delicately to eye the Major and beg for coffee. She was often both amazed and annoyed that no matter how much the Major drank the night before, he was always up early and never seemed the worse for wear. She really must learn his secret, but for now coffee would do the trick.

Feeling refreshed and ready to take on the day, they had agreed to a leisurely morning of sunbathing followed by lunch and later a bike ride to Victoria Park. One thing Kiddie loved about Bermuda was how different stories about the royals were woven into its rich history. While she had some reservations about their bike riding, she was excited to visit Victoria park named after the golden jubilee of Queen Victoria in 1887. It was Kiddie's understanding that the park had a bandstand and military bands often performed there for tourists and natives alike. The park covered a full city block from Victoria Street to Cedar to Washington to Dundonald Street. Kiddie almost wished they could just walk to the park, rather than rent bikes, but riding bikes would be a new adventure for them both.

As they picked out their bikes to ride, the Major casually asked Kiddie if she had ever ridden a bike when she was a kid. She remembered once riding her cousin's bike around the grounds at Grand Prospect Hall, but Kiddie had not really been a fan. The Major on the other hand had loved riding his bike as a kid, using it to get down long dirt roads to his friend's houses as well as many trips to the river. Out in the Boonies there were no cabs to hail and walking got hot fast on humid summer days in Missouri.

Watching Kiddie now, the Major laid his hand on her arm, "Kiddie are you sure you want to ride? We can always walk to the park." he said kindly.

Hiking her dress up and swinging one leg over, Kiddie smiled back, "Major I'm always up for an adventure. I'll be fine." The Major shrugged, deciding Kiddie knew best.

The weather in Bermuda was nonstop perfection. The nights cooled off enough to warrant snuggling, but the sun warmed back up nicely by afternoon. Today was no different and Kiddie was enjoying the sun on her arms, the breeze ruffling her dark curls as they pedaled through the streets of Hamilton. She was following the Major hoping he knew where they were going, moving slower than he was. She could see him stop every so often, looking back to check on her and make sure she was still behind him. She was happy to notice they finally turned onto Victoria Street knowing it couldn't be far now.

Entering the park there were lots of places to park their bikes. They could see from all the bikes it was a popular destination for tourists. Kiddie wondered if anyone ever came back from walking the grounds to find their bike missing. She knew that wouldn't break her heart if that should happen to theirs. The grounds were beautiful as they walked through them, Kiddie resting her hand through the Major's bent arm. She almost felt like royalty herself as they moved through the park, the Major debonair in his suit and hat as usual. Kiddie leaned her head on his shoulder, her way of letting him know how much she was enjoying the moment.

As they retrieved their bikes, Kiddie gave a rather dramatic sigh. "Kiddie are you ok?" the Major asked. She was feeling a little worn out, but to be fair, it had been a crazy busy week since the Major had first suggested they get married last Friday.

"Major, can we stay in tonight and eat at the hotel restaurant? I think all the sun is starting to get to me." Kiddie said.

The Major smiled wickedly, "and all the champagne and all the things that come after champagne." Kiddie laughed and acknowledged that too with a smile. It briefly crossed the Major's mind that maybe Kiddie was already pregnant as he had never known her to ask for a break in their adventures before.

Heading back down to the harbor, traffic was much busier as people were moving about more, getting ready for afternoon tea and an early dinner. The Major moved through the horse drawn carriages and other bikers slowly, trying to make it easier for Kiddie to keep up. Kiddie appreciated the Major keeping a slower pace, feeling more relaxed than on their journey to the park. As she coasted down the hill, she was so busy looking around her that she never saw the pothole until it was too late. Her tire fell deep into the hole, projecting Kiddie into the air. Hearing a kid yell, "lady look out!" the Major turned just in time to see Kiddie fly over the handlebars of her bike before landing with a hard thud on the pavement. He quickly stopped to drop his bike to run to her side.

Frantically the Major asked the crowd to stand back and for someone to get help. As Kiddie's head rested in his lap, he took in her limp body, her pale face and for a moment worried she was dead. Checking her pulse he was relieved to find she was not. Waving to the crowd, more urgently now, he shouted for someone to go get help. He realized he had blood on his hand and that Kiddie had suffered a gash to the back of her head. Taking out his handkerchief, he gently applied pressure to her wound. Finally a police officer came around, telling the Major they had sent for an emergency vehicle to get her to the hospital.

Riding beside Kiddie, the Major was relieved to learn Bermuda did have a hospital, King Edward VII Memorial. He quietly sat beside Kiddie, shushing her gently when she started to stir. Briefly she had opened her eyes, mumbling the Major's name before losing consciousness again. After what seemed an eternity Kiddie was rushed through the hospital doors, a nurse stopping the Major before he could follow her into the examining room. Checking in at the front desk, the Major was asked to fill out some paperwork. He told the nurse they would need to call Kiddie's father as he was a doctor in New York City and would want to know precisely what her injuries were and the treatment given. The Major sat in the rigid chair, his face grim while he himself waited to hear about Kiddie's injuries.

A doctor finally emerged, searching the room until his eyes met the Major's. Walking up to him he asked politely, if he was Kiddie's family. The Major paused for a moment before informing the doctor he was Kiddie's husband. The doctor let the Major know she would need to stay most likely a couple of days to recover. They were concerned with how extensive her internal injuries were and waiting for results from her preliminary tests to come back. The doctor also confirmed that she had a nasty head wound and concussion. All in all the doctor thought she was one lucky young lady. He offered for the Major to go in and see her, reminding him she would need to rest. The Major asked one more question before finally asking the doctor to contact Kiddie's father as a professional courtesy. The doctor kindly let the Major know he would go and take care of both things now.

The lights were low as the Major walked to Kiddie's bedside, taking her small hand in his. She still looked quite pale and fragile and it took all the Major's will power not to scoop her up and hold her. The doctor had let the Major know she had been awake and could tell them her name and what day it was. He realized, as with any concussion patient, nurses would be waking her every so often to check on her. He wanted to be there the next time she was awake and reassure her everything was going to be ok. Seeing a chair in the corner, he dragged it over to sit beside her bed, holding her hand. It was a long miserable night, Kiddie giving them all more concern when she spiked a fever in the wee hours of the morning. They were watching for infection although it most likely stemmed from the trauma to her body. The Major often paced the room, anxious for signs of improvement in Kiddie's condition. As the long night finally slipped away and daylight broke, the nurse let him know her fever was gone as well.

It was some time mid-morning that Kiddie finally woke up enough for a brief conversation. She opened her eyes to find the Major's gaze on her. She smiled at him, wondering if he had willed her to wake up. Realizing she was really awake the Major moved up close to her face and took her hand.

"Hi." she said weakly. She could see the exhaustion and worry in his face and never doubted for a minute he had been by her side all night.

"Kiddie how are you feeling? You have a concussion and several bruised ribs, but you are going to be ok. In a day or two you'll be out of here and back to lounging on the beach. I promise."

"I'm so sorry Major. I've ruined our honeymoon." Kiddie said sadly.

He returned her gaze unwaveringly. "Nonsense! Nothing could ruin time spent with my beautiful wife, whether she's in a hotel bed or a hospital bed!" the Major teased.

The Major had been beating himself up all night, the depths of his exhaustion making him feel like he should have somehow prevented Kiddie from hitting that pothole. Now he said to her, "Kiddie it was an accident that could happen to anyone. Remember, we signed up for better or worse."

Kiddie smiled a little, squeezing his hand slightly. "Yes we did Major, so I guess this is on you."

The Major gave a little laugh, relieved to hear Kiddie banter words with him. He kissed her gently on the top of her head and told her she should rest. Closing her eyes she willingly complied, a slight smile still lingering.

It had been almost forty-eight hours since Kiddie's bike accident and the hospital was finally willing to let her go. The doctor had spoken to

Kiddie's father, keeping him abreast of her injuries and they both agreed she should be good to go as long as she continued to rest. Both men had no doubt the Major would see to it, and the staff wished Kiddie well as a car rolled up ready to take them back to the Princess Hotel. For once the weather was cloudy, and both Kiddie and the Major slept soundly through the afternoon.

When Kiddie awoke, it took her a minute to realize she was back at their hotel. Fearful the car ride would be painful on her bruised body, the doctor had given Kiddie a healthy dose of pain medication just as she left the hospital. The Dr. had also given the Major a bottle of the pills to help Kiddie survive her voyage home. Trying to carefully sit up in a bed, Kiddie now called out the Major's name. As if on cue, he opened the door carrying a large tray of food Kiddie assumed was dinner. There were tuna fish sandwiches, fresh fruit, salad, and sweet tea. Kiddie wasn't really all that hungry, but realized it would help the Major feel better and most likely her too if she ate something.

As Kiddie started to throw off her covers, the Major was immediately by her side. "Kiddie what do you need? I can get it for you." Kiddie paused from untangling her legs in the covers.

"Major I need to get out of bed. I want to sit in a chair on our balcony. Can you help me to the balcony, please?" Kiddie asked pleadingly.

The Major did not have the strength to argue with Kiddie and putting his arm around her waist, helped her move slowly out onto the balcony. She winced as she sat down, the impact on her body just enough to make her body talk to her.

"Maybe you should stay in bed?" the Major asked hesitantly.

"I've wasted enough of our time in bed, Major! I want to see the ocean, the people, watch the sun go down! Will you join me?" Kiddie asked, softening her half cross tone.

The Major all but smiled as he pulled up his own chair beside Kiddie's. This was the Kiddie he knew and loved and he had missed her over the past couple of very long days.

"I would be happy to Kiddie," he said simply. Exhausted by her little outburst, Kiddie looked at him gratefully.

Reaching for his hand, trying not to grimace, Kiddie kissed the top of it. "Thank you Major for taking care of me. Bike or no bike, it's been the best honeymoon ever. I love you and being Mrs. Major."

It was the Major's turn to kiss the top of Kiddie's hand now, adding "I love you more Mrs. Major."

They sat side by side, holding hands, taking in the sailboats dancing on the turquoise water, marveling at the pink sand, easier to recognize from their small balcony. Eventually the Major brought a plate of food to Kiddie, watching her move it around until she finally ate something. Kiddie did not argue with the Major when he announced it was time for bed, allowing him to help her move from the balcony back to the bed. She mildly protested modesty when he offered to help her into her nightgown, but reneged when he reminded her that by now he knew every inch of her body like the back of his hand. He was careful not to bump Kiddie's head wound or her wrapped ribs and was thankful her father would be checking on her upon their return to New York City. The doctor had suggested another pain reliever at bedtime to help her get a good night's sleep. Kiddie recognized sleep was her best friend during this time of healing, right after having the Major by her side.

The Major lay on top of the covers, afraid of jostling Kiddie and causing her any pain, but he lay facing her, stroking her head and thankful she was going to be okay. The Major suddenly stiffened when Kiddie asked ever so softly, "Major why did you think I was pregnant? Were you hoping I was?"

Kiddie's eyes were on his and he knew that despite her somewhat medically induced fog, she wanted a real answer. "Kiddie I just thought it was something the doctor should be aware was a possibility given your condition. I had to think of every way I could to protect you. It had briefly occurred to me when we were headed home and you asked to stay in for the night."

Kiddie searched his eyes, before answering, "Careful what you wish for right Major?" She took his hand, "Major even if I was and now I'm not, that's the way it was meant to be. Right now we're writing our own stories, yours, mine, and ours and that's all the story I'm ready to be writing for now. We have plenty of time to write our family story." Kiddie finished softly.

She was fading fast, her eyes closed, her breathing slowing. The Major thought about what Kiddie said, happy she brought it up, knowing what she said was true. The Major was working on becoming a sports writer people recognized as talented. Kiddie was due to sit for another painting with Edna Crompton later in September and the Major knew Kiddie hungered for the same public recognition he did. They were just starting to write their own story, a beautiful start minus this one glitch. They had plenty of time to think about children. The Major carefully rolled out of bed, grabbing his cigarettes to go smoke out on the balcony.

As he stood on the balcony enjoying the early evening light, his mind whirled with how the next few weeks were going to play out. They had one more day in Bermuda before they would set sail for home. Arriving home presented its own set of dilemmas, starting with where Kiddie should stay. He knew work would be calling, expecting him front and center as the Yankees and Giants seemed to be destined for another subway series this fall. His boss had been gracious, giving him two weeks to get married and honeymoon, but expected his full attention upon his return. He was not good with Kiddie being home alone, and her things were not even moved into his apartment yet. It was most likely best for her to stay at her family home, where there would always be someone around to check on her, but that seemed to defeat the purpose of them getting married to begin with. The Major reminded himself it was only temporary and he couldn't be happier to be married to Kiddie.

The Major liked his small one bedroom apartment well enough, but he knew Kiddie would need more. Her family home in Brooklyn wasn't a mansion per se, but it was close. The Major was grateful Kiddie was all about living in the city, preferably on Morningside and close to the Columbia campus. He wondered if Kiddie had really thought through what it would be like to live away from her family. He worried how she would take his long work days, when he was sometimes writing late into the night, leaving her to entertain herself. If it all got to be too much she was still only a cab ride over the bridge from home. There was a lot to think about, but for now the Major was going to find a way to help Kiddie enjoy the end of their honeymoon.

Putting out his cigarette the Major went in, quietly closing the balcony doors behind him. He had not laid beside Kiddie since the accident and he looked forward to being in bed tonight, knowing she was there and she was safe. Afraid he might jostle her, he lay on top of the covers, watching her sleep and wondering if she had any idea how much he loved her. Her color was getting back to normal and he had been somewhat impressed she had actually eaten a little bit for dinner. She had already insisted they go down to the beach to sunbathe tomorrow and he had finally relented. It was their last day and he understood Kiddie needed to leave their sweet honeymoon on a happy note.

Over dinner she admitted to him her head throbbed less from her concussion, but admitted her ribs were tender with almost every move she made. She was playing it tough though and waved it off, announcing "I'll live!" Thank god for that the Major thought, as he brushed her with a kiss goodnight on her cheek.

The Major stood at the rail, knowing they would be the first ones off the ship due to Kiddie's injuries. Their luggage sat beside them, everything packed somewhat haphazardly, as the Major had done it by himself. At first Kiddie had tried to direct from the bed, but eventually decided she should let the Major take care of it all in his own way. Kiddie was gingerly sitting on her tall trunk, searching the dock for her family. She wondered who would be picking them up, expecting at the very least it would be Iris and her mother. As the ship's horn announced their arrival, Kiddie finally spotted Iris waving to them wildly. Her father stood beside Iris and Kiddie teared up a little, thankful to see them both. She looked up at the Major as he came to stand behind her, his hands resting lightly on her shoulders.

He smiled down at her and said, "I told you we were worried." Her father's presence there on a Thursday afternoon more than confirmed it to be true.

Kiddie was grateful for the pain pills as Iris hugged her, trying to be ever so gentle. It was more like stepping into her father's embrace rather than hugging him, and Kiddie enjoyed the familiar scent of his pipe tobacco and soap as she leaned into him. Kiddie smiled as Iris gave the Major a big hug and then he shook her father's hand, her father using his free hand to pat him on the back. Soon they were all in the car, Iris chatting nonstop, filling her in on all the little details Kiddie had missed while they were away. Resting her head against the back of the seat, Kiddie realized she had never been away from her family for so long, if ever. It had been a wonderful honeymoon, but it felt good to be home.

The double doors flew open as the car pulled up to the house. Her mother, Freddy, and even Cook came out to welcome the newlyweds home. There were gentle hugs all around while the Major and Freddy hauled their luggage into the house. The Major had taken Kiddie's big trunk up to her room, finding Kiddie's mother waiting patiently at the bottom of the stairs, not letting him pass without a strong hug and a soft "thank you" in his ear. The Major smiled and had to admit it did feel good to be home.

As they finished a delicious dinner of all their favorites, the Major was relieved to hear Kiddie's father announce Kiddie would need to be heading upstairs to get some rest soon. It felt good to have someone else be in charge and the Major almost laughed when Kiddie protested, "But Father we haven't even had our carrot cake for dessert yet!"

"Or seen the surprise we have waiting for you in the sitting room!" Iris announced joyfully. Kiddie and the Major exchanged glances wondering what Iris could possibly be up to now. Bernie laughed as Iris pleaded with their father on Kiddie's behalf. "Can't we just show them the surprise? It will only take a minute!"

Kiddie held her own as her father stared her down, trying to assess her level of pain and exhaustion. She was relieved when he announced sternly Iris could show them the surprise after they had their cake. Iris went to get small plates while Kiddie's mother carved up generous portions of the moist carrot cake, the frosting at the side tempting a quick swipe with one's finger. The family took their time over cake and coffee while Kiddie and the Major shared stories about their honeymoon. Finally it was time for Iris to lead Kiddie and the Major into the sitting room, both of them humoring her by closing their eyes as they shuffled to the doorway, Iris leading the Major and her mother leading Kiddie.

"One, two, three, open!" Iris shouted. She clapped her hands with glee seeing the couples utter shock at what sat before them. There were presents everywhere, all different sizes and shapes, all wrapped beautifully with cards attached under big bows.

"Surprise!" Iris said dramatically. Kiddie looked from Iris to her mother to the Major. She could see he was as surprised as she was.

Kiddie's mother, who was still holding her arm and smiling at them both said, "You two have a lot of people who love you and wanted to celebrate your big day with more than a steak dinner and a glass of champagne!"

Iris was walking around the room excitedly pointing out this present was from this person, that present was from that person. Kiddie could tell Iris had spent a lot of time with the presents and seemed to have them memorized. She pointed to a rather large one and turned to the Major announcing excitedly, "This one Major is from your boss at the *New York Times*! I bet it's something fancy!"

Seeing Kiddie get emotional, the Major gently put his arms around her to hug her and said, "How lucky can one couple be?" Kiddie and the Major realized it had never occurred to either of them that their newlywed status would carry over after the honeymoon.

Kiddie's father spoke up from behind them, with an announcement of his own. "I know it's exciting, but these presents will have to wait another day or so. Right now I want you upstairs Kiddie getting ready for bed. Iris, you go with her to help and I'll be up to check on you." Suddenly her father realized the Major was standing there, the Major not sure whether to be amused or offended. "I mean if that's ok with the two of you?" he added, gesturing to Kiddie and the Major.

The Major stepped aside as the two girls headed up, Kiddie telling Iris she would have to go slow. The Major grabbed the rest of their luggage and followed them up, keeping a watchful eye on Kiddie. Having deposited the luggage Iris shooed him away and he realized they needed some sister time, just the two of them.

As the Major descended the stairs Freddy poked his head out of his father's study to ask the Major if he could use a stiff drink. Walking into the room, Kiddie's father handed the Major a healthy shot of bourbon in a small glass. He could tell by the color of it, it was the good stuff.

"Major, it was a whirlwind the week you two got married, but now I would like to make a toast to you. If ever there was a man who can keep Kiddie grounded and let her soar at the same time, it's you Major. Her Mother and I are proud to welcome you officially into the family and thank you for loving our little girl. To the Major!" As they clinked their glasses together, the Major bowed his head modestly and thanked him for his kind words. This night was full of surprises and the Major appreciated the calming warmth the shot of bourbon brought with it.

The Major didn't give the girls much time before he was respectfully knocking on Kiddie's bedroom door. It seemed like Iris had spent hours with Kiddie leaving only to let their father examine Kiddie for himself. The Major called into his office letting them know he would need one more day before returning, sharing about Kiddie's accident. He also called and checked in with his own family, filling his mother in on their trip and answering all her questions. She asked if they had opened the family gift to them and insisted the Major go and get it to open while they were talking on the phone. Feeling somewhat guilty his family had not been able to participate much in the wedding festivities, he did as she asked. It was a beautiful wedding ring quilt done in pinks and greens. His mother informed him almost everyone in the family had worked on it at some point given their rush to get married. The Major assured her Kiddie would love it and it would look beautiful on a bed.

Now it was finally the Major's turn to check on Kiddie and get her tucked into bed. He brought her a glass of water so she could take another pain pill. He could see she was exhausted and ushered Iris out in no uncertain terms. Knowing the Major was right, Iris kissed Kiddie on the top of her head and closed the door behind her. It had been a whirlwind since they had come home and Kiddie was grateful to have the Major there, ready to protect her peace and quiet so she could sleep. Kiddie snuggled deep into her pillows and blankets, so happy to be sleeping in her own bed. The Major turned out the light and crawled into bed beside Kiddie. Letting her mind drift, it occured to Kiddie this was the first time the Major had ever really been in her room. It felt comforting to Kiddie and she mumbled to the Major, "Goodnight, Major, love you."

The Major wasn't sure she heard him, but he answered back, "Goodnight my love, sweet dreams."

It was late in the afternoon and Kiddie sat propped up on the Major's couch reading magazines, right where Iris and her mother had left her. She had not seen the Major since their first full day home. They had slept in late and then taken hours to open all their wedding gifts, Kiddie moving about slowly and taking breaks every so often. Iris had been wonderful, writing down who gave what so Kiddie could write thank you notes later. Kiddie was touched that her parents had bought them their own Victrola and several records to go with it, including their favorite from Victor Herbert. Work finally caught up to the Major and he had stayed in the city the last two days, first attending playoff games for the Giants and then having late nights writing his stories for the paper. They hadn't been married that long yet, but Kiddie had become used to having the Major around and she missed him.

Over breakfast, Kiddie had insisted to her family she was "fine" and needed to be with her husband. She planned to surprise the Major by being at his apartment when he got home, knowing both the Yankees and the Giants had the night off. Under her protests, Iris and her mother helped Kiddie pack her bag like she was a hundred years old. She was getting tired of all the redirects "you should be resting!" although she suspected it had something to do with her father and the Major being too overprotective.

Cook thoughtfully made plenty of dinner for the night, then packed a basket of food for Kiddie to take with her. Iris had snuck in a couple of bottles of wine, not sure if the Major drank anything other than the bathtub bourbon readily available. As soon as Iris and her mother returned home, Iris called the paper, asking politely to be put through to the Major's office. She wanted to make sure Kiddie didn't sit there alone too long, unsupervised.

Kiddie never heard the Major's key turn in the lock as she slept peacefully on the Major's couch, curled up with a blanket Iris had brought, her magazine still open in her lap. The Major had been annoyed she was there at first, worried for her wellbeing, but relented when Iris explained how much Kiddie missed him and she had really left them no choice. He knew Kiddie adored her family so it felt good for her to choose him. Now he sat down on the end of the couch, sipping his bourbon and watching Kiddie sleep. The Major turned on a lamp beside him as the room was starting to darken, finally causing Kiddie to stir. She gave a sleepy smile seeing him there.

"Well my love, I see you escaped from home despite my requests to keep you in bed resting." The Major said as Kiddie stretched out, putting her legs across the Major and letting her magazine slide to the floor.

She could feel the Major watching her closely and squashed her grimace when her ribs painfully protested her movements. "Sir I am fine and ready to report for my wifely duties, Major, sir!" Kiddie said playfully.

"Is that right?" the Major asked lazily. "So I can expect you to clean the house and cook my dinner every night? Keep my shirts clean and my pants pressed?" He was smiling, the Major amused to think about Kiddie doing any of those things.

"Well actually no." Kiddie replied slowly. Kiddie tossed her blanket aside, sitting up carefully to move closer to the Major. Laying her head in his lap, she continued. "Remember Major, I'm a modern woman, and my skills in the wife department basically include witty repertoire over a glass of wine, but I would be happy to help you with your pants." It had been a week since the accident and it felt good to Kiddie to flirt with her husband. She was rewarded as his eyes darkened and he bent down to kiss her. She could feel his hunger for her as he kissed her gently, but deeply. Kiddie knew her husband was a very disciplined man, and could feel his control, knowing it would be a while before her body was healed enough for anything more.

"It's good to have my wife back, but I think we should move onto safer things like dinner. Did you bring food with you?" the Major asked hopefully. Kiddie sighed knowing the Major was right.

"Cook was an angel, you should go see for yourself all the food she packed! Pull out whatever looks good to you, I'm famished!" Seeing the Major turn to look at her, as if surprised to hear that, Kiddie added with a smile, "I told you I was better!"

As September rolled into October. Kiddie was finally feeling recovered, eventually getting back to class and going out on the town when the Major wasn't working. The Major had been very busy as the Giants and the Yankees both won their championships, securing their places in a second subway series. Kiddie went home often, not yet used to spending nights home alone in the Major's apartment. The Major loved coming home on those late nights, thankful Kiddie had her family to feed and entertain her, but also happy she was always waiting in bed for him. Sometimes she would sleep right through him crawling into bed beside her and other nights she would move over to snuggle with him, knowing there would be a price to pay for his snuggles. As the days grew shorter, and the nights longer, Kiddie and the Major relished in their marital bliss.

After the World Series finished, they finally set up domestic shop, moving into a new apartment not far from campus and still within walking distance to all their favorite places. They had debated on a one bedroom or two, but finally settled on a two bedroom. They had high hopes as the Major became more established at the paper, making $40 a week and almost that much more writing stories for the paper at $8 a column. Kiddie was busy too, keeping up with her classes at Columbia and events scheduled with the Columbia Art League on campus. She was even more excited to have occasional appointments scheduled with Edna Crompton even into the new year. Iris was busy modeling for

Edna as well, although she was mostly focused on counting down to her wedding day.

Finally it was November and Iris and Bernie's wedding day arrived. Kiddie and the Major could not be happier for them, toasting the couple the night before and wishing them their own happily ever after. Iris looked absolutely stunning as she came down the grand staircase at Prospect Hall in her floor length, long sleeve floral lace dress. Her chiffon veil was long and flowing, a statement in itself. Kiddie and another friend stood beside Iris, while Bernie was flanked by his two best friends from childhood. Kiddie looked beautiful in her pale yellow dress, holding a bouquet of roses to match. She tried to focus on Iris and Bernie, but could not resist stealing looks at the Major, looking handsome as always and sitting on the front row with her family. She smiled to herself to see the Major always returned her gaze, his dark eyes warmly meeting hers. Once he put his fingers to his lips briefly, causing Kiddie to nearly blush, knowing full well what his intent was.

The Hall, decorated in palms and overflowing bouquets of bride roses, was packed with both sides of their family and friends. Dinner was served banquet style, followed by champagne and dancing that lasted well into the night. Kiddie and the Major stayed in Brooklyn catching a ride home with Freddie when the festivities finally came to an end. Iris and Bernie had only to go upstairs, their bridal suite ready for them, a chilled bottle of champagne waiting for them beside the bed.

The next morning Kiddie recruited Freddy and the Major to go with her and retrieve all the gifts locked in a room at Grand Prospect Hall. Iris and Bernie would be coming by later for lunch and Kiddie wanted to have all the gifts arranged and displayed in the sitting room when they arrived. Kiddie remembered how excited Iris had been for Kiddie and the Major to see their gifts and wanted to do the same for her little sister.

The wedding rolled through Thanksgiving into Christmas into the new year. Kiddie and the Major agreed not to get each other gifts for Christmas as they already had so much to be thankful for. After dinner with her family, Kiddie and the Major spent New Year's Eve on Broadway, waiting for the ball to drop with hundreds of other New Yorkers. They walked home hand in hand, a bottle of champagne waiting for them and their own private celebration to welcome 1923. It had been quite the year for the two of them and they couldn't wait to see what the new year would bring.

CHAPTER FOUR
=1923=

*"IN CASE YOU EVER FOOLISHLY FORGET: I AM
NEVER NOT THINKING ABOUT YOU."*
—VIRGINIA WOOLF

K iddie finished reading part one of "Fires of Ambition" by George Gibbs in her latest *RedBook* magazine, quite taken with Mary Ryan and her determination to use her youth, smarts, and good looks to find success in the big city of New York. Kiddie could relate to Mary's ambition, and supposed at age nineteen she too had been somewhat as naive as Mary. When Mary's date had taken her to a cabaret, Kiddie was reminded of when the Major had taken Kiddie once after a movie. Unlike Mary, Kiddie had enjoyed the music and dancing while sipping cocktails. Maybe Mary was not as naive as Kiddie thought as Mary found herself focused on the harsh realities of the cabaret, finding women to be more objectified than celebrated. Kiddie never thought about it like that before, realizing it was hard for a woman to be employed in a way where the woman was valued for her mind rather than her looks. Kiddie frowned to herself, thinking this is what she was doing, then brushed it aside, telling herself gracing magazines was a much more respectful way to go about it.

Looking around their apartment, Kiddie was happy with the life they were creating. It was a comfortable place they called home, the Major's somewhat shabby furniture balanced by the newness of their wedding gifts splashed around. One of Kiddie's favorite pieces was the Victrola her parents had given them as a wedding gift. Kiddie went to it now to find their Victor Herbert record she would be playing later tonight.

Sighing, she decided it was time to face the challenge she had set for herself today. She went to her book bag to retrieve the piece of paper her teacher gave her in French class. Kiddie had been gifted classic cookbooks as wedding gifts such as *The Boston Cooking School Cook Book* and *Selected Recipes and Menus for Parties, Holidays, and Special Occasions*. She would peruse through them often wondering how hard it would be to make recipes like Calumet Quick Cake or Deviled Crab, but could never commit to the challenge of actually cooking them.

She finally became motivated to try her hand at cooking dinner when her French professor had shared a recipe for Coq Au Vin. It was something different from American cuisine and Kiddie was excited to cook a very traditional French stew with chicken. Kiddie knew what a meat and potatoes kind of man the Major was, and felt certain he would love the taste of it. It had half a bottle of dry red wine in it, so Kiddie was certain she too would enjoy it. Upon Kiddie's request, her professor had written the recipe out for her. Kiddie was somewhat daunted by all the steps involved, but the ingredients themselves she was mostly familiar with. Her teacher had assured her she could do it and that it was the perfect dish for her husband to come home to on a cold winter's night. Kiddie smiled wryly thinking how she had volunteered "why not?"

Kiddie had gone to the market yesterday after class and spent what seemed like an eternity finding all the ingredients. She had a newfound appreciation for Cook and all the trouble she went to, to keep Kiddie's family fed. Finding the meat and vegetables had not bothered Kiddie, it was hunting down the small pearl onions and fresh herbs that had tried her patience. Today everything sat ready and waiting for Kiddie to orchestrate into a mouth watering masterpiece. Kiddie decided to open the wine first and pour herself a small glass of courage to ease the pressure.

She remembered months ago opening pots and pans with the Major as wedding gifts and thinking how disappointing it was. Yet, now here she was with them all out on the table, not yet sure which ones would be crucial to the success of her first home cooked meal for the Major. Kiddie appreciated that the Major did not expect her to cook and clean like she was sure his mother did. The Major had taken care of himself for a while now and was always ready to go out, unless Kiddie brought home leftovers from her parent's house. Cook had been most gracious teaching Kiddie and Iris how to do basics like boil potatoes, make deviled eggs, and roast a chicken, showing them how to turn the leftovers into chicken salad sandwiches. Kiddie had become an expert at toasting bread, although she was thankful for the little bakery down the street when she wanted something more than sliced bread. It was a monstrosity to sit on their counter, but the fancy toaster was one of Kiddie's favorite wedding gifts, from the Major's boss himself.

Kiddie finally got started by first sauteing bacon, enjoying how good the apartment smelled already. That would be sure to get the Major's attention when he walked in. She quickly learned the hard way that bacon is best cooked over a low heat, or the fat causes it to burn to a crisp in no time. Fanning the smoke from the kitchen, Kiddie was not deterred and quickly cut up more bacon to try again. Kiddie was a big fan of bacon and needed this part to be just right. Kiddie was thankful her teacher had walked her through the recipe so she knew words like saute, sear, and garnish. Kiddie had given herself plenty of time to cook, loving that the Coq Au Vin would have been simmering for hours when the Major walked in. Her only last minute items would be to boil the potatoes and saute the mushrooms, before adding them and the pearl onions to her stew. Kiddie knew the Major loved mashed potatoes and was sure to have plenty of potatoes washed, peeled, and ready for cooking, just in case filler was needed.

At last Kiddie's chicken stew sat simmering, and Kiddie felt proud of what she had accomplished. The kitchen had not fared so well, dirty dishes piled up everywhere. Kiddie grimaced as she poured herself the end of the wine and put a record on the Victrola. If she was going to clean, she would need liquor and music to motivate her. Having finally got everything washed, dried, and put away, Kiddie wondered if the Major would realize how much work she had gone too. Checking on her dish one more time, she turned the Victrola off and went back to the couch to find another story to read in her magazine. She had plenty of time to rest and later change before the Major would be home from the paper. Thinking about it made her smile as she covered herself with the blanket and settled into another short story.

K iddie awoke with a start, wondering why the room was dark. Her magazine fell to the floor as she sat up on the couch and realized she had fallen asleep. For a minute she panicked wondering how late it really was. Reaching to turn the lamp on beside her, Kiddie anxiously checked the clock. It was just a minute after six and Kiddie was thankful the clock chiming had most likely jogged her awake. She knew the Major should be leaving the paper now, a brisk fifteen minute walk home ahead of him. Kiddie ran to start the potatoes boiling, knowing that would take the longest time. She prepared her mushrooms for sauteing and then rushed to set the table with their fancy new dishes and table service. Making sure to leave the mushrooms on low, Kiddie went to quickly change her dress. Kiddie's mother had taught her girls long ago that you didn't have to go out to dress up for dinner. Besides the Major would be in his suit and tie.

Kiddie had just hooked the clasp on the back of her dress when she heard the key in the lock. She hurried over to the door to open it for the Major and greeted him with a warm hello. Hanging his coat on the rack, the Major looked around their apartment, taking in the set table and smelling something delicious.

Kiddie kissed the Major on his cheek before hurrying over to stir her potatoes and mushrooms. "Kiddie did you cook?" he asked with surprise.

She smiled back at him proudly, "I did! Dinner will be served. . .well um shortly" Kiddie announced assessing how much there was left to do. She pulled out another bottle of red wine and took it to the Major. "Major do you mind opening this?" she asked almost apologetically.

She was rewarded with "Of course, seems like the least I can do." from the Major.

Kiddie added the mushrooms and pearl onions to her Coq Au Vin and butter to her potatoes. While she let the butter melt, she went to light the candles on the table and put their favorite record on the Victrola. She held out two glasses to the Major as he pulled the cork from the wine bottle.

Setting the bottle down, the Major turned back to Kiddie to toast her, "To a home cooked meal my love!"

The Major went to wash up while Kiddie set the creamy mashed potatoes and fragrant chicken stew on their dining room table. She was beaming as he came to join her. Kiddie watched nervously as the Major dished up hearty portions to his plate. When Kiddie told him what it was he had paused for just a minute, taking in her explanation of how she came about the recipe. Kiddie was thankful she had served it into bowls as she had noticed her sauce was not quite as thick as expected. She had been told how to thin the sauce, but alas not how to thicken it. She decided to not mention it to the Major and watched him carefully as he took his first bite. She was relieved when he announced "Wow! This is really good! Kiddie you really went to all this work?" Kiddie nodded blowing on her own spoonful.

Trying her Coq Au Vin, Kiddie decided it wasn't bad, enjoying the chicken, the bacon, and the savory sauce. She decided the herbs blended nicely into the tomato paste and the chicken broth Cook had shared with her from home. By far the mashed potatoes were her favorite and she wondered if the Major felt the same as he reached to fill his bowl with more.

After dinner, the Major had been more than happy to help Kiddie clean up the kitchen, imagining how bad it looked hours ago when she had finished her culinary masterpiece. Knowing how hard Kiddie had tried, made it an instant favorite with the Major. Now the Major was holding Kiddie close to him, their bodies swaying to the music playing from the Victrola.

He kissed the top of her head and said, "Thank you Kiddie for making such a special night for us. I'm impressed the princess of my dreams can cook and clean after all." he added teasingly.

Kiddie looked up at the Major, answering back, "Don't get any ideas Major. I'm not the most motivated wife a man will ever marry, but luckily for me you promised for better or worse."

The Major pulled Kiddie even closer to him, kissing her neck, her cheek, until finally finding her mouth. "I suppose as your husband I should be better at motivating you." His words in her ear made her shiver in anticipation.

"Major, you should know I need a lot of motivating, but I'm confident you are just the man to do it." Kiddie answered back.

The Major went to blow out the candles and grab their wine as Kiddie started the record over. Following him into the bedroom, Kiddie wondered if she had underestimated how good domestic life could be.

K iddie lay sleeping while the Major laid in bed thinking about what a whirlwind it had been since they said I do that Friday afternoon. The Major was happy to have some down time from the office as the winter weather curtailed the usual sporting events. He was starting to hear rumors of a fight to be scheduled between the heavyweight champion Jack Dempsy, who would be defending his title against Tommy Gibbons. The location was still up for grabs, but out west somewhere seemed to be most likely. The Major was fairly certain he would be going, he just wasn't sure when and for how long. He worried about Kiddie and how she would handle him not being around for more than a couple of days.

For tonight he enjoyed their time together, thankful Kiddie put in the time and effort. The Major realized Kiddie had stirred and was awake and watching him. She moved closer to him, resting her head on the Major's shoulder, her arm draped across his stomach. Kiddie let out a heartfelt sigh and kissed the Major's chest, her lips soft on his skin.

"What is it Kiddie?" he asked.

"I was just thinking that this is my favorite place to be in the whole world, lying in bed with you holding me." Kiddie said softly.

The Major turned her face to his and kissed her on the mouth before agreeing with her. "I feel the same my love."

Kiddie reached up to touch the Major's cheek and asked, "What are you thinking about Major? You look so serious."

He turned to face her and said softly, "I'm thinking about all the work you went to for us tonight. Kiddie that really did mean the world to me that you made us dinner tonight. Thank you my love. I'll always remember this night."

"I love you Major and I want to do things for you. I know how hard you work to provide this home for us and to take care of us. So thank you," Kiddie added dramatically at the end.

"I'm happy to do it Kiddie." The Major said, pulling her back to him.

It was the first of June and Kiddie's birthday was a few days away. The Major was packed and ready to take his wife out before he caught the train early in the morning. They had dinner reservations at the Cascades, The Biltmore Hotel's rooftop dining experience and Kiddie's favorite place to eat. They were meeting the crew later at the RedHead, one of their favorite places to go now. He and Kiddie planned to spend the night at her parents house and he would slip out early in the morning to go directly to Grand Central Station to catch his train. He was packed physically, but dreading to leave Kiddie in the morning, knowing he would be gone for more than a month.

It had only been a few days since the Major had come home and shared the big news with Kiddie he would be heading west. They had gone out for burgers and he had casually told her about his latest story assignment. He was relieved she had seemed surprised, but taken it well. The Major was headed to Shelby, Montana for what his boss was calling "the last great fight in the west." World heavyweight champion Jack Dempsey would indeed be defending his title against Tommy Gibbons. The fight was scheduled for July 4th, but his boss had decided he needed to go out now, a month early. He wanted the Major to get to know Shelby, the contenders, and the fans motivated to make the trek out west and see it for themselves. Just before he left work for the day he had been sent to the cashier's office to pick up his spending allowance. The Major had been stunned to find a thousand dollars cash in his envelope. Although he hated to leave Kiddie, he was excited to make his first adventure out west, finding it particularly sweet as it was on the paper's dime.

Kiddie too was surprised how much money the paper trusted the Major with, realizing this really was a big deal her husband had been asked to go. Tonight Kiddie chose to wear the same dress she had worn a year ago, a most memorable night, causing the Major to be most attentive at dinner.

They had a lovely dinner under the stars before heading to the West Village to join their rowdy crowd of friends. Their group was lively, and Jack and Charlie were always happy to see them. As the drinks flowed, Kiddie seemed to be putting on quite the show, loudly demanding attention from everyone in their group, yet choosing to ignore the Major. Eventually the Major grew tired of it and took Kiddie firmly by the arm, telling everyone they were going to get some air. Even Iris, who was usually louder than Kiddie, nodded it was a good idea.

Kiddie could feel the Major's controlled energy as he walked her to the side of the building. Kiddie, thinking the Major was mad, was caught off guard when he leaned her up against the brick wall and kissed her so deep she felt it all the way to her toes. With one hand on the building behind Kiddie's head, the Major used his free hand to trace Kiddie's neckline, pausing in his favorite spot.

"Kiddie I can see you're going to be just fine without me, but you're going to need to save some of this for me. I'm not going to see you for a month and I don't care where we sleep tonight, but we will be up until the wee hours of the morning. Can you do that Kiddie, save some for me?" the Major asked in her ear, leaning his body into hers.

The Major knew Kiddie wasn't really that drunk, but was putting on a show, which he assumed was because he was leaving her in the morning. He hoped she was proud of him, but knew she worried that a month could be a long time. He supposed she thought tonight she would show him how independent she could be, trying to make him mad or jealous or both, but the Major rarely angered.

Kiddie knew the Major was right, she didn't want to waste tonight acting like a spoiled child who hadn't gotten her way. Looking into his eyes she answered simply, "Yes Major, I can do that." Smiling, he released her and took her hand to go back into the tea room. He kissed the palm of her hand before opening the door for them to rejoin the others.

Handing Kiddie a teacup, Iris asked her if she were ok. Taking her French 75 from Iris, Kiddie smiled and said, "Of course."

The rest of the evening flew by quickly, but still Kiddie and the Major were happy when Iris and Bernie dropped them off at Kiddie's parent's house. They tiptoed up the stairs, trying to not wake anyone. The Major closed Kiddie's bedroom door softly behind him, his dark eyes focused on Kiddie. Without a word, Kiddie turned her back to the Major, letting him unzip her dress. For just a second the Major wondered who would be helping Kiddie with her dresses while he was away. Just as quickly he dismissed it as Kiddie turned to face him, pulling her dress off her shoulders and letting it fall to the floor. She stepped out of her dress and went to sit on the bed.

Patting the bed beside her, she said softly, "Well Major, come see what I've saved for you." He was happy to comply.

I t was very early in the morning, the light of dawn just starting to push in and as he promised, Kidde and the Major had gotten very little sleep. Kiddie didn't care in the least thinking she could sleep for the next month. They enjoyed each other, taking their time and making it last. Afterwards they cuddled, talking softly for hours about anything and everything. The Major let Kiddie know he had left her a present for her birthday, hidden in their closet. Kiddie let the Major know how proud she was of him to have this assignment. Way too quickly the Major was up, getting dressed, calling a cab to take him to the train station.

Now Kiddie stood at the little window to the side of the front door, her head pressed to the glass. She watched him get into the cab, smiling when he turned one last time to the house, knowing she was there watching.

"A month will go by fast Kiddie, you'll see." Her father's voice behind her made her jump and she quickly wiped her tears away before he could see.

"Father! You gave me a fright! Why are you up so early? Are you headed to the hospital already?" Kiddie asked.

Handing her a cup of coffee, he smiled at Kiddie. "I'm always up this early Kiddie. I make coffee and eggs for breakfast and then I sit and read the paper. Holding the side door open for her, Kiddie followed him out to the back garden. They could feel the warm day ahead of them, but for now the air was still cool and felt refreshing to Kiddie's worn out self.

Kiddie sat beside her father, sipping her coffee and marveling at how she had never realized her father could be so self sufficient. Of course in a house as big as theirs, someone was always doing something the others were oblivious to. It was a big part of how Kiddie and Iris had gotten away with things over the years. She was even more surprised when he patted her leg kindly and asked her how she was doing.

Glancing at her father sideways, Kiddie announced glumly she was doing alright. She was thankful to have the coffee in her hand for a distraction as she fully planned on climbing back into her bed and having a good cry.

"Kiddie I don't think I've told you lately, but I'm proud of you." her Father said quietly.

Kiddie turned to look at him, a little startled. "Why do you say that?"

"Kiddie you're Mother and I are both proud of the young woman you've become. You're learning how to think about someone else's needs while at the same time learning how to take care of your own. Not everyone is able to figure that out so quickly. You're growing up on us Kiddie."

Kiddie forgot about her coffee while she thought about what her father said. She supposed he referred to supporting the Major in going out west, which was definitely putting the Major before herself. She wondered how he thought she took care of her own needs and respectfully asked him if he could explain what he meant by that.

"Kiddie the Major is very talented in his writing. This may be the first time he's leaving you to answer the call for work, but it won't be the last. The Major has a knack for writing a sports event into a story. He doesn't just tell us if it was a win or loss, but he makes us care about the people who won or lost. He's going places Kiddie and he's going to be lucky to have the love and support of a good woman beside him."

Kiddie was stunned. Her father had not talked to her like this since she was a kid navigating friendships on the playground. She was proud that her father read the Major's stories and she knew he was right. She loved the Major and this is what she had signed up for, supporting him for better or for worse. Her father continued, not giving Kiddie a chance to respond.

"Kiddie you've taken your classes seriously at Columbia and wiggled your way into the world of art. You've found something that you love to do and you're doing it, taking care of your own needs too. You're a strong, independent woman and the Major loves that about you. Among other things I'm sure," he added dryly.

Kiddie knew her father was right and she felt proud of herself. She would miss the Major, but she shouldn't waste a whole month pining away for him. Kiddie understood her father was encouraging her to make her own way while at the same time supporting her husband as he made his way too. Kiddie was thankful the Major encouraged her to do the same and realized he needed her to do so. It would be an impossible burden to be responsible for someone else's happiness and Kiddie realized she was the one who needed to make her own happiness. It was tedious and time consuming work, but Kiddie did love posing and being sketched into magazines. She liked to think she might even inspire other girls to follow their dreams..

It suddenly occurred to Kiddie she was more like her mother than she had ever thought. She turned to her father thoughtfully. "Is that what you love about Mother? Her independence, her passion for her writing?"

He smiled at Kiddie, nodding, "It's one of the things I love about her Kiddie."

Kiddie had always thought she was just like her father, inheriting his independent, artistic side. Now Kiddie thought about all the dinners, the family games, all the things her father missed over the years because of his work. Her mother never acted like it was a burden and Kiddie didn't remember ever feeling cheated of her father's attention. Kiddie realized it was her mother who should get the credit that she and her siblings had the best childhood a kid could ask for, always knowing they were loved by both of their parents. Kiddie's mother had never coddled her three children, believing mistakes and independence were important to growing up into happy, competent adults. In her own quiet way she modeled for Kiddie and Iris how to take care of a home, your family, and yourself by being a strong, independent woman. She followed her passion as a writer, seeming to easily balance both her personal and professional life.

Of course Kiddie acknowledged that was easier to accomplish with Cook in the house. Cook had been part of the family as long as Kiddie could remember and she realized her father appreciated Cook for more than the authentic German dishes she would serve to the table. Having Cook there allowed for the doctor's wife to pursue her own happiness and not just keep house, making for a happy marriage as well. Kiddie appreciated her father was smart enough to know this, but wasn't sure the Major would ever make that kind of money. Besides, Kiddie wasn't sure she wanted children, let alone three. She assumed that would change as she got older.

"Thank you Father," Kiddie said sincerely. "I'll remember this, especially on my hard days." Kiddie stood up to stretch, kissed her father on his cheek and headed back to bed. The sun was fully up and the birds were chirping, but Kiddie was oblivious as she slept soundly until noon.

The days mostly passed quickly as Kiddie's father had promised, Kiddie's schedule busy with modeling and finding ways to entertain herself. The Major wrote Kiddie letters as he had promised, but more often he would call and talk to her. During the week Kiddie stayed at their apartment, often inviting Iris to come into the city to go shopping or see a movie or out to lunch. Over the weekend Kiddie would go home to give herself a change of pace. On Saturday nights Bernie escorted Iris and Kiddie out on the town, although they usually stayed close to home in Brooklyn. The hardest part for Kiddie was the Major's empty chair at Sunday dinners and of course, his empty side of the bed.

Together, Iris and Kiddie became pros at modeling, teaching themselves mental tricks for sitting still so long, distracting themselves from aching backs and ignoring how slowly the time would pass. One day Kiddie was surprised to find Edna had laid out a winter weather outfit for her to wear in the middle of June. Edna assured her magazines plan out their covers way before a season even starts. Kiddie understood and as Edna painted Kiddie in her coat with a matching blue hat and scarf, Kiddie learned how to ignore the sweat that trickled down her back.

Kiddie's commitment and hard work paid off when she found herself introduced to Arthur William Brown, a commercial artist from Canada. Arthur, or "Brownie" as his artist friends nicknamed him, often sketched pictures for stories in the Saturday Evening Post and The New York Woman. Familiar with his work, Kiddie was more than flattered when he asked her to pose for him as well. Kiddie found Brownie, as he insisted she call him, quite energetic and understood his life motto of "ninety percent of life is just showing up." Kiddie's work for Mr. Brown was less tedious as he sketched quickly with his artistic pencils. Something new for Kiddie was that she also posed with at least one other person, usually a man or even as part of a small group. It was awkward at first, but Brownie's energy often left them all smiles.

The Major himself was having quite the adventure out west, although not all of it was sports related. Shelby turned out to be the prairie side of Montana, where there were few trees let alone any mountains in sight. The Major enjoyed the only room boasting a bathtub in the only hotel in town, the bleak two story Rainbow Hotel, his new home for the next month. As the big wigs headed into town, he got bumped from his room, the bathtub becoming a necessity for icing down beer. His new roommate was a bartender from up north and he had brought plenty of supplies with him. The nights were loud and rowdy, with plenty of liquor, gambling, and saloons to entertain anyone.

During the day, the Major worked to get to know the right people and stay busy, knowing the office would be expecting his stories to be telegraphed back to the paper. The Major had a front row seat as Shelby went from a small sleepy town to a town overflowing with fortune seekers rather than boxing fans. It was too bad the stands sat mostly empty on fight day, because Tommy Gibbons put up a helluva fight, lasting all fifteen rounds against Jack Dempsey. Happy to board his train early the next day, the Major was headed home with lots of good stories to tell, but mostly ready to get back to Kiddie and civilization.

K iddie checked the clock one more time, having memorized the Major's schedule and hopeful his train had no delays. He should be arriving within the hour and then a short cab ride to their apartment. She had debated on going to meet him at the train station, but decided being at home worked just as well. She sat dressed in one of his favorite dresses, the apartment clean, and the small refrigerator stuffed with Cook's good home cooking. To be fair, Kiddie had spent the day with Cook helping her prepare all the Major's favorites. Kiddie wanted everything to be just right for the Major's homecoming.

Kiddie was half way through her *RedBook* story when she heard the slam of a cab door. She tossed her magazine aside and ran to open the door. "Major! Welcome home!" she said excitedly.

She barely gave him a chance to get his luggage in the door before she was wrapping her arms around him giving him a big hug. Stepping back to look at him, the Major slipped his arm around her waist and pulled her close for a proper greeting.

"It's good to be home Kiddie." he added happily.

As Kiddie took his hat from him, she could see the Major was exhausted. She knew the train ride had been a long ordeal from Shelby to New York City and wondered how much sleep the Major got on the train.

"What do you want to do first? Cook and I made all your favorites yesterday. Are you hungry? Do you need a drink? A glass of wine?"

The Major smiled at Kiddie's exuberance. "I would love a piece of chicken if you have any? And mashed potatoes? And I'm drinking whatever you're drinking," he added at the end.

Kiddie smiled delighted that she had all the Major's favorites. She had put a dish of chicken, potatoes, and homemade rolls in the oven to heat just thirty minutes ago. She pulled it out of the oven now, and filled a plate for the Major before pouring them each a glass of wine.

"Welcome home Major," Kiddie said, raising her glass to toast him as he ate.

"Dinner was just what I needed! That and a good bath!" the Major said. "Kiddie do you mind if I go for a quick tub? I need to get this layer of train dust off so I can get the layer of Shelby dust off me."

Of course Kiddie understood and went to fill the tub as the Major took his luggage to their bedroom. He left it on the floor, pulling out only the essentials he needed. "I won't be long," he told her as he kissed her on the cheek in passing.

It had been a good forty minutes since Kiddie closed the door on the Major getting into his bath. Kiddie ate her own plate of food and was about to pour herself her third glass of wine, thinking the Major better hurry if he was needing another glass. Feeling restless, Kiddie got up and walked to the bathroom door, finding it slightly ajar and the bathroom empty. She went to the bedroom door and slowly opened it. She smiled to herself to see the Major on top of the covers, sound asleep, and softly snoring.

Disappointed she went back to the couch, poured herself the rest of the wine, and finished reading her *RedBook* story. As the hours passed and the Major continued sleeping, Kiddie decided she might as well go to bed too. It was not the homecoming she imagined, but still it would be good to sleep beside the Major tonight. Kiddie changed from her dress into her soft cotton nightgown in the dark, not wanting to disturb the Major. She wanted so badly to curl up against the Major, but decided against it seeing that he obviously needed his rest. She settled for having her foot resting on his closest leg, and was soon sleeping soundly herself.

Sometime in the wee hours of the morning, the Major finally awoke. It took him a minute to realize he was home and he smiled when he realized it was Kiddie's foot on his leg and not some critter that had wandered into the hotel. Now in the moonlight he could see her leg sticking out from under the sheet, her foot on his leg. He realized he had planned to rest his eyes for just a minute after his bath, but never got back up. He regretted that Kiddie must have been disappointed and he shared that sentiment with her. Now he turned to face Kiddie, first stroking her leg, then slowly working his way up to her thigh, to her hip, continuing to move up her body. At some point Kiddie woke with a start, the Major shushing her, kissing her, and apologizing for falling asleep.

Now he was going to make it up to her, in the dark and all she had to do was lay there and enjoy it. He could see her smile in the dark, her eyes still closed, as Kiddie allowed him to gently roll her onto her back, getting reacquainted with every inch of her, tracing her curves first with his fingers and then his lips. Kiddie kept her eyes closed, letting him take her along for the ride.

Later they lay in each other's arms, happy to be back together, their five weeks slipping away in no time. At some point Kiddie got up to get the glass dish of carrot cake Cook had sent, two forks, and a large glass of cold milk for them to share. They sat in bed eating, talking and laughing until too soon the dark receded, replaced by a dreary rainy day, perfect weather for a lazy day in bed. The Major had been given a day to recover from his trip before reporting back to his office. Pulling Kiddie back under the covers, he was thankful they had no place to be, but right there.

They woke around noon, neither of them in a hurry to get dressed and start their day. The Major went to the kitchen bringing back scrambled eggs, toast, and fresh fruit. Together they lay in bed talking, catching each other up on the five weeks they had been apart. Kiddie told the Major about how Iris was doing most of the modeling with Edna for magazine covers and about her new gig with Brownie, a renown sketch artist. She told him about her new peer group, a professional group of other models she was getting to know. She admitted it had felt different at first, like she was not being true to the Major, when she posed with another man as part of a couple for the first time. She told the Major how Brownie was a pro at making them laugh, thereby getting the best poses to sketch and hopefully sell.

The Major told Kiddie he would have to meet this Brownie character in the near future. He added to her story of not feeling true to her by telling her stories of his bartending roommate, who had this talent of sleeping with a lit cigar in his mouth and yet had managed to not burn down the one and only hotel in town. He shared stories of the small town in Montana, who despite all the tent homes, lemonade stands, and rodeos, was sure to go bankrupt after all the cheating and misdeals hosting a major boxing event had brought on them.

Eventually they got dressed for a long walk around Central Park, the rainy day giving way to a cool afternoon of sunshine and humidity. They had worked up an appetite and wandered into P.J. Clarks for burgers and a drink. The Major had been home for just twenty-four hours and it seemed they were finally all caught up on life and each other. The Major could see Kiddie had survived without him, feeling a mixture of both disappointment and relief. He was proud of Kiddie for working so hard, but he admitted to himself he wanted Kiddie to miss him too.

When they got back to their apartment, Kiddie put on their favorite record and opened a bottle of wine. She lit a candle and took the Major's hand and led him into the bedroom. Putting her arms around his neck, she let him know in between her kisses that tonight was her turn to show him just how much she had missed him. It was good to be home.

It was a hot Sunday at the end of July and the Major's birthday. Kiddie had planned a surprise for the Major, dragging people from the office into her scheme. Kiddie was excited she had bought tickets for the Major and some of his buddies to go to the Yankees game. Today the

Major could enjoy sitting in Yankee Stadium as a Babe Ruth fan and not a sports reporter for the *New York Times*. Of course the Major had been in the new stadium a few other times, his most memorable opening night back in April, when Babe had hit three home runs sending the Boston Red Sox home in a hurry. It had taken nearly a year for them to build their own ballpark, but now Yankee Stadium sat as the jewel in the Bronx, on the Harlem River, across from the Polo Grounds. People liked to call it "The house that Ruth built" and the Major was a little disappointed he hadn't been the one to coin the phrase.

Now for his birthday, Kiddie bought four tickets to the Yankees second game in their double header against the Chicago White Sox. She had invited some of the boys the Major was always sharing stories about, ones she had met here and there during one or more of their nights out on the town. She told the Major she was taking him out for lunch, although he was unaware his friends would meet them there and then she would announce they had tickets to the game.

Kiddie was happy to see the boys were already there when they walked into the pub. They greeted each other loudly, shaking hands and slapping each other on the back. As the Major turned to introduce them to Kiddie, he could see from her smile she wasn't surprised to see them there.

"Happy birthday Major!" She said as she pulled out the tickets from her purse.

The Major was truly surprised and touched that Kiddie would go to so much trouble for his birthday. Looking from the tickets to his friends, the Major noticed there was one extra ticket. Seeing their confusion, one of the guys offered that Frank had a sick baby at home and his wife had said in no uncertain terms was he going anywhere today, but to take the other two children to church. Without missing a beat, the Major boomed that meant Kiddie should join them for the afternoon. Kiddie tried to decline, not wanting to step on the boy's toes, but when the Major insisted, she acquiesced. It wasn't like they were playing the Giants, so what could it hurt to cheer on a homerun from Babe Ruth himself.

The bartender had the first game on the radio and as the small group celebrated the Major's birthday over burgers and beer, they realized the Yankees were about to lose game one of this double header today. They already knew they had lost last night's game too, but the boys had enough beer in them to believe the birthday boy would be their good luck charm in game three of the series. One of the boys paid their tab and they went to hail a cab to take them over the bridge to Yankee Stadium. This stadium could hold more fans than any other stadium and the Major gave a hefty tip to their driver as he maneuvered around all the fans, bringing them right to the main gate. The group settled into their seats behind home plate, the Major spotting Babe Ruth warming up in no time. As the national anthem was sung, the Major squeezed Kiddie's hand with his free hand.

It wasn't a Cardinals game with his Uncle Crutch, but it was a very close second as a great place to be. The game ended as a huge win for the Yankees, the final score 8-2. Much to Kiddie's delight, the boys gave the Major all the credit, and thanked Kiddie for including them on his birthday surprise. Kiddie was happy to surprise the Major on his birthday, but saved the best for last, a private party for two.

A few weeks later Kiddie decided she would not be going back to Columbia in the fall, feeling like she had done all that she could with her classes. Kiddie also learned that some of the sketches Brownie was doing of her were getting bought for publication in papers for stories as well as advertisements. She was excited to have her efforts pay off, particularly as her checks started to come in. The Major told Kiddie she should spend it on herself, that it was his job to take care of them financially. Kiddie found this a little insulting, that the Major seemed to be saying her money wasn't good enough to contribute to their expenses. Kiddie and the Major ended up having their first big fight, over money no less.

Kiddie knew she wasn't the typical wife that kept house, but she always thought of herself and the Major as partners in their marriage. It was important to Kiddie to contribute in ways other than cleaning house, having dinner on the table, and having babies. When Kiddie did those things it was because she wanted to, not because she was expected too. Kiddie also knew she enjoyed spending money on a new dress or a pair of shoes, but that didn't mean she couldn't be responsible with her money. They spent a few frosty days agreeing to disagree until finally the Major realized he was supporting an old-fashioned sentiment and decided to relent. Kiddie was proud the day they went to the bank to open a checking account with both their names on it. Walking out of the bank on the Major's arm, Kiddie realized how difficult it could be for a single working girl to open her own account in 1923. Although Kiddie considered herself a modern girl, she realized she was still spoiled in a lot of ways.

A month later Kiddie and the Major celebrated their one year anniversary. They had drinks at the Plaza before heading to the Biltmore for dinner. Sitting under the stars at the Cascades the happy couple wined and dined with some of their closest friends, including Iris and Bernie. It occurred to Kiddie that Iris did not seem her usual glam self, and was unusually quiet and looking tired around her eyes.

Following her into the bathroom, Kiddie asked Iris if she was ok, which she immediately responded with, "Of course Kiddie!"

Getting back to the table, Kiddie was quickly distracted as another round of drinks was brought and the Major started telling stories about their honeymoon in Bermuda. As the evening came to a close, the Major surprised Kiddie with the honeymoon suite, a chilled bottle of champagne sitting on the table beside the bed. They might not be newlyweds anymore, but they seemed to be making the most out of married life, and that was most definitely something to celebrate.

As Kiddie and the Major rolled through September, the Giants and the Yankees were in the middle of their playoffs. It seemed for the third year in a row, the Giants would be playing the Yankees in yet another subway series. Unexpectedly the Major and the New York City papers found themselves in the middle of a pressmen's strike, using their union to advocate for fewer hours with better pay, and improved work conditions. To the surprise of many, some of the city's major papers collaborated together to print one morning paper and one evening paper for their readers. Stories printed had to be the best writing of the most pertinent information. Although the sports section was slim, not even a strike could keep New Yorkers from getting their sports news during playoff season. The Major was proud and happy one of his stories made one of the morning papers while the newspaper industry worked to resolve the issue with their printers. Eventually the papers got back to printing their own papers and the Major could breathe a little easier.

Depending on who you were rooting for, New Yorkers either enjoyed or suffered through the Yankees winning the World Series in October. For the first time ever, the Yankees kicked off the series in their own stadium, but still lost to the Giants by one run. In the second game, the Yankees beat the Giants at the Polo Grounds by two runs. One of the largest crowds of the series watched as the Giants defeated the Yankees in their own stadium yet again. Much to the delight of Yankee fans everywhere, it would be the last win for the Giants as the Yankees won the next three games played in both ball parks. For the first time in baseball history, the Yankees were the World Series Champions and the fans celebrated the Yankees and Babe Ruth everywhere. Kiddie was torn between her lifelong status as a Giants fan, and not being able to resist the Major's enthusiasm for watching Babe Ruth play. It was hard for Kiddie to resist joining the Major and half of New York in celebrating the Yankees sports milestone.

As Kiddie and the Major settled back into their regular routine, it occurred to Kiddie she had not seen Iris for a while, other than Sunday family dinner. It was hard to talk one on one when everyone was at the table, as their family conversations were often loud and lively. Early in October, the family celebrated Iris as she made yet another cover on *Modern Priscilla*.

She looked beautiful, her eyes somehow haunting yet demur in her hat and red scarf. Kiddie was proud of Iris and was anxiously waiting for her own next cover with *RedBook*. Although Kiddie posed more frequently for sketches, Kiddie considered getting the cover of a magazine much more prestigious. Edna had told her she believed she would be the January cover, sporting her blue hat and scarf, but Kiddie would just have to wait and see.

It was late October as Kiddie finished another appointment with Brownie. After her setting, he had let her know one of their sketches would be featured next week as part of a story in *The Saturday Evening Post*. The story titled *"The Wives of Great Men Oft Remind Us,"* had made Kiddie smile. Kiddie knew some great men and wondered if the story would remind her of them. As Kiddie was featured more and more, it occurred to her that *RedBook* and *The Saturday Evening Post* weren't limited to just New York City. It made Kiddie proud to think maybe hundreds of people on the east coast would see her face somewhere, used to help tell a story or sell a product.

Today Kiddie was waiting to meet Iris for lunch, sitting at a nice table tucked into a corner where they could eat and chat with some privacy. Outside the Halloween-like weather was wet and chilly, promising of winter days ahead. Winter was never Kiddie's favorite as it made her want to eat and then hibernate for the winter, tucked in with wine and good books. Kiddie waved to Iris as she blew in the door, her overcoat wet with big fat raindrops.

As she settled into her chair, Iris asked their waiter for a hot tea. Seeing Kiddie's raised eyebrow, she mumbled it was the perfect drink for such a dreary day. Iris smiled at their waiter as he sat it down before her, asking if she needed honey or sugar. Stirring the honey into her tea, Iris finally gave Kiddie her full attention, a big smile on her face, asking her what's new with her and the Major. As Kiddie watched Iris go through her production of getting her tea, she thought Iris looked different. She didn't seem as tired, but there was still something Kiddie couldn't quite put her finger on. She wondered what was new with her and Bernie, and if they were enjoying their domestic bliss like her and the Major.

"Since the World Series finished, there's not been much going on in the city. I've already started counting down to Thanksgiving though and when I can officially start eating all our favorite holiday foods. What's new with you and Bernie? Do you have plans for your one year anniversary?" Kiddie asked.

For a minute Iris looked startled, as if she had forgotten all about their anniversary. As they ordered their sandwiches and sides, Kiddie wondered how Iris was really doing. "Do you have any more appointments scheduled with Edna before the end of the year?" Kiddie asked.

Iris shook her head, chiming in she was going to leave all that to Kiddie for a while. Kiddie was stunned and unable to cover it, asked Iris why.

"Don't get me wrong Kiddie, I love seeing my face on the cover of magazines, but it's a lot of work and takes a lot of time and there are other things I can be doing at home." Even as she said it to Kiddie, Iris knew this sounded like a poor excuse. She shifted her gaze to Kiddie's chin, deciding now was as good a time as any to tell Kiddie her news.

Kiddie tried hard to cover her surprise and even disappointment. "Iris is it Bernie? Does he not want you to work?"

Now Iris looked Kiddie in the face and announced, "No Kiddie, it's because I'm pregnant."

This time Kiddie could not hide her surprise and sat in stunned silence for a minute, collecting her thoughts on what would be just the right thing to say. "Iris! That's so exciting! Right? You're excited?!" Kiddie mustered up.

To both their surprise, Iris started to tear up. "Kiddie I wasn't planning on this so soon. Someday sure, but I'm only twenty! Some days it's all I can do to take care of myself!" Iris bowed her head, wiping her tears discreetly, thankful they weren't sitting at a table in the middle of the room.

Kiddie's big sister instincts kicked in immediately. Taking Iris's hand she told her it was going to be ok, she would be right beside her and Bernie all the way. Seeing Iris's expression, Kiddie asked, "What does Bernie say?"

"I haven't told him yet Kiddie. You're the first to know. I can hardly admit it to myself let alone go out and tell the world!" Iris said.

"Iris, why weren't you using protection if you're not ready to be pregnant? I know Mother had the talk with us and you and I talked about it too!" Kiddie answered back.

"I was using my diaphragm, but somehow I still got pregnant!" Iris said defensively. "You also know Mother always said abstinence is the only birth control that's one hundred percent guaranteed!"

Hearing this news, startled Kiddie as she wondered how she would feel if she were sitting in Iris's shoes right now. The Major did his part to take precautions, but still there were times when in their drunken state, their lusty greed for each other got the better of them. Kiddie made a mental note to work harder on that.

Now she said to Iris, "How do you think Bernie will take the news? Is he ready to be a father? Are you scared to tell him?"

Iris shook her head. "Not scared exactly, but once I say it, there's no turning back, for better or worse. Right now it's just me and it," Iris said rubbing her belly. "And now Aunt Kiddie too!" Iris laughed seeing Kiddie's expression. "Yes Kiddie, you're going to be an auntie!"

This news made Kiddie smile too. Iris and Kiddie came from a large family on their father's side and they loved the big holidays when all the aunts, uncles, and cousins added to their family chaos. For sure they couldn't all be her favorites, but she did have a couple of aunts she could talk too about pretty much anything. Now Kiddie would be the aunt. She squeezed Iris's hand with a big smile.

"Iris, maybe you should tell all the family at Sunday dinner? Then I can be there to support you and distract anything crazy."

"Kiddie I don't know if Bernie would appreciate that. But I am going to tell him right before we come over for dinner. I want him to be a part of this, I can't do this without him! Or you Kiddie!"

As Iris started to tear up again, Kiddie realized how scared Iris must be. She knew it must have been quite a shock and felt bad her little sister had been going through this without her.

Now she handed Iris another napkin and asked her softly, "Iris why didn't you tell me sooner? I could have been there for you!"

Wiping more tears away, Iris answered back, "Kiddie I didn't want you to be disappointed in me. I know how much you want to be a career girl and you want that for me too. And well. . .this isn't what we planned."

Kiddie felt guilty Iris would think that, but she also worried Iris was projecting her own disappointment onto Kiddie. Iris was young in many ways and Kiddie could only hope Bernie would be excited and give Iris and the baby all the support they would both need. Once again she squeezed Iris's hand.

"Iris, I'm so sorry you would ever think that, but you know I love you more than anything and you should know you can always come to me about anything!" Kiddie could feel her own eyes starting to water and decided it was time to lighten the mood.

"Besides, you know I've never been disappointed in you! Well except for that time when you were four and ate that ladybug one of the Gillette brothers dared you to eat!" Much to Kiddie's relief this made Iris laugh.

The waiter had been watching, discreetly waiting for a lull in their conversation to bring their food to them and the girls thanked him as he finally had a chance to set their plates down on the table. Kiddie realized Iris was eating for two now and encouraged her to dig in. For the first time in weeks, Iris was famished.

She felt better now, having finally shared the burden of her pregnancy with Kiddie. In a few days she would finally tell Bernie too, although it had been hard to hide her throwing up, her tiredness, and her changing body from him. She suspected he already knew on some level, but was giving her the space and time to tell him when she was ready. She wondered how her parents would take it, but was certain Freddy would be ecstatic to be an uncle. Dot, a long time friend of the family, was hanging out with Freddy a lot these days and Iris supposed she should be a part of the big news as much as anyone. She couldn't wait for everyone to know, and she would no longer have to hide it, worried and alone.

K iddie lay in bed, her mind moving around like a hurricane with Iris's pregnancy at the center of all her thoughts flying around.

It was a late night for the Major at work and she knew she had a few hours before he would be home. Kiddie and Iris had walked to the car together, Iris giving Kiddie a ride home before heading to her own home in Brooklyn. Kiddie had given Iris a big hug and told her everything was going to be ok. She had tried to reassure Iris that having a baby didn't mean she couldn't ever work again, but saying it and believing it, were two different things. Kiddie knew Iris and Bernie had plenty of money and Iris would not be tied down to the house if she didn't want to be. But who knew, maybe this was Iris's path and she would love mother-hood. Whatever Kiddie's thoughts were on motherhood, Iris needed to choose her own path. That was part of being an independent woman, that a woman could make her own choices and answer to herself with-out worrying about judgement from others.

It was this last thought that Kiddie was stuck on. Once you had a child, weren't you supposed to put their needs ahead of your own? Wasn't that what good parents did? Kiddie worried she might not ever be ready for that.

She wondered how serious the Major was about becoming a father. She felt fairly certain he would be a good father, but she also knew he wasn't going to be the father with an 8-5 job, home for dinner every night. It would be up to Kiddie to pick up the slack, as mothers were expected to do for husbands all over the world. Kiddie was serious about her career and was just starting to get busy with appointments, particularly with Brownie. She thought about all the magazines and papers she read and never once had she seen a pregnant woman as part of a cover or ad or story.

Kiddie padded into the kitchen in her slippers and robe to get another glass of wine. She knew if she was awake when the Major got home he would make certain assumptions. When Kiddie wasn't in the mood, she would pretend to be asleep and the Major would gently kiss her on her shoulder and whisper "good night my love." But tonight Kiddie didn't think she could fake being asleep and she was in no mood for the Major to touch her. She couldn't wait to share this news about Iris with the Major. She was very curious what his reaction would be, feeling like it would be indicative of how he felt about them getting pregnant.

That was something else she was worried about. For over a year now, the Major and Kiddie enjoyed their adult privileges that go with a healthy, loving marriage. Kiddie wondered if they too should be worrying about their own little bunny, given that they often made out like bunnies. Kiddie knew it's not easy for every woman to get pregnant and wondered if that was going to be the case for her. Of course they did take precautions, even to the point that both Kiddie and the Major knew her monthly cycle and when she was ovulating.

Kiddie knew her mother had waited a while to get pregnant although that had more to do with her mother marrying her father later in life. In the first four years of their marriage, Kiddie's mother had three children. Just thinking about that made Kiddie sweat. It was no wonder Cook seemed like such a part of their family, as she had been hired when Kiddie was born. With or without the help, Kiddie wasn't sure she would ever agree to having three kids, but quite possibly somewhere down the road, one little Major running around could seem doable. Thinking about that did make Kiddie smile. By the time the Major got home, Kiddie was sleeping peacefully, her face a welcome sight at the end of the Major's long day.

Kiddie awoke to their room flooded with sunshine and the smell of toast and eggs cooking. It was the Major's specialty and Kiddie knew if she laid there long enough, the Major would bring it to her in bed. She stretched and then rolled over to the empty side of the bed. The best part about the Major working late, was that he always went in to work late the next day. Yesterday came rushing back to Kiddie as her mind cleared the cobwebs away, and she wondered if she wanted to have this conversation at the dining room table or in bed. Taking too long to decide, the Major walked through the door with a "good morning my love" and his tray of breakfast for two. In addition to the toast and eggs, there was fresh fruit and coffee.

Kiddie smiled at the Major as she sat up in bed, taking the hot coffee before settling back into her pillows. "Thank you Major." she added.

The Major sat on his side of the bed, the tray of food between them. Kiddie loved when the Major did this, feeling like she really was the princess of his dreams. She was famished and realized she had never really had dinner last night, just her wine. In between her bites of toast and eggs, she asked the Major how his night was. He was happy to announce the newsroom was so slow, his boss had unexpectedly given them all the day off. His eyes glowed over the rim of his coffee cup, Kiddie was torn between her anticipation of things to come later and her anxiety over Iris being pregnant. She decided to jump right in and announced, "Iris is pregnant!"

The Major sat his coffee down on the tray. Kiddie could see he was as stunned as she had been and was trying to wrap his own brain around it.

Not giving him time to say anything Kiddie blurted out the whole story.

"We had lunch yesterday and she told me there. Bernie doesn't know yet, but she's going to tell him soon and then all the family at Sunday dinner. She wasn't planning on getting pregnant, but apparently her diaphragm failed her. She was crying and she's scared, but I told her it's all going to be ok. Right Major? It's all going to be ok? What do you think Bernie will say?" Kiddie finished in one big breath, watching the Major closely for his reaction.

"Wow! No wonder there's an empty wine bottle sitting out. I can imagine how you must have stayed up and worried all night. I'm sorry I wasn't here. I think Bernie will be fine. I think Bernie is just as interested in Iris being a mother as he is with her on the cover of a magazine, but I could be wrong." The Major shrugged, going back to his coffee.

Kiddie narrowed her eyes and asked with a frown, "What do you mean by that Major?"

Kiddie could see the Major was choosing his words carefully. "Kiddie you know we are out with Iris and Bernie often and I feel like he will be okay with it. They have money and it won't be a burden for them to maintain their social life. The important thing is that we support them and Iris knows she is going to be ok. Iris is young, but she's a good person with a big heart, and what kid doesn't want that in a mother?"

Kiddie relaxed a little, knowing the Major was right. "Iris is a good person with a big heart and she will figure this out. We will be there as she figures it out. Besides, I'm going to be an auntie! And you are going to be an uncle!"

The Major smiled, "I am going to be an uncle! And you are going to make an excellent auntie." The Major took the tray of food back to the kitchen. Coming back to Kiddie, who still sat with her arms across her knees, her face still somewhat anxious. The Major could see there was more on Kiddie's mind. Propping his pillows up, the Major sat beside her, taking her hand in his.

"What else are you thinking about my love?" the Major asked softly.

"I'm wondering how that would work for us if I was the one pregnant. I'm just getting started in my career and I don't know if I could be a mother and a career girl! Who would take care of the baby when we're both at work? I'm not ready to be a mother, but I love being your wife, but I don't want to be pregnant. It's a lot to think about Major."

"Kiddie you know we're careful and we're not planning to get pregnant anytime soon. We both have careers we're chasing and we don't have the time to be chasing around a little brown eyed baby girl with dark curls bouncing everywhere. We'll know when the time is right and until then, we know it's important to be careful and we will be."

Kiddie smiled then thinking about how the Major imagined a little Kiddie running around, while she imagined a little Major running around. It made her wonder if Iris was having a boy or a girl. Either way it was going to be big news at the dinner table on Sunday. Talking to the Major made Kiddie feel better and she could only hope Iris was feeling better about it too. Releasing a big sigh, Kiddie laid her head on the Major's shoulder.

"Thank you Major. You always know the right thing to say." He squeezed Kiddie's hand in his and kissed the top of her head. He could see this day wasn't going to go as he had hoped, but he was okay with that. The beauty of living in the city was that there was always something else to do.

I t was early November as Kiddie and the Major took their table at Club Fronton. They were greeted by Jack, one of the owners and someone they now considered a friend. Kiddie and the Major had become regulars at the RedHead, their tearoom, until it had burned down not that long ago. Now the boys were relocated across the street on Washington Place. Jack and his cousin Charlie had reinvented themselves, going from a tearoom to a spanish themed speakeasy. They had added a small kitchen and even live jazz music most nights. Being that Jack and Charlie had been college students when they opened the RedHead, they often attracted the college crowd to their establishment. Now, being older and wiser, they were hoping to cater more to artists and writers, a more mature group who could hopefully afford to pay their tabs. The Major might be a mere sports writer, but the boys made him and Kiddie feel right at home.

Kiddie and the Major were lively tonight as they were both celebrating recent professional events. Kiddie had again appeared in *The Saturday Evening Post*, a lovely sketch of her and another gentleman used for the cover story's picture. Kiddie liked to save copies of her work, signing her name at the top. "The Wives of Great Men Oft Remind Us," had piqued Kiddie's interest, but Kiddie had been more impressed with Brownie's sketch than the actual story itself. Still, she was in the *Post* and Kiddie was proud of that. She had been reading stories in the *Post* for years, her current favorite author being F. Scott Fitzgerald. In his stories like *"Head and Shoulders"* and *"Bernice Bobs her Hair,"* Mr. Fitzgerald created characters Kiddie became invested in. She could relate to his characters who were often young and ambitious, and falling in love. Kiddie had learned recently through a conversation with Brownie, that Fitzgerald's story *"Winter's Dream,"* had featured one of Brownie's sketches. Kiddie wondered if she would ever be so lucky as to be the model in a sketch paired with a Fitzgerald story.

The Major was also celebrating having recently made the first page of the *New York Times, Sunday Edition* with one of his stories. He had been assigned his first trip to Covington, Kentucky, to cover the Old Latonia Horse Race. The Major had been somewhat disappointed the "blue grass" was over advertised and the November weather cold and dreary. However, he had been rewarded with the opportunity to write his first story on horse racing, a race that turned out to be quite the four legged version of a sports upset. Zev had been the favored horse to win, having won the Kentucky Derby back in May. However, In Memoriam, a local horse had come from behind to win by an impressive six lengths. The Major had learned a few lessons along the way, such as betting isn't a sure thing nor are jockeys that prolific, even after a major win. He was most definitely smitten with horse racing now and could only hope he would be assigned to the Kentucky Derby next year.

Before they knew it, Kiddie and the Major were saying good-bye to the year, ready to welcome in the new one. They celebrated at her parent's house with all the family, making it easier on Iris. Kiddie sat on the couch between Iris and the Major, Iris with one hand on her baby bump while Kiddie sat with one hand on the Major's leg. It had been a busy year full of milestones, the biggest one being Iris was having a baby in the spring. The family was supportive of Iris and Bernie's big news, Bernie hoping for a boy to name after his father. His father had died unexpectedly when he was young, and he really wanted a son to carry on both their names. Only time would tell. For now it felt good to already have something to look forward to in the new year.

Even though they were almost always cautious, Kiddie and the Major's love life had definitely taken a hit from the news of Iris being pregnant. Iris was the first person Kiddie had ever known personally to be pregnant. It was daunting to Kiddie to listen to Iris tell stories about her changing body and her worry about childbirth, sure to come sooner or later. Most nights now Kiddie was more adamant about not getting pregnant than she was about satisfying her basic instincts. But still, there were other nights when the Major knew her sweet spot well and he knew she could not say no to him. In some ways it had become better between them as when they were together, they took their time with each other, wanting to make it last.

Kiddie was thankful her cycle would allow them to bring in the new year the best way they knew how, later tonight with their own bottle of champagne. As if reading her thoughts, the Major picked up her hand and kissed her palm. She could see it in his eyes, he was anticipating their private celebration later tonight too. She snuggled into the Major as she held her glass out for Freddy to pour her more wine. He was happy to oblige as Iris asked for their mother to go to the piano and play something..

Her mother played while most of them sang, waiting for midnight. As was tradition, she ended their evening with *"Auld Lang Syne,"* knowing it by heart. It always made Kiddie's mother tear up, her heart overflowing with love and gratitude for all the blessings bestowed upon them throughout the year. Kiddie shared her sentiment, agreeing it had been a good year and she could only imagine what the new year would bring for all of them.

CHAPTER FIVE
═ 1924 ═

"THE BEST PROTECTION ANY WOMAN CAN HAVE IS COURAGE."
—ELIZABETH CADY STANTON

K iddie and the Major lay in bed together, busy reading *The New York Times, Sunday Edition*. Since the Olympics had started at the end of January, they both became obsessed with keeping up on what country medaled for what event. It was the Major's job to keep up so as to write stories to both inform and entertain New York's Olympics fans, fans like Kiddie. They each had their favorite events, their favorite athletes, but mostly they enjoyed rooting together for team USA. Kiddie was even more obsessed because the Olympics were taking place in Chamonix, France, a half day's travel south of Paris. It was the first winter olympics to ever be held and sixteen countries had gone to France to compete. There were sixteen events in six different sports including hockey, skating, and skiing.

After twelve days of competing, the Major was not surprised to see Norway and Finland win the most medals. The United States came in fourth place after Great Britain. Charles Jewtraw, an underdog in the 500 meter speed skating event, had been the first to win a gold medal for the USA. While the Major focused on the hockey game between Canada's powerhouse and the US, Kiddie became a huge fan of skaters Sonja Henie and Herma Szabo, two of the eleven women competing in the games. Even though she scored poorly, Kiddie was impressed with the audacity of eleven year old Sonja Henie from Norway. Herma Szabo from Austria had dominated her competition and that impressed Kiddie too.

As the winter games wrapped up, Kiddie looked for other ways to entertain herself when she wasn't modeling. As Edna predicted, Kiddie was the January cover of *RedBook*, a great start to Kiddie's year. Kiddie was not a fan of winter, finding the cold, dreary weather an annoying challenge to go out for any reason. The Major was an understanding husband often stopping off somewhere to pick up food for dinner on his way home from the office. Kiddie was an understanding wife, realizing he would enjoy a whiskey or two while he waited for their food to be cooked. She supposed most wives were expected to have dinner on the table every night, but the Major didn't seem to mind how it worked for them. Kiddie did make an effort a couple of times a week, Coq Au Vin becoming her specialty and a dish Kiddie loved to make when friends came over.

Tonight Kiddie had decided to cook something new for the Major. Thanks to a temporary lull in the winter weather, Kiddie spent most of the day out, walking Central Park, having lunch with Dot, and going to the market. Kiddie's recipe was actually one of her own favorites that Cook made often. Tonight Kiddie was making meatloaf, mashed potatoes, green beans, with homemade bread from the bakery nearby. Kiddie was sure this would hit the spot as the next winter storm blew in with the Major that night.

"Welcome home Major!" Kiddie said as she greeted him at the door with a kiss on his cheek, and taking his coat to hang up.

"Kiddie whatever you're cooking for dinner, it smells delicious!" the Major said as he took off his wet shoes.

The Major came over to Kiddie to give her his own greeting. She could feel the winter cold in his hands on her hips, and his kiss on her lips.

"Major I can pour you a drink while you get out of your cold, wet clothes." Kiddie said helpfully. The Major was happy to comply.

The Major returned to find candles lit at the table, a record playing, and a glass of red wine waiting for him. He sat down to his plate of hot food, thankful Kiddie had cooked dinner. He was a fan of Cook's meatloaf as well, and appreciated when Kiddie brought the catsup to the table with a simple, "I know it might be a little dry, so doctor it as you will Major."

The Major resisted the urge to doctor his meatloaf with catsup, and let Kiddie know dinner was delicious. After they finished eating and cleared away the dishes, they went to sit together on the couch. Kiddie refilled their wine glasses while the Major flipped the record over. Now with her head on the Major's shoulder, their feet up on the coffee table, Kiddie knew all her hard work was worth it. She supposed if she cooked dinner every night, it would get easier, but no less tedious. Kiddie was okay with not being known for her cooking talents, as long as she had one or two signature dishes for nights like tonight. Her meatloaf would improve, but it was hard to improve on this night.

Taking a sip of her wine, she turned to look at the Major. "Thank you Major, for not tying me to a kitchen every night. And thank you for helping me clean up, when we both know you didn't need to."

The Major chuckled. "Kiddie my love, I couldn't tie you to a kitchen if I tried and I'm happy to spend a few minutes cleaning up after you take the time to put hot food on our table." he said, kissing her on the top of her head.

Kiddie didn't know how, but somehow when the Major talked like that he touched her sweet spot. When he put effort into them, let her be who she was, it was more of an emotional sweet spot than a physical one, but the result would be just the same in the end.

It was almost Valentine's Day and Kiddie was struggling with what to get the Major. It wasn't her favorite holiday and they hadn't done gifts in the past, but shopping gave her something to do. Of course she could find plenty of things to buy for herself, and she had to stop and remind herself to be responsible with money. In the end she bought him a nice blue tie, something to bring color to all his dark suits. It would be perfect in the Spring, if this dreadful winter ever moved on. Walking home Kiddie smiled to herself knowing the perfect way to present the Major's tie to him, a gift he wouldn't soon forget.

Kiddie had only been home for a few minutes when the Major walked in. Surprised to see him so early in the afternoon on a Tuesday caused Kiddie to run to the door to greet him. "Major is everything alright? Are the roads getting bad out?" Kiddie asked. It was a typical blustery winter day in New York City, and the Major shook off his overcoat before hanging it up.

"I have a surprise for you Kiddie! We're going out this afternoon!" the Major said excitedly. "But you are going to want to get dressed up for this!" he added as an afterthought.

Kiddie looked concerned. "But Major it's practically a winter storm out there! Can't we do it another time?"

The Major was propelling Kiddie to their bedroom, "Actually we cannot and we need to leave in the next thirty minutes, but it will be worth the winter weather my love, you'll see."

Kiddie went to do as she was told, finding her dark emerald velvet dress to wear. She found the pearls the Major had given her for her birthday last summer, the present he had hidden in their closet as he had packed to go out west for a story. The necklace was a beautiful double row of pearls with one large pearl as the clasp. Kiddie liked to wear it at the back or the front, depending on her dress.She added some perfume and lipstick before finding the perfect hat to cover her short dark curls.

As she walked out to the Major, he let out a long whistle. Kiddie laughed appreciatively and apologetically at the same time. The Major wore his suit and tie to the office everyday, but if Kiddie wasn't going anywhere she had to admit she threw on something warm and comfortable to putter around the apartment in. Hearing the Major's whistle made Kiddie realize they hadn't really been out much lately and she probably hadn't looked this good since New Year's Eve.

She took a bow before saying, "Why thank you kind sir."

The Major came to take her face in his hands and kiss her. Smiling at her he said, "The pleasure is all mine mademoiselle."

Kiddie sat in her fur coat snuggled up to the Major in the back seat of the cab. Although they usually walked wherever they went in Manhattan, it was too cold for that today. She suddenly realized they were stopped across from Aeolian Hall on West 42nd street in midtown. Kiddie clutched the Major's arm excitedly, "Major, we aren't!"

He took her hand on his arm and squeezed it, "We are my love!"

Kiddie and the Major ran across the street after the Major generously tipped the cab driver for his efforts in the winter weather. Despite the frigid temperatures, it was mayhem around the entrance as people were lined up trying to buy tickets or even just to get into the Hall and out of the weather. Kiddie had never been to Aeolian Hall before, but walking up to the third floor, she assumed it would be much like the other venues she had been in.

As they walked to their seats Kiddie was aware of the very eclectic group of people assembled for the premier of "Rhapsody in Blue." Among the elite and famous, she was most impressed to see Victor Herbert there, her favorite musician. As they took their seats, Kiddie asked the Major how on earth he had acquired their tickets for such a prestigious event.

"I have my ways." the Major answered with a smile.

Waiting for the show to start, Kiddie went through her program, a masterpiece created by Paul Whiteman. They had seen Paul Whiteman perform before with his Palais Royal Orchestra. Tonight George Gershwin would play the piano, joining the "King of Jazz" and his orchestra. Mr. Whiteman touted the performance as "An Experiment in Modern Music," promising a unique performance of his orchestra's jazz talents blended with George Gershwin's classical notes. Not only were there celebrities in the audience, but he had orchestrated a plethora of musical celebrities on stage as well. Kiddie was delighted to be here, to experience it first with this group of music lovers who had braved the winter weather. She noted that "Rhapsody in Blue" would be the next to last song performed.

As the curtain went up, the audience was pleasantly surprised to find a stage set with as much drama as the music promised. The stage was decorated with a Chinese theme, highlighted by two large pillars and even a large gong. Mr. Gershwin's piano sat left center stage while the orchestra played to the right of him. Kiddie was enjoying herself, although at times the songs blurred into each other during the long program.

The crowd came to life though when the long awaited "Rhapsody in Blue" was finally performed. The audience clapped excitedly as a clarinet began with a hook that would delight the most particular music critic. Kiddie was mesmerized by Gershwin's animated tapping of his keys, the music taking her along a jaunty path of music, enhanced by Whiteman's orchestra. While the Major was also enjoying the music, he mostly loved watching Kiddie's face, her expression a reflection of how the music made her feel. Feeling her joy and delight, the Major couldn't resist kissing her hand, happy to be there sharing this musical masterpiece with her.

All too soon the performance was over and the crowd stood cheering wildly in a well deserved ovation. Although it became tedious eventually, Kiddie and the Major were both impressed with the five standing ovations this crowd bestowed on the musical magicians on stage. Both the Major and Kiddie realized they had been part of something special and understood the crowd's reluctance to let it end.

As the house lights came on for good, Kiddie turned to the Major to give him a kiss on the cheek, and say, "Thank you Major! I will never forget this afternoon!"

The Major smiled, squeezing Kiddie's hand. "You're welcome my love. Now where should we go for dinner?" he asked as he followed her to the doors, headed back downstairs and out into the winter weather.

Naturally Shanley's seemed the place to go, the newer location just a block over from the music hall. It seemed Kiddie and the Major weren't the only ones with that idea, and they followed a crowd right in the double doors. It was still relatively early in the evening so they were able to be seated in the Empire Room with only a short wait. They were happy to dine on lobster while sipping champagne, a perfect ending to their perfect afternoon.

It was getting late a few days later as Kiddie waited for the Major to make it home from work. She had baked a carrot cake for the Major and had champagne chilled and ready to pour. As she had planned, she now sat on the couch in one of the Major's white work shirts, only a few buttons closed, the blue tie hanging strategically right where she wanted it. Kiddie wondered how many wives were happy to give themselves to their husbands for Valentine's day. Kiddie knew some wives considered it a chore to satisfy their husbands, but this only convinced Kiddie they weren't going about it the right way. Kiddie thought of Iris with her baby bump growing bigger every week and completely understood how that negated a couple's sex life too.

Kiddie had also heard that keeping up your sex life became a challenge as your marriage moved along and the responsibilities piled up. The husband worried about the bills, the wife worried about what's for dinner, while they both worried about children they were committed to putting before their own needs. Kiddie wondered if it made them selfish or bad people as she and the Major mostly worried about where to go out for dinner and what drink to order to go with it. The truth was Kiddie loved her life with the Major and she could only hope they would always be this happy.

Kiddie thought about how seeing "Rhapsody in Blue" had made her feel anything but blue. Despite being in a good place with the Major, Kiddie was struggling through this winter and the isolation she often felt. She had nearly teared up when the Major had acknowledged it over dinner. This winter Kiddie was struggling to keep herself busy without the structure and routines of college life, missing the camaraderie and intellectual challenge going to class at Columbia brought with it. But tuition wasn't cheap and Kiddie knew not going was one way to save them money.

The Major never seemed to worry about money, but she knew he didn't just throw it out the window either. She knew it was expensive to wine and dine like they did, which made her feel even more proud to put her checks in the bank. She had a general idea how much money the

Major made each week, but she really had no idea what their monthly expenses were.

While Kiddie waited for the Major, her mind continued to wander, thinking again of Iris. Kiddie had been appalled to learn from Iris that society expects pregnant women to be talked about and not seen, and as such she and Bernie had rarely been out with them this winter. She could only hope that would change back once the baby was born, but Kiddie wasn't sure how. Kiddie called Iris often and when the weather was reasonable, would take a cab over to Brooklyn to see Iris and check on her baby bump. They were happy to spend time together, but they were in very different places in their lives and they didn't always feel connected. It reminded Kiddie of when she had started college and dating the Major, and Iris had felt so left out. Kiddie wondered if she would feel left out after the baby was born.

Kiddie was grateful when she was able to work, but there was no predictable pattern, working some weeks and other weeks spent waiting by the phone. The Major didn't work 8 to 5 like Bernie did, but Kiddie enjoyed that the days didn't all blur together, his schedule different from day to day. Her favorite part of winter was that it was the Major's down time of the year and he was usually always close to home. Kiddie wondered how that would change as the Major became more successful at the paper.

So much to think about as she sat and waited for the Major. Feeling restless she got up and poured herself a glass of champagne. She hadn't eaten since lunch and it was well past dinner time. She had just given up on the Major and was cutting into the cake when she heard his key in the door. She sat at the table trying to decide how she was going to play him being so late, especially on Valentine's Day.

The Major came in the door in a rush, already apologizing, "Kiddie I'm sorry I'm so late, but. . ." he trailed off upon seeing how Kiddie was dressed. He took in the opened champagne bottle and piece of cake on her plate, her fork loaded and ready to delight her taste buds. Kiddie had temporarily forgotten how she was dressed, but seeing the way the Major looked at her, she could well imagine he was sorry.

Dropping his coat, he walked over to where she still sat at the dining room table. He stood smiling at her, taking all of her in, her legs bare, one tucked up under her, his shirt covering her yet open enough he could see her curves, and then a blue tie he had never seen before hanging around her neck, before falling into her lap. Bending down to kiss her on the cheek, the Major paused for a minute to pointedly enjoy the view she offered him.

"Please tell me I haven't missed your private party for two." he said in her ear. Kiddie turned her face up to look at him.

"To be honest Major, I got thirsty waiting for you and then I got hungry waiting for you, so I hope you don't mind that I started without you." Kiddie said with her own little smile. Handing him his glass of champagne, Kiddie tapped his glass and added, "Happy Valentine's Day."

As they both emptied their glasses, the Major reached to pour them more champagne before cutting himself a piece of cake and joining Kiddie at the table. Kiddie was playing it cool, but he could tell she was a little miffed with him and he decided to tread lightly. Kiddie felt a little better seeing his eyes take in how she was dressed, enjoying the effect it was having on him.

"Like what you see Major?" Kiddie asked, crossing her legs and extending them out to his chair, like an invitation. "Perhaps you should have Edna paint my picture or better yet, Brownie could sketch me. He's very good at making a woman look good." she added saucily. Kiddie had not missed how the Major's eyes had narrowed ever so slightly, clearly not entertained by this idea. Kiddie decided to drive her point a little harder.

Standing up she turned her chair around and then straddled it just out of reach of the Major. She slowly unbuttoned a button so she could pull the shirt just off her shoulders, but still mostly covered. "Or maybe this look would be better. What do you think, Major?" Kiddie asked softly.

Kiddie could feel the heat between them, wanting to push the Major's buttons, but wondering how far would be too far. Thinking about another man seeing Kiddie in this way, gave the Major a slow burn, but he knew Kiddie was trying to get a reaction so he sat like a cat, ready to pounce when she had pushed far enough.

Feeling quite impetuous, Kiddie stood up and came to stand between her chair and the Major's. Her eyes were locked into his and she didn't say anything as she unbuttoned the last two buttons of her shirt, letting it fall open to reveal nothing but the blue tie on her bare skin. Not able to resist her any longer, the Major was quick to use the tie to pull her down on his lap, before kissing her hard on her lips.

Still holding on to the tie to keep her close, he asked, "Are you finished with your show Kiddie?"

Kiddie traced the Major's lips with her finger, her eyes blazing. In a deep husky voice she answered, "Actually Major, I'm just getting started."

In a flash the Major was standing, carrying Kiddie to the bedroom, her legs wrapped around him. Closing the door behind him, the Major was one very happy man.

March in the sports world can only mean baseball and for the Major, he was about to hit his first journalistic home run. He had learned only yesterday that he had been assigned to cover the Brooklyn Robins for the season. As any true baseball fan would be, he was excited to be headed to Florida for spring training and on the *Times* dime no less. His biggest worry was how many suits to pack and how to tell Kiddie. He would be gone not quite a month before the team moved back home to start their season opener in mid April against none other than the New York Giants.

The Robins played at Ebbets field, located in Flatbush, Kiddie's part of Brooklyn. The field was named after one of the owners and current president of the organization, Charles Ebbets. Although the Robins were definitely the lesser talked about baseball team of New York, it wasn't for lack of talent. The Major had been doing his homework and found out the team boasted a deadly baseball pitching combination of Burleigh Grimes and Dazzy Vance. In addition Zack Wheat was a force to be reckoned with out in left field. The Major was looking forward to heading south and seeing the boys in action.

For now the Major was headed home, hurrying to pack after telling Kiddie his big news and then hopefully taking her out on the town for dinner and dancing. He was home early with a bouquet of roses in one hand and a bottle of champagne stashed under his overcoat as he unlocked the door to their apartment. He was disappointed to find Kiddie out and he assumed she was still working on her sitting with Brownie. The Major decided to go ahead and start packing, not wanting to do it later when he and Kiddie could be enjoying their time together. His train left early in the morning and he wanted to be packed and ready way before that final call.

He hadn't gotten far when he heard Kiddie call his name. She walked into their apartment surprised to see roses on the table beside a bottle of champagne. She was happy and curious to hear what they were celebrating. Kiddie paused her smile as she walked into their bedroom to find the Major packing.

"Are we celebrating or are you running away from home Major?"

"Kiddie, my love, I've got big news! I've been assigned to cover the Brooklyn Robins for the season! The hard part is that spring training starts in a few days in Florida and I have a train to catch first thing in the morning." He walked over to her, taking both of her hands, eagerly looking into her face, wanting her to share his excitement.

Being a Brooklyn girl, Kiddie was familiar with the Robins, although her father often touted them as a lesser team. Kiddie had never been sure why and had always chalked it up to as part of being a Giants fan. She could see the Major was excited and wanted to share in that with him, but still she was afraid to ask how long he would be gone this time. As if reading her mind, the Major spoke before she could say anything.

"Kiddie I'll be gone for a month, but with Iris's tea to plan and Brownie demanding your presence, you'll not even have time to miss me!"

This made Kiddie smile as she found her voice. "Major, I'm so proud of you! I know you've been waiting for this and what true baseball fan doesn't dream of going to spring training? I'm happy for you! Should we open the champagne and celebrate?"

Kiddie had already turned and was headed to the kitchen to get their coupe glasses out of the cabinet, the Major following close behind her.

As the Major went to open the champagne he asked, "Are you really okay with me being gone Kiddie?"

Keeping herself together, knowing it didn't matter one way or another, Kiddie answered with a kiss to his cheek, "Of course Major! You caught me by surprise, but you're right, there is a lot to do to get ready for Iris's tea and the baby coming. I'll be fine, but I will miss you!"

Kiddie expectantly held out her champagne glass, eager to move on and down her first glass. She didn't want to waste their last night together worrying about dinner for one and sleeping alone right now.

As the Major poured and handed her glass to her Kiddie said proudly, "Cheers to you Major! I know you'll knock it out of the park!"

The Major laughed at her play on words and bowed his head to her as he clinked his glass to hers. He took her empty glass to sit on the table beside his, before he pulled her to him, this time kissing her before asking her where she would like to go out to dinner.

Kiddie smiled and answered, "You pick Major, it's your news to celebrate."

The Major wasn't sure which way he should take that, but returned her smile, kissing her hand gallantly before answering, "Leave it to me, my love, I've got the perfect night planned for us. We need to be headed out in an hour, if that works for you?"

"I can make it work because I have the perfect dress to wear." Kiddie answered while pouring another glass of champagne and handing it to the Major, before taking the bottle with her to the bedroom.

She stopped at their door when the Major called her name, watching as he walked over to her with her glass, before handing it to her with a quiet, "Don't forget your glass." She took it from him, despite knowing full well she would be drinking from the bottle.

Kiddie had taken her time soaking in the tub, finishing the champagne. She was thankful she had a late lunch with a friend after her setting with Bernie, knowing it would buffer her champagne well. She was trying hard to be excited for the Major, but really just wanted to sit and pout. She knew it was only a matter of time before the Major would be sent away on assignment again, but still the news had caught her by surprise. Taking a deep breath, she got out of the tub, finally ready to get dressed and embrace her night with the Major.

Of course she had chosen the dress that she knew would drive him crazy, and a sure sign of how she expected to end their evening. She would let him wine and dine her as he should before he went off to sunny Florida, doing what he loved and getting paid to do so. Kiddie envied him not only the beach and sunshine, but how lucky he was to be in such a position. A month was hardly a blip in time except at the end of the day when she laid in their bed without him. The first time he had gone away it had seemed natural to spend more time at home, but now she was all grown up and used to living her adult life, her life with the Major. She would go to see Iris, but as Iris was very pregnant, their time together had its limits. As her aunt had told her on more than one occasion, it was time to pull up her big girl pants and move on.

Kiddie was just adding her double pearl necklace to her dress when the Major came in to see if she was ready. It tugged at her heart to see him standing there so handsome in his suit, ready but patient.

Walking up to him, she kissed him on the cheek before saying, "I'm all yours Major, take me where you will."

She turned back to him as he took her arm, bringing her back to him before kissing her on her mouth. "Kiddie you look beautiful. You know what this dress does to me!"

Kiddie smilied, "I'm counting on it Major."

I t was barely light out as the Major stood outside waiting for his cab to the train station. He was still thinking about last night, Kiddie in her dress, smiling as he thought about how late they had eaten dinner. He had not been able to resist her and in the end she had refused to put her dress back on, suggesting he go out and get dinner so they could have dinner in bed, among other things. It was the among other things that kept Kiddie close in the Major's heart and his head. He knew she had played him well last night and he was happy to let her. He also knew she had been sad this morning as she kissed him good-bye and that he regretted. Once again they had promised to write to each other, although he knew he would be better at it than she would. This seemed only fair to him, knowing she relied on him to use his pen on her behalf as well as for the *Times*. As he got into his cab he glanced up at their apartment one last time.

He paused seeing Kiddie standing beside the curtain, returning her wave with a kiss from his lips and said, "until next time my love."

After watching the Major's cab pull away from the curb, Kiddie crawled back into bed, pulling his pillow close to her, embracing the smell of his hair gel. It made her feel better he had looked up to see her there, blowing her a kiss. She could almost swear he had said "until next time my love," but couldn't be certain. She was certain he would be thinking about her most of his train ride down to Florida, smiling as she thought about how he had not been able to resist her in her dress even long enough to go out to dinner. In the end it had been nice to have a night at home, in bed, laughing over oysters Rockefeller among other things.

Kiddie had nothing on her agenda for the day except going back to sleep and calling to check on Iris and her baby bump later in the day. She was happy she and her mother were throwing Iris a "Tea" to welcome the baby and shower them both with presents. Planning and preparing for it would give Kiddie something to do. She knew it was a good distraction for Iris and realized now it would be for Kiddie too.

It finally felt like Spring as New York settled into late April. The Major had been back for a few weeks now, but had jumped right into the season with the Robins opening game series with the New York Giants. The Major had been impressed the team had held their own against the Giants, the series ending in a tie, each team able to claim two of the four games in victory. As promised, the Robins pitching team had given the Major plenty to write about and for that, he was happy. Kiddie was happy to have her husband home although his schedule was dependent on the Robin's latest game series. The Major would be traveling with the team, but the afternoon home games usually left time for late dinners and time well spent together. Kiddie didn't mind too many late nights for the Major, as he often graced her with coffee and breakfast in bed the next morning.

Today Kiddie and her mother were busy setting vases of tulips and daffodils out on the dining room table. It was almost time for Iris to arrive and Kiddie hurried to finish adding plates around the table, the floral pattern bringing the crisp white tablecloth to life. Cook brought out pitchers of tea, one sweet and one unsweetened.

As her mother lit the candles, Kiddie went to greet Iris, their guest of honor, at the door. "Iris, welcome to your tea party!" Kiddie said hugging her happily.

Iris looked beautiful in a loose pink floral dress, her baby bump obvious underneath. She hugged Kiddie before following her into the dining room. She took in the cheerful table set with the fresh spring flowers, glowing candles, and her mother's good china. The buffet set full of finger sandwiches, deviled eggs, fresh fruit, and a platter of cupcakes. There was another table set up under the front window, and Iris noticed the two gifts wrapped in paper. She went to hug her mother and Cook too, her eyes watering slightly.

Concerned, Kiddie grabbed Iris by the hand and asked, "Iris what's wrong?"

Laughing sheepishly Iris replied, "Nothing's wrong silly! I'm touched that you and Mother are hosting this tea for me and the baby today. I hope the family doesn't mind coming." she added.

It was their mother who dismissed that idea. "Nonsense darling! Your family loves you and we're all happy to celebrate you and our soon to arrive newest family member!"

After much deliberation on how and when, Kiddie and her mother had decided to host an afternoon tea for Iris to shower her and the new baby with love and presents. They knew some people considered it presumptuous to celebrate a baby before it was born, but Kiddie and her mother had decided Iris needed something to take her mind off of her impending childbirth. They both knew she was scared and Kiddie had to admit she was a little scared for her. Still, their mother had given birth three times and assured Iris, women all over the world gave birth everyday and it would all be okay one way or another.

It still annoyed Kiddie to no end that society needed to be protected from seeing a pregnant woman out and about, as if the reminder of how she got there was too appalling to endure. She mocked society's stupidity that without women giving birth, life would eventually cease to exist quite literally. Kiddie pushed her annoyance aside and led Iris to her seat at the head of the table, while their mother went to answer the door and welcome their first guests.

Before long Iris sat surrounded at the table by her aunts and cousins, Bernie's mother, and even her grandmother. Everyone marveled at how good Iris looked, hugging her, and sharing their excitement for the newest family member. Iris was happy to listen to all the small talk at the table, enjoying the chance to be involved socially for a change. As they all finished eating, Kiddie and her mother cleared the table, pouring more tea and bringing the platter of Cook's delicious cupcakes around. Cook's sister had cleverly decorated each cupcake with either a pink or a blue safety pin made out of fondant. Now Aunt Emma turned to her and asked, "Iris do you think you're having a boy or a girl?"

Iris caught Kiddie's eye before answering, "A girl I think!" Iris knew Bernie hoped for a boy, but also knew he mostly hoped for a healthy baby. She and Kiddie talked about it often and they agreed it felt like a girl, but Iris declined to share any baby names feeling that could jinx them all.

Soon it was time to open gifts, Kiddie happy to bring them to Iris and watch her showered with so many ooh and aah's over each one. The gifts ranged from practical to fancy, a good mix of diapers, bottles, blankets, towels, and even baby clothes. Iris's crown ewels came when Iris's grandmother gave her a silver spoon for the baby and Bernie's mother gave her the christening gown that Bernie had worn. Iris's immediate family had bought a crib for the baby, the deep cherry wood beautiful to look at.

As the various family members departed, Kiddie and her mother began packing all the gifts up for Bernie to load in the car. He arrived soon and was impressed and grateful for the family's generosity. Iris gave Kiddie and her mother a big hug and a thank you before waddling down to the car. Kiddie offered to come over later and help her put it all away, the baby's room mostly ready and waiting to look lived in. Bernie promised to have the crib all set up when she came, so she could admire it for herself.

As April rolled into May, Iris became consumed with her impending delivery. Kiddie sympathized with her, but for once had no sisterly wisdom to impart on her, other than she was stronger than she thought. Despite society's distaste on the subject, the Major was surprised how often the conversation at Sunday dinner revolved around the numerous options Iris had available for consideration. The girls trusted their father's medical expertise as well as their mother's experienced opinion to help Iris make the best choice. Bernie wisely left this decision up to his pregnant wife, just wanting everyone to be safe and healthy.

She could give birth at home with a doctor or a midwife, or she could go to the hospital when the time came. Twilight birth was becoming a popular option where the woman was basically in a sleep like state, while the baby was pulled out with forceps. As big fans of the royal family, Kiddie and Iris wondered if it was good enough for Queen Victoria, wasn't it most likely good enough for Iris. Ultimately it was about giving birth to a healthy baby in the safest, least painful way. Although giving birth was a natural event for a woman, one could not argue the statistics of how many women and babies died during childbirth even in the 1920's.

As Iris's baby bump grew daily, her father advised she had better make her decision soon or it would be too late and others would be making it for her. After many conversations with a variety of people, Iris finally committed to giving birth at home with an attending physician, knowing her family, particularly her father would be available as needed. Iris trusted her doctor who had explained how her body would naturally take over when the time came, his task to support her with modern medicine as he managed her pain and was ready to catch the baby. While more and more women were heading to the hospital for their deliveries, it was important for Iris to know she could ask for and have her family members right there as she wanted. Kiddie was thankful she wouldn't be Iris's first ask for, deferring to her parents first for support.

It was a beautiful day in May when Iris's water broke. She was at home with Bernie's mother, who quickly rallied the troops, Bernie being her first call. It was time for the baby to be born and everyone knew exactly what to do. This well rehearsed plan of action had been crucial to Iris surviving the past few weeks, waiting to go into labor without being too anxious about it. Kiddie arrived just before the doctor, going to the bedroom to check on Iris and give her the best pep talk she could. She squeezed Iris's hand and kissed her on the forehead before allowing herself to be ushered out. At first, Iris and Bernie's home was a hive of activity, collecting towels, blankets, hot water, all the paraphernalia required to deliver a baby. Iris's mother sat with her while everyone got themselves organized and prepared around her, but in the end Iris had asked for only Bernie to be in the room with her and the doctor. Now everyone sat or paced or alternated between the two, waiting for the cries of a baby to ring out into the quiet house.

As the minutes crawled into hours, Kiddie tried to occupy her time flipping through Iris's collection of magazines. Her mother busied herself with cleaning, which Kiddie rarely saw her do. Bernie's mother was the gracious host, making large pots of coffee and pitchers of tea and lemonade. As the sun started to set, Kiddie helped her turn a roasted chicken into chicken salad sandwiches. Together they sat out pickles, olives, and deviled eggs alongside the sandwiches. Kiddie offered to make plates for people, but noticed people nibbled on next to nothing, their anxiety or anticipation curbing their appetite.

Occasionally Bernie would come down and update them, using words like dilated and effaced. Seeing Kiddie's confused expression, her mother explained it to her so she would understand where Iris was in her delivery. The hardest part was hearing Iris moaning through her painful contractions, Kiddie cringing as it became more frequent and resounding as the afternoon wore on. Her mother promised Kiddie this was a good sign as her contractions were getting closer together, a sure sign the baby was closer to being delivered. Kiddie felt both appalled and in awe of what her sister was going through and wished with all her heart it would be over.

As the evening grew late, the family realized the house had become very quiet. Kiddie instinctively went to stand by her mother, taking her hand. She said to Kiddie quietly, "Either Iris is in trouble or the baby is here." Kiddie turned to look at her father, his eyes glued to the stairs.

"But if Iris were in trouble, the doctor would come to get Father, right? Right Mother?" Kiddie was almost in tears, the anxiety of the day weighing her down. She wished the Major was there for her to lean on, then immediately felt like a selfish baby when Iris was the one in so much pain. Iris's family and Bernie's mother stood around together waiting for Bernie to come tell them some news, good or bad, they just needed to know what was happening.

Suddenly they heard the sounds of a baby's cries, weak and tiny, but announcing their own arrival to the family. In one move the family stood at the bottom of the stairs willing Bernie to come out. As if feeling their wishes, he suddenly appeared at the top of the stairs.

"It's a girl! She's here and she's beautiful! I'm a father! We have a daughter!" Bernie was beside himself with emotion, a mixture of tears, joy, and disbelief.

As if speaking for the group Kiddie yelled out, "That's wonderful, but how is Iris? Is she okay?"

Bernie paused as he was about to go back in to say, "Iris was amazing! I can't believe what she just did!" Kiddie was thinking that wasn't really an answer, but he was gone, back to Iris.

Finally Kiddie's mother was summoned and she anxiously went to see her daughter and brand new granddaughter. Bernie came downstairs as she went up, going to hug his mother and the rest of the family. Kiddie was anxious to see Iris and yet afraid she would fall apart upon seeing her. Now as she stood in the kitchen, she took a deep breath, willing all her anxiety to wash away and wishing more than anything the Major was there.

The team was on the road, seemingly for the whole month of May traveling from Chicago to St. Louis and currently to Cincinnati. The Major had been in St. Louis the last time he had called her. He had been melancholy at the thought that Uncle Crutch wouldn't be in the stands while the Major was getting paid to be there, his dream come true. Kiddie had wished she could put her arms around him then, just as she wished he could do for her now. His presence made her feel safe and warm, as she hoped hers did for him.

"Your mother and I made chicken salad," she said as Bernie came in.

Suddenly Kiddie realized her mother was at the top of the stairs, announcing the doctor would allow another family member to come up.

Glancing at Bernie, Kiddie said quietly, "Bernie you should take your mother. After all, it's her first granddaughter too."

"You're right Kiddie. We'll be quick about it I promise." Bernie said. As an afterthought she grabbed his arm causing him to pause.

"Bernie, tell Iris I'm so proud of her and I can't wait to meet my new niece!"

Bernie nodded and gave Kiddie a hug before heading up the stairs. "And ask her if she's hungry!" Kiddie added as his mother followed him up.

It was very late in the evening as Kiddie sat in the rocker holding her niece, Iris smiling to finally see the two of them together. She was exhausted, but still riding the high of having her baby girl finally here. When Kiddie finally had her turn to see Iris, they had both teared up, Kiddie rushing to give Iris a big hug, thankful she was okay.

Sitting on the side of her bed Kiddie said to Iris, "I have never been more proud or amazed by you Iris! You did it!"

Then Bernie's mom was handing the tiny bundle to Kiddie, showing her how to support her head with the crook of her arm. At first Kiddie felt incredibly awkward, but as she sat in the rocker, she started talking softly to her new niece.

With her eyes still on the baby, Kiddie asked Iris, "What are you and Bernie going to name her?"

Iris smiled shyly. "Consuelo. We're not sure about her middle name yet, but we like the name Consuelo. It means in consolation. She's my prize for enduring all that horrific pain," Iris said with a grimace.

Taken aback by the uniqueness of the name, Kiddie was mulling it over in her mind, understanding Iris's choice better as she explained. She had only heard the name one other time, in a magazine article about the Vanderbilt family, remembering William and Alva Vanderbilt had named their only daughter that years ago.

Iris was still talking. "Bernie said after what I've been through, it was my choice and I chose Consuelo."

Kiddie smiled at Iris and said, "I love it." Taking the baby's hand in her fingers, she said softly, "Welcome to the world Miss Consuelo! Your aunt Kiddie is very happy to meet you."

Kiddie handed the sweet sleeping baby back to Iris. She understood Iris must be exhausted and her time was up. She kissed Iris on the top of her head, telling her "I love you Iris." before leaving the room.

Iris and Bernie nicknamed the baby Lelo and everyone quickly fell in love with the latest addition to the family. Kiddie added a new routine of going to see them at least a couple of times of week. Someone in the family had bought them a stroller so Kiddie and Iris often walked the baby, talking about everything from feeding schedules to Kiddie's latest sitting with Bernie or Edna. Kiddie was quite busy, her magazine covers less frequent, but Bernie's sketches often appeared in a variety of places, including *The New York Woman*. Currently the Major was back to a home schedule, but some days it seemed they were ships passing in the night as Kiddie would get home from working just as the Major was headed out to cover a game. Kiddie was thankful they were both night owls, and didn't mind the late nights catching up on life and each other over late dinners and drinks.

Just as the Major had traveled most of May, the team played at Ebbets field most of June. The team played against the Pirates on Kiddie's birthday and the Major acquired complimentary tickets for Kiddie, Iris, Bernie, Freddy, and Dot. Although not true Robins fans, it had been a fun afternoon as the team won their game with six runs. They had all been impressed with Dazzy Vance as he pitched several strikeouts in a row. Kiddie knew the Major was proud to have them there, their seats better than his as they sat behind home plate. The Major had written his story as the game progressed, although he would have to eventually go in to finish it up.

After the game they all headed to the family home for dinner and Kiddie's favorite coconut white cake Cook graciously still made for her every year. Saying goodnight to the parents the rowdy crew had later taken over Club Fronton, practically another birthday tradition for Kiddie now. The Major kept her glass filled with her favorite drink there, the French 75, before eventually pouring her into a cab and heading them home. After getting her tucked into bed, he walked the five blocks to the office to finish his story and call it a day.

Before they knew it, it was the end of July and they were celebrating the Major's birthday. The Major had traveled with the team through most of July, so they were both happy he was finally home by the end of the month. He spent some of his birthday at the Robins game against the Cincinnati Reds, rewarded with a shutout courtesy of Burleigh Grimes to write about. Back at the office he quickly got his story out before meeting Kiddie and some friends for a late dinner. As the Major often did for her, Kiddie kept the party going, his drink never empty before pouring them both into a cab and getting him home and into bed.

It was a roller coaster of a summer as Kiddie and the Major adjusted to his new schedule. When he was home, Kiddie was a happy wife. When she would find his bag out, all packed and ready to catch the train in the morning, not so much. Living out of suitcases and riding train cars for two to three weeks at a time was exhausting for the Major. He had never been one who needed much sleep or would turn down a party, but he did enjoy his own comforts of home and that included Kiddie. He knew it was starting to wear on her too, but he wasn't sure what to do about it, since after all, it was what he had signed up for, and without realizing it, so had Kiddie.

Despite not always getting the usual press the Yankees and the Giants received, the Brooklyn Robins were having a good season, maybe even good enough to go to the World Series. The Major was hopeful, but didn't have the heart to tell Kiddie the season of one hundred fifty four games could be extended into October. He would cross that bridge when and if they got to it. Right now he was trying to figure out how to tell Kiddie he would be in Philadelphia for their anniversary, the Robins scheduled for two days of double-headers against the Phillies. The train ride was just short of ninety minutes, but with double-headers they would start early and finish late. The Major thought about asking off for the day, but it was a lot of baseball to ask off for during a crucial time in the season and he decided against it. He thought about having Kiddie come to Philly, but didn't want to worry about her being bored in the hotel by herself or even at the ballpark. There seemed to be just one thing to do, he would promise to make it up to her next year, and hope that he could.

It was Labor Day weekend and the Major was finally home. Kiddie knew he still had games to attend and stories to write, but he would be there when she woke up in the middle of the night and reached for him. Besides, their anniversary was actually on Labor Day this year and how could that not be a good thing? Kiddie didn't even try to keep up with the Major's schedule anymore, waiting for him to tell her a few days out of him leaving town.

Tonight they were meeting Iris and Bernie after he finished his story, heading out to Club Fronton, Kiddie wanting a tall drink all weekend long. She was thankful for Iris and Bernie as they often let her tag along when they went out. She was thankful for Bernie's mom too who seemed happy to stay home with little Lelo. Sometimes it was hard to be the third wheel, but it was better than sitting home alone wishing the Major would call. At times it was clear Iris and Bernie needed some couple time and Kiddie would go sit at the bar, trying not to attract any-one's attention but the bartenders. Other nights she could feel she was the buffer between the two of them, and it would be Bernie who would get up and go to the bar. The best nights were when the Major was there, his presence bringing balance to their group. Kiddie was looking forward to tonight, a new dress hanging in her closet and begging to be worn. She had found it on sale at Macy's the other day when she and Iris had been out shopping.

Now Kiddie sat at the bar, the first to arrive at Club Fronton, waiting for them to set up their table. Freddy had decided to join them too, bringing Dot along. Kiddie smoothed down her skirt, before sipping more on her French 75. Her dress was a navy chiffon, stylish in the front, with a low v in the back. She was just about to order another cocktail when the bartender handed her a fresh drink. Seeing Kiddie's puzzled expression, he let her know the gentleman sitting at a table had bought the drink for her. For a moment Kiddie was flattered, but as she turned to look at him she made sure her stony expression said no thank you, annoyed when he merely smiled and raised his glass to her anyway. She was relieved to see her group walk in just as Jack came to show her to their table, making a point to leave the drink on the bar. Jack observed her interaction with the man and assured her he would make sure it didn't happen again.

There were hugs all around as the group sat down, and Kiddie could only hope the Major would be there soon. The group went ahead and ordered dinner, Kiddie ordering for the Major, but requesting they hold his food until he arrived. Their food arrived only minutes before the Major did, Kiddie jumping up to greet him with a kiss on the lips. She wasn't sure if the stranger was watching her, but she hoped he had seen that too. Jack himself went to get the Major's dinner, as the Major thanked Kiddie for thinking ahead, knowing he would be starving. The lively group of six were enjoying themselves, their food delicious and the drinks flowing. The Major sat close to Kiddie, his arm around her, whispering private side notes into her ear every so often, making her laugh. Kiddie's siblings exchanged a glance between themselves, happy to see their sister glowing for a change. They knew how much Kiddie missed the Major when he was gone, but there wasn't a lot they could do about it.

Too soon everyone was headed home, their happy group closing down the bar after the final call for drinks. Bernie played big man on campus picking up the tab for everyone. Seated in the back of their cab, Kiddie snuggled up to the Major, her head resting on his shoulder, her hand on his leg. The Major was a fan of Kiddie's new dress and the effect of it wasn't lost on him. She looked beautiful and sophisticated from the front, but the low v in the back seemed like an invitation. He too had noticed the man watching Kiddie from afar and had discreetly asked Jack to ask him to leave, tipping Jack generously for his trouble. The Major would never question Kiddie being faithful to him, but he did worry about her safety when she was alone so much. He shook it off now as he followed her into the bedroom, happy to know he was the one she wore the dress for and happy to be the one to get her out of it.

The sun was shining as Kiddie stretched under the covers. She could smell the coffee and hoped the Major was fixing a cup to bring her soon. Her eyes noticed her dress flung over the back of the chair in the corner of their bedroom. She smiled to herself thinking about their private party for two once they got home, knowing it would be hard to top last night on their anniversary. The Major soon appeared with plates of bacon and eggs, toast and jelly, and cups of hot coffee.

"Good morning my love," the Major said as he set the tray down on the bed. Kiddie was happy to see him and leaned over to kiss him.

"Thank you Major. You always do make the best breakfasts!" Kiddie realized she was hungry and dug into her bacon and eggs happily.

She knew the Major would be watching the Robins play the Giants in the last game of the series today, but she realized he hadn't said when or where he was headed to next. She pushed it aside as the Major pulled out four tickets for today's game. It would be tricky to root for both teams, but Kiddie didn't mind, she was just happy to have plans.

"A messenger just brought them by. I'm happy you want to go. I asked the group last night who would want to join you, and all but Dot can make the game." The Major said with a smile.

"Sounds like a perfect afternoon. Do you have to go in before the game or are you all mine until then?" Kiddie asked mischievously.

It was now or never, and the Major braced himself as he broke the news to Kiddie. "Actually I'm all yours. Kiddie I'm headed to Philadelphia in the morning for a series with the Phillies." The Major winced as Kiddie paused her fork halfway to her mouth. He had seen the look before she could shut it down.

"You're leaving in the morning?" Kiddie asked, her voice light but needing him to clarify.

"I am." The Major answered somberly. "Kiddie I'm so sorry I'm going to miss our anniversary! I've been trying to think of a way we can be together, but it's two full days of double headers. I promise I'll make it up to you." He picked up her hand and kissed her palm.

Kiddie retrieved her hand and was moving the tray away so she could get out of bed. Keeping her voice light Kiddie said. "I understand Major, you have a commitment to the paper and your story. We had a great time last night and we can make the most of our day today. I'll get dressed and we can go for a walk."

Kiddie would save her meltdown for later, pushing it deep down where it wouldn't ruin their day. Avoiding his gaze, she went to the closet and pulled out a dress before heading to the bathroom.

"I'll be ready in a jiff Major." she said airily.

The Major knew Kiddie was disappointed, but she was not going to show him that. Her comment about his commitment to the paper wasn't lost on him, although he hoped she didn't question his commitment to her and their marriage. He would see to it that they had a wonderful day.

It was longer than a jiff, but finally Kiddie was ready to go. She had picked one of her favorite pink dresses to wear, willing it to coat her like an emotionally free armor. She really did want to enjoy her day with the Major and knew he wanted the same. As they went to walk out the door, the Major stopped her and pushed her hat up enough to kiss her deeply on the lips. "I love you Kiddie and nothing makes me happier than to be married to you." Then he fixed her hat, kissed the palm of her hand, before tucking it into the crook of his arm. Kiddie was grateful the hat shielded her eyes somewhat while mentally cursing her dress for not being the armor she needed. He hoped she didn't notice her wipe her eyes with her free hand as they headed down the stairs and onto Morningside.

It was a beautiful day and the Major moved their conversation along comfortably as they walked. The fresh air felt good, more crisp like fall than humid like summer. Kiddie was enjoying herself and was happy to have this new maturity to keep herself together. They stopped at P.J. Clark's for lunch, indulging in thick juicy burgers and greasy fries topped off with discreet shots of bourbon disguised in thick chocolate milkshakes. Soon their cab was headed over the bridge to Ebbets Field where they would be meeting Kiddie's family. It was the last game in the series with the Giants, the Robins already with two wins under their belt. The fans had packed the stands, hoping for another win as Kiddie's family hoped for a loss for the Robins. Unless you were the Giant's batter standing at the plate trying to get a piece of their pitches, you had to admit the Robins pitching team was pure magic, regardless of which team you rooted for.

At times the game was slow as baseball games can be, but eventually the Robins were rewarded with a 3-2 win. It was a beautiful day and Kiddie couldn't think of any place she would rather be. Being so close to home, Kidde and the Major were happy to join the family for Sunday dinner before heading back over the bridge and into the city. The Major was thankful to hear Iris ask Kiddie if she would join her in taking Lelo to her first parade, the Memorial Day parade in the morning, which Kiddie happily agreed too.

Reality set in as Kiddie and the Major returned home, the Major headed to the office to write his story for today's win. Kiddie did not realize the Major had packed while she had been in the bathroom this morning, trying to keep herself together while getting dressed. He promised he would be back soon with a swift kiss and a quick smile. Kiddie flipped through a magazine before heading to bed. It was late and Kiddie knew from experience the Major's "soon" could easily be a couple of hours. Besides she was tired, too tired to hold herself together any longer and wanted to be asleep when the Major got home. She had also promised to meet Iris at 8:30 to walk the few blocks to the parade with little Lelo in her stroller.

The Major didn't know if he was relieved or disappointed when he got home and Kiddie was asleep. It had been hard work putting up a light and breezy front all day, but the truth was he was tired too. He loved his job, but he was ready to get off this baseball roller coaster and be home for more than two or three weeks at a time. He truly was disappointed not to be home with Kiddie on their anniversary. Laying in the dark beside her, he thought back to their honeymoon, their time together there so special. He thought how he had almost lost her when her bike had crashed. It would be a long day tomorrow, but he knew it would be worth it for both of them. He kissed Kiddie on her shoulder, before whispering "good night my love."

The Major set his alarm extra early so he could lay in bed with Kiddie and hold her for a little while. He could tell by her breathing she was awake too and as he pulled her to him he whispered "Happy anniversary, my love." He kissed her on the top of her head, grateful to feel her snuggle into his chest.

He smiled when Kiddie whispered back to him, "Happy anniversary Major."

Too soon he was out the door, suitcase in tow, blowing her a kiss and sending "Until next time my love" back to her at the window before climbing into his cab. Remarkably Kiddie went back to sleep, thinking of Iris and Lelo who would be waiting for her in a few short hours. Kiddie found it amusing that Iris wanted to take a four month old baby to a parade, but she was also grateful for the distraction. After the parade they would go and have lunch and do some shopping together at Macy's. Ever since the store had taken over an entire city block, the girls were impressed with their redesign and fashion forward styles for all ages, including Lelo. Kiddie's last thought was it would be a good day to buy her niece a new dress.

The day passed quickly, a perfectly lovely day despite Kiddie missing the Major and knowing it was their anniversary. She had to admit she enjoyed herself, trying to find things to be thankful for. Now as she got to her door, she saw a dozen red roses waiting for her, a card tucked down into the flowers. Kiddie took her packages and flowers inside, stopping short of reading the card, afraid it would unravel her. Instead she went to the cabinet and pulled out her favorite red wine and a glass. She thought about the first time she and Iris had to open a bottle of wine, a couple of teenagers trying to survive a pandemic.

Kiddie went to the record player, looking through their records, wanting to find Victor Herbert. Even if the Major was gone, she wanted to hear *"The Princess of my Dreams"* on their anniversary. She thought about how sad she had been to hear Mr. Herbert had died unexpectedly in May. Listening to the familiar words, Kiddie remembered the first time she heard this song with the Major. Starting to tear up, Kiddie went to get the Major's pillow from their bed, chiding herself she was being a baby. She knew the Major was disappointed too and she had made sure she didn't make him feel bad about them not being together. As she poured herself another generous glass of wine, she could see her pile of magazines calling to her to come read. Ignoring them, she decided to curl up with the Major's pillow and her wine and throw herself a pity party instead.

As the day turned to dusk and the apartment became dark, Kiddie turned on the small lamp beside her on the end table. She thought about rummaging through their small icebox for some dinner, but decided another glass of wine was all she needed tonight. She was disappointed to find the bottle already empty, but then thought why not open another bottle? If the Major were here, they would go through two anyway. She could drink for both of them she thought wryly.

Kiddie listened to the music, drinking her wine, her head propped up by the Major's pillow. She had no idea what time it was, but that it was late. She knew she couldn't sleep in their bed alone tonight so she might as well get comfy on the couch. She sat her wine glass down and went to flip the record back to side one before retrieving the blanket off of the back of the couch. She was vaguely aware the phone was ringing just as she drifted off half way through *The Princess of my Dreams.* She assumed it was Iris calling to check on her, but she mumbled to herself she was fine, just fine.

He entered the apartment quietly not wanting to startle Kiddie, but wondering why she hadn't picked up the phone. The joke would be on him if he had caught the last train out of Philly to come home to an empty apartment. The roses caught his attention first and he sighed as he picked up the unopened card. It seemed so long ago he had written, "Wait up for me my love, I'll be home before midnight. Love, the Major" Instinctively he checked his watch, the time reading 11:27. He wasn't surprised to see an empty wine bottle beside the flowers. It took him a minute to realize the scratching sound was a record on the Victrola. He smiled to see it was their record by Victor Herbert that Kiddie had been playing. He was more surprised to see a second bottle of open wine than to see Kiddie sleeping on the couch. Picking it up he was grateful to see it was still mostly full. He picked up Kiddie's empty glass and poured himself a glass. For a few moments he enjoyed sipping his wine and watching his wife sleep.

He could imagine how this scenario had played out and understood why Kiddie hadn't answered his call before he hopped on board the train bound for New York City. He was exhausted, but seeing her laying there made it all worthwhile. He realized she had no idea he was coming home and wondered the best way to wake her. Sitting on the couch beside her he caressed her cheek with the back of his hand. When she didn't move he leaned over to kiss her on the cheek. He paused for a moment realizing she had his pillow, the smell of his hair tonic very recognizable.

Now he gently started to shake her shoulder, saying her name softly at first. When she started to stir, he became a little more forceful, needing her to wake up. He realized she was mumbling his name and decided to sit her up. He knew she had a lot of wine, but no idea how long ago. He did know he was going to get her awake even if it was just to say "happy anniversary my love" to her one more time today. Suddenly Kiddie's eyes were open, looking around her frantically like she was trying to remember where she was. He smiled as she realized he was home, watching her face turn from confusion to joy to tears. She was reaching for him and he almost laughed out loud as he took her into his arms.

"Happy anniversary my love!" He said gently into her hair.

Still tearful, Kiddie pulled back to say, "Major I can't believe you're here! How did you get here? Why are you here?"

The Major took her face into both hands and kissed her. "I'm here because the princess of my dreams is here. Where else would I be on our anniversary?" Then he scooped her up and carried her to the bedroom, before gently laying her on their bed. Kiddie was awake enough to crawl to the middle of the bed and wait for the Major to come join her. He realized between her drunken state and his exhaustion that sleep would be best for both of them. Kiddie snuggled into the Major, still in her dress. Resting her head on his shoulder she said with a yawn, "Thank you Major for coming home. I love you, I love us. Happy anniversary Major." Kissing the top of her head, the Major said, "Happy anniversary my love."

The Major was about to wrap up covering the World Series, even though his team, the Brooklynn Robins had just missed beating the Giants and moving onto the World Series. The Major had been disappointed for the team, but they had felt some much deserved appreciation when their pitcher, Dazzy Vance, had won The National League's Most Valuable Player for the year. Dazzy had won the triple crown in pitching, having pitched three hundred and eight innings in thirty five games. The Major and the team had developed their own bond over the year, appreciating how the Major put pen to paper to share their wins and losses. They all appreciated there were way more wins to write about than losses.

The Major enjoyed his free access and front row seat in the press box for the World Series, still expected to write stories for the *Times* and report highlights from the games. Surprisingly the Washington Senators had held on against the New York Giants, and the series sat tied, three wins for each team. Today, in game seven, the Senators were hoping to beat the Giants and claim their first World Series title in club history. The game had been tied at the end of the ninth inning forcing fans and players alike to struggle through three more innings in over-time. The Senators finally hit a grounder allowing a Senator to round all the bases to home plate and score the winning run. Despite many New Yorkers' disappointment over the loss, it had been the Major's plea-sure to write his story for the *Times*, his version giving the Washington's pitcher, Walter Johnson the credit he deserved. Although his story got tucked into page nine, column five, the Major still felt it was a great story and an even better way to end the season.

It wasn't that much later that the Major was covering the football game between Princeton and Harvard, that he caught up with one of his writer buddies from his Montana boxing adventure. His buddy let him know that he had heard Bisbane of the Hearst paper was wanting to move him from the *Times* to his paper, *The Journal*. The Major was surprised to hear this, asking him what would prompt him to do so. His friend didn't seem to know and the Major let it go. Standing in the press box later in the day, the Major was even more surprised, but pleased to hear others talking about it. The Major was thankful he never said any-thing to Kiddie though, as he never heard from Bisbane and the Major decided it was a rumor afterall.

T hanksgiving Day was starting out much different than usual as this year, Kiddie and some of her family attended the first ever Macy's Christmas Parade. It was an early morning, with plenty of sunshine and children galore lining the streets all the way from 145th street near Harlem to Herald Square, front and center of Macy's, now known as the largest store in the world. The modest crowd was rewarded with bands playing, animals on loan from the Central Park Zoo, and Macy's employees dressed as clowns, knights, and cowboys. To match their Mother Goose windows, there were floats of Mother Goose favorites such as Little Miss Muffet and Little Red Riding Hood. The parade was short lived, ending with Santa Claus himself in his reindeer driven sleigh on a large icy float.

Most of the men had deferred from attending the parade, but when the Major had come up with tickets to the football game at the Polo Grounds, they were happy to participate. The game was between Syracuse and Columbia, and of course Kiddie and the Major went to support their alma mater. For once, the Major was not working the game, but enjoyed it as a mere spectator like the rest of them. Disappointingly Columbia lost by a field goal to Syracuse in front of a crowd of forty thousand football fans.

Kiddie's family was now gathered around their festive table, passing around dishes piled high with hot food and delicious smells. The family was lively as an Al Jolsen record played on the Victrola, while they took turns sharing what they were thankful for. The Major always found this awkward, but went along, always saying he was thankful for Kiddie and her family.

Thanksgiving had run late this year, leaving little time for December shenanigans. The Major was attending an event hosted by the National League at the Waldorf one afternoon, when he ran into his friend Fick, who immediately brought up the rumored offer from Bisbane at the Hearst paper. The Major started to believe there was some validity to the story, as Fick shared how Bisbane had thought a story had belonged to him, when he had to tell Bisbane it was a guy named Corum who had written the story. The Major was even more excited to hear it was his story about the Senators winning the World Series that had gotten his attention. The Major asked his friend why he thought Bisbane hadn't reached out to him yet, to which he promptly replied "He's waiting for baseball season to start again."

The Major had to admit this made sense to him, but still he wondered if an offer would actually come to pass. The Major was happy with his job at the *Times* and he was making decent money, so he tried not to worry about it too much.

Before they knew it, Christmas was a week old memory and New Year's Eve was upon them. Kiddie and the Major played it close to home this year, celebrating the new year with Kiddie's family as they had many times before. They drank the usual amount of wine and champagne, nothing out of the ordinary for the two of them. Kiddie wasn't sure if it was her or the Major or both of them, but they hadn't seemed to be able to get reconnected since the Major had finally finished baseball season in October. Now Kiddie and the Major were headed home in their cab, sitting close together, both of them lost in their own thoughts.

It had meant the world to Kiddie when the Major had taken the train home on their anniversary, even if he had to be back on it early the next morning. It had been hard having him gone so much over the six months of baseball season. The holidays had been fine enough, but Kiddie felt like on some level they were both going through the motions. The on again, off again nature of the Major's traveling had disrupted the rhythm of their relationship and Kiddie wasn't sure how to get it back. It had been a long year and Kiddie worried if more of the same lay ahead for them in the new year.

The Major looked over at Kiddie and picked up her hand to kiss it before asking, "What are you thinking about my love?"

Kiddie was grateful to the Major that he reached out to her and took it as a sign. Scooting even closer to him, she laid her head on his shoulder.

"Actually Major I was thinking about the new year and hoping 1925 will be good to us. What are you thinking about?" Kiddie asked.

Even in the dark the Major could tell Kiddie was being serious. Squeezing her hand he answered her with, "The same Kiddie, the same."

CHAPTER SIX
═1925═

"WHATEVER YOU ARE, BE A GOOD ONE."
—ABRAHAM LINCOLN

K iddie realized the bedroom still seemed quite dark, but it had to be late in the morning. She wondered where the Major was and why it was so quiet. She had been in no hurry to get up as there was very little on her agenda today. She knew the Major would go to work at some point, but it shouldn't be a late night. She had thought about cooking her signature dish and gone out to get all the ingredients yesterday, despite it being New Year's Day. With a big sigh she finally rolled herself out of bed, grabbing her robe from the chair. She went to the window to confirm the dreary day for herself.

She was surprised to see more than a couple of inches of snow on the ground and more falling heavily. She shivered instinctively to see the way it was blowing, at times a horizontal snow. She was wide awake now wanting to know the time and where was the Major? She found it was just after ten and a note on the dining room table, "Good morning my love. Went to work early to beat the snow, back as soon as possible. Love, Major" The last part made her worry, knowing for the Major "as soon as possible" could mean hours later. For now she would hope for the best.

Kiddie wondered how long it had been snowing and assumed it must have been when the Major walked to work. Thinking about being snowed in with the Major could be what they both needed, but he would need to be home before it got too bad. She decided she would cook her Coq Au Vin afterall. She was not a fan of winter weather, but she was a fan of being stuck at home with the Major. As she made herself a piece of toast, she started a mental to-do list. She would start cooking after she cleaned the apartment. She would round up their candles feeling it was a good possibility they would lose their electricity. She was thankful she had raided her parents' wine cellar at Christmas, using the gifts they brought home to disguise wine, knowing it wasn't illegal to drink the wine, only to transport it. Energized with her plan for the day, Kiddie went to get dressed, finding it odd to be excited to play the housewife.

An hour later, as Kiddie surveyed the clean apartment, she had to admit she felt a sense of pride in her accomplishment. The apartment felt cozy, the perfect place for them to be holed up through one of New York's infamous winter storms. Now she went to the kitchen to start her cooking, wondering if it was too early in the afternoon to pour herself a glass of wine to drink. It seemed a shame to pour it only into her stew, but she knew it would keep for later too. She was relieved to have plenty of wine to get even heavy drinkers like Kiddie and the Major through the storm.

Hours later Kiddie finally had the Coq Au Vin in the oven and the kitchen cleaned. She went to set the table, checking the time as she went to retrieve plates and table service for two. She was surprised to see it was already getting close to three and worried why the Major wasn't home yet. She went to the window to see how much snow had accumulated so far. She realized there was very little traffic braving the mix of snow and sleet at the mercy of the howling wind. Reluctantly she decided to call the office to check and see if the Major knew when he would be home. As soon as Kiddie was put through to the Major, she regretted she had called. She could tell he was busy, and maybe not annoyed, but not happy to be interrupted in his work.

"Kiddie I will be one of the last to leave as we literally live blocks from the paper. We already sent home all the folks who live in the burroughs. A skeleton crew of us are here and as soon as we get the paper to print, I'll be home." When she didn't say anything, he added as an afterthought, "I'll be home in time for dinner and don't worry, I'll be safe." With that he was gone. Kiddie hung up the phone, but continued sitting there, trying not to get herself stirred up.

Of course he would have to be the last one to leave, his sense of duty to the paper greater than to his own safety. She wondered if he had even looked outside recently and if he thought he would be taking a cab home. Kiddie decided to pour herself a glass of wine and take a hot bath, hopeful that between the two, her annoyance would dissipate.

Kiddie was finally out of the tub and dressed in a comfortable, but attractive wool dress. She walked around the apartment turning on lamps here and there, noticing them flicker ever so often and willing them to hold. Dinner was done as she added the finishing touches, but she left it in the oven to stay warm. Her potatoes were peeled and ready to be cooked, the butter out softening and waiting to be spread over homemade rolls from the bakery. Kiddie did not like having to sit around and wait, and she realized she wouldn't even know when the Major left, let alone when to expect him.

She told herself the Major was a grown man and could very well take care of himself. She poured herself a half glass of wine and curled up with a blanket and a magazine to read, determined to not worry just yet. Checking the time she decided she wouldn't really worry until it was after six. She had thirty minutes to entertain herself before things started to get ugly in her headspace. It wasn't long before Kiddie finished reading her story and went to check the time again. It was five minutes past six. Feeling her stomach knot up, she went to look outside. To her it looked like a blizzard, but maybe in the darkness, looks were deceiving. She started to pace the small apartment, debating on whether she should call the office again. She went to the window to watch the weather taking place outside, hoping the Major was on his way home.

Kiddie checked the street lights to see how heavy the snow was falling now. It was dark out, but the Major had walked these streets in the dark hundreds of times before, just not in blizzard like conditions. He would be fine she told herself for the hundredth time. She wasn't sure what to do with herself, so she stayed at the window, watching and waiting. Kiddie shivered as the cold wind howled, flickering the lights and trying to sneak into their warm apartment. Kiddie went to light some candles and then to get a sweater to put on over her dress. Maybe some music would calm her nerves paired with another half glass of wine.

Kiddie chose a Paul Whiteman record, thinking of that wintery day last year when the Major had surprised her with tickets to see Rhapsody in Blue. That night over dinner, the Major had explained how his boss had the tickets, but when his wife called him too sick to go, he had generously offered the tickets to the Major, knowing that Kiddie loved a show of any kind. The rational Kiddie could understand how the Major had so much loyalty to his boss, his work ethic beyond reproach of any kind. Sometimes though, the emotional Kiddie would take over and wish she would be the Major's priority more often. Kiddie decided it was hard to be married and think like an adult all the time.

As she went to the kitchen to check on her dinner in the oven, she checked the time once again. It was almost seven. Kiddie took a deep breath and went to the window instead. Staring into the dark night, the street lights were dimmed by the heavy snow moving across them, nearly white out conditions. For the first time she let her mind worry about what would happen if the Major got stuck at the paper, the weather too severe for him to make the four or five blocks home. Kiddie also worried what if the Major lost his way, and never made it home at all. She could feel the worry creeping into her sensibilities, her emotions ranging from frustration to fear to wishing the Major would be home already.

She was about to go check on dinner when she realized there was a dark blob struggling against the wind to move toward her. She peered into the dark, hoping it was the Major and wondering who else would be crazy enough to be out in this weather. Her eyes were glued to him, sending her strength, her encouragement to him, foolishly hoping he could feel her energy. She almost cried out to him when he stumbled and fell into the snow. She watched as he lay there, taking too long to get back up and for a moment she worried he wouldn't.

Not being able to take it any longer, Kiddie grabbed her boots and fur coat and headed out into the dark. She gasped as the wind savagely embraced her, knocking the breath from her and stinging her eyes with the cold snow. She paused a moment regaining herself and then went to him. He barely looked up, allowing her to guide him as he moved stiffly beside her, both of them bowing down to the power of the storm. As Kiddie opened the door for him, he all but fell into the apartment, his body covered with snow from head to toe. Kiddie hurried out of her things to help him to get out of his. She could see he was struggling to even move, and was grateful to let her help him off with his things.

Kiddie felt scared when the Major was so quiet and finally she said to him, "Major are you going to be okay?"

Shivering badly he turned to her with a wan smile, "I told you I'd be home for dinner and it smells delicious."

Kiddie's relief washed over her, even knowing the Major was most likely suffering from hypothermia and had a long way to go before he would be eating dinner. Kiddie went to start a warm bath for the Major, leading him into the bathroom and helping him out of his wet clothes. Leaving him to soak and thaw out, she brought blankets to set on chairs by the open oven door. She took the chicken stew out, turning the oven on high, and starting her potatoes to boil. She took a shot of whiskey to the Major, checking his color anxiously and asking him if he was warming up yet.

The Major gratefully accepted the shot from Kiddie, throwing it back quickly. As she turned to go the Major grabbed her hand and said, "Kiddie thank you for coming to get me. I knew I was close, but I don't know if I would have made it without you there to guide me through the last little bit."

Kiddie smiled at the Major and said huskily, "You're welcome Major. I'm glad you made it in one piece. One frozen piece!" she added, trying to make light and away from how tragic it could have been.

She was cleaning up the wet clothes and throwing snow into the sink when the Major emerged from the bathroom. His color was starting to come back and he was bundled in his robe and slippers over his socks and pajamas. Kiddie hurried to get him another shot and a warm blanket from the oven door as he went to sit in a chair at the table, close to the oven's warmth. The Major took the shot from Kiddie and then took her into his lap. He buried his head into her shoulder, just holding her. It was then Kiddie realized how scared the Major must have been out there, fighting to get home. She put her arms around him, holding him back while Rhapsody in Blue played behind them, adding drama to their embrace and bringing Kiddie to tears of gratitude.

She gently broke the Major's hold, moving off his lap to go and mash the potatoes. She loaded a plate for the Major full of steaming hot food and a full glass of wine. Putting it on the table in front of him, she took the blanket to switch it out with the other one, rewrapping him in the fresh warm blanket. She poured herself a full glass of wine and made a plate although her nerves told her stomach she wasn't really that hungry.

She realized the Major was watching her and picking up her glass said, "Welcome home Major." The Major clinked his glass to hers more than grateful to be home.

Kiddie opened another bottle of wine and put on their favorite record, happy to cuddle with the Major on the couch. Eventually the electricity succumbed to the weather and they sat under a blanket together in the quiet glow of the candlelight, Kiddie's head resting on his shoulder. Neither of them said much of anything, just taking in the wine and each other. Kiddie finally took the Major's empty wine glass and pulled him up off the couch. She knew he was exhausted and needed to get some sleep. She worried about his possibly frostbitten toes as he walked stiffly to the bedroom, and went to the kitchen to switch out blankets once again. She covered him in several layers before crawling in beside him. She could see his face in the white light the snow pushed into their room and she reached up to gently trace his chin line, so strong and sweet to her all at the same time.

The Major reached to take her hand and kissed her palm. "Good night my love."

"Good night Major." Kiddie said with a smile. He was home safe and tomorrow he would be all hers. She turned her back to him, backing up to him and smiled again as he turned to pull her even closer and hold her tight. It had been a rough start, but maybe this year would be a better year than she anticipated.

In the morning Kiddie woke up to the Major bringing her breakfast in bed and almost a foot of snow. That wasn't a crazy amount for New York, but enough to cause everyone to pause while the city brought the streets back to life. The smell of coffee caught Kiddie's attention first, and then the Major appeared shortly with his usual tray of bacon and eggs, toast and coffee. They sat in bed together, enjoying the Major's culinary efforts and knowing they had the whole day together.

Kiddie noticed the Major was still sporting his robe over his pajamas and worried maybe he was still not feeling up to par. Pausing over her toast and jelly she asked the Major if he was feeling all recovered from yesterday and his battle with Mother Nature. Finishing his bacon and eggs in one forkful, he took the tray and set it on the floor before taking off his robe and getting back into bed.

"Actually Kiddie I'm feeling recovered, but this dark dreary weather makes me want to come back to bed and snuggle with my best girl."

The Major lay on his side looking at Kiddie expectantly, watching her finish her toast. Kiddie brushed the crumbs off her hands dramatically before using her napkin to wipe her mouth delicately. Then she too scooted down in the bed, laying on her side facing the Major. Once again she used her finger to trace his face, this time focused on his lips. He took her hand to his lips and moved closer to her.

"What are you thinking, my love?" he asked gently, seeing her somber expression.

"I'm thinking how scared I was for you when I saw you out in the snow last night. When you fell and didn't get back up, I was worried you wouldn't ever get back up." Kiddie was being honest, keeping her eyes on the Major's chin.

He used his hand to lift her chin, wanting her eyes to meet his. "I was scared too, Kiddie. I never should have waited so long, but then I couldn't not come home to you. I was never so happy to see you as last night in your big fur coat, guiding me the rest of the way."

He kissed her on her forehead before pulling her to him. She snuggled into his chest mumbling "I love you Major."

He answered her back with a simple "I love you too Kiddie."

Kiddie rolled away from him, laying on her back beside him. Clearly she knew he loved her, but she worried about his all consuming sense of responsibility to the paper. Last night could have ended much worse.

Kiddie could no longer resist asking the Major her number one question, "Major why did you wait so long to come home?"

"Kiddie I knew it was dangerous last night, but I had to come home to you. I know we need this day together. I should have left earlier than I did, but I have responsibilities at the paper I can't disregard. I hope you understand that?" the Major asked.

Kiddie was focused on a spot on the ceiling, choosing her words carefully. She was torn to even say anything, knowing his commitment to her also played a part in last night. "Major, I know you have responsibilities and I know that's what puts a roof over our heads and pays our bar tabs at the end of the night. I'm grateful for that. When I go to work, I enjoy it, but it's really something I do to stay busy. When you go to work, it's not just what you do, but it's who you are. There's a difference and to be honest, sometimes I'm jealous of that."

Kiddie was surprised by her own words, realizing the conversation had taken an unexpected turn. Thinking about it, Kiddie knew there were some things she needed to say so they could finally move forward again.

The Major took her hand and kissed it. "Go on," he said quietly.

"When you're on the road I know you miss me, but at the same time you're doing something you love, something you were born to do. I'm at home trying to fill my days with something besides what's in my glass and it's hard." Kiddie was close to tears, but her confession to the Major felt good to get off her chest. "I know it's not something you can fix for me Major, it's something I have to figure out myself and that's the hardest part of all. I want to hold it against you, but actually I'm letting myself down." Kiddie hadn't realized this last part until she actually said it to the Major.

The Major pulled Kiddie into him again. He knew things hadn't been right between them for a while now, but he wasn't exactly sure how to fix it. That's why he had walked home in the blizzard, knowing they needed this time together today to reconnect. It made him hurt for Kiddie, but he was happy to hear her say her piece. Now he tried his best to make her feel better.

"Kiddie I don't blame you for holding it against me. I know baseball season took me away a lot and when we got married, it was hard to know that was coming. I worry about you when I'm gone. I want to know you're happy and safe and it kills me that something might happen and I would be a train ride away. Whatever I can do to support you and your happiness, I'm here to do. When I'm gone I want you to go out and do the things you love to do. Except today, today you're stuck with me and nowhere to go!" The Major teased Kiddie in the end trying to lighten the mood. Kiddie laughed and snuggled into him even closer.

"I would be stuck with you any day Major. Remember that's what we signed up for, for better or worse, stuck with you?" Kiddie asked softly.

The Major kissed the top of Kiddie's head. "I told you years ago you would be stuck with me forever and I will always mean that. I'm the luckiest man in the world Kiddie that I get to go out and do what I love and then I get to come home to you. This home you've made for us, when you cook dinner for us, have a glass of wine waiting for me, our records playing, you need to know all that is what gets me through the long road trips."

Kiddie thought about what the Major was saying. She had always poo pooed the housewife, but in the end she guessed she was one after all, even if she was doing it in her own way. The truth was she did depend on the Major to take care of her financially just as her mother and Iris depended on their husbands in their homes. She thought about her mother, and how she took care of their home and yet took time for her writing as well. Maybe she misunderstood the term housewife and needed to give housewives the credit they deserved. She realized when Elizabeth Stanton had fought for women's rights, it wasn't to sit and judge each other, but to support each other and lift each other up to be the best version of themselves, whatever that looked like. Of course Kiddie wasn't naive enough to think all men thought like the Major, and realized there were women in the world being held back by men, particularly in the workplace.

Kiddie wondered what the Major's boss would say if she decided she wanted to write stories for *The New York Times*. Maybe Kiddie should get involved in a women's organization, and put her time and energy into supporting women's rights. She winced realizing last year would have been a perfect opportunity to support women and their right to vote for the next president. She had been happy to have Iris and her Mother go with her again, all three of them relishing in the thought that their vote counted. Kiddie had been impressed last fall as two women had been elected governors in their home states of Montana and Texas.

Kiddie realized there were lots of ways to make better use of her time. She would always want the Major to be home, but she felt better about what she brought to the table, and appreciated the Major listening to her and giving her the credit she didn't give herself.

Kiddie sat up on her elbow to look at the Major. "Thank you Major."

"For what Kiddie?" he asked.

"For loving me, for being a supportive husband, for trying to help me be the best version of myself." Kiddie answered back.

The Major rolled onto his side, putting his hand to Kiddie's cheek. "It's the least I can do considering you do the same for me. I should be thanking you Kiddie."

Kiddie smiled. "You're right Major and I know just the way you can show your appreciation!" Seeing the Major's quizzical look, Kiddie pressed on.

"Since I basically saved your life last night I think it's fair to make today Kiddie day. Whatever I want, you can't say no to. Deal?"

The Major was smiling, happy to see Kiddie's mood lighten. "Well if that will make you happy, I can get on board with that. And what do you want to do first my love?"

As Kiddie reached for him under the covers, the Major's smile broadened. "I guess a husband's gotta do what a husband's gotta do." he said as he pulled them both under the covers.

It was a wonderful day with the Major. After they finally climbed out of bed, they poured more coffee and sat down to play chess, a game Freddy had given them for Christmas. Kiddie wasn't that good, but she didn't mind even when the Major took so long to figure out his next move. Later they sat reading together, their backs at each end of the couch, their legs intertwined under a blanket in the middle. They never had lunch and decided to brave the cold, going to get burgers at P.J. Clark's just before dark. Walking home hours later, they held hands, the cold air making it impossible to talk.

Now they sat snuggled on the couch, each of them with a glass of wine, listening to their favorite records. The electricity had been back on since early morning, but now they had a candle lit, the lights off. When *"The Princess of My Dreams"* came on, Kiddie sat her glass down and asked the Major if he would dance with her.

Gallantly he stood up to take her hand, bowing with "as you wish my love." Kiddie rested her head on his shoulder as the two of them swayed to the music. When the record ended the Major kissed Kiddie on the lips before picking her up and carrying her to the bedroom.

Sometime later, Kiddie slid out of bed worried about the candle they had left burning. She went to blow it out and carried their glasses to the kitchen, downing the end of her wine before setting it beside the sink. Now as she stood in the dark, she surveyed their apartment, thinking about what the Major had said about how she had made it a home. She realized for the first time that's how she should see it too, instead of the prison cell she had pouted about last summer. For the first time in months Kiddie felt connected to the Major again and for that, she was the most thankful.

T he Major struggled to get himself and the box he carried out of the cab against the gusty March wind blowing. Balancing the box, he paid the driver and hurried up the stairs and into their apartment. He had called home earlier to make sure Kiddie was out, knowing it was her usual afternoon to visit with Iris and the baby. He wanted to surprise her with his package and have it all set up by the time she got home. He felt pretty certain that she would be as excited as he was to have a radio in their home. The Major was usually more about spending money on experiences rather than possessions, but he knew a radio was something every home would have sooner or later. He hoped it would keep Kiddie company and give her something else to do when he was on the road. Spring training was right around the corner and he was hoping this season would take less of a toll on both of them and their marriage.

Kiddie walked in just as the Major found a radio station, adjusting the volume to the perfect level for both conversation and entertainment. He stood in front of it as Kiddie breezed in the door. She was surprised to see the Major home so early, but could see from his expression that something was up.

"Hello Major! Why are you home so early?" Kiddie asked, going to kiss him on the cheek.

"Kiddie I have a surprise for you! Well it's for both of us, but I think you will find it a nice surprise." Watching her expectantly, the Major stepped aside, proud to show Kiddie the new radio.

"Major, you bought a radio?" Kiddie was surprised.

"I did Kiddie! What do you think?" The Major was smiling from ear to ear.

"I think it takes up a lot of our table. Is this where we're going to keep it?" Kiddie asked cautiously.

The Major waved Kiddie off, disappointed she wasn't more excited. "We can put it wherever makes you happy, my love. But won't it be wonderful to have radio stations to listen to music and programs? To hear world events as they happen, not just read about them in the paper?"

Kiddie turned to the Major, "What world events? You mean like the World Series?"

The Major took both of Kiddie's hands, needing her to feel his excitement over this new contraption he brought into their home. "Not just sports events, but national events. Did you know in just a few days, President Coolidge's inaugural speech will be broadcast for the first time in history? We can listen to every word Kiddie!"

Kiddie kissed him on the cheek, wanting to show some appreciation, but still not sure about how much she would use the radio. Kiddie and Iris had been teenagers when their father had brought one home. He loved to sit and listen to it after dinner, the music seeming to wash away his long day.

"Major, it's a lovely surprise. It will be nice to have when you're out on the road, a box to keep me company." Kiddie said with a smile.

For a second the Major frowned, feeling annoyance with Kiddie's lack of enthusiasm and not sure how to take her last remark. He quickly shook it off and went to turn the radio back up. He now realized Kiddie had grown up with a radio and so it wasn't the novel idea he thought it to be. Sometimes he forgot how privileged Kiddie had been growing up, a far cry from his small town life in Missouri.

Kiddie was going through the mail, and turned to ask the Major, "What's this?" This time she was the one smiling from ear to ear, holding a magazine out to him.

The Major smiled, realizing he should have known Kiddie was far more about print and her love for reading magazines. "That my love is New York's latest magazine, *The New Yorker*. Harold Ross is publishing it to showcase New York's opportunities socially and culturally with a story thrown in here or there. I thought it was just your style and bought you a subscription for a year."

"A subscription?" Kiddie asked, flipping through the pages. "Like the newspaper gets delivered? How often is it published?"

The Major went to Kiddie, a smile on his face. "You will now be getting *The New Yorker* every week my love. I hope you enjoy it! It takes a lot of moxy and money to start a weekly magazine. Luce and Hadden set the trend a few years ago when they started printing *Time* as a weekly magazine, but they seem to be doing well. *The New Yorker* seems to be striving for something in between your magazine *RedBook* and a news magazine like *Time*, something with a little more edge, like you my love."

The Major laughed as Kiddie threw her arms around him in a big hug. "Oh thank you Major! I'm sure I will love it!" Now he had her attention, he thought to himself.

After dinner that night, Kiddie and the Major sat together on the couch, the Major enjoying music from radio station KDKA in Pittsburgh while Kiddie read about New York's nightlife and who was busy enjoying it. The Major's choices in stations were limited for tonight, but he had heard rumors of Westinghouse's plan to use new technology to create a market wide open for more stations in the near future. Kiddie read *The New Yorker* voraciously beside him, taking in everything from short stories such as *"Say It With Scandal"* to features such as *"Talk of the Town."* Kiddie could see what the Major meant, the stories in *The New Yorker* a little edgier and perhaps more likely to be appreciated by men and women alike.

Hours later as Kiddie lay in bed listening to the Major softly snoring, she wondered how and when they had become like her parents. Kiddie smiled at the thought, relishing in the fact they could spend an enjoyable quiet night at home. She knew the Major would be leaving in a few weeks for the Robins spring training in Florida and she would take all the cozy nights together she could get before then. Although cozy was good, Kiddie still needed her nights out on the town too. She was looking forward to going out tomorrow with Iris and Bernie, ready to throw back a few French 75's at their favorite speakeasy. Of course the Major had promised her dinner at her favorite restaurant at the Biltmore on his last night, just the two of them, before he caught his southbound train in the morning.

Kiddie realized she hadn't been anywhere by train for quite some time and maybe it was time to change that. Maybe, thought Kiddie, she would make her own trip down to Florida and surprise the Major one night. But she wondered if it would really be worth the long tedious ride down for a night together. Kiddie smiled to herself thinking about the beach, the waves crashing up to cover her toes. As Kiddie drifted off she promised herself to work harder to keep herself busy and happy this baseball season, whether the Major was home or not.

K iddie sat across from the Major, their glasses full of champagne, a candle between them, the stars shining above them. The Cascades was one of Kiddie's happy places, and even though she had to tell the Major good-bye in the morning, tonight was no different. While Kiddie was enjoying her creamy lobster bisque, the Major seemed preoccupied over his own food.

"Major, what are you thinking about? Missing me already?" Kiddie asked teasingly.

The Major smiled and reached for Kiddie's hand before answering, "I am missing you already my love. It's nothing I can't figure out for myself."

"Why don't you share and maybe I can help." Kiddie offered.

"It's about my writing and getting recognized for my work. It's rather annoying the paper doesn't let us put our names on our work. How are my readers going to know how good I am, if they don't even know who I am?"

Kiddie was surprised to hear the Major's frustration, but she could see his point. While she was thankful to grace magazine covers it was only the artist's name who was given credit for the work.

"So what can you do to change that? Have you talked to your boss about it?" Kiddie asked thoughtfully. "It seems like a fair request to me and you can't possibly be the only writer who feels that way." Kiddie added.

The Major paused his fork full of food to look at Kiddie, before nodding his head to her. "Kiddie you're absolutely right! What can it hurt to ask?"

Kiddie smiled, happy to be helpful, but curious too. "So what precipitated this need to suddenly have your name on your work?"

The Major hesitated, but only for a second. "I found out a while back there are rumors that the *Evening Journal* wants to hire me. The story goes that their head guy loved my story about the Senators winning the World Series, but thought it was written by a buddy of mine until he set him straight. Since I've never heard from the *Journal*, I'm not sure how much truth there is to the rumor, but it made me realize that I can't move ahead if my name isn't on my work!"

Kiddie was stunned to hear the Major had been sitting on this for so long and never said anything to her. "Major, why didn't you tell me this before? That must be frustrating in so many ways!"

The Major put his fork down and looked at Kiddie. "I've thought about it so many times, but if it's just a rumor, why worry you about it too? I make good money at the paper and I'm not looking to leave *The New York Times* to write for someone else. I love what I do and I don't want to be greedy about it. I do want my name on my work, but I don't want it to be a deal breaker."

Kiddie was watching the Major, listening to him intently, wondering how much he worried about his job. She knew the schedule coming up was much harder on him than it was on her, but how much pressure did he feel to get his stories out there. Getting his name on his stories was a big deal because it was only fair for the readers to know the man behind the typewriter. Having his name under his byline could be a game changer.

"Major, I think it's a fair question to ask your boss. It could be a game changer for you and your career when people can put your name to your stories." Kiddie said, wanting to both encourage and support the Major.

Kiddie raised her glass, waiting for the Major to join her. "To you Major, and a new season, and to possibly a new chapter in your career. If ever a man should be recognized for his work, it's you."

The Major clinked glasses with Kiddie, then sipped his champagne. "Thank you Kiddie. Your support means everything my love." he added sincerely.

Walking back to their apartment, they were both quiet, enjoying the beautiful spring night and lost in their own thoughts. As they snuggled in bed later Kiddie asked the Major how hard it would be for him to take a night off from spring training to take her to dinner and enjoy a hotel on the beach together. The Major loved the idea and encouraged her to come down, if she were up for the long train ride, more than a day away and over a thousand miles. Kiddie admitted this was a factor, but she would love to see the ocean and could easily entertain herself during the day sitting on the beach reading. The question was could the Major be free to wine and dine her in the evenings. The Major promised to check into it and Kiddie felt excited at the idea of a getaway for them, even if it was short.

K iddie's train was about an hour away from the Clearwater train station. She was scheduled to arrive early evening, the Major hoping to meet her there if he was done with baseball training for the day. It had been a long trip down, but now Kiddie felt excited for a change of scenery and some time with the Major. Kiddie had some trepidation about making the trip by herself, but Iris had encouraged her to go anyway. She had even teased Kiddie that she could talk the talk, but not walk the walk of an independent woman of the twenties. Kiddie thought of all the young girls who came from small towns all over the states to find their new life in New York City and had decided Iris was right. Now here she was, a day and a half later, ready for her Florida adventure. The Major had been gone for almost three weeks, plenty of time for them to miss each other.

Kiddie did her best to freshen up in her sleeping car, hoping the Major wouldn't notice her slightly rumpled dress and dark circles under her eyes. She had seen this very look on the Major many a time after he came home from a long train ride for whatever story he had been pursuing on behalf of baseball. Kiddie finished repacking her suitcase and took it to go and sit in the dining car, watching out the window for signs they were approaching Clearwater.

As scheduled, within the hour she was rewarded with sight of the Major standing at the platform, along with other people waiting for their train to arrive. Seeing the Major standing there holding his hat, dressed in his suit and tie brought an immediate smile to Kiddie's face. Just like that the long ride was washed away and the prospect of her weekend ahead gave her joyful anticipation. As the train decelerated, she waved to him from her window, but wasn't sure he had seen her.

Kiddie was lugging her suitcase down the train steps, grateful when someone reached out to help and take it from her. She was startled when a second hand reached for it as well, realizing it was the Major, dismissing a young man with a smile.

"I can get my wife's suitcase, son, no worries." the Major said amicably.

As Kiddie took the last step down from the train, she went to give the Major a big hug, greedy for his embrace. She was delighted when he took her face in both hands and kissed her full on the mouth, oblivious to the people having to go around them as they hurried to catch their own trains. The Major had a cab waiting for them, and now her suitcase sat tucked beside the Major's in the back, the two of them sitting close, holding hands as they took the bridge from Clearwater to Clearwater Beach.

Within minutes the Major was checking them into the Clearwater Beach Hotel, one of the few hotels actually on the beach. The beach looked beautiful, calling to Kiddie to come walk the pristine white sand. The water too was beautiful, the gulf's clear blue water promising to refresh her and the Major during their short getaway. Kiddie was reminded of their trip to Bermuda for their honeymoon, almost three years ago. Bermuda was much more established than Clearwater Beach, the Major filling Kiddie in on how the area was booming with people hoping to get rich quick, making real estate deals and planning to cater to the tourists.

Finally they were in their hotel room, happy to be alone. The Major understood Kiddie's need for a hot bath before they went anywhere or did anything. As she unpacked, she was happy to see the two bottles of wine had safely made it from her parent's wine cellar to their hotel room. The Major was appreciative and decided to go in search of food, happy to relax from their room, enjoying the view of the sun setting on the ocean from their own veranda.

Kiddie waited until she heard the Major return before leaving the warm bath. She started to throw on a dress, but then thought better of it and instead wrapped herself in only her towel. Opening the door, she went to stand casually in front of the Major, who was laying on the bed reading the paper. He quickly ditched his paper upon seeing Kiddie in her towel, pulling her down to him, and making her laugh when he growled to her "come to me my love!"

Later they lay together in bed, sipping wine and feasting on the random snacks the Major found at the local drugstore down the street. The Major had noticed something different about Kiddie and now as he watched her, he asked her, "Kiddie have you been doing something different?"

For a second Kiddie froze, surprised but pleased the Major had noticed. She asked coyly, "What do you mean Major? To my hair? The way I wrapped my towel I was wearing?"

The Major smiled, but continued to watch her intently. "Ms. Kiddie, I know every inch of your body and somehow it's different."

Now Kiddie smiled and confessed, "When you left for spring training, I started a little training of my own. I've been working to tone up and get my wine riddled sorry butt in shape. Actually I'm surprised you can tell Major, after only three weeks."

It was the Major's turn to be surprised. "First, there is nothing sorry about your butt and second, how did you come up with that idea?"

"I read about it in one of my magazines and then I went and bought some arm weights. I usually do a long brisk walk everyday and then exercises I learned from my magazine. Spring training isn't just for baseball players Major, lots of women are doing it. And it gives me some routine to my day," Kiddie added.

The Major was watching her. "Well as the one who gets to enjoy your efforts, let me give you a big thank you. I'll have to think of some way to show my appreciation," he added. Kiddie laughed as he pulled them both back under the covers, happy to let him.

The next morning Kiddie felt a relaxed happiness she hadn't felt in awhile. The Major had left their veranda doors open and Kiddie embraced the ocean breeze blowing in, the crash of the waves therapeutic. She assumed the Major was off getting coffee somewhere and decided to laze in bed a little longer, grateful for her new surroundings for the next couple of days. Kiddie had left New York on Monday morning, the Major telling her the week was less busy for him than the weekends. Today was Wednesday and she would be catching the train back Friday afternoon. Iris had offered to pick her up from the train station early Saturday evening, wanting to go out to dinner and hear all about her Florida adventure.

Kiddie was standing on the veranda in her robe when the Major walked in with fresh coffee and egg sandwiches. They were both hungry having missed a real dinner last night. The sandwiches were made with thick biscuits, stacked with slices of bacon and fresh fried eggs, topped with a hollandaise sauce. They were devine and just what Kiddie needed to start her day.

"Kiddie I've given myself a sick day so that we can spend the day together. I've asked around and it appears there is a restaurant over in Tampa that would be worth the drive. We can spend the day on the beach and then head over there late this afternoon. How does that sound?" The Major was smiling, welcoming Kiddie's excitement.

"It sounds perfect Major!" Kiddie announced as she finished her biscuit. "I'll go get dressed."

Kiddie went to the bathroom to freshen up and put on her black Jantzen suit, pleased with herself that it fit even better than on their honeymoon. She threw a white cotton dress over it, ready to enjoy the beach and their day together.

They walked the beach first, before finding a quiet spot to stretch out on a large blanket Kiddie had packed, usually reserved for their picnics in Central Park. Later they put their shoes back on and walked the small town, Kiddie taking note of the library and theater. They went back to the drugstore to buy bottled lemonade and sandwiches which they took back to their blanket, enjoying the ocean view while they feasted on ham and cheese, trying their best to keep the sand out. It was hard to let their fabulous day go, but the Major promised dinner would be worth her patience.

Kiddie dressed for dinner in one of the Major's favorite dresses and one she had worn on their honeymoon. The yellow strapless dress accentuated her newly toned arms, her skin glowing after their day in the sun, it's shorter length highlighting her shapely legs and high heels. Now as they sat in their cab, the Major couldn't take his eyes off Kiddie as she seemed to glow from the inside out, her happiness abundant. The Major realized he traveled all the time on the paper's dime, but that he and Kiddie really should get out of New York more often. It had been three years since their honeymoon and this trip was way overdue. Impulsively he picked up Kiddie's hand from the seat and kissed her palm.

Kiddie smiled at him, busy watching out the window as the cab carried them across the long bridge over the bay into Tampa. It was rather a long drive, but depending on where you might be going in New York, not unreasonable. Kiddie loved how the ocean sparkled in the late sunlight, seeming to applaud their efforts to go the extra mile for a dinner adventure. Kiddie pointed excitedly when she spotted a school of dolphins jumping and putting on quite the show, enjoying the ocean and sunshine in their own way. It was with equal excitement that Kiddie took in their dinner destination as their cab pulled up to the The Columbia Restaurant.

The Major had informed Kiddie that The Columbia Restaurant, opened in 1905, was a family owned place with a Spanish flair. They were well known for their coffee, cuban sandwiches, and large salads. Kiddie noted the big mahogany bar to the left as they entered, hopeful there would be a cocktail in her future. She was even more delighted to see outdoor seating, their wood deck decorated with round tables dressed in crisp white tablecloths, contrasting nicely against the blue of the ocean, small lit candles blowing in the breeze. Sitting oceanside across from the Major, Kiddie was reminded again of their honeymoon in Bermuda. There was something about the ocean that felt so refreshing to Kiddie, and she was soaking up every minute of this beautiful night with the Major.

Before long they were sharing the large salad and enjoying their authentic cuban sandwiches. The fresh cuban bread was loaded with salami and roasted pork, topped with swiss cheese, slices of dill pickles, and buttery yellow mustard. Kiddie had never tasted anything like it, loving how toasting the bread melted and blended all the flavors into deliciousness. Too soon the Major was paying their tab and they were in a cab headed back to their hotel. Kiddie's head rested on the Major's shoulder, both her heart and stomach happy and full.

"Thank you Major for the most lovely day," Kiddie said softly. The Major took Kiddie's hand and kissed it.

"You're so welcome, my love," he said.

As the cab pulled up to their hotel Kiddie impulsively asked the Major if they could walk along the beach for a little bit. It was a beautiful night, the moon full and a soft breeze blowing. He was happy to comply, understanding her need to not let their day end just yet. They were both quiet as they walked holding hands, carrying their shoes in their free hand. Suddenly the Major stopped Kiddie, turning her to look at him. "I love you Kiddie." Standing under the full moon he kissed her long and hard.

Suddenly Kiddie squealed when a cold wave snuck up on them both, the wave washing over their bare feet. Kiddie laughed as the Major picked her up, acting like he might throw her in, and hoping he didn't fall. Kiddie couldn't stop smiling as they walked along the beach, back to their hotel.

The next day was another beautiful, sunny day and Kiddie was happy to make the most of it, even if the Major had work to do. When the Major headed over to Clearwater, Kiddie walked the block to the local library. She stopped to read the plaque near the door, informing all those who entered and took the time to read it, that the library existed thanks to a grant from Andrew Carnegie in 1916. Kiddie had always loved the library at Columbia University and was happy to explore the stacks and stacks of books in this small local library.

On her way back to their hotel, Kiddie stopped at the Capitol Theater to see what might be presented tonight. She promptly bought two tickets when she discovered it would be the motion picture *"Monsieur Beaucaire"* starring Rudolph Valentino. Kiddie had read the book by Booth Tarkington years ago and seen the movie late last summer with Iris. Happy to have plans for the evening, Kiddie went back to the hotel to get her book and go read on the beach. She found a quiet spot where the Major was sure to find her easily when he returned from his work day. She was looking forward to their evening and then time together in the morning before Kiddie boarded her train and the Major went to the ballpark.

Way too soon Kiddie was back on the train, headed north to New York City. Before boarding the train, the Major had taken her out to lunch after a lazy morning in bed enjoying their view and each other. He was happy to hear Iris would be picking her up at the train station, and that Kiddie already had something to look forward to. Now as she sat in the dining car, it was easy to tell herself the Major would be home in a few weeks, ready for the Brooklyn Robins home opener. Her time with the Major and a change of scenery had been good for Kiddie, the two of them making memories that would last her for awhile and making the most of her short trip. Kiddie felt confident too that there would be more trips for them to Florida in their future after their conversation last night.

After dinner and then the movie, they sat on the beach and had talked for hours last night, discreetly sharing a bottle of champagne the Major confiscated somewhere along the way. Kiddie and the Major agreed having time out of their routines and New York was good for both of them and their marriage. They agreed that spending money on possessions like a house didn't seem as important as spending money and time on enjoying life. It was a big world out there and Kiddie realized she loved to explore it. They agreed exploring new places and enjoying quality time with each other was where they needed to focus their resources. The reality for them was a very demanding schedule for the Major, and one neither of them could argue with. Thinking back to their conversation, Kiddie felt good knowing they were on the same page and striving for the same goals.

Kiddie had sat and listened as the Major talked about his goal to be a sportswriter all of New York recognized. He might not be a F. Scott Fitzgerald, but still he wanted to be known for his work. He planned to go to his boss and ask him about getting his name on his stories as soon as he got back from spring training. He had mentioned it to some of the writer's he was working with here in Florida and they all agreed it was a reasonable request and wished him all the luck.

It was still early, but the train was already moving to their dim lighting, the night rapidly taking over outside the large dining car windows. Kiddie decided to head to bed early, hoping the train's rocking motion and her tiredness would lead to a good night's sleep. She was grateful the beds on the train were tight so maybe she would not miss the Major's presence as much. She lay in bed reliving the past couple of days, the sun on the water, their walks on the beach, the Major and her in bed together. Sweet dreams, Kiddie thought to herself, sweet dreams.

The Major was just back from spring training yesterday and it felt good to be home. True to his word, the Major talked with his boss earlier in the afternoon about getting his name on his stories. The Major felt good about their conversation, although a little nervous to be dismissed with "I'll let you know." Tomorrow he would write his first official story as the season opened for the Brooklyn Robins against the Phillies.

The Major was patient waiting to hear back from his boss. He wasn't sure who made a big decision like that so he let it ride, assuming he would find out when his boss had a decision to share. The Robins started their season off strong, lucky enough to still have their dynamic pitching duo. Dazzy Vance pitched the Robins into a 3-1 win for their opening game, happy to not disappoint the twenty thousand fans that had come out to watch the team play ball on a chilly April afternoon.

The Major was just about to turn in his story and head home for the night, when his boss called him into his office. The Major searched his face, but his expression remained the same as always, hard to read. Having no choice, he stood at his desk patiently, but hopeful.

"I hope you haven't turned in your story yet so that you can go back and add your by-line. Make sure it's a good story for you to attach your name to for the first time. It looks like other papers will follow suit and from now on, people will know who's sports stories are worth the read. Be sure and let the others know, if you don't mind."

The Major was grinning from ear to ear. "Yes sir, thank you sir! I appreciate the opportunity!"

The Major hurried back to his desk to type in By M.W. Corum. He couldn't be more proud to know his name would be in the paper tomorrow and was grateful he had a win to write about. Before he left for the night, he also stopped to make a quick phone call home, happy to share the news with his mother before he hurried home to share the news with Kiddie, ready to take her out on the town and celebrate.

They wined and dined until the wee hours of the morning, some of the Major's sports writer friends joining them to celebrate. As he deserved, they gave the Major credit for bringing their names to their stories, while at the same time cursing him that they would have to step up their stories now to keep up with his writing. The Major knew they were just giving him a hard time, but wondered how many writers wouldn't make the cut once their name was attached to their stories. Either way, the Major was happy.

The Major was still celebrating having his name under his story title when tragedy took hold a few days later. Charles Ebbets, one of the owners of the Brooklyn Robins and the President for the team died. Mr. Ebbets had not been well for a couple of weeks and died of heart failure.

The team was playing at home that day, suffering more than a loss on the field against the New York Giants. The day of Mr. Ebbets funeral, all National League games were suspended, showing the respect and honor Mr. Ebbets had earned within the sport of baseball. Mr. Ebbets had not just been an owner, but also an advocate and visionary for the sport. Determined to make the game the best it could be for fans and players alike, he came up with concepts like Ladies Day, lengthening the season to include fourteen more games, the "rain check" for games rained out, and the 2-3-2 games now played for the World Series. The Major had quite the legacy to write about as some declared Mr. Ebbets the best loved man in baseball. As the team struggled with five losses in a row, the Major could only explain it as the team was heartbroken over their loss. Eventually the Robins found their baseball spirit again, winning two of their games against the Phillies in Pittsburgh a week later.

Lightning struck twice when Mr. Ebbets' successor, Ed McKeever, another owner of the Robins passed away as well. Mr. McKeever had caught pneumonia at Mr. Ebbets funeral and died only days later. The Robins struggled not only on the field, but in team operations as well. Over the next month the team had as many wins as they did losses, trying to keep their head in the game and focus on winning. The Major struggled to write the best stories he could, giving *The New York Times* readers motivation to read his stories. Just like the competition on the field between the Robins and the Giants, the Major had plenty of competition for who was getting their stories on the front page in the sports section. It kept the Major awake at night trying to think of a hook that could get his name out there, and give people something to talk about besides the weather. The two deaths in the Robins franchise had rattled the Major, reminding him life moves fast and you better be moving fast too, if you don't want to get left behind.

B eing assigned to a baseball team means a steady gig in the sports world, but can leave you overlooked for other sports stories with way more meat and interest to your reader. The Major was a little frustrated to not be going to the Kentucky Derby yet again. Since he was a boy growing up in Missouri, he had always known someone who would make the trip to Louisville for the Kentucky Derby. The Major had always loved all the Derby traditions from the bugle call to the blanket of roses bestowed upon the winning horse. He was happy to learn the race would be broadcast on the radio this year for the first time. He decided this could be his way into the Derby, but needed to get Kiddie on board first.

It was a beautiful Sunday morning in May and the Major was busy making their usual breakfast in bed. When the Major wasn't on the road, he enjoyed this time with Kiddie before heading out for the day's baseball game. Today he had an agenda as he had decided he and Kiddie should host a party for the Kentucky Derby. Being broadcast live on the radio, would allow people everywhere to participate and have a feel for the race. As with any sports event, the pregame was as important as the sports event itself, especially when the event only lasts two minutes, give or take. Doing his research the Major had some ideas on how to create a memorable event for their guests.

Giving the Major time to bring her breakfast in bed, Kiddie lazed about in bed. This Sunday tradition was one of the things she missed the most when the Major was on the road. It was a quiet time, just the two of them, as they recalled their Saturday night and made plans for the week ahead. The Robins had suffered a loss in the Giants stadium yesterday afternoon, but the Major hoped for a win today over the Phillies before they headed to Boston for a four game series with the Braves. The Major would be home for most of the month, including May 16th, the day of the Derby. Ironically the Robins would be playing the Cardinals that weekend, games the Major enjoyed the most as it was always a win-win for the Major, regardless of which team came out on top. As the Major watched Kiddie sip her coffee, he decided to jump right in.

"Kiddie, I was thinking we could have a party for the Kentucky Derby this year. It's going to be broadcast live on the radio so we could have people over to listen, have some food, some drinks, some fun. What do you think?" He could see her mulling the idea over as she focused on her coffee.

"When is the Derby Major? And invite who? What kind of food would we need?" Kiddie asked.

The Major knew Kiddie would have questions and he was prepared. "It's in two weeks, May 16. I plan to ask for the day off. I have some traditional recipes they serve in Kentucky that we could use. We can find something to mix with bourbon. I'll make a list of the horses running so people can think about who they want to cheer on to a win. We'll need bouquets of roses too, since the Derby is really the run for the roses Kiddie!"

Kiddie did love a good party, she just wasn't used to hosting them. She hadn't really had bourbon before, but she would leave that up to the Major. She supposed she could learn a new recipe or two and it might be fun to bet on the horses and then cheer on your favorite while they listened to the race on the radio.

"Hmm, a run for the roses you say. You know I love a good party and roses and horses so I say, it's a grand idea Major! How did you find the recipes and how difficult are they? Will I need Cook to help me?" Kiddie asked, cautiously committing to cooking food for other people.

Now for the hard part. The Major had sold Kiddie on the idea, but he hadn't told her the big news. "Actually my mother was quite helpful. She has a friend that's been lots of times and she shared some recipes with me."

Kiddie's radar was suddenly on high alert as she sensed there was more to come. "How kind of her." Kiddie mumbled into her coffee as she braced herself.

The Major jumped in. "Mother has decided that weekend is a perfect time for her to visit New York. She has always loved the Kentucky Derby and the Robins are in a series with the St. Louis Cardinals too. She hasn't been here since last fall and I couldn't tell her no Kiddie. She mentioned my aunt Maddie coming with her too so she has company on the train."

"And at her hotel?" Kiddie asked hopefully. The Major smiled, knowing that meant Kiddie would survive a visit from his mother.

"And at her hotel." the Major confirmed with a smile. He sat quietly on the bed, giving Kiddie time to process everything he had thrown at her, having braved it over scrambled eggs rather than a bottle of wine.

"Well if your mother is going to be at the party, then I should invite mine too. They seem to get along well enough." Kiddie added. "I feel like I should start a list. How many people are we talking about, Major? And what are these recipes you have for me? And I wonder how bourbon would taste with lemonade?" Kiddie was on a roll now and the Major was happy to go fetch paper and a pencil.

Together they sat in bed, making a guest list, looking over the recipes the Major had typed up per his mother's instructions. The Major was happy to give Kiddie a quick history lesson about the Derby, or the run for the roses as he had called it. The Major realized that would be a great line to write in his story as he competed with stories from writers who were actually at the Derby. Before they knew it, he was headed out the door to Ebbets field for the game. He promised to meet Kiddie at her parents for Sunday dinner after the game. It was going to be Lelo's first birthday, and the Major was happy to be reporting from the home field this year. As his cab crossed the bridge into Brooklyn, the Major had a smile on his face. It felt good to have something to look forward to besides baseball.

The Major was impressed with how well Kiddie handled his mother coming to New York. He had actually offered for her to come, her trip a gift from him for Mother's Day, but not at all oblivious to his mother's hints she wanted to come. He knew his mother wasn't Kiddie's biggest fan and vice versa, but it was important to him to have time with his family too. The recent deaths of the Brooklyn Robins owners reminded the Major that life was fragile and not to be taken for granted. He didn't want to have the same regrets with his mother he had felt when he lost Uncle Crutch. He offered for his father to come too, but much like the Major, it was hard for him to walk away from his job as postmaster.

Later that night as Kiddie and the Major snuggled in bed, a cool spring breeze blowing through their window, the Major replayed his day. Although the Robins secured a win over the Phillies, the Major had only a mediocre story to write with their 2-1 win. Little Lelo had been so cute, diving into her birthday cake with both hands. She had opened presents while Iris and Bernie sat on either side of her, giving her assistance and trying to redirect her from one present to the next. The Major had watched Kiddie, wondering if she were any closer to wanting a baby for the two of them. Since it had never come up in Florida, the Major doubted she was. He was okay with that as well, wanting to focus on advancing his career. He was looking forward to their Derby party and wanted it to be memorable for all those who came. He had invited some of the writers he worked with earlier this afternoon and they had invited Kiddie's family over dinner. Although he looked forward to their party, the Major wondered when it would be his turn to go to the Derby, and see the run for the roses for himself.

It was Derby day and Kiddie was trying to stay calm and cool as she went through her party list of to-do's. The apartment was clean, a huge bouquet of roses adorning their dining room table. She had gone to Macy's and bought a few things such as a white linen tablecloth and two glass pitchers. The Major had brought home plenty of bourbon and she tried not to think about what bathtub it had been concocted in. She had a bowl full of lemons, ready to mix one regular pitcher of lemonade and one pitcher of bourbon lemonade. Kiddie wondered where their guests would sit, knowing they had all accepted their invitations, but the Major dismissed her concern telling her that would be a bore of a party and that standing room only was the way to go.

Kiddie had just finished making her Benedictine sandwiches, covering the platter before sticking them in the refrigerator. Trimming all the crusts off the white bread was time consuming, but the sandwiches looked mostly presentable. Kiddie also made a carrot cake, a family favorite and always a tasty treat. It was the Burgoo that Kiddie wondered about the most. Cream cheese could make anything taste delicious, but Kiddie wondered how this traditional Kentucky stew would go over with their New York crowd. It was easy enough to make, a combination of meats, barbeque sauce, Worcester sauce, vegetables, and seasonings. It had been simmering for hours now and the smell of it filled the apartment. As Kiddie stood taking in the apartment, she felt pleased that they had thought of everything to make this Derby party memorable. She smiled wryly to herself as she wondered which thing the Major's mother would comment about. She hurried to get dressed before the Major returned with his mother and aunt.

Kiddie often limited her dress shopping since she and the Major had taken their vows, but if ever Kiddie wanted a new dress, it was for this party. The Derby was as famous for it's fashion as the blanket of roses the winning horse would wear in the winner's circle. She knew loose waistlines were all the rage, but Kiddie had found something a little more fitted, with a higher hemline. The dress was a light blue and the Major was wearing his blue tie to match. The color was stunning with Kiddie's dark hair, and she felt confident her light makeup and curves would not go unnoticed with the Major.

She knew the Major had a lot on his plate today balancing his numerous guests while also giving his attention to the details of the race. He hoped to write a story that would make his boss take notice, a story that would actually get him to the race next year. Kiddie felt she had done her part as they blended their families with work friends as guests. Since the Major invited some of his colleagues, Kiddie invited Brownie and some of the people she often modeled with. It was bound to be an interesting group for sure and Kiddie could only hope the race would live up to the Major's big talk.

Kiddie was just sampling the bourbon lemonade when the Major walked in with his mother and aunt, Kiddie's mother, Iris and Bernie not far behind. It was time to get this party started as Kiddie glanced around the apartment once more before going to greet everyone. Kiddie was happy to see her mother had come, her green dress and pearls complimenting her dark hair beautifully. The Major's mother was dressed impeccably in red and Kiddie was thankful for her mother's voice as she greeted her in-laws warmly.

"Kiddie the apartment looks wonderful! The roses make such a statement on the table, and whatever you're cooking smells divine!"

Kiddie thanked her mother while basking in the Major's appreciative glance over her from head to toe, turning her cheek to his kiss as his mother looked on.

"Why thank you Mother! How does it feel to not be the one hosting for a change?" Kiddie asked, taking her mother's arm and guiding her to the kitchen.

"Different but lovely just the same. I don't know much about the Kentucky Derby, but this definitely feels like a party! Kiddie you've always loved horses since you were a little girl. Remember riding at the stables?"

Just as Kiddie was about to pour her some lemonade, her mother turned abruptly to Bernie. "Bernie do you have the package I brought for Kiddie?"

As Bernie went to fetch it from the car, Kiddie was busy filling glasses with lemonade. Iris and the Major's aunt and mother had come to join them in the kitchen.

"What are we drinking today Kiddie?" Iris asked expectantly.

"I've made lemonade and bourbon lemonade too. Apparently they drink a lot of bourbon during the race. Drinking it straight seemed harsh so I added it to lemonade." Kiddie explained as she handed a cup to Iris.

"I'll try some of that bourbon lemonade too Kiddie." her mother said with a smile.

Kiddie was startled and glanced at Iris who looked equally surprised. They had never seen their mother drink anything more than half a glass of wine at dinner, and maybe a glass of champagne on New Year's Eve.

Looking at her two daughters, Kiddie's mother laughed, "I thought this was a party! Or is your special lemonade only for the young people?" She then turned to the Major's mother and said, "Viva won't you join me in some bourbon lemonade?"

It was the Major's mother's turn to look startled, but she recovered quickly. Never one to back down from a challenge, she answered lightly, "Kiddie I would love to try your bourbon lemonade as well."

Kiddie turned and asked graciously, "And you as well Aunt Maddie?"

Kiddie glanced at the Major as he came to join the group of women. He was equally surprised and amused as the group of women cheered their cups of bourbon lemonade together. Seeing Iris down hers quickly, her mother followed suit. Kiddie had poured just enough for a taste and smiled as she refilled cups all around. Clearly no one was going to be left out today and it promised to be more interesting than Kiddie had thought.

As if reading her mind, the Major announced graciously there was plenty of bourbon to go around. As Bernie handed the package to Kiddie, he turned to the Major,

"If that's the case, I'll have some of the straight stuff Major, thank you!" The Major pulled out his decanter of bourbon, filling a glass with ice before pouring bourbon over it and handing it to Bernie.

"Mother what's this?" Kiddie asked curiously.

"Open it and see Kiddie. It's just something from your room at home that I decided should be with you on a day like today."

As Kiddie tore away the brown wrapping paper she realized it was the picture of her as a teenage girl with her favorite horse at the stables. The picture had been hanging in her room for years and Kiddie was happy to have it. She went to put it by the radio before thanking her mother with a big hug. Looking over her shoulder, the Major was reminded of what a horse girl Kiddie had been not that long ago. It was symbolic sitting there by the radio as if waiting patiently for the horses to be announced.

The Major suddenly remembered he had typed up the list of the twenty thoroughbreds competing in today's fifty-first running of the Derby. He had typed up several copies so their guests could look over the names of the horses before predicting who would be the winner. He had pencils handy so guests could write their name and circle the winning horse.

As the small apartment filled with guests, the party overflowed with Kiddie's delicious food, bourbon lemonade, and laughter. Some of the guests were competitive in choosing their winning horse, turning to the

Major for the inside scoop, but the Major remained impartial letting everyone make their own choices. The horses had interesting names from Broadway Jones to Prince of Bourbon to Flying Ebony, making that the deciding factor for most of the choices guests made.

Before long the Major turned on the radio, tuning into their usual station out of Pittsburgh. The Major got goosebumps as he stood close to the radio, listening to the bugle call signaling riders up. He could imagine the horses parading to the starting gate, as the crowd sang the traditional ballad of "My Old Kentucky Home." The Major buzzed with excitement as he focused on the announcer's words. It soon became apparent the crowd had been showered with a fast heavy downpour just minutes before the riders mounted their horses and they now faced a sloppy track.

Kiddie shushed her mother as the shot went off signaling the race had started. The apartment fell quiet as they listened to the announcer call the race, his excitement contagious. Within minutes he was announcing Flying Ebony the winner, his jockey Earl Sande supposedly smiling from ear to ear as the blanket of five hundred and sixty four roses was bestowed upon his horse. While it was all well and good to hear it on the radio, Kiddie wished she could see it too. She could better understand the Major wanting to be at Churchill Downs for himself, but for Kiddie it seemed highly unlikely there would ever be something worth standing out in the rain for.

Kiddie jumped when her mother suddenly started shrieking "my horse won! Flying Ebony was my horse!"

The Major was the one smiling now, calling for someone to get that lady a drink! A huge cheer went around the room as he added, drinks for everyone! Like the horse himself was presented with roses, so the Major presented Kiddie's mother with a small bouquet of roses too. He then walked around the room handing out a single rose to the other ladies, starting with his own mother and Aunt Maddie.

It felt like the party was winding down until *"Yes Sir, That's My Baby"* came on the radio, someone turning the radio way up. One of Kiddie's model friends was quickly in full swing with her husband doing the

Charleston, claiming it was their favorite song. Before long a circle had formed around them, some clapping to the music and others joining in. Kiddie was delighted when Iris grabbed her and they joined in the fray of kick steps and swaying arms. Kiddie could feel the Major watching her and she worked hard to keep up with the music.

Kiddie knew the Major would never join in the fancy footwork, but couldn't resist when Iris yelled in her ear the mothers should learn how to do the Charleston. Iris was just crazy enough to go and grab the Major's mother, while Kiddie went to get her own. The Major's mother had just enough bourbon in her lemonade that she eventually succumbed to Iris's insistence that she join the dance floor. Kiddie's mother was delighted to be asked and tried to focus through her own bourbon fog on the girls steps.

The girls explained that the Charleston was a fast eight count, but they would start slow to teach them the steps. They started with a touch and step before moving to the kick step then to the heels in and out before finally adding in swinging arms. The mothers were behind them, following their moves slowly before hitting it full tilt. It was all in good fun and before long Kiddie and Iris's mother had gone freestyle throwing her kick steps and swinging her arms wherever she pleased. The Major had come and rescued his own mother deciding maybe a cup of coffee was more appropriate for her.

As the party finally wound down, the food gone, the pitchers of bourbon lemonade dry, Kiddie and the Major were left cleaning up. The Major had put his mother and Aunt Maddie in a cab hours ago, while Iris and Bernie took their mother home, still the life of the party. Now as they sat on the couch together, the music still playing Kiddie was tired, but happy. She sat with her head on the Major's shoulder, wondering just how late it was.

"Kiddie my love, you outdid yourself today. Everything was perfect, especially the bourbon lemonade!" the Major chuckled.

Kiddie smiled, thinking of her mother, and seeing a new side of her today. Kiddie wondered how much of that had been the bourbon and how much had been way overdue. Sometimes she worried her mother spent too much time alone writing, her father often working his own long hours. It seemed like Sunday dinners were the only thing on their social calendar these days. The picture of Kiddie with the horse caught her eye and she got up to go look at it again. Standing there looking at it, Kiddie felt an unexplained sentimental sadness for times gone by.

As *"It Had to be You"* came on the radio, the Major came and offered his hand to Kiddie.

"May I have this dance please?" The Major asked with a bow.

Kiddie graciously accepted his hand, always impressed with how light on his feet the Major was as well as handsome to look at. It was annoying and charming all at the same time how the Major was good at so many things, even things he didn't do often. As a big yawn overtook Kiddie, the Major reminded her in her ear that he still had a story to go write. Kiddie nodded, knowing that would be the case. She didn't protest as he led her to bed, helping her unzip her dress and tucking her into bed, kissing her on the lips and then her forehead. Kiddie barely heard him as the Major locked the door and headed to the paper, Kiddie already drifting off to sleep.

B efore they knew it, summer was upon New York and Kiddie's birthday had rolled around again. The Major was on the road in the last week of May, first to Philadelphia and then to Boston. Now he was home as the Robins played in a series with the New York Giants, winning only the last game out of three. The Major had the day before Kiddie's birthday off before he headed to Chicago and was then on the road for the next couple of weeks. They took advantage of their time together and spent the day doing some of their favorite things, picnicking in Central Park and visiting the Metropolitan Museum of Art. As was tradition, they had dinner at The Cascades, the stars twinkling down on them and their coupe glasses full of champagne before meeting their rowdy group at their favorite speakeasy, Club Fronton.

As the Major kissed Kiddie good-bye early in the morning, he surprised her when he told her he had hidden a gift in their apartment somewhere for her birthday. Trying to look all of her soon-to-be twenty-three years, Kiddie told the Major she wasn't a child anymore and he didn't need to worry about lavishing gifts on her. But still, Kiddie went back to bed, a smile on her face, grateful to the Major for always thinking of her and her happiness. The day passed quickly as Kiddie slept late before meeting her mother for an early lunch. Having the time at home now, Kiddie searched their apartment to eventually find the Major's present hidden under the last towel in the bathroom. It was a beautiful long strand of pearls, a perfect compliment to the choker strand he had gotten her a few years ago. Kiddie lounged after lunch, reading her latest issues of *Vogue* and *The New Yorker* before taking a cab over the bridge to her family home in Brooklyn. Kiddie's mother insisted she come for birthday dinner and now Kiddie was happy to see all her family there to celebrate with her.

Kiddie tried to keep her long summer days busy, focused on her workouts and staying in shape. She and Iris played tennis three to four times a week, a workout of a different kind. She was always ready to work when she would get a call from Brownie or Edna, but it was sporadic and Kiddie worried she missed calls when she wasn't home to answer the phone. Kiddie was making a point to enjoy her time at home, even when the Major was gone. She kept their apartment tidy, but often opted for a glass of wine over cooking dinner for herself. She was always grateful to Cook when she sent Kiddie home with leftovers from Sunday dinner.

Since their Kentucky Derby party, Kiddie started meeting her mother for lunch once a week, sometimes in the city and sometimes in Brooklyn. It was a new chapter in their relationship as they both shared about husbands with busy jobs and how to stay productive when no one needed you to do so. Kiddie shared about her workouts and encouraged her mother not to spend so much time sitting at a desk writing. Her mother asked about the latest fashion trends and Kiddie was delighted when she asked Kiddie to take her shopping one after-noon to update her closet. Kiddie and Iris were always doing things together, and Kiddie realized they should include their mother more often. Sometimes Kiddie's mother would talk about selling their big family home and moving to a smaller house, but Kiddie would always brush the idea off, not taking her mother seriously.

For once the Fourth of July turned out to be over the weekend and Kiddie's family decided to go to the beach. They left early on Friday, planning to return late Sunday afternoon. Iris was excited for Lelo's first trip to the beach, while Kiddie managed to get the Major to take a day off. The Robins had a double header with the New York Giants on the Fourth, but the Major caught the train down with the family on Friday, knowing he would be getting back on the train early Saturday morning. Kiddie and the Major enjoyed a long walk on the beach, dinner out for fresh seafood, and sitting by a fire on the beach with the family. They were a large, boisterous group, Freddy's friend Dot and Bernie's mother even joining the fray. The Major could not imagine his own mother with sand in her shoes, but then again they had never talked about a trip to the ocean before.

A few weeks later, when the Major came into the office to write his latest story, he found a little blue envelope sitting on his desk. Inside the envelope was an invitation to come and see Mr. Brisbane at his office. As the Major walked over, he wondered if this was finally the offer he had been waiting for, almost a year later. The Major wondered no more as Mr. Brisbane got right to the point and asked if he had any interest in working for the Hearst paper. While the Major was trying to think of an intelligent response, Mr. Brisbane pulled out *The New York Times* paper, searching for something written by the Major.

"*The Times* has always taken good care of me." the Major finally said as Mr. Brisbane read his piece in the paper.

"I like your nice short sentences Corum. I can offer you a three year contract for one hundred fifty dollars a week. Are you in?" Mr. Brisbane asked pointedly.

The Major was impressed with the offer, mumbling "That's quite an offer sir."

As Mr. Brisbane turned to his desk, he came back with three contracts, extending them with a pen to the Major. "So that's a yes Corum?" The Major was all smiles as he signed his name on the dotted line.

The Major headed back to the *Times*, trying to think of how to best explain his departure. The people at the *Times* had always taken good care of him and he didn't like to think leaving was about money, but it was hard to argue with a contract offering almost twice as much money as he made now. The Major couldn't wait to get home and share the big news with Kiddie. It would be a night to celebrate for sure.

In the weeks that followed, the Major transitioned to *The New York Journal* and was assigned to cover the New York Giants. He was proud as his first story for the Giants posted on July 21, and thankful to be able to write about their win over the Cincinnati Reds. The Major spent most of the next three weeks on the road with the team traveling from Boston to Chicago to St. Louis to Cincinnati to Pittsburgh. In a strange turn of events the Major was home for a day when the Giants faced the Brooklyn Robins in a single game right before his birthday.

It was the Major's thirtieth birthday and Kiddie had toyed with the idea to have a party for the Major, but in the end decided there wasn't enough time to do it right. Instead they went out to dinner and came home to cake and champagne. Although Kiddie planned a private party for two, she knew she would be sending the Major off later to his favorite watering hole, The Tavern. She had made a few calls to let his friends know it was a big birthday for the Major, and if they weren't out of town writing their own stories, that was where the Major would be. The Major was a man who required very little sleep and Kiddie knew he often spent time at the Tavern after he finished writing his stories. A few years ago Kiddie had insisted on going to the Tavern one night with the Major, and after that, had never bothered him again. It was a man's bar and full of writers who could talk about sports and writing all night long. It had been awkward and boring and Kiddie had regretted it, feeling she should have trusted the Major when he told her that from the beginning. In the end the Major was a happy man, having the best of both his worlds for his birthday.

By mid-August, the Major was finally home for a while as the Giants faced their opponents at the Polo Grounds. Looking ahead in the schedule the Major was happy to report to Kiddie he would have no game on their anniversary this year, but would be headed to Philadelphia early the next day. On impulse Kiddie asked if they could celebrate their anniversary in Philly as she had never been there before. She trusted that the Major had been there enough times to know a nice hotel and restaurant where they could celebrate their three years of marriage. The Major readily agreed and began asking for recommendations for a romantic dinner for two.

Kiddie didn't often find herself in Grand Central Station, but today she felt excited that for once, she and the Major would be getting on the train together. As they checked the chalkboard in the Biltmore Room to make sure their train was on time, the Major told her that the North River tunnel had been built under the Hudson River, getting trains from Manhattan to New Jersey to Philly in ninety minutes or less. They were soon enjoying the view from the dining car as they traveled south, the Major wondering out loud how the Giants would do against the Phillies in their quest to finish first in their division. Kiddie had been a Giants fan her whole life thanks to her father, and now thanks to her husband, she often knew more than she wanted about their season at any given time.

Getting off the train, Kiddie could immediately feel the big city energy of Philadelphia. The train shed was a masterpiece of steel and glass, people getting on and off trains in a bustle of activity. The Major carried their luggage while he pointed out the Farmer's Market, and other buildings of semi-importance. As they took a cab to their hotel, the Major explained they would be within walking distance of historical Independence Hall, a place he wanted to see for himself. Kiddie could feel the energy of the city shift as their cab seemed to take them back in time and the area became decorated with beautiful colonial buildings, including the Morris House Hotel, built in the late seventeen hundreds. Kiddie loved the crisp white trim in contrast to the red brick pavers that had stood the weathering for so many decades. It was clean and lovely and elegant, giving Kiddie a sense of peaceful anticipation for their stay.

Having checked in, they walked through the beautifully crafted hotel to their room, Kiddie taking everything in including a glimpse of a courtyard and garden. She smiled at the Major as he unlocked their door and led them into a room that was quaintly luxurious, promising comfort in style. Kiddie was most taken with the fireplace and wondered if they would be able to light it later tonight. They deposited their luggage and freshened up quickly before heading out to explore the history of the city.

This was a new experience for both of them as they never played tourists anywhere that wasn't oceanside. It was a warm fall day as they walked and explored along the cobbled paved roads, getting a history lesson first hand. Kiddie was surprised to see the effect Independence Hall had on the Major as they stood admiring the bell tower, the clock below it, and the other architectural elements of the building. She admired the archways and could well imagine the horses and carriages pulling up as men like Benjamin Franklin and George Washington arrived.

The Major shared a short history lesson of how the Constitutional Convention had transcended into the creating and signing of the Declaration of Independence. He inspired Kiddie to imagine that day in 1776 when the first public reading had taken place to a crowd of hopeful Colonists. They had celebrated the document with cannons and fireworks, unaware of the harsh war ridden days ahead of them. Kiddie did not know the RedCoats had taken over Independence Hall as their headquarters while they occupied Philadelphia until the battle of Bunker Hill had sent them running back to England and King George.

Seeing Kiddie's look the Major responded with, "Did you think I only know about sports?"

As they walked along the hall from front to back, the Major gravely informed Kiddie that when you spend time defending your freedoms in the name of the United States, a place like this has tremendous meaning. Thanks to WWI, he knew firsthand how it felt to stand in combat beside your friends and peers, praying for safety and resolution during a war. It was easy for him to imagine what it must have felt like in battle while trying to birth a nation in the name of freedom and the pursuit of happiness.

Eventually they realized it had been a while since breakfast and ducked into a place called the Bell in Hand. As they sat at their table enjoying ice cream, the Major told Kiddie about his plan for dinner tonight. An Italian restaurant had been highly recommended to him, a short cab ride away from their hotel, in an area called Bella Vista. The Major had been promised Kiddie would love it, the perfect destination to celebrate their anniversary. Although the Major had been to Philadelphia many times, his experiences were limited to the ballpark and whatever hotel the paper was willing to pay for. He was happy Kiddie had asked to spend their anniversary here and hoped she was enjoying it as much as he was.

It wasn't long before they were dressed up and ready for their night out on the town. Kiddie dressed for the occasion in a lovely light pink dress of satin with a big bow at the back of her neck. She doubled the long strand of pearls the Major had given her for her birthday and paired it with her shorter strand, making her dress look that much more elegant. The Major himself was debonair as always in his black suit, sporting a bow tie for the night.

Kiddie immediately fell in love with the romance of the restaurant, admiring the dark wood floors and tall windows, enhanced as the sun was setting in a colorful bouquet of soft pinks and yellows. They were led to a table covered with the traditional white linen, a small glowing candle and rose bud welcoming them. As they looked over their menus both Kiddie and the Major struggled to choose between all the pasta dishes, most of them served with Italian gravy. In the end they went with Osso Buco, enjoying a classic Italian comfort food made with lamb shanks and vegetables in a wine sauce. They opted for mashed potatoes in addition to the classic gremolata, a sauce in its own right, a blend of lemon zest, parsley, and olive oil. It was heaven when mixed into the creamy potatoes.

After dinner the Major announced he had a surprise as they stood under the stars waiting for their cab. He shared with Kiddie about a theater club called The Mask and Wig Clubhouse where students from Penn University put on a show of music, comedy, and dancing. Tonight they would see Joan of Arkansas performed. The Major told Kiddie the clubhouse had made history in the spring as the performance became one of the first electrical albums recorded. Kiddie and the Major discovered the interesting thing about the show was the all male cast playing both men and women parts. It was a fun change of pace from the showgirls which typically embellished performances on Broadway. As they walked out of the club, Kiddie asked the Major if they could walk back to their hotel, wanting the night to last as long as possible.

The Major accepted Kiddie's request by offering Kiddie his arm with, "Of course my love."

Taking the Major's arm, Kiddie asked him, "Major how do you do it? You always know just the right places to take me to and just the right things to do. I'm lucky to have such a thoughtful husband!"

"The pleasure is all mine, my love. I know I challenge your patience when my work is so demanding, and I want to make sure our time together is memorable, in the pursuit of our own happiness." he added.

Kiddie reached up to kiss him on the cheek. "Thank you Major!" He stopped them under a tree, the light unable to reach them, pulling Kiddie to him to kiss her full on the mouth in a long deep kiss.

"Happy anniversary my love. I hope your day has been perfect!" the Major said to her softly.

"Happy anniversary Major. It's been the most lovely day. But there's one thing I'm still looking forward to!" Kiddie's eyes danced as she went on. "It involves you, me, the bottle of champagne I snuck in, and that fireplace."

"And don't forget the bed Mrs. Corum," the Major growled in her ear. Kiddie laughed as they headed into the hotel to their room, stopping only long enough to make sure it was okay to burn the wood in their fireplace. The Major was quick to start the fire, the dry wood starting up in no time under the strike of the Major's long match and wishful thinking.

The Major woke Kiddie the next morning with the scent of fresh coffee from Tacconelli's Bakery. The Major had taken a cab to bring Kiddie their famous fresh baked bread with honey to drizzle over it. Kiddie's train would be leaving for New York just after lunch, about the time the Major would need to be reporting to the ballpark for the Giants and Phillies game. As they lounged in bed enjoying the bread and coffee, the Major asked Kiddie what she would like to do for the morning.

"Major, I think we need to visit Gimbel's! Will you go with me? You need some new ties and perhaps a new suit to celebrate your new job at *The New York Evening Journal.*"

"Kiddie we can do that in New York. Are you sure that's how you want to spend your time?" Even as he looked into Kiddie's excited face, he knew her mind was made up.

Kiddie jumped up with a quick "Thank you Major!" hurrying to the bathroom to get dressed before he could change his mind.

It took less than an hour to work their way through the men's department at Gimbels. The Major agreed to some new ties and shirts, but declined to go all out and get a new suit. Checking his watch for the time, he led Kiddie over to the jewelry counter and asked Kiddie to pick something out. Kiddie hesitated not having any idea what to get, but quickly changed her mind when the Major pointed out a pair of pretty clip-on pearl earrings.

"Kiddie these would look stunning on you and go with your birthday necklaces." the Major said, not having to work that hard to convince her.

Kiddie was smiling from ear to ear as the lady wrapped them for her. "Major, you are too good to me." she said with a kiss to his cheek.

The Major leaned into her ear and said softly, "You can show me how good when I get home in a few days." Kiddie's skin tingled as she smiled up at him.

"Something for us to look forward to Major," Kiddie responded, her eyes dancing.

With plenty of time left for lunch, the couple hailed a cab to McNally's Tavern, a place known for its cheesesteak sandwich. Rose McNally herself greeted them, seating them at a table by the window where they could watch the midday bustle of Philadelphia walk by. The room was noisy with locals enjoying their lunch breaks.

Too soon Kiddie was on her way back to New York City and the Major headed to the ballpark, a reality check for both of them. It had been a wonderful trip, and Kiddie sat in the dining car, a smile on her face. The time flew by as she perused the latest issue of *The New Yorker*, having tossed it in her suitcase last minute when they packed a few days ago.

It was late in the day as she unlocked the door to their apartment, lugging her suitcase in after her. Pouring herself a glass of wine, she went to unpack her suitcase, hanging up the Major's new ties and unwrapping his new shirts. She checked the mirror, turning from side to side as she admired her new pearl earrings, a lovely anniversary present from the Major and souvenir from their trip to Philly. Kiddie sipped her wine and listened to *Rhapsody in Blue* on the Victrola, while she soaked in the bathtub, feeling content to be home. The Major would be home in a few days, for a few more games at the Polo Grounds before finishing the season on the road. Even as Kiddie got into bed by herself that night, she was grateful to have had a memorable anniversary with the Major. Kiddie knew not every husband traveled as much as hers, but she was pretty sure not every husband worked as hard to make their time together count as much as hers either. She fell asleep with a grateful heart.

B efore they knew it, Thanksgiving passed them by and Kiddie was out shopping all over Manhattan for Christmas presents. The Major settled into his new job nicely with *The New York Journal*, while Kiddie kept busy posing for Brownie and sometimes Edna when they called. Her magazine covers were few and far between, but her sketches with Brownie were consistent and kept her busy. When they weren't working, Kiddie and Iris were going out to a show or a bar and living the good life. They became quite taken with their latest show, *The Phantom of the Opera* having seen it at the Astor Theater on Broadway just before Thanksgiving. Like so many other women, they fell for Lon Chaney and his portrayal of a devil versus a saint, or more importantly, a lover versus a hater.

The Major himself became quite taken with the third and newest version of the venue known as Madison Square Garden. Having recently reopened, this indoor arena was now at a more uptown location at Eighth Avenue and 50th Street in Manhattan. The new owner, Ted Rickard, a boxing promoter, promised a sports arena like no other. The house that Ted built had seating on three levels and would offer spectators boxing, basketball, and hockey. The Major was happy to attend Ted's first event early in December as the Garden hosted a basketball game between the Celtics and the Washington Palace Five, the Celtics winning by four points. Days later the Major attended the light heavyweight match between Paul Berlenbach and Jack Delaney. The defending champion Berlenbach was knocked down several times, but always rallied against Delaney. Later in December the Major attended his first hockey event as the New York Americans were defeated by the Montreal Canadians by 3-1. Between the three sports, there was always a reason to be at the Garden, just the way Rickard had planned it.

The Garden drew crowds on a regular basis and proved to be a mecca for the sportswriter, especially one in his off season from baseball. Kiddie herself was not such a fan of the Garden as suddenly she had competition for her and the Major's dinner and drinking routine she enjoyed in the off season. Unlike baseball, which had to be played on an afternoon outdoors, the Garden's activities were held indoors at night to give the working man ample opportunities to attend. In addition, it seemed like a natural extension of the game to go and have a beverage or several, somewhere after the game, to rehash the event. Like Kiddie, many wives did not appreciate this new distraction and eventually it became an issue between Kiddie and the Major.

It was brought to the Major's attention a week before Christmas, when the Major came home from his latest Garden event and found their bedroom door closed and locked. He had been drinking, but was sober enough to recognize his pillow and a blanket on the couch. He was not sober enough however to take the pillow as a win and proceeded to bang on their door.

"Kiddie, the door's locked! Can you kindly come open it please?" The Major was doing his best to act as if nothing was amiss.

When there was no answer, he pounded louder on the door and repeated himself. The Major rarely lost his cool, but decided if ever there was a time for it, this was it. He would not sleep on the couch believing he had done nothing wrong. He pounded loudly on the door again, demanding Kiddie come and open it at once.

Fearing the Major would wake the neighbors at the unreasonable hour of two in the morning, Kiddie finally went to the door.

"I don't know what you're bellowing about Major. You have everything you need right there on the couch. I'm sorry if I don't have a basketball or a puck to tuck you in with, but be sure you do not want to go rounds with me tonight!" Kiddie's eyes were flashing, her tone icy as she made her biting announcement to the Major. It felt good to finally speak what was on her mind after laying in bed saying it over and over to herself for the past two hours.

The Major was taken aback for a moment, caught off guard by Kiddie's demeanor and confused about her point. But before he could say anything, Kiddie slammed the door in his face and relocked it. The Major stood there for a moment, willing his sensibilities to take over the situation. In the end he left Kiddie alone and went to sleep on the couch, assuming there would be plenty of time to sort it out in the morning.

The next morning Kiddie waited for the Major to make the first move, hoping for his sober knock on the door. Kiddie herself had been drinking last night and was thankful they hadn't gotten into an emotional verbal battle fueled by alcohol. The morning was dark and dreary and finally when Kiddie could wait no longer, she opened the door to make a beeline for the bathroom. She kept her eyes focused on the bathroom, afraid to make eye contact with the Major. It was time to make a plan B as Kiddie realized the Major was not going to come to her. She freshened up in the mirror, giving herself a mental pep talk that it wasn't too much to expect your husband to be home once in a while and that she for sure better come before hockey or basketball!

When Kiddie opened the bathroom door her eyes were immediately drawn to the Major. He had a cup of coffee waiting for her on the table and he reached out to hand it to her.

"I take it you have something you would like to share with me, Kiddie?" the Major asked in even tones.

Kiddie accepted the cup of coffee and went to sit on the other end of the couch. She focused on her first sip, willing it to give her the words to say the right thing in a reasonable voice and not a naggy wife voice.

"Major, I feel like you're spending all your time at Madison Square Garden since it opened. You're at the office all day and then out all night. I'm not ok with that." Kiddie added the last part softly, willing him to understand her point.

The Major was looking at her and she could see he was trying to choose his own words carefully while she waited for him to answer her.

"Sometimes I'm home in the mornings Kiddie, but you've been so busy with Brownie, you're out the door and I hardly see you." the Major finally said.

Kiddie was stunned this was the way he was going to play it. "Major you know I'm working. You know I want to be available for Brownie as much as possible."

Kiddie suddenly stood up as she realized she had an appointment with Brownie in an hour. She stood staring the Major down, challenging him to have more than a stupid comeback for that.

"But Kiddie you don't have to work. I make more than enough to take care of the two of us." And there was his stupid comeback. As soon as he said it, the Major knew he had said the wrong thing. It didn't really matter if he wanted his wife home when he was home, she wasn't at his beck and call. And for sure he was gone plenty when she was home alone.

Kiddie could not think of anything she could say to him without screaming it at him so instead she stood as tall as she could and walked to the bedroom, closing and locking the door once again. The Major sat down on the couch and decided he would wait her out. When she emerged twenty minutes later he was not expecting to see her all dressed up. She usually tried to look her best when she went to pose for Brownie, but this morning she had gone all out. Without even a glance his way, she picked up her purse and put on her coat, closing the door firmly behind her. She liked to think it was the cold air making her eyes sting, but she knew it would take all her willpower to not cry. Seeing a cab sitting on Morningside across from Central Park, Kiddie tapped on the window to signal she needed a ride. Numbly she gave Brownie's address to the driver and willed herself to focus on her work ahead of her.

Kiddie tried her best to get through her morning without thinking too much about the Major. Brownie seemed happy enough with her work although one of her friends noticed something was amiss. When Kiddie declined to comment, her friend gave her hand a squeeze, but respectfully let it go.

It was early afternoon as Kiddie sat in a cab headed over the Brooklyn Bridge, home to have her usual weekly lunch with her mother. Now Kiddie was trying to decide if she should share the Major's stupidity with her mother or just pretend everything was fine.

As Kiddie entered the house and greeted her mother with a hug, she knew she wouldn't be able to pull off an "I'm fine" routine. The December weather was nasty enough outside that Kiddie's mother had already decided they should stay in and let Cook surprise them with whatever leftovers she wanted to dispose of. Kiddie was grateful for the divine intervention, clearly the goddess looking over wives with stupid husbands watching over her. She was even more convinced when Cook showed up with chicken salad sandwiches and deviled eggs, two of Kiddie's favorites.

"Well Kiddie, do you want to talk first or eat first? Clearly you have something on your mind. Is everything ok?" her mother asked, getting right to the point.

Kiddie poured herself some tea and fixed her plate, trying to decide where to start. Holding her plate in her lap would give her something to do while they talked. Kiddie realized she never had breakfast and was actually quite famished. Kiddie's mother followed her lead, fixing her own plate before leaning back into the couch, looking at Kiddie expectantly, her feet tucked up under her, with her plate balanced on her legs. Kiddie took a deep breath and jumped in.

"Mother have you heard about the new Madison Square Garden opening?" Kiddie was going to start at the beginning.

"Well of course darling, I read the paper." her mother answered.

"Well it turns out the Major can't get enough of that place and has spent more time there lately than in his own home! Suddenly he's a big fan of basketball and hockey, and not so much of me!" Kiddie finished, trying not to sound like a petulant child.

"I see." her mother replied with a thoughtful look on her face. "And why do you think that is Kiddie?" her mother added as an afterthought.

Kiddie looked startled by her mother's question. "Mother, what do you mean? Why what?" Kiddie was confused. This didn't sound like the support of someone in her corner.

Seeing Kiddie's confusion her mother added, "Tell me more about what happened Kiddie."

Trying to keep a long story short Kiddie shared how she had made dinner for her and the Major only to have him call her and let her know plans had been made at the last minute to be at Madison Square Garden for yet another sporting event. Kiddie had been so annoyed she couldn't even remember what it was. She had gone to some trouble to fix dinner for the two of them and had been looking forward to a nice quiet night at home. Kiddie left out how she drank her dinner instead, eventually giving up on the Major coming home and going to bed with a closed, locked door.

Kiddie's mother listened and added, "That would definitely be frustrating Kiddie. Did the Major know you had cooked dinner? What happened this morning? Did you talk it out?"

Kiddie took a minute to collect herself. "This morning the Major acted like I'm the reason we're not seeing much of each other. When I told him it's because I'm busy working for Brownie, he asked me why I'm even working when I don't need to because my big man on campus can take care of us!"

Kiddie's mother paused her sandwich in midair and then sat it back down on her plate. "Oh dear, I can't believe the Major would say that! I know that had to hurt Kiddie!"

Finally! Kiddie nodded her agreement. "It was awful Mother! I can't believe he would say that to me, to dismiss what I do isn't important! How dare he!"

Kiddie put her plate down on the coffee table and stood up to pace. Moving her hands around dramatically, she unleashed a plethora of frustrations she had been shoving down over the weeks, trying to be the supportive wife, the understanding rock by his side. Kiddie's mother watched, flashing back to when Kiddie was a little girl and her patience would reach its limit with her sister Iris. Finally, out of words, Kiddie dropped to the couch, her eyes on her mother, waiting for her to say something to help her feel better.

Kiddie's mother patted her hand. "Kiddie, I know firsthand how hard it is to be married to someone who is so devoted to their career. As their wives we work to keep ourselves busy and productive so that when it's our turn for their attention, we have something interesting to say. And not only do we want to have meaningful conversations with them, we want them to think we're pretty and the only girl in town. We want to feel like we're as important to them as their careers, but more importantly, that we come first. When that balance is broken, it hurts."

Kiddie's eyes filled with tears. She leaned over to hug her mother. She wanted to shout "YES!" That's exactly how it is!" but clearly her mother already seemed to know. Kiddie's mother handed her a napkin to wipe her tears and rubbed her back just briefly.

"Kiddie darling, your husband is a good man. If he's gone off the deep end like this, then there must be a reason. You need to talk to him and explain your side, but also try to hear his side too. Then the two of you have to find a compromise, something that can work for both of you."

Kiddie supposed her mother could be right. The Major had never hurt her like that before and she had seen the regret sweep his face even as he said it. Still, that sentiment had to come from somewhere and for that, Kiddie would hold on hard to her side of the story. Kiddie sat finishing her sandwich and one more deviled egg, trying to decide if she should go home.

As if reading her mind, her mother said, "Kiddie you know you're welcome to stay as long as you like, but you'll have to go home sooner or later."

Kiddie sighed and acknowledged her Mother was right. "I know Mother. I guess I might as well go now. Thank you for the talk Mother. And for lunch!"

Kiddie hugged her mother at the door, the cab waiting for her at the curb. "It will work itself out Kiddie, you'll see. Talk to the Major. He loves you Kiddie and wants you to be happy."

Her mother's words rang true to Kiddie and she knew what she needed to do. When she got home she would reheat dinner and assume the Major would be home at a reasonable time tonight. They could have an adult conversation and Kiddie would accept his apology, assuming he made one.

It was late afternoon by the time Kiddie's cab dropped her at her own door. She hurried up the stairs out of the cold, turning the key quickly to let herself into their apartment. Kiddie was immediately struck by two things. First, the Major was in the same spot she left him this morning and second, the apartment smelled like the lasagna she made last night for dinner. Kiddie turned to greet the Major, but he was first to talk.

"Kiddie, where have you been?" the Major asked, his voice a mix of concern and annoyance.

"What do you mean Major? How long have you been home from work?" Kiddie asked.

"Kiddie I never went to work. I've been waiting for you to come home so we can sort this out." The Major was looking at Kiddie expectantly.

"I had a job with Browne and then I had lunch with my mother. Why would I ever think you didn't go to work Major? How did they survive without you for the day?" Kiddie added sarcastically.

Kiddie saw the Major's jaw tighten. "That's fair. I guess I deserve that," He said quietly. "I found the lasagna you must have cooked for dinner last night. I'm sorry Kiddie! You're right, I have been spending too much time at Madison Square Garden. I never thought how it might affect you and I'm sorry."

He was standing before her, his hands on her arms, his face so earnest. Kiddie didn't know what to say except to go with her mother's advice.

"So why have you been spending so much time at the Garden Major? I understand you enjoy boxing, but since when have you been a fan of basketball or hockey?" Kiddie asked as the Major poured each of them a glass of wine.

Handing her a glass, Kiddie allowed the Major to guide her over to the couch to have a seat beside him. She could see the Major was choosing his words, hesitant to share with her. She waited patiently, giving him the time he needed.

"You know Kiddie, this job isn't so new anymore, but I still feel like the new kid trying to prove himself. I'm thirty Kiddie, thirty! I'm not fresh out of school where people give me room to grow and improve, but I've also not been writing long enough to have the respect, the contacts, the experience it takes to be a top man on the team. I'm still trying to find my way and hanging out at the Gardens is one way to work my way in. I'm sorry I never thought how that would make you feel Kiddie." the Major finished.

Kiddie had never thought about the Major struggling with turning thirty or having transition pains to *The New York Journal*. Kiddie could almost see her mother prodding her on. She was surprised by the Major's words, but she could see his point.

"Why haven't you talked to me about any of that before now Major? I'm here to listen and support you. I can understand how you would feel like that, but I still need you at home at night, especially when baseball season is done. I need you to choose just one of the sports to obsess about at Madison Square Garden, and then I need you to obsess about me." Kiddie said the last part softly, looking the Major in the eyes.

He picked up her hand, ignoring her slight resistance to his touch and kissed it. "Kiddie, you should know I'm always obsessed with you! When you left dressed like that this morning, it's all I've been thinking about all day! When you didn't come home, I was worried about you!"

Kiddie gave the Major a minute to let his words sink in. Withdrawing her hand she said to him in an even tone, "I would know a little about how that feels, wouldn't I Major?"

Quite unintentionally Kiddie had given the Major a taste of his own medicine and she could see the moment on his face when he realized the irony of his words. The wondering, the waiting, the annoyance, and lastly, the eventual worry was something Kiddie experienced as he worked long hours and would then sit drinking with the boys from work rather than come home to bed.

"Kiddie I'm so sorry. I don't even know what to say. I want you to be happy and I promise to try to limit the Gardens to boxing matches. I love going out on the town with you and our quiet nights at home too. Kiddie I never should have insulted you like that this morning about your work. If anyone deserves support and patience for their work, it's you."

Hard as she tried, Kiddie could not keep from tearing up. "You hurt me Major. You of all people should understand how important my work is to me. You know I don't do it just for the money!"

The Major pulled her to him, holding her and kissing her on the top of her head. "Kiddie I'm sorry! Brownie is lucky to have you and you've worked hard to make a name for yourself! I was just mad about sleeping on the couch. I'm proud of my working girl. Can you forgive me Kiddie?"

Kiddie took a deep breath and released it, letting go of all the wear and tear from the last twenty-four hours. Her mother was right, the Major was a good man and Kiddie believed him when he said he would do better. The Major could feel the change in Kiddie's body, and decided they should move on.

"I made us dinner if you're hungry," he said with a smile on his face. It was then that Kiddie realized why the apartment smelled like the lasagna she had made last night. She decided to play along.

"Did you? My, my you must be exhausted after all that effort! It smells fabulous. I could eat." Kiddie quipped back.

The Major reached for the blanket from the back of the couch, covering Kiddie as he said, "Kiddie let me wait on you tonight. You relax and I'll fix our plates."

For the first time Kiddie smiled. "Thank you Major, that would be nice."

As the Major refilled her wine glass, he said, "I'm happy to do it my love."

Kiddie watched as the Major pulled her lasagna out of the oven. He had even put bread into warm, which he now lathered in butter, knowing that was just the way she liked it. He brought their plates over to the couch, a lovely presentation of lasagna, Cook's leftover green beans, and warm bread. Before he sat down to join her, he went to the record player and put on one of her favorite records, *"Rhapsody in Blue."* Sitting down beside Kiddie, the Major held his glass up for a toast.

"Cheers to your delicious lasagna and to a better evening my love." the Major said with a smile. Kiddie clinked his glass, happy to drink to that.

A week later, as an early Christmas gift, Kiddie and Iris took their mother to see the new show, *The Roxyettes.* The show had been a good time, a glamorous group of sixteen girls forming a meticulously synchronised chorus line with stylish costumes and high kicks for days. The girls applauded the efforts of both the choreographer, Russell Markert, and Roxy Rothafel, the man who had insisted on creating the group of dancers in New York. After seeing the Missouri Rockets from St. Louis perform in the Broadway show, *"Rain or Shine,"* Rothafel knew he needed to create his own group of dancers in Manhattan.

Kiddie's mother enjoyed the show immensely, and was happy to go along when her girls insisted they all go out after the show. Determined to show her a good time, they took her to Club Fronton where Kiddie introduced her to the refreshing French 75. After a while, the boys joined them one by one, the Major, Freddy and Dot, and Bernie rounding out their group. No one was surprised Kiddie's father was busy with his doctor duties, and impulsively the Major offered to take them all out to dinner. Manhattan was a glow with holiday cheer and the small group relished in the season and being together on that cold, crisp night. It was a perfect end to the night, as they came out of The Plaza to find snow falling.

In no time at all, they were toasting with champagne for New Year's Eve. After dinner and shenanigans at Kiddie's parents house, they stopped by Club Fronton for a round of drinks, before heading home for their private party for two. It had been a big year for the Corums and Kiddie felt a sense of accomplishment as they celebrated mostly highs for the year. The big highs for Kiddie were the trips she got to enjoy with the Major and that she was busy working so much. Brownie's sketches were popping up everywhere in advertisements and stories in magazines and newspapers.

Now as the Major refilled their coupe glasses with champagne, Kiddie asked him what had been his highs for the year. The Major started with getting his name on his stories before moving to the Kentucky Derby party they had in May. He had been proud to see his Derby story posted in *The New York Times* as his phrase "run for the roses" received quite a bit of attention. The Major was also proud to now be writing for *The New York Evening Journal* and making more money than he ever had in his life. But mostly, the Major told Kiddie, their trips together had been the best part of his year. As their champagne bottle sat empty on the floor, they were happy to welcome in the new year snuggled in bed together, wondering what adventures 1926 would bestow upon them.

CHAPTER SEVEN

$=1926=$

K iddie checked her watch one more time, as her train passed through Clearwater. Kiddie smiled thinking about her trip there a year ago, a fun few days with the Major during his spring training with the Brooklyn Robins. This year however, her destination was another hour further south as the New York Giants held their spring training in Sarasota. It had been three weeks since the Major had left for spring training and Kiddie was looking forward to the sight of him.

Winter continued to have it's chilly grip on New York City, ignoring that the calendar finally said early March. Kiddie was anticipating warmer weather and at the very least, lots of sunshine on the beach. She was definitely in need of a change of scenery, and always a fan of an ocean view. The winter for Kiddie and the Major had been nothing to write home about, just following their usual routines of balancing work with couple time. Since getting to Sarasota, the Major had been good about calling Kiddie almost daily, but it wasn't the same and she tried not to worry that the time and distance would take a toll. Now as she watched the countryside sweeping past her dining car window, she could feel the nervous excitement she got when she was about to see the Major after time apart.

As the train finally pulled into the station, Kiddie swept the waiting crowd for signs of the Major. Gathering her luggage, she struggled to disembark from the train as gracefully as possible. She was grateful when a strong hand reached down to take her big suitcase from her, a big smile on her face as she turned expecting to see the Major. Her smile froze as she looked into the face of a stranger and he followed her as she turned and walked to search once again for the Major.

"Kiddie! Kiddie!" the Major was shouting as he rushed up to her, wanting her to see him in the swarming crowd. "Thank you, I can take my wife's bag now," the Major said, waving the stranger off. Kiddie had a sense of deja vu as the Major reached to hug her first, then kissed her on the lips.

"Kiddie I'm sorry I'm late! The game went on forever and then my cab moved at a snail's pace. We can get a new one over there. Welcome to Sarasota my love!"

Kiddie was calming her anxiety, willing her sleep deprivation not to take over. She was relieved to see the Major and the sight of him was washing her worries away. Taking a deep breath she said to the Major, "Thank you Major! I'm happy to be here and off that train!"

As they sat in the cab together the Major explained that there were limited hotel choices at the moment in Sarasota, but given all the construction, there would be more choices in the future. The Major had made reservations at the Sarasota Terrace Hotel, built in the last year by Charles Ringling. He pointed out the eleven story structure, sitting pretty on the number one green of the golf course.

"Kiddie I've been promised beautiful water views and glorious sunsets. The best part is there's a rooftop garden where we can have dinner and listen to the Sarasota Terrace Orchestra play. How does that sound?"

Kiddie turned to the Major, his handsome face happy to see her, his anticipation evident. "It sounds wonderful Major!" The Major picked up Kiddie's hand, kissing the top of it as the cab pulled up to the hotel entrance.

It wasn't long before they were checked in and unpacked, ready for their couple of days together. Kiddie had bathed and dressed for dinner while the Major went in search of champagne. They were both looking forward to dinner on the rooftop, just a few floors up from their own room. Their terrace opened out to a beautiful view of the Gulf of Mexico and Kiddie could feel herself starting to relax as they stood together taking it all in, each of them with a glass of champagne in their hands. The Major held his glass up to Kiddie to toast her.

"To my beautiful wife, thank you Kiddie for coming all this way to see me!" the Major said as he tapped his glass to Kiddie's.

Finishing her sip Kiddie added, "To see you and this view Major!" Her eyes were dancing and the Major wondered if there was some truth to her teasing dig.

"Touche, my love, touche!" the Major said with a smile. "Shall we go to dinner? I'm sure you're famished!"

Kiddie admitted she was and was grateful when they were seated promptly. It was a beautiful spring day and Kiddie relished in the slight breeze blowing her hair, the late afternoon sun warming her face. Kiddie and the Major took their time over dinner, starting with an appetizer before moving onto their real food. Kiddie was enjoying her pasta, but her attention was focused on the Major and having the time to catch up with each other. They enjoyed the music of the orchestra for a while before agreeing it was time to give their table to the next couple.

Back in their room, Kiddie stood on their terrace taking in the green trees which led out to the Gulf of Mexico. It was a different look than in Clearwater, but the Major had assured her they weren't that far from the beach. The Major stood behind her, his body embracing hers, his arms wrapped around her waist. She smiled as she could feel him breathing in the smell of her hair before moving to her neck, taking in her perfume. As the Major planted a kiss on her neck, Kiddie could feel her skin tingle and she turned to the Major to kiss him back. Taking his hand she led him back into their room, turning her back to him so that he could unzip her dress. Kiddie could feel the Major behind her, his hands warm and gentle as he relieved her of her dress. As they fell into bed together, this, thought Kiddie, this was worth the long train ride.

K iddie was still laying in bed, enjoying the warm breeze coming in through the opened terrace doors. Looking around the room, for the first time she was able to appreciate the beauty and elegance of the Venetian Renaissance style of their hotel. The Major was nowhere to be found, but Kiddie felt confident he was out finding coffee and breakfast. Kiddie knew it was late in the morning, but then again, they had been up until the early hours of the morning catching up on this and that. As Kiddie rolled to her side, seeing the empty champagne bottle made her smile. She was grateful that she and the Major were able to reconnect last night, the change of scenery adding to their enjoyment of each other.

Kiddie sat up in bed, pulling the sheet up with her as the Major came in bringing hot coffee and a stack of waffles. "Kiddie, I want you to know that Charles Ringling himself recommended these waffles as he and his wife Mabel were having them for breakfast themselves."

Kiddie looked delighted. "Waffles? I haven't had waffles in years Major! Cook always made the best waffles, but let's give these a go and see if your Ringling man knows what he's talking about!"

Balancing her plate carefully on her knees, Kiddie's first bite was heaven. The thick syrup and butter graced every crevice of her waffle, which was light and airy in itself. She nibbled on her bacon, enjoying the sweet and salty of the two. The Major smiled at Kiddie's obvious agreement that they were indeed some of the best waffles.

In between forkfuls Kiddie asked the Major, "So what's on our agenda for today Major?"

Sipping his coffee the Major looked thoughtful. "I thought we could spend some time on the beach and then go on a cruise before sunset. Apparently there are two yachts, *The Black Cat* and *The Blue Lantern*, that take you out into the gulf and let you drink to your heart's desire.

Because you're out on the water, the sheriff has no jurisdiction. How does that sound Kiddie?"

Kiddie loved the idea and finished her waffles quickly so she could go get dressed for the beach in her new Jantzen swimsuit, throwing on a white cotton sleeveless dress as her cover up.

It wasn't long before their picnic blanket was spread out and the two of them were lounging beside each other, enjoying their ocean view. The Major had been in Sarasota for just three weeks and had yet to get this close to the water. Most of his time was spent at Payne Park watching the Giants or at the bar of his hotel where he and other writers sat and enjoyed drinks before heading up to their rooms. The Major was sharing a room with a fellow named Arthur Mann, about Kiddie's age, full of passion for baseball and a pen that could write the stories to prove it. It wasn't a bad way to spend your work week, but it could get old eventually and the Major was happy to take a day off and enjoy some time with Kiddie.

It was a beautiful day to sit on the beach and now, just hours later, to be on the water thanks to *The Blue Lantern*. Kiddie and the Major sat at a table for two, their cocktails flowing. The yacht was definitely a party and they were enjoying themselves and the beautiful sunset to go with it. Kiddie could feel herself getting tipsy, but enjoyed the fact the Major was there to take care of her. When she and Iris went out to the clubs, she always tried to not get to where she couldn't keep herself safe. Tonight she could let her guard down and enjoy this time with the Major. Kiddie was glowing, her French 75 cocktail an easy recipe for the bartender to follow given the Major's directions. The blend of gin and champagne gave Kiddie a smile for days. The Major himself was enjoying the cuban rum *The Blue Lantern* was famous for smuggling into Florida waters.

After the cruise Kiddie and the Major headed back to the rooftop garden of their hotel for dinner. It was convenient for them to have only one destination after leaving the boat, and the food and views had been perfect the night before. They ordered oysters Rockefeller as an appetizer, one of their favorites they often had at The Plaza. The Major loved the rich toasted butter, cheese, and watercress over the half shell. For dinner they both savored the fresh catch of the day with baked potatoes, while listening to the house orchestra. After dinner, Kiddie was delighted when the Major danced with her, holding her close to sway to the music. Eventually they called it a night before heading back to their room, bringing another perfect day to an end. Later, as Kiddie lay watching the Major sleep, she was sad to be leaving in the morning, but looked forward to the Major being home soon for the opening day of baseball.

Before Kiddie knew it, the Major was starting his new season. Ironically the Giants opening day was against the Robins, and the Major enjoyed seeing some of his favorite baseball people. Although he wasn't a fan of writing about a loss to open the season, he was happy to see the Giants pull out wins for the other two games in the series. Before long the Major was back on the road as the team headed first to Philadelphia, then to Boston, to Chicago and eventually on to St. Louis. The Giants started their season off strong with seven wins in a row, but eventually lady luck turned her back on them and it became anyone's guess who would claim the win for the game.

The Major was in St. Louis, covering the Giants, when he got word he was headed to Louisville to cover the Kentucky Derby, his first official Kentucky Derby. It seemed that his "run for the roses" phrase had caught a lot of people's attention, including his new boss. He caught the train from St. Louis and would later catch up with the team in Cincinnati. It had been a proud moment for him when he called Kiddie and shared the big news with her. He told her this was just the beginning and that someday she would see for herself the parade of magnificent horses mixed in with the latest hats in fashion at Churchill Downs.

When the Major finally arrived at Churchill Downs, he could not take it in fast enough. The twin spires stood out like beacons, calling to horse lovers from around the world. The paddocks were pristine, the horses taking in the people milling about, waiting patiently for their opportunity for glory. The Major could not believe he was finally at the

Derby after all these years of hearing stories about it. He had been to more than one horse race before, but for him, this was the mecca of horse racing. The only thing that could make it better was if he were to run into Colonel Matt Winn himself, the man responsible for making the Kentucky Derby the race it was today.

The Major had seen a lot of press boxes at ballparks, but nothing compared to the energy of the Kentucky Derby Press Box. The Major got goosebumps as the horn signaled riders up. He got a little misty as the crowd sang loudly *"My Old Kentucky Home,"* the song making him nostalgic for his own home. He stood at attention as the parade of thirteen horses walked by with power and grace to the starting gate, their eyes and ears on point, taking it all in, ready to answer the call of the bugle. The Major couldn't help but admire the horses as they shot off from the gate with a surge of power, their muscles rippling underneath their shiny coats, their tails flowing behind them, the crowd cheering them on.

It was an interesting story to write for sure when Colonel Bradley's horses won both first and second place. This had happened only five years ago, when his horses had the same good fortune to smell the roses up close, Behave Yourself gracing the winner's circle. For today though, Bubbling Over left no doubt who was boss, easily winning the race by five lengths. Later he pranced his way to the winner's circle, a beautiful horse on which to place the garland of roses, his jockey Albert Johnson proud and honored to have ridden such a magnificent horse in the run for the roses.

It was a fast forty-eight hours for the Major to be in Louisville. He had checked into the Brown Hotel, but was really too busy to enjoy the English Renaissance style of the sixteen floor structure. He heard rumors in the lobby that Queen Marie of Romania had been there for the race and entertained in the hotel's Crystal Ballroom the night before the race. He noted the hotel had a dinner dance most nights and made a promise to himself, one day he would bring Kiddie to enjoy it and all the southern charm and hospitality of Louisville.

After the race, the Major was lucky enough to enjoy more than one of the Hot Brown sandwiches the other fellows in the press box had gone on about. The open-faced turkey sandwich with bacon, two types of cheese, and a delicate white sauce on toasted bread had been just what the Major needed to get him through his long train ride to Cincinnati. He was thankful to travel at night as the peaceful train car allowed him some time to regroup mentally and switch from horses back to baseball. The Kentucky Derby had been everything he thought it would be, loving every minute of his first run for the roses.

Kiddie could hear Iris calling her name, but she refused to answer. She was sitting on the floor in the middle of her childhood bedroom surrounded by a variety of memories, all expected to be packed into boxes. Kiddie's face was red, her eyes swollen from crying. She quickly wiped tears away as Iris burst into her bedroom.

"Kiddie! I've been calling you! Why didn't you answer?" Iris asked crossly.

Seeing Kiddie's face, she quickly relented and went to sit with her on the floor, hugging her from the side.

"Kiddie, it's going to be ok, I promise! It's the end of an era, but that doesn't mean there won't be more happy times!" Even as Iris said it, she knew it sounded hollow.

It had been only three weeks since that dreadful Sunday family dinner after Kiddie's birthday, that Kiddie and Iris's parents had announced that their house was sold and they were moving to Hollywood. Kiddie and Iris had been stunned and even more appalled to learn their brother Freddy would be moving with them. Apparently her father planned on doing plastic surgery for Hollywood's starlets and Freddy wanted to try his luck in the film industry.

Kiddie and Iris had not known what to say and finally Bernie had chimed in with a lame "congratulations." After taking some time to absorb the news, Iris asked questions, demanding her answers. Where would they live? When would they see them again? Do you know how far away California is?! She had all but screamed the last part before pushing her chair back and leaving the table. Kiddie had sat silently, mindlessly going through the motions of eating her dinner, wishing more than anything the Major was there with her. She was torn between wanting to share in their excitement for such a big, new chapter, yet she completely agreed with Iris and her concerning questions.

After dinner Kiddie had gone to find Iris crying her eyes out in her old room. Kiddie had laid in bed with her like they had so many times growing up, sharing secrets, life ambitions, and stories about boys. Eventually their mother came to find them and inserted herself between the two of them, their heads in her lap, while she stroked their hair. She told them it would be okay, that it wasn't forever, just something they needed to do right now. Iris had not been convinced and demanded again to know when would they see them again? Would they come home for Thanksgiving? For Christmas? What if something happened to one of them? Kiddie could only imagine the train ride to California had to be a good 5-6 day trip and she could not imagine being that far from her family. Their mother tried to reassure them they would be fine, they were both grown women with families of their own now, but they were not convinced.

Freddy and Bernie both offered to drive Kiddie home later, but Kiddie wasn't speaking to Freddy just yet and she didn't want Bernie to face the awkward silence of not knowing what to say. In the end she hugged both her parents telling them she loved them and climbed into a cab by herself. She sat in the back seat, tears streaming down her face, wishing more than anything the Major was coming home soon. He had left just yesterday for Chicago and would be gone for a good three weeks, on the road with the Giants.

Kiddie had not wanted to tell the Major over the phone the bomb her family had dropped on her and Iris, but in the end he could hear something was wrong in her voice and demanded she tell him. Kiddie had barely been able to get the words out, before losing her composure. The Major was equally stunned by the news, and worried how Kiddie would fare through this without him there. He called her every day and tried not to worry when she didn't answer, hopeful she was staying busy.

Kiddie had cancelled her appointments with Brownie for a couple of days, apologetic but telling him she was not feeling well, wondering how long it would be before her eyes lost their red, puffy look from all her crying jags.

Iris came over one afternoon and they reminisced, going through a variety of emotions together from disbelief to anger to sadness to finally resignation. It had taken several hours and glasses of wine for them to work through it, but in the end they agreed to wish their parents and Freddy well. When Iris left, Kiddie had laid on the couch, feeling more alone than she ever had in her twenty three years. Iris had a family and between Lelo, Bernie, and Bernie's mother, there was almost always someone in the house with her. The same was not true for Kiddie, and she felt her feelings of betrayal start all over again. In her head she knew she was a strong woman and she would be fine, but in her heart she was sad and needed a day before she could move on.

Now, a few weeks later, today was the day to clean out her bedroom, choose any piece of furniture she would love to have, and say goodbye to the house. Tomorrow her parents would load the car and start driving for California. She worried about them making the trip, but was thankful that Freddy would be there to help when needed. While Iris had a big house to fill, Kiddie and the Major had only their two bedroom apartment. Kiddie had asked if she could have the dining room buffet, thinking that would be a nice addition to their modest dining room. Her mother had a pile of things to give away and/or trash and reluctantly Kiddie added things to her piles. She gave herself two boxes to pack, knowing they would fit into the spare bedroom closet. Kiddie was grateful when the Major agreed to throw out his college bed and replace it with Kiddie's beautiful bedroom furniture. Freddy had found a truck to borrow and in a few hours, he and the Major would be moving the furniture to their apartment.

After it was all said and mostly done, they would have one last Sunday family dinner together. Cook went out of her way to fix everyone's favorites, but no one had much of an appetite. Kiddie's mother asked Cook to join them for dinner, but she refused saying today was not the day to start. The Major did his best to support Kiddie and her family during this difficult time for all of them. He had grown close to Kiddie's family over the years, and felt a sadness of his own.

After they got home that night the Major had watched Kiddie worriedly as she wandered around the apartment looking at all the new pieces they had acquired. When she finally went to bed, he held her while she cried into his shoulder, her sadness almost more than he could bear. He hated to leave her in the morning and tried to talk Kiddie into joining him in Boston for the few days he would be gone. She was stoic as she kissed him good-bye early in the morning, assuring him she would be fine.

Kiddie kept herself busy cleaning like she had never done before. She washed every linen in the house, dusted every piece of furniture, and moved dishes around putting her most cherished items in the family buffet they moved just yesterday. By late afternoon she had exhausted herself and decided to treat herself to a glass of wine and a piece of carrot cake Cook sent home with them. When the Major called he was relieved to hear she sounded more like herself as she told him about her productive day. She and Iris had made plans to have lunch and see a movie together the next day and then the Major would be home from Boston, the Giants having games at home until after the Fourth of July.

As planned Kiddie and Iris had lunch together the next day before going to the movie theater to see *The Great Gatsby*. Kiddie had read the book when F. Scott Fitzgerald released it, and was curious to see which one she liked better. The movie had been released a couple of months ago, and Kiddie and Iris were lucky it was still even in theaters. Iris told Kiddie over lunch how Scott and Zelda dismissed the movie saying it did not do his book justice. This piqued Kiddie's interest even more as they bought their tickets and headed into the dark theater. The movie was full of glitz and glamour from the beginning as only it could be, but in the end, was a testament that life can catch you by surprise and leave you crying like a baby. Kiddie kept herself in control, paying no attention to Iris's sniffles here and there.

After the movie they decided to go to Club Fronton and enjoy dinner and their favorite cocktails. Waiting for their cocktails, Iris reminisced about bringing their mother there last Christmas after a show and how much fun it had been.

Seeing Iris's look of dismay Kiddie added, "We will need to bring her here again when they come home for Christmas, won't we Iris!"

Iris smiled gratefully, tapping Kiddie's glass with her own before agreeing, "I'll drink to that Kiddie!"

June finally gave way to July as Kiddie and the Major did their usual baseball season routines. The Major would be home for a while, reporting on the Giant's wins and losses for the afternoon and then heading out for a late dinner and drinks with Kiddie after he finished writing his story. When the Major was gone, Kiddie would often take a cab over the bridge to Brooklyn to have lunch with Iris or recruit her to go shopping or see a show with her. Kiddie went out on the town when she could, tagging along with Iris and often Bernie, reluctant to be home alone. Kiddie and Iris could turn their fair share of heads wherever they were. Other times she would put on her big girl pants, finding ways to entertain herself at home. Kiddie always started her day with a brisk walk, the routine keeping her negative space to a minimum inside her head. On those nights Kiddie was home alone, it was hard pouring wine for one at the apartment, and Kiddie worried she often indulged more than she should.

Although Kiddie found herself going through the motions at times, Kiddie did her best to stay busy and productive. She missed her parents and Freddy too, but was relieved they made it in one piece and were adjusting well to their new life. For now they were living in a hotel, enjoying the sunshine and learning their way around Hollywood. Somehow Kiddie's mother had met and been hired by the famous actress Marion Davies and was currently her executive assistant. Kiddie talked with her mother on the phone often and could hear in her voice she was enjoying the new challenge. She missed her mother, but knew her mother deserved a new chapter more than anyone.

It was a muggy day in July, the Major once again in St. Louis, when he received news that starting immediately, he would be writing a daily column for the *Journal*. The Major was both startled and flattered to hear the news, and he immediately set about choosing a name that would intrigue readers enough to check out what he typed up on a daily basis. He recruited opinions from some of the other writers he traveled the baseball circuit with as well as from Kiddie. He had debated on waiting to tell her in person, knowing he would be home in a week, but in the end he could not contain his nervous excitement enough to not tell her. It was after a particularly grueling loss against the Cardinals, 1-6, that the Major finally got to spend some time on the phone with Kiddie.

"Kiddie I have big news! I've been assigned to write a daily column for the *Journal* starting as soon as possible! Can you believe it?" The Major shared with Kiddie, trying to play it cool, but failing miserably.

Kiddie was stunned, but was quick to congratulate the Major. "Major, that's wonderful news! Of course I can believe it given how good you are at writing your stories! What is your first story going to be about?"

The Major was taken aback having not even thought about his content yet. For just a moment he wondered if he really was the right man for the job, quickly reaching out to Kiddie for the support he needed.

"Kiddie I haven't even thought about that yet. I'm still trying to figure out what to call my column. Any ideas my love?"

"Hmm, it needs to be edgy, but with some grit too. How about "Corum's Capers?" No that's too juvenile. How about "Sports According to Corum?" Major that is going to be a tough call! What do the boys say? They're writers, they can help you out!" Kiddie announced.

"You're right, they were eager to share their ideas. Which one do you like better, Kiddie? "According to Corum" or "Take If From Me?" As the Major said them out loud, he wondered if both of them missed the mark, but was eager to hear what Kiddie thought.

Kiddie wanted to support her husband and told him what she thought he wanted to hear. "Major I think it's important to have your name in there, so "According to Corum" sounds better." It was close to something Kiddie suggested herself, and she did think it should include his name.

That night, as Kiddie shared the big news over dinner and drinks with Iris and Bernie, she tried to ignore the small warning bell going off in her head. Laying in bed later, she finally let her mind explore the possibility this could be more time away from her, more time on the job. Kiddie was proud of the Major, but worried how it would work out for their relationship.

The Major had his first column in the *Journal* the day before his birthday. It turned out he had little say in the column's title as all the ideas he had submitted were dismissed and traded for simply "Sports." The Major wasn't impressed, but went with it having no choice in the matter. The Major was further taken aback when his sports editor decided he wanted to change the Major's name from M.W. to simply Bill. The Major was still trying to decide how he felt about it all when he got home to Kiddie.

Kiddie greeted the Major at the door looking divine and dressed for dinner in an emerald green dress of satin. The Major told her his first column would be in today's paper so she was prepared for them to go out to dinner and celebrate. Seeing the Major's face though, Kiddie paused her exuberant welcome home and asked the Major what was wrong. Kiddie heard the Giants had been shut out by the Pittsburgh Pirates, 0-6, but had assumed the prestige of his first column would override the loss.

"Major, what's wrong? Did something happen to your column?"

"My first column is in the books Kiddie and goes by the name of "Sports!" I'm not sure we could be any less obvious if we tried. But I'm here to do as I'm told, right my love?" The Major came to her and kissed her on the cheek, clearly preoccupied.

"Major I'm sorry! Are you that disappointed?" Kiddie asked.

"Actually Kiddie, it was something else that happened, that I'm not sure how I feel about it. I got my own initials, M.W. changed to Bill today. Mr. Farnsworth would like me to sign my name as Bill Corum from now on to all my work! Who changes another man's name Kiddie?"

Kiddie was surprised by this news and wasn't sure what to say or do to help the Major feel better.

"That seems a little presumptuous to me Major! What did you say?" Kiddie asked.

"That's just it Kiddie, I was so stunned I didn't really say anything. I didn't ask why, I didn't protest the change, hell I might have even said thank you sir! Is that not the craziest thing Kiddie?" the Major turned to Kiddie, his face telling her he needed her reassurance. She had never seen the Major like this before, and she wished she could get her hands on Mr. Farnsworth and share an opinion of her own with him. For now she focused on her husband.

Kiddie went to stand in front of the Major, her hands on his arms. "Major, do you trust Mr. Farnsworth? Does he know what he's doing?" Kiddie asked earnestly.

The Major looked into Kiddie's face and thought about what she was asking. He answered her slowly, "Yes Kiddie I trust him. He's one of the best at what he does for sure."

Kiddie smiled reassuringly, "Then Major you have to trust in his decisions and assume he's watching out for you and your career writing sports. Ultimately your success is his success. He obviously believes in you or he wouldn't have given you the daily column in the first place."

The Major took Kiddie's face in both his hands and kissed her on the forehead. "Smart and beautiful! Kiddie my love, you're absolutely right! Bill it is, one fine writer for the daily column called 'Sports!'"

Kiddie laughed, happy to see the Major get back to himself. "Shall we go to dinner? Start at The Plaza and work our way around Manhattan?" he asked, extending his arm to her.

Kiddie took the Major's arm, giving a little curtsey. "Why I would be delighted to join you Major! It's time to announce to New York you've arrived, a soon to be sports legend in your own right!"

It was the Major's turn to laugh and he was happy to escort Kiddie out into the warm summer night, the sun just starting to set. He was thankful to have Kiddie's support and that she had found just the right thing to say to make him feel better. He could only hope she was right, that he really was on his way to something big, even if he was signing his name as Bill.

After dinner at The Plaza, Kiddie and the Major met friends and family at Club Fronton. The Major was on a roll for sure as he celebrated his new column and his birthday tomorrow. Lady luck had smiled on him, giving him his birthday off, the Giants having no game for him to cover. After they said their farewells to their lively group, they headed to The Tavern, the Major's favorite place to get a drink. Kiddie didn't usually join him here, but tonight was special and she was out until he was ready to go home. When the bartender realized it was his birthday, he was happy to pour a round of drinks on the house. The Major was all smiles, feeling grateful for so much love and the bourbon in his glass.

Eventually the Major was ready to go home and Kiddie decided maybe a cab would be safer at two in the morning. Kiddie got the Major into bed thinking he would pass out quickly, but the Major had been watching her all night, having his own plans once Kiddie was out of her dress. As Kiddie crawled into bed and reached up to kiss the Major goodnight, she felt him pull her back.

"I believe you owe this birthday boy more than that Mrs. Corum." he said into her ear.

Kiddie shivered as his breath tickled her ear. "Are you sure the birthday boy is up for that?" she asked playfully. "I thought at your age, all that bourbon would be all you could handle!"

Hearing that the Major pulled Kiddie even closer to him and growled, "Just for that, you can add an extra happy to my birthday!"

Even though he would always be the Major to her, Kiddie laughed and said suggestively, "Whatever makes you happy Bill, whatever makes you happy."

The Major was drunk, but not so much as to not be able to appreciate Kiddie's banter. Hearing her say Bill in that way, he decided that name would suit him just fine afterall.

It was late August, almost their anniversary and the Major was finally home to stay for a while, both of them looking forward to going out tonight. Kiddie had a quick job to do with Brownie this morning and then her day was free. She had learned only a few days ago from Edna that she would be the September cover for *RedBook* and she was excited to tell the Major over dinner tonight.

The Major came to stand behind her in the bathroom as she added lipstick to finish her look. She met the Major's eyes in the mirror and smiled.

"Kiddie, the Giants will be in a series with the Robins this weekend and I thought I would see if you and Iris and Bernie would like to be my guests for tomorrow's game? Then we could all go out to dinner. How does that sound my love?"

"That sounds wonderful Major! I'll check in with them today and see if they're up for the game tomorrow. As for tonight, what would you like to do?" Kiddie asked, turning to the Major and wrapping her arms around him.

"Tonight Kiddie I would love to have dinner with you wherever you want. You choose!" the Major said.

"It's a beautiful night for The Cascades Major! Does that work for you?" Kiddie asked.

"Of course and over dinner we can discuss our anniversary plans!" the Major added, "I have no games after this series until the Giants play the Braves here at The Polo Grounds."

Kiddie was happy to hear this news. The Major walked her to the door and stood facing her, ready to see her off to her job with Brownie.

"That is excellent news Major! I'm happy you're home!" Kiddie said before reaching up to kiss him on the cheek. The Major brought Kiddie back to him and kissed her on the lips before saying, "I'm happy to be home Kiddie!"

I t was getting late and Kiddie was beginning to wonder where the Major was. Growing worried and impatient, Kiddie poured herself a glass of wine.

She had been dressed for dinner an hour ago, thinking the Major would be home much sooner. She worried he was out with the boys, which would be a relief and annoyance at the same time. She went to the window to see if she could see him coming. She was reminded of that January day when she had stood at the window, waiting for him to come home in a blizzard. Kiddie took her glass of wine and sat on the couch to flip through her *Vogue* magazine for the hundredth time.

Not able to focus, she threw the magazine on the couch, and went to the bathroom to check herself in the mirror yet again. Her short dark curls contrasted nicely with the light blue dress she was wearing. Normally the blue would make her brown eyes dance, but tonight they accentuated her mood, her stormy irritation evident. Her pearls swung forward as Kiddie leaned into the mirror to add more lipstick, a shade deeper than pink, but just short of red.

Hearing the door open and close, Kiddie quickly closed her lipstick and went to see the Major. As soon as she saw him she could tell the Major had been out drinking. Before she could say anything, he rushed to defend himself as he went to the couch to take off his shoes.

"Kiddie, my love, I got a call I couldn't refuse! My buddy was at The Tavern and guess who showed up, but Babe Ruth! I've been trying to get an interview with him since I got my daily story." The Major was making himself comfy on the couch, apparently oblivious to the fact that Kiddie was dressed for dinner. She wasn't even sure what to say to him as he pulled a pillow to him and closed his eyes.

Finding her voice, Kiddie said not so casually, "Of course it's about work! That makes sense Major, a perfectly good reason to stand your wife up for dinner after she hasn't seen you in two weeks!" Her biting words finally brought it to the Major's attention that something was amiss.

He opened his eyes and looked at Kiddie, "Oh yes, we have a dinner date! You look beautiful as usual my love. I just need to rest my eyes for a minute and I'll be right with you!"

Kiddie stood with her hands on her hips fuming. Was he serious with this? "Don't bother Major, I can take myself out to dinner!" Kiddie said icily.

She poured herself another glass of wine and sat at the kitchen table, trying to resist the urge to go and throw it on the Major. As Kiddie sat watching him sleep, his guard down, she could see the exhaustion in his face. For a split second she felt concerned for him, before she pulled herself back to highly offended. She knew all the days on the road added up for the Major and maybe a night at home would have been a more reasonable expectation. Yet still, he hadn't wasted any time drinking with the boys!

Kiddie was all dressed up and nowhere to go, her least favorite position to be in. Finishing her glass of wine she toyed with the idea of calling Iris, but decided she didn't feel like sharing the story with her. It wasn't even eight o'clock yet and Kiddie decided impulsively to head to Club Fronton on her own. At this time of night there should still be a spot at the bar and she could sit and chat with Jack and Charlie while she sipped her drink. Making a face at the Major and grabbing her purse, Kiddie locked the door behind her. Within seconds a cab pulled up to her and she gave them the address for Club Fronton in Greenwich Village.

As Kiddie predicted, there was a barstool available for her and Jack was there to greet her with a friendly smile. The bartender was happy to pour her usual cocktail for her, her French 75. Kiddie wasn't sure if it was her or the champagne, but somehow her drink tasted flat tonight.

"Hey Kiddie! Is the Major meeting you here later? Or are Iris and Bernie on their way?" Jack asked casually, making conversation.

Kiddie played with her pearls, trying to be flip and yet shut the conversation down too. "I'm flying solo for now Jack, but we'll see who shows up!"

Jack had talked to a lot of women at his bar over the years and he knew when to leave well enough alone. He switched gears thinking sports would be safe. "So how about those Giants? Does the Major think they'll make it to the World Series this year?" he asked.

Kiddie mumbled into her drink, "I'm sorry, I don't have a clue." before downing her drink and signaling for another. Jack looked at

Kiddie curiously, certain something was amiss, before taking drinks out to a table.

Kiddie spent a good part of an hour staring into her drink, making small talk only when someone required it of her. She was just thinking she should go home when a fresh drink was placed in front of her.

"Compliments of the gentleman at the table over there." the bartender announced, pointing with his head in the direction of her admirer. For a moment Kiddie sat frozen, trying to decide how to play this. In the end Jack made the decision for her, picking up the drink and taking it over to his table. She could hear him say in no uncertain terms, "Mrs. Corum is not interested."

Kiddie watched the exchange as discreetly as possible, recognizing the man as someone who had tried to play this game before. She was grateful to Jack for stepping in and decided it was definitely time to go home. She signaled her bartender she was ready to pay her tab, and tried not to look like the loneliness she felt. She jumped just slightly when someone touched her on the back, bringing her out of her reverie.

"I'm sorry to startle you, miss. Do you mind if I sit here?" he asked casually.

Kiddie glanced at him briefly before answering, "It's a free country, do what you want."

He signaled the bartender for a drink and sat down beside Kiddie. Noticing her drink was all but finished, he added, "And another drink for the lady on me."

Kiddie said back icily, "I'm buying my own drinks tonight, thank you!"

He seemed undeterred by her attitude and persisted in starting a conversation. "I'm surprised to see such a beautiful young woman sitting here alone." he observed.

Kiddie answered back, "Well, when people let you down, it's good to know how to take care of yourself. I'm getting pretty good at it actually."

Jack stood watching this exchange from the side, not sure if he should interfere or not. He could see Kiddie was struggling emotionally, yet she was handling herself at the same time.

He said to Kiddie softly, leaning into her just slightly. "I bet the idiot who let you down, is very sorry and regrets it ever happened."

Kiddie sat for a minute, taking it in, deciding she was tired of this and it really was time to go home.

"I wouldn't know." Kiddie said as she left her money on the bar for her drinks. She paused to look him in the face when he took her by the elbow, escorting her out.

"I can get you a cab, it's the least I can do. Do you mind if I share it with you?" he asked.

Kiddie gave a brief nod to him, too tired to have the energy to debate the sensibility in that.

They sat in silence, neither of them knowing what to say. When they arrived at Kiddie's door, he jumped out to open her door for her before paying the cab driver.

As Kiddie went inside she tried to head straight for the bedroom, but he was quick to deter her, taking her arm and turning her around to face him.

"Kiddie we need to talk! I'm so sorry I stood you up tonight! I have no excuse you will want to hear and you deserved better than that! Can you please forgive me?"

Kiddie was trying to hold onto her anger, but in the end they both knew he had hurt her deeply as she fought to hold back tears.

Kiddie stood there not sure what to do next. Seeing her hesitation, the Major went to put his arms around her, pulling her into him. "Kiddie I'm so sorry I let you down like that. I promise I'll make it up to you."

Kiddie let herself be held, wanting to stay mad, but needing to understand how that had happened to begin with. "What happened Major?"

The Major sighed and led Kiddie to the couch. "Kiddie I couldn't pass up the opportunity to meet with Babe Ruth today. I didn't expect it to take that long or for us to drink so much."

When Kiddie sat in silence, the Major continued. "I'm sure this seems silly to you, but writing this daily column is a lot of pressure. It can't just be did the Giants win or lose, but sports in general. Every single day I need a story and I'm out there trying to find one. My boss gave me a lot more credit than I deserve and I don't want to let anyone down, especially you. I need my stories to be good, really good every single day and it's hard." the Major finished lamely.

Kiddie sat for a minute thinking about what he was saying. "I get that Major, but you need to know your boss is no fool and he knows you're more than capable of doing your job and doing it well. Every single day." Kiddie added.

The Major pulled Kiddie to him and sat back on the couch. "Kiddie what would I do without you? It means everything to know how much you believe in me, but I worry too, Kiddie, trying to balance my stories with our relationship. I know it's a lot to ask of you." the Major was leaving it all out there and Kiddie felt herself start to tear up again.

There it was, her number one worry always. How long could the Major balance his demanding schedule with a meaningful relationship with Kiddie. It both scared her and made her feel better to hear him say it too. The Major was never going to have the forty hour work week that Henry Ford was currently promoting. His job would always be ongoing, right around the corner, not just what he did, but who he was. But still, Kiddie loved the Major and she knew he loved her. They would find a way to make it work.

"Major we just need to work that much harder to balance us with your busy schedule. Just don't ever stand me up like that again!" Kiddie added.

The Major turned Kiddie's face to look at him. "I promise Kiddie, I love you and I always want to do everything in my power to make you happy."

Kiddie laid her head on the Major's shoulder and said, "You better Major, because I'm holding you to it."

K iddie and the Major were celebrating their four year anniversary, dressed to the nines and ready to head out on the town. They spent the day together, the Major even taking Kiddie shopping for a new dress for tonight. She settled on a midi length white satin gown with a ruched bow cinched perfectly on her hip. The Major himself was sporting a black suit complete with a bow tie. He refused to tell her where they were going, only promising it would be a night to remember. Kiddie trusted him as the man always delivered a good time.

Kiddie sat beside the Major, holding his hand, excited to see where this night would take them. The street signs eventually became less familiar as she craned her neck to see where they were, until she suddenly realized they were in Harlem. Kiddie turned to look at the Major, who was watching her, enjoying first her anticipation and then recognition. There was no way to ignore the bright lights, the plethora of cabs dropping couples at the door, the feel of glitz and glamour in the air.

Seeing Kiddie's look of anticipation, the Major laughed and then kissed the palm of her hand. "Happy anniversary my love!"

Kiddie and the Major arrived just after nine o'clock, the Major paying the cab driver before escorting Kiddie inside. She took it all in as they walked in, relishing in the elegance and glamour down to the most minute detail. Kiddie could feel it was going to be a special night and turned to smile at the Major, squeezing his hand in anticipation. Kiddie had heard stories of the clubs in Harlem, well known for their talented jazz bands and swinging dance floors full of happy couples.

Kiddie and the Major were happy to find champagne flowed freely, their waiters dressed in red tuxedos more than happy to serve them. They spoiled themselves with caviar as an appetizer and later ordered venison steaks for dinner. The music was continuous as two bands were lined up for the evening and Kiddie was delighted when the Major took her hand to lead her to the dance floor. As the music played, Kiddie was happy to be in his arms while he moved her around the floor.

Having danced and dined, they were ready when the show started after midnight, when tables had been cleared and coupe glasses sat full of bubbles. The club was well known for having a plethora of high caliber musicians play, swinging between jazz and blues greats. Tonight Kiddie and the Major enjoyed the stylistic sounds of Fletcher Henderson and his jazz band as he sat at his piano in his bow tie and tails. Kiddie knew Mr. Hernderson was known for working with some talented artists including Bessie Smith, Nina Simone, and Louis Armstrong.

It was in the wee hours of the morning that Kiddie and the Major finally made it home as once again the Major delivered a memorable anniversary. As the Major came out of his bow tie and suit, he watched with his own anticipation as Kiddie first released the big bow on her hip, then unhooked the dress wrapped around her slim torso, before stepping out of her dress and into bed, ready for the perfect ending to their celebration of four years of marriage.

It was October and the World Series took center stage for the Major as his beloved St. Louis Cardinals were in the series against the New York Yankees. The Major had been back and forth, watching the games first in St. Louis before moving back to New York before back again to St. Louis. Today was the final game in the series, each team boasting three wins so far. The Major sat with thirty-eight thousand fans, holding his breath to see who would come out on top, winners of the World Series. The Cardinals managed to secure three runs, all in the fourth inning, while the Yankees had only two runs under their belt. Both teams were getting hits in, but could not complete the deal. In a nail biting last inning, the Cardinals held their breath as the Yankees were unable to secure any more runs and the Cardinals became World Series Champs for the first time in franchise history. The Major was overjoyed, sure that Uncle Crutch had been watching too, and may have even had something to do with their win. Writing for a New York paper, the Major did his best to console the Yankee fans and his friend, Babe Ruth writing "there's always next season!"

Kiddie put the finishing touches on her makeup, expecting the Major home any minute. It was New Year's Eve and Kiddie and the Major were trying something new to ring in 1927, having invited people over tonight.

Kiddie stood for a minute to check herself one last time in the mirror. Kiddie and Iris had been practicing their finger curls and Kiddie thought her dark wavy hair complimented her silk emerald column dress with a sweetheart neckline perfectly. She wore more makeup than usual tonight, donning a smokey eye and painting her lips to look like Clara Bow's. Kiddie's pale skin only highlighted her eyes and lips, and she decided this was a good look to ring in the new year with.

The apartment glowed and Kiddie hoped her guests would enjoy her efforts. The buffet sparkled with candlelight while dishes of olives, mixed nuts, and deviled eggs sat in between, just as it had in her family home on many a New Year's Eve. Kiddie had covered their table with a white linen tablecloth, added more candles and platters of cheeses, baked ham, and rolls from the nearby bakery. She was most proud of her chocolate icebox cake, although truth be told, Cook had been kind enough to come over and help her make it. There was champagne in the icebox and Gin Rickey's waiting to be made, the drink recently made popular by Scott Fitzgerald's *Great Gatsby*.

It had been the Major's idea to host the party as they worked to create new versions of holiday traditions. Her parents and Freddy made the long trip back to New York for Christmas, but it was different going to Iris's house to celebrate. It was better than Kiddie anticipated, but different just the same. Cook had been kind enough to come and cook with Kiddie and Iris the day before they arrived, so they could surprise their mother with all the family holiday favorites. It had been hard letting them leave the day after Christmas, not knowing when they would be home again. A few days later, the Major suggested that they host a party for New Year's Eve, hoping it would give Kiddie something else to think about besides missing her family. At first Kiddie had resisted, but with Iris's encouragement decided it could be fun. Together she and Iris planned the menu, keeping in mind Kiddie's culinary limitations.

Now as Kiddie double-checked everything, she was relieved to see the Major finally home. She knew better than anyone the paper never takes a day off, and made a point not to protest when the Major had to go into the office to write his last sports story for the year. Kiddie could see him taking in everything around the apartment, his eyes finally coming to rest on her. He gave a low whistle as he looked her over from head to toe.

"Kiddie, my love, you look stunning! And the apartment couldn't look better or be more inviting if you tried." The Major noticed Kiddie had everything discreetly set up for the Gin Ricky's, the soda water, limes, gin and simple syrup ready to go.

Kiddie went to kiss the Major on the cheek. "Thank you Major for suggesting this party tonight. It's been a fun distraction and no matter who shows up tonight, I'm happy to start a new year with you."

The Major went to the icebox to pull out a bottle of champagne. Kiddie gave a little screech as the cork popped loudly, then went to the Major as he handed her a glass of the bubbly.

"Happy New Year, Kiddie. It's been a helluva year for sure, but I wouldn't do it with anyone other than you." The Major pulled her close with his free hand and kissed her long and deep.

Kiddie smiled into the Major's face. "I agree Major, for better or worse, being stuck with you is the only thing that works for me. I love you Major."

She was reaching up for another kiss when the doorbell rang. Kiddie went to welcome their first guests in and get their New Year's celebration underway, as the Major went to make the first batch of Gin Ricky's. Kiddie had to agree, it had been a helluva year and she wondered what would be ahead for them in the new year, knowing only time would tell. Kiddie was okay with that, because time was something she had plenty of.

CHAPTER EIGHT

=1927=

"NEVER LET THE FEAR OF STRIKING OUT KEEP
YOU FROM PLAYING THE GAME."
—BABE RUTH

K iddie flipped back over to her other side for the hundredth time, annoyed she couldn't sleep when she felt so tired an hour ago. It was midnight and not that late, and she was expecting the Major to be out for another couple of hours. Kiddie finally hauled herself out of bed to go find a snack. She padded out to the kitchen in her socks and robe, opening the icebox to pull out what was left of the icebox cake from New Year's Eve. She toyed with having a glass of wine, but in the end decided she was craving a glass of milk. Kiddie left the lights off, a candle lighting the small apartment, making it feel warm and cozy in it's glow. As Kiddie sat enjoying her milk and cake at the table, her thoughts continued to wander around just as they had when she lay in bed, tossing and turning.

Kiddie was thankful her mother had finally called her a few days ago, their journey back to California complete. She found it a little depressing to wonder when she would see them again. She couldn't imagine suffering through the long five day train ride from New York to California. Then again, it's not like she had a lot on her plate at the moment and if she stayed long enough, it might be worth the ride.

She thought about their New Year's Eve party, not even a week ago, happy that it had been a good time for everyone who showed up. There had been a good mix of friends for both Kiddie and the Major and of course, Iris and Bernie. They had brought in the new year over snacks and ham sandwiches, Gin Rickeys and champagne, music and dancing. Kiddie smiled thinking of how the Major had saved the last dance for her, long after midnight when the apartment was just theirs again. It wasn't the same as all the New Year's celebrations with her family over the years, but it had been good, even better than Kiddie anticipated.

Kiddie sighed trying to resist another piece of cake, when she jumped suddenly hearing someone at the door. For a moment she sat frozen, hoping it was the Major. He came into the apartment in a blast of cold air and surprisingly, snow. He had his own startled expression as he realized Kiddie was sitting at the table, her face glowing in the candlelight.

Recovering faster than Kiddie he said, "Kiddie, my love, why are you up?"

Taking her plate and glass to the sink she answered, "I couldn't sleep Major and this cake was calling my name, so I decided I might as well get up. It's not like I have anywhere to be tomorrow."

The Major came to stand beside her, his hand on her back, kissing her cheek before pausing her busy hands, "Kiddie before you get that put away, I would love to have a piece."

Kiddie smiled, happy to get the Major a fork and plate topped off with a generous piece of cake. They both sat down to the table, the candle between them. Kiddie watched as the Major enjoyed his cake, happy to see him home so early, early for him anyway.

The Major looked up from his cake, returning Kiddie's gaze. "Would there be any ham left by any chance Kiddie?"

Kiddie laughed and went to the ice box to pull out leftover ham, olives, and deviled eggs, bringing it all over to the Major.

Kiddie tilted her head at the Major thoughtfully. "Major why are you home so early?"

The Major paused his fork, smiling at Kiddie, "Well my love, it's cold enough out there you could milk a cow for ice cream, and I decided to hell with that when I've got a beautiful wife at home keeping my bed warm. So here I am."

Kiddie laughed at his expression and said, "Only I'm not in bed. Sorry about that Major."

"No worries Kiddie. I'm happy to sit here with you in the candle-light, snacking and talking. By the way, did you ever go ice skating when you were a kid? Some of the boys were talking about how ice skating is big in New York City and it made me wonder."

Kiddie arched an eyebrow at the Major. "Really? That must be the real reason you're home if that's the best conversation you had tonight!"

The Major laughed as he got up to put his plate in the sink and all the food back in the icebox. Then he reached for a bottle of wine, pour-ing each of them a glass before rejoining Kiddie at the table.

"With all those ponds you have, didn't everyone ice skate when you were a kid Major?" Kiddie asked curiously.

"Actually, you're right Kiddie. I grew up playing ice hockey with the boys on old man George's pond as soon as it froze over enough to be safe. Where did you skate?"

"Well Major, we do actually take our ice skating quite seriously around here. The boathouse at Prospect Park was always turned into a skate house during the winter. We would know the ice was ready when we would see the red flag hang at Grand Army Plaza. They would even post signs on the front of the trolleys. Iris and I could skate circles around those silly boys Freddy hung around. They were better off chas-ing stones around the ice for curling than trying to catch me and Iris!"

The Major was smiling, seeing Kiddie's face light up recalling her winter adventures from the past. He asked curiously, "Kiddie are you saying that kids would do curling on the ice? Or do you mean ice hockey?"

Kiddie took a sip of her wine. "Major I know the difference between a puck and a stone. It was fun to watch the men play, all dressed up, sliding the stones around. They even played ice baseball, even some of the girls Major!"

The Major was surprised. "Ice baseball?' Kiddie how have I never heard of this before now?"

Kiddie shrugged. "It never came up, Major."

"Kiddie I have an excellent idea! This would be a great sports story for me to write. Will you go skating with me tomorrow at Central Park? The boys were talking about how they were draining the pond before Christmas to make sure it's just the right level for freezing and skating on safely. Will you go with me Kiddie?"

The Major knew Kiddie was not a fan of winter, but maybe this would be something new for them to do together.

"But Major, we don't have any skates!" Kiddie protested, but inside her head she was already imaging the two of them on the ice, holding hands and later warming up together on the couch while sipping hot chocolate.

"Kiddie I'm sure there's a place at the park to rent them, right?"

The Major knew it was a plan when he saw Kiddie smile. "Ok Major, if this will help you write your story, the least I can do is show you what a real skater looks like." Kiddie boasted.

It was the Major's turn to raise an eyebrow at Kiddie. "Really? I hope it comes back to you better than riding a bike!" the Major teased.

For a moment Kiddie looked startled, then realized he was teasing. She picked up her wine glass and tapped it to the Majors. "Touche Major, touche!"

As agreed, the Major and Kiddie were headed to Central Park the next day, cautiously checking for signs the ice was safe. They joked together that part of them hoped the ice wasn't ready, while the other part of them hoped it was. The Major was impressed when Kiddie pulled out her old wool skating skirt, adding it over lots of layers to stay warm, adding her fur coat and a hat last to complete her ensemble. Kiddie had even called Iris to see if she wanted to join them and bring little Lelo for her first try on the ice.

It was a frigid day in New York's Central Park, but the sunshine and laughter warmed them all up. Iris and Bernie brought Lelo, her little white skates adorable under all her layers. The adults rented their skates, happy to have someone else's years of wear to break the skates in, helping them fit in all the right places. If Kiddie remembered anything about skates it was you had to tie them up tight. They all stumbled around at first, but eventually it came back to them, their skates holding them up, gliding around on the ice mostly with ease. Kiddie enjoyed seeing the Major's usual laid back self turn into a ten year old boy out on the ice. As they went to turn in their skates, the Major noticed a group of boys starting a game of ice baseball. He watched, more than interested to see how batting a ball on ice skates, let alone skating the bases, actually worked. Kiddie waited patiently with him, having already told Iris and her family good-bye.

Feeling Kiddie shiver beside him, the Major took her hand in his arm, finally ready to head for home. "Kiddie I hope you had as much fun as I did today, thank you! I can't wait to write this story, a little different for my readers, but hopefully relatable."

Kiddie smiled at the Major, "It was nice to do something different for a change Major and make some memories!" The Major nodded and squeezed Kiddie's hand, "It was Kiddie, it really was."

Kiddie and Iris sat in the dark theater, eagerly anticipating the movie they were about to see. Clara Bow was starring in "It," a silent romantic comedy, but better known as a novella written by Elinor Glyn. Kiddie had read it months ago when the story was first published in a series for *Cosmopolitan*. Kiddie was a big fan of Clara Bow, admiring her style and sassy spunk in her films. Kiddie loved that the Major liked to boast she was his "it" girl, her face lighting up magazines and advertisements for the world to see for themselves.

It was a given they would head out for dinner and drinks after the movie, expecting the boys to meet them sooner or later. You couldn't just go home after that and carry on with your own boring routines, as that would be too disappointing, even on a good day. After the movie, they headed out to Puncheon, the new Club Fronton. It was a perfect night to be out as the girls were already dressed and primed for a night out on the town. Seated at their usual table, the girls sipped happily on their cocktails, chatting about the movie. Clara had worn one particular dress that really caught Kiddie's attention and they were discussing where she might find it. It had a ruffle mock turtleneck and ruffled long sleeves, two of Kiddie's favorites in her wardrobe. Growing short on possibilities, they turned their attention to what Elinor Glyn had meant when she used the word "it." In the movie, 'it' had been described as *"self-confidence and indifference as to whether you are pleasing or not, as well as something in you that gives the impression you're not cold either."* The girls both had self-confidence, but had to admit, they liked to dress to impress, although to be fair, they were indifferent as to whether you liked their look. They agreed that their indifference was part of their self-confidence and that perhaps they dressed to impress themselves and their husbands more than anyone.

Eventually the boys arrived, jumping into their discussion of what an "it" girl was. The Major was the gentleman telling the girls all they needed to do was look into a mirror to see an "it" girl.

Bernie heartily agreed, tapping his drink to the Major's, a big smile on his face. "Touche, Major, Touche!"

Kiddie leaned over to kiss the Major on the cheek with a "Thank you Major," while Iris rolled her eyes at all three of them. Before she could add her own comment, the waiter came to take their orders for dinner.

Having a fresh round of drinks on the table and dinner on the way, the Major asked Kiddie and Iris when they had heard from their folks last. The Major didn't miss Kiddie's face change as Iris jumped in, ready to share their latest news.

"Apparently Mother has been hired to be the executive assistant for Marion Davies, another famous starlet who made it from Brooklyn to Hollywood!" Iris boasted. "She said some days Marion's driver drives them all the way to Santa Monica and they spend their day working at her mansion on the beach! I told Mother she should send for me if any other positions come open!" Iris quipped.

The Major watched Kiddie focus on her cocktail, regretting he had brought them up. He quickly changed the subject much to Kiddie's relief.

"Speaking of beaches, I leave for the Giants' spring training in Sarasota in a few days. Kiddie, I hope you're planning to join me for a rendezvous again this year?" the Major asked, picking up her hand and squeezing it.

Kiddie turned her attention from her cocktail to the Major, squeezing his hand back gratefully. "Major you know I would love to see some sandy beaches for myself! Of course I'll come down!"

Sensing her sister needed a change in the conversation, Iris said lightly, "So tell us about Sarasota. I've only ever been to Daytona." Their dinner arrived and the table fell silent for a moment as they all dug into their hot food. Kiddie shared about her trip last year and they all ended up sharing some of their favorite beach stories while they ate.

Hours later, Kiddie and the Major jumped out of Bernie's car, waving goodbye and giving out one last thank you for the ride. The Major swung the door open for Kiddie, who immediately climbed out of her pumps before shedding her fur coat. Pulling Kiddie towards him, the Major gave her a hug, holding her in his embrace by the door.

"Kiddie are you alright?" the Major asked, looking into her face earnestly.

"Of course Major, why wouldn't I be?" Kiddie asked, dismissing his concern.

"How about a glass of wine before we turn in?" the Major asked as he headed to the kitchen.

Kiddie followed him, standing quietly at the table while he opened the bottle, holding her glass up for him to fill.

Carrying his glass in one hand, he took Kiddie's hand in the other and led her to the couch. "Spill Kiddie, what's on your mind?"

Kiddie took a sip of her wine before answering airly. "Nothing Clara Bow or I can't handle."

The Major kept his gaze on Kiddie, silently willing her to share her real thoughts. She finally succumbed to his silent stare. "Major, I know it sounds crazy, but who's going to watch over me? With my parents so far away and you about to start a new season, I feel so alone."

Kiddie couldn't meet the Major's eyes, embarrassed that she sounded like a whiny child at age twenty four. There were plenty of girls younger than Kiddie living by themselves in New York City, far from their homes and family. Kiddie thought about the Major and how far he was from home, but somehow it seemed different.

The Major pulled Kiddie to him, embracing her head on his shoulder with a kiss to her forehead. "I know this is hard on you Kiddie and I worry about you when I'm gone. Iris and Bernie would do anything for you and you know it. I know you miss your family, so do I, but you still have grandparents and aunts and uncles and cousins here. Reach out to them, they love you and would be there in a minute for you. And what about Dot? She must be missing Freddy."

Kiddie sighed. She knew the Major was right, and she grimaced as she felt he confirmed she did sound like a child. "I'm sorry Major, you're right, I'll be fine. I do miss my family and I always miss you when you're gone. It's a good idea to reach out to Dot, I'm sure she does miss Freddy."

The Major could feel there was more. "And?" he said in her ear.

Kiddie continued, "Major who watches over you? Riding all those trains around the country makes me worry about you too. What if something happened to you?"

"I know Kiddie, I do ride a lot of trains, but I don't even think about it. Today's trains are safer than riding in cars these days. And it won't be long now before we're flying on planes to our destinations."

The Major was matter of fact, trying to put Kiddie's worries to rest, but not wanting to dismiss them. Years ago, Kiddie had told the Major about the worst train accident in New York City, the subway train accident of 1918. The accident had happened not far from her home in Flatbush and her father had rushed to the scene to help care for the victims. While hundreds of people were injured, a hundred people had died. Iris and Kiddie had learned years later, one of them had been Bernie's father. The Major knew Kiddie remembered the accident well, feeling her community's devastation at such a tragedy so close to home, where almost everyone had known someone in the accident.

"If it makes you feel better Kiddie, I like to think that Uncle Crutch and my Grandma America are watching over me and you too my love. It's late and I'm bushed, let's go to bed."

After that last glass of wine and snuggling with the Major, Kiddie agreed it was time. Often the Major would go out later for a drink with the boys, but tonight he sensed Kiddie needed him home, beside her, his presence under the covers warming her physically and emotionally. The Major was looking forward to another season of baseball, but he had to admit it was hard to be away from home so much, for Kiddie and for him.

K iddie was thankful to see her train finally pull into the Sarasota station. She was smiling as she got off the train, quickly spotting the Major waiting for her. Magically he was beside her, taking her suitcase as she struggled to get it down the stairs. Kiddie was happy to see the Major as he pulled her into him for a big hug, before kissing her on the lips.

Kiddie watched eagerly out her cab window, taking in all the new hotels which now stood at attention, ready to embrace their weary travelers. The Major told Kiddie the Giants were staying at the Sarasota Terrace Hotel this year, and decided they should stay at the Mira Mar Hotel, a premier hotel on Palm Avenue. The white stucco building with it's red roof promised elegance as the many palm trees swayed in greeting. The apartment complex behind the hotel made the hotel seem bigger and grander than it really was. Kiddie also noticed the Mira Mar Auditorium across the street. Kiddie was most excited a sea view would be offered. She was in need of some sand and sun after the winter New York City had dumped upon them this year. Kiddie enjoyed the high ceilinged, expansive lobby full of more palm trees and abundant sunshine from the many windows, while the Major checked them in, their luggage in tow.

Before long Kiddie was all refreshed and she and the Major were headed out to dinner, to the rooftop restaurant at the Hotel Sarasota. The Major predicted that Kiddie would most likely meet John McGraw tonight, the manager of the New York Giants, as he often enjoyed the bar area after a day of baseball at Payne Park. The Major told Kiddie about Mr. McGraw being kind enough to organize a tour of the Roth Cigar Factory for all the sports writers hanging at the park.

They were quickly seated for dinner, and soon sharing a plate of pasta with a basket full of fresh bread for dinner. They were happy to enjoy their wine while listening to the Sarasota Orchestra play lively jazz tunes. They had their fair share of wine and a dance here and there, and were about to call it a night, when the orchestra started to play *Someone to Watch Over Me.* Kiddie turned to the Major, her hand outstretched. He smiled and took her to the dance floor, waltzing her around the floor, his embrace warm and comforting as her head rested on his shoulder.

When the song ended, Kiddie and the Major applauded the orchestra's efforts as they walked back to their table to collect their things. The Major leaned into Kiddie's ear to say, "It's time to make this a private party for two."

Kiddie smiled in agreement with him, taking his arm as the two of them left the restaurant. As they walked out into the night, the warm air felt refreshing and lovely. Kiddie took a deep breath as they walked back to their own hotel, the full moon outdone only by street lights here and there. After a short walk, the couple found themselves back in the privacy of their room. Kiddie went to open the balcony doors, happy to admire the moonlight on the bay. Kiddie smiled as the Major called to her, bringing her back into their bedroom, leaving the doors open behind her. She enjoyed the Major's gaze as she stepped out of her dress before crawling into bed beside the Major, grateful to be in her happy place.

The week was flying by, a perfect blend of sunshine, beach time, and outings with the Major. Kiddie was used to walking all over Central

Park and didn't mind the walk to the beach when the Major worked. She laid on the beach and read, happy to soak up the warmth of the sun and the sound of the waves hitting the beach. They had been to dinner every night, and cruised on *The Black Cat* yesterday before sunset. Kiddie was particularly looking forward to tonight as they were to be guests for a party at John and Mabel Ringling's mansion which they fondly referred to as Ca' d'Zan.

Now as the cab took them to their residence, Kiddie was thankful she had packed her green dress she had worn on New Year's Eve. She knew she looked stunning, the two of them bound to turn heads as they entered the party. The Major had met John Ringling several times and even had a hand in getting the team into his hotel for spring training. Tonight the Major greeted him cheerfully as he kissed Mabel's hand, before turning to introduce them to Kiddie. Kiddie was delighted as Mabel and John both made a fuss over her, happy to meet her after all the stories the Major had shared about her.

Leaving the Ringling's to greet their many guests, Kiddie and the Major walked around the Venetian styled home admiring the many exquisite items the couple had collected from their travels around the world. Eventually they collected a glass of champagne and wandered out under an ornate archway onto the marbled terrace overlooking the Sarasota Bay. Here they found John McGraw and to the Major's surprise, his wife Blanche. As the Major and McGraw introduced their wives, Kiddie's night got even better when Blanche recognized her from her magazine covers with *RedBook*. Leaving the two women for a moment to discuss New York's latest fashion trends, the men went to find another round of drinks.

Kiddie was happy to see the Major back with a fresh glass of champagne, as he came and put his arm around her. "Kiddie, John here is regaling me with stories of when he joined Charles Comiskey to take their teams on tour around the world.

"Oh John, you're not!" said his wife Blanche.

"What's not to share? Kiddie I was telling your Major here that in 1913 Comisky and I took our teams to Europe before finishing in Japan.

We played forty four games of which my Giants won only twenty, but Cominsky was footing the bill, so it all worked out in the end." he added with a smile.

It was the Major's turn. "And then you did it again in 1924, is that right?"

"Well we tried, but it seems like Europeans didn't take to baseball after our first trip and we ended up coming home early. Too bad you weren't assigned the Giants back then, Corum, you could have been along for the ride!" McGraw added.

The Major turned to Kiddie, "Probably best I wasn't. That's a long time to be that far from my girl Kiddie here. You would have to send me home early!"

Blanche turned to comment before Kiddie could. "Well aren't you two sweet! Better hold onto him Kiddie. Not every man is smart enough to know when he's got a good woman!"

She laughed as McGraw took her hand and kissed it. "Blanche you know I would be lost without you!"

Kiddie was saved from responding to her comment as John and Mabel came out and joined their conversation. They were quick to compliment the Ringling's on their beautiful estate and thanked them for the invite to their party tonight.

Mabel dismissed them with an "Of course, the more the merrier we always say." She then turned to Kiddie. "Kiddie the Major tells us you took art classes at Columbia. I would love to take you on a tour of our Art Museum tomorrow if you're available." She turned to Blanche and added, "And Blanche you too of course. I assume these boys will have some baseball to tend to. I can have the car pick you both up at noon to have lunch here first and then we can walk over to the museum. How does that sound ladies?"

Kiddie smiled as Mabel made an offer she assumed would not be declined. Glancing at Blanche, they both nodded in appreciation. "That would be lovely Mabel, thank you for the invite!" Kiddie said quickly.

"Speaking of cars, we better get these people home Mabel. It's getting late and some of us have work in the morning!" John announced.

"Oh poo, we have time for another glass of champagne, don't we?" Mabel asked, her gaze sweeping the group.

They all agreed heartily, and were thankful when Mabel led them to be seated at a table, the view of the bay breathtaking in the moonlight. After many glasses of champagne, Kiddie and the Major were finally back on their own balcony, enjoying their alone time before calling it a day.

"Kiddie my love, did you enjoy yourself? Do you mind going to have lunch tomorrow and seeing their museum?" the Major asked.

"It was a lovely night Major. Thank you for telling me to bring my green dress. Quite the lives those two men have led. I felt like we were kids at the grown up party and I was just trying to keep up with the conversation!" Kiddie said teasingly. "You know I love art, so I'm more than happy to go to the museum tomorrow. What I didn't know was how much you talk about me. You do miss me don't you Major?" Kiddie had come to sit on the bed beside the Major, her hand on his back as he was getting out of his fancy evening wear. He paused for a moment to turn to Kiddie.

"Kiddie did you ever doubt it? I love to talk about you. And I love that you're here." the Major added. "Now why am I the only one getting out of these fancy clothes. It's time for bed my love!"

"Yes, Major." Kiddie said happy to join him.

K iddie's train was pulling into Grand Central Station, her Sarasota visit soon to be a memory, and a good one at that. It was already dark in the city and Kiddie was happy to have Iris and Bernie meeting her at the station. As Bernie stowed her suitcase in the back of the car, Iris turned to Kiddie to ask her about her trip. Kiddie filled her in on their highlights, particularly the Ringlings, and their stunning venetian mansion and impeccable museum filled with everything from paintings to sculptures to decorative arts from around the world. Kiddie had enjoyed herself immensely during the tour, after a beautiful lunch spread they had shared out on the marbled terrace. Kiddie and the Major made the most of her last night in Sarasota, rolling their night into morning sharing a blanket, sitting snuggled together on their balcony as they watched night turn into dawn. Kiddie didn't mind at all, using her train ride home to catch up on her sleep.

Kiddie thanked Iris and Bernie for bringing her home, as he carried her suitcase into the apartment for her. Iris suddenly jumped out of the car and called to Kiddie, "Come join us for the night Kiddie! We're headed to Puncheon! You'll have plenty of time to unpack tomorrow!"

Kiddie turned to Iris in astonishment. "Iris look at me! I've just spent two days on a train. I need a hot bath and. . .well, maybe I could use a couple of French 75's tonight. But you don't want to wait for me!" The girls laughed as Bernie went to turn the car off and walked back up the stairs with Iris.

"I promise Bernie, I'll hurry!" Kiddie said as she went to her closet for a fresh dress. "And help yourself to a drink!" she added, knowing full well they would.

In less than an hour the three of them were seated at their favorite table, drinks and food in front of them. Kiddie had picked a blue dress, going for a more casual look tonight since the Major wouldn't be there. She was starving, not a fan of train food and thankful Iris had talked her into coming out knowing her icebox sat empty after she had been gone all week.

The Puncheon was hopping tonight, full of well dressed couples as well as sequinned flappers out ready to meet and mingle. The music was loud and rowdy, the drinks flowing. Kiddie was starting to miss the Major and feeling restless, decided to go to the bar to get another drink. As she stood there with the crowd waiting her turn, a man walked up and tapped her on the shoulder. With a big smile on his face, he was trying to hand her a drink.

"French 75 right?!" the stranger yelled, trying to be heard above the crowd. Kiddie recognized him from other times he had tried to deliver a drink to her, but tonight Jack was too busy to run interference for her.

"No thank you! I'm buying my own drinks tonight!" Kiddie said icily.

"Why would a gorgeous woman like you ever need to buy herself a drink?" he asked, still holding the drink out to her.

"I'm a happily married woman! Go give it to one of those flapper girls out there!" Kiddie was trying to move away from him as she talked, but he persisted in following her.

"Girls are a dime a dozen. I need a woman like you! And if you're so happily married, where's your other half?" he said with a mild sneer.

"Please go away!" Kiddie said. Having caught Jack's eye at the bar, she could see him trying to make his way over to her.

Just as Jack was about to reach her the doors burst open, sirens started going off, and cops were suddenly running around all over the place. Kiddie stood stunned not sure what to do, when the stranger grabbed her arm and led her out through a side door.

Kiddie instinctively started to struggle, "Take your hands off me! Let me go!" she said to him.

"Kiddie, it's a raid. I'm helping you! You don't want to go downtown tonight do you?!" He said, clearly expecting her to be grateful.

Kiddie started to shiver in the cool spring air, more from fear than from the temperature change. "How do you know my name? Why do you insist on this when clearly I'm not interested!" Kiddie said aggressively, trying to sound tougher than she felt.

The stranger laughed. "Kiddie you're here all the time. I've had my eye on you for years. I'm just waiting for you to dump that boyfriend of yours."

Kiddie was trying to think fast. He still had his hand on her arm, his fingers digging into her as he was trying to lead her down the alley, away from Puncheon. Outside lights were flashing everywhere, the pandemonium obvious. Kiddie thought of Iris and Bernie and wished they would come.

Kiddie was trying to pull her arm free and yelling, "Let go of me! I don't want you to touch me!" Turning to face him she gave him a mighty kick in the shin, heading back to Puncheon as he bent over, howling in pain. She stood at the door, becoming frantic when she realized it didn't open from the outside except with a key. She was about to start running when the door opened and she heard someone yelling her name.

"Kiddie! Kiddie!" Iris was calling her, Bernie right behind her. Kiddie went to Iris while Bernie took one look at the stranger and went to chase him. "Oh my god, Kiddie are you okay? Did he hurt you? Bernie was trying to get to you and then all hell broke loose! It's a raid. Kiddie, are you okay?" Iris asked, holding her at arm's length, checking her over.

Kiddie was shaking, but she was okay. She was thankful Iris and Bernie came out when they did. Iris was wrapping her coat around her, handing her purse to her, and then latching onto Kiddie's hand. Bernie was back within minutes, madder than Kiddie had ever seen him. He took both of the girls by the arm and steered them to the street away from Puncheon. He tucked both of them into the car before he said anything.

Slamming his hand on the steering wheel, he started to curse. "If I ever see that no good son of a bitch again I swear he'll be shitting glass for a week after I stuff his cocktail down his throat and don't bother to pull it out of his ass! Kiddie are you okay?"

Both of the girls sat silently, Kiddie nodding yes and mumbling "Bernie please can I go home? I want to go home."

Grimly Bernie started the car and headed to her apartment. Iris and Bernie both got out of the car to walk Kiddie up the stairs. "Kiddie you're sure you're okay? Do you want to stay with us tonight? Why don't you stay with us tonight?" Iris asked.

Kiddie had collected herself during the car ride home. It had been a fluke event and Kiddie really was fine. It wasn't the first time some guy had hit on her, but the chaos of the raid had turned it into more than it should be. She just wanted to curl up in bed and get some sleep. It had been a week since she'd been home and she was sleeping in her own bed tonight.

Kiddie went to hug Iris, "Iris, I'm fine I promise. I'll call you in the morning."

Then Kiddie went to hug Bernie. "Bernie, thank you for watching out for me. That guy is lucky you didn't get a hold of him."

The two of them stood at the car watching her go to her door. As the door swung open, she turned and gave them a final wave. "I'm fine, I promise! Goodnight! I'll talk to you tomorrow Iris! Love you both!"

She closed the door on them and then sank to the floor after she locked all her locks, well aware they were the only thing standing between her and the crazies in the world. She was determined not to cry and instead went to the phone to call the Major. She had already talked to him earlier letting him know she made it home, so she wasn't surprised when he didn't answer.

Kiddie didn't feel scared as much as all alone. The apartment was too quiet so she went to turn the radio on, grateful for the background noise. She changed out of her dress and brought blankets and her and the Major's pillows to the couch. She missed her bed, but tonight she missed the Major more. Sleeping on the couch somehow felt safer, more comforting. She lay there all covered, her arms wrapped around the Major's pillow. Kiddie finally let the tears flow as the song *"Someone to Watch Over Me"* came on the radio. Kiddie told herself it was more from exhaustion than anything else and she was entitled to a little pity party. It had been awhile since Kiddie cried herself to sleep, and for that Kiddie was thankful. Tomorrow would be a new day, and she would be just fine.

K iddie sat in the dining car of the train reading her book. The Major sat beside her watching her read, loving that she had agreed to join him on his trip to the Kentucky Derby this year. He had been on the road for a while, but had finagled his way home to accompany Kiddie to Louisville. She would head back to New York after the race while he would be meeting the team in Cincinnati, but for the next five days, she was all his. Sensing his stare, Kiddie marked her place in her book and looked up at the Major.

"What are you thinking about Major?" Kiddie asked.

"I'm thinking how happy I am you're all mine for the next couple of days my love." the Major said with a smile, picking up her hand to kiss it. "I can't wait for you to experience the Derby Kiddie!"

Kiddie smiled back at the Major. "I know Major. I'm looking forward to it too. Jack mentioned the other night, our fearless Mayor Walker is supposed to be here this year."

Watching the Major, Kiddie noticed his eyes flicker just slightly when she said Jack's name. It had been more than a month now since the raid and somehow the Major held what happened to Kiddie against Jack. She had been back to the Puncheon less than a week later, insisting to Iris it was the thing to do. Something about when a horse throws you, you have to get back on it so it knows who's boss, which was exactly how Kiddie felt. Jack had rushed over to their group, hugging Kiddie first and then Iris, clearly happy to see them. They in turn expressed concern over Puncheon surviving their raid. Jack waved it off explaining they had an intricate system set up to where it looked like they were pouring out the good stuff when actually it became well hidden within a matter of seconds. After the first round of drinks were brought to their table, Jack had pulled Kiddie aside to talk to her in private.

He had apologized profusely about what happened to her, even as Kiddie had explained he wasn't responsible for her safety, just her cocktails. He refused to let her laugh it off, spilling the beans when he said, "If anything ever happened to you not only would the Major never forgive me, I wouldn't be able to forgive myself!"

"Jack, what does this have to do with the Major?" Kiddie asked, her face serious. "You are not responsible for me. I'm a big girl and I can take care of myself."

Only then had Jack's face relaxed. "The Major said you would say that! Kiddie, the Major asked me and Charlie years ago to always watch over you when he's out of town. He knows you like to go out and you guys are like family now. It's an honor that he puts that trust in us!"

Flabbergasted, Kiddie had stirred this news around like the drink in her hand, trying to decide how to react. On one hand she did not need a babysitter bartender, she could very well take care of herself. On the other hand, it made Kiddie smile to think that in a roundabout way the Major was trying to take care of her from wherever he was. Still Kiddie wasn't about to let Jack feel responsible for her.

Before she could say anything, Jack jumped in. "Kiddie I want you to know that person isn't welcome in our establishment anymore. He's been stalking you for years and we should have put a stop to it a long time ago. I don't blame the Major for being mad."

"You talked to the Major about this? Jack you don't need to worry about me like that! I am perfectly capable of taking care of myself! I bet he's still hobbling around after that bruise I left on his shin! Please don't worry about me, or the Major." Kiddie said, her hand on his arm, looking Jack in the eye.

Jack knew he wasn't going to win this argument so he did the next best thing he could think of. "Kiddie please let the house buy you drinks tonight! It's the least we can do!" In the end Kiddie agreed, hoping it made Jack feel better about the situation.

Kiddie never had a conversation with the Major about it, feeling the moment had passed by the time he was home and she could tell him the story. Still, after her conversation with Jack, she knew the Major knew. Now seemed as good as time as any for them to hash it out.

Kiddie turned to face the Major. "Major, do you expect Jack and Charlie to be responsible for my safety when I'm at their place?" Kiddie decided to hit this head on and get straight to the point.

The Major looked down at his hands, wanting to say the right thing. "Kiddie I need to know people are watching out for you when I'm not there to do so. Jack and Charlie are two people I trust to do just that. I'm sorry if that offends you, but it's reasonable for a husband to worry about his wife."

It was Kiddie's turn to choose her words carefully. "I understand that you worry about me Major, but you can't put that on them. Like it or not, I'm a grown woman and able to take care of myself, regardless of where I am."

The Major took Kiddie's hand again and kissed it, wanting to put this behind them. "Kiddie I know you're a grown woman and very independent. "

Kiddie watched him as she asked, "I know you know about the incident the night they were raided. Are you mad at Jack? Because he was on his way over to help, but then the raid happened." Kiddie wanted to make sure he understood Jack wasn't to blame.

"I wish you would have told me about it yourself. I know it was just one of those things and I'm not mad at Jack." the Major wanted to add "any more," but he held his tongue.

"I tried calling you that night Major, but you were out. Then when you were home again, it was old news and I was fine." Kiddie said defensively.

The Major flinched when Kiddie told him he was out when she tried to call. "I'm sorry about that Kiddie and I thank god you were okay. You can't blame me for worrying about you." the Major said, squeezing her hand.

They were thirty minutes out of Louisville and the Major was ready to let it go, not wanting to start their weekend in an argument. Kiddie had never been west before and the Major wanted to make sure Kiddie had a great time, embracing the charm and horse culture that Louisville had to offer.

Kiddie relented, believing the Major was moving on. "I know, I get that Major. As soon as you're home we need to go to Puncheon and have drinks with the gang." The Major did not object, agreeing it would be good so that he could have his own conversation with Jack. It wasn't perfect, but when the Major thought about that guy putting his hands on Kiddie, he knew it was the best he could do for now.

It occurred to Kiddie one of her favorite things in the world was to be standing in a beautiful lobby of a hotel, waiting for the Major to check them in. Today they were checking into The Brown Hotel, one of the newest prominent places to stay during the Kentucky Derby. Located on the corner of Fourth Street and Broadway, the hotel did not appear to Kiddie as anything special from the outside. She was happy to discover a lavish two story lobby, where she couldn't help but admire the grace and beauty of the coffered ceilings, marble floors, and sparkling chandeliers.

Having arrived late in the day, Kiddie and the Major were quick to freshen up and leave their train look behind. They headed to the popular dinner dance the hotel was becoming famous for, where they could draw crowds of more than a thousand people a night. Kiddie chose a light pink dress with rose colored sequins and fringe.She was going all out with her flapper look tonight and even added a feathered headband to her look. Kiddie thought of Clara Bow and decided she was giving her "it" look tonight. While Kiddie always loved to turn a few heads, she mostly wanted to get the Major's attention tonight. The Major had spent the majority of the last couple of months on the road, and Kiddie was happy for their time together, even if half of it was spent on the train. The Major would start his official sports writing tomorrow, so for tonight he was all Kiddie's. The Major was looking quite dapper himself in his suit and bow tie, and with Kiddie on his arm, they headed to the ballroom where the dinner dance was hosted.

As they walked into the ballroom, Kiddie felt that sense of anticipation when she's about to experience something for the first time. The tables were crisp and inviting in their white linens, glassware sparkling in the candlelight. Bouquets of roses sat on every table, in honor of the Kentucky Derby, making it colorful and lovely. The room was arranged with tables around the dance floor, their house orchestra set up just off from the center of the dance floor. The Major had made a reservation and they were quickly seated.

Kiddie smiled at the Major as he discreetly ordered a glass of wine for each of them and assorted canapes for an appetizer from their menu. Later he was happy to order a Budweiser beer to go with his ribs while Kiddie ordered the young duckling veronique. She was impressed there were so many potato choices including sweet potatoes, but in the end she went with mashed and a side of new peas. She finished her delicious dinner with a chocolate souffle pudding. Kiddie could only hope the Major planned on dancing with her tonight, as she absolutely needed to work off some of her dinner.

The Major was happy to oblige Kiddie and they danced to several songs. At one point they literally bumped into Mr. Jimmie Walker, the mayor of New York City, dancing his wife Ally around the dance floor as well. The two men gave a nod to each other, acknowledging the other's presence, but not stopping to make small talk. Hours later, Kiddie and the Major walked back to their hotel room, hand in hand. It had been a long time since they danced that much and Kiddie was happy she made the trip with the Major. She could only wonder what tomorrow would be like as she got her first real taste of the run for the roses.

K iddie and the Major were up early and after a hearty breakfast at the Brown Hotel Coffee Shoppe, they were ready for a full day of horses and racing. Kiddie had carried on with her pink theme and today wore a light pink linen dress with a drop waist pleated skirt and white peter pan collar, and coordinating cloche hat. The weather was cool and cloudy and Kiddie was thankful she brought her coat along with her. There were thunderstorms in the forecast and Kiddie had already warned the Major she did not want to be caught in a downpour. He understood that and already had a place in mind where they could wait out any storm.

For now the rain was holding off as the Major took Kiddie around to see the horses waiting patiently in the paddock of Churchill Downs. The Major used his press pass to get them as close as possible, but the truth was there were lots of people milling around. Being around the horses took Kiddie back to her riding days in Prospect Park Stable. As a teenager, she had spent many an afternoon after school riding the three and a half mile bridle path through the park. Kiddie realized horses had been part of both their teenage years, knowing the Major had ridden horses growing up as well, even riding horses during his time in the Missouri National Guard. Clearly he still had a soft spot for them today, and after all the baseball games and several fights, Kiddie enjoyed seeing this side of the Major.

Suddenly, with but one loud clap of thunder to warn them, the rain started to pour. The Major grabbed Kiddie by the hand and ran with her under the concrete bleachers, joining lots of other horse fans. They were both wet, but not that bad and Kiddie followed the Major through the throngs of people, thankful he was holding her hand tightly. Before long he was greeted loudly by men that Kiddie assumed were also sports writers, quick to notice they had drinks in their hands.

"So this is where the real party starts!" the Major announced cheerfully.

Peering around the Major, one of them gauffed, "Bill I believe you snagged a looker along the way! How'd you get that lucky?"

"Too bad your vision is better than your writing Runyon!" The Major rallied back good naturedly. "This, my friends, is my wife Kiddie." Kiddie smiled and gave a little wave to the group in general, wondering if the Major had noticed their drinks.

"Nice to meet all of you," Kiddie said before turning to the Major and asking, "Major do these friends like you well enough to pour us one of whatever they're drinking?"

The men laughed, and the one Major had referred to as Runyon brought them each a drink, a big smile on his face. "Careful, Kiddie, we try to use this for good only, but we have been known to get carried away. I apologize in advance."

The Major held his glass up to Runyon and Kiddie, the three of them tapping their glasses with a "To the Derby!" before they each took a swig. Kiddie tasted hers gingerly, assuming it was bourbon and powerful stuff even for what she was used to drinking.

As the group stood around chatting, Kiddie noticed Mayor Walker walking up to them. "Runyon! I should have known I'd find you down here somewhere!" The two men shook hands before Runyon turned to introduce the Major to the Mayor.

"Mr. Jimmie Walker, our mayor extraordinaire, meet Bill Corum, a sports writer of equal talents, and his lovely wife, Kiddie." Mr. Runyon said, presenting the two men to each other.

"Ah yes, you have the daily sports column for *The New York Evening Journal*. I read it almost every day." the Mayor said, jumping in first.

The Major gave a modest bow, and said, "I'm an equally big fan of yours sir. With the work you've done with the garbage system and our parks, you're clearly a man with a vision to make life better for all New Yorkers."

The Major and Kiddie both knew they would often see the Mayor at Jack and Charlie's establishments over the years, but wisely kept this to themselves. As the Mayor moved on, one of the men walked over to their group. "It's time to break this party up and move it to the pit!" he said with a big smile.

"The pit? But what about the rain." Kiddie asked in concern.

"Aww that's moved on by now. These thunderstorms pop up, drop a little rain trying to dampen our day, but most definitely not our spirits. Major, shall we move on?" Runyon asked, a gleam in his eye.

Kiddie could see the Major was hesitating and she wondered why. She turned to the Major, waiting to see what he had to say.

"Kiddie the pit gets a little wild. This may be a dry state, but just like New York City, there's little policing out in the pit. We can head to our seats if you would rather?" The Major said, leaving the choice up to Kiddie.

Kiddie reached for the Major's arm, checking the time on his watch. Don't we still have two hours until race time? That's plenty of time for the pit. Major, you know I love a good party!" Kiddie said with a smile.

Runyon linked arms with the Major first and then turned to offer Kiddie his other arm. Kiddie finished her drink before she happily accepted it, and they started toward the pit, the fellows following behind with "To the pit!"

It turned out Kiddie had never seen anything like the pit before. Men and women alike dressed to the nines, were standing in small groups, stretched out on blankets, or just wandering around. There was a buzz in the air and she could quickly tell who was drinking. A band played lively jazz music, food vendors were selling hotdogs, and clearly someone, somewhere was selling alcohol. Kiddie took it all in, the pit being the biggest party she had been to since Time Square on New Year's Eve. She thanked Runyon again as he handed her and the Major another cocktail.

Kidde stood sipping her drink as the men carried on about the horses and jockeys, discussing who would be the winner for this year's run for the roses. Clearly they were all sports writers and quite a lively group of men. Suddenly the Major touched Kiddie's arm and asked her who she would bet on to be in the winner's circle. Kidde had only been half listening, taking in all the activity around her, but she still managed to come up with an answer that seemed worthy.

"Personally Major, I don't know that much about this group of horses so I'm going to trust the men who have already placed their bets. Whiskery seems to be the favorite to win, and with a name like that, what's not to love? But then again, a horse named Jock seems like a confident long shot, so why not place bets on both?" Kiddie asked as she handed her empty drink to Runyon with a smile.

The Major and Runyon were both smiling. "Kiddie I believe you have an excellent plan. Shall we go place our bets?"

The Major was holding his arm out to Kiddie who took it with a nod and a "Gentleman." to the group. Standing in line with the Major, Kiddie could see how people got caught up in the Derby. There were a lot of moving parts that kept one wondering what was next.

As if reading her mind, the Major leaned over and said in her ear, "And you haven't even seen them race yet my love." Kiddie smiled up at the Major, taking hold of his arm to confirm her enjoyment of the day.

Before long Kiddie and the Major were at their seats, although Kiddie quickly discovered very little sitting was going to take place. Kiddie felt a shiver of excitement upon hearing the bugle call the riders up and was moved watching the crowd sing my *"Old Kentucky Home"* by Stephen Foster. She watched in anticipation as the fifteen three year old horses pranced their way to the starting point. As the horses started their run, Kiddie was impressed to see Osmand take off like a shot, quickly establishing a significant lead, then delighted when Jock and Whiskery came thundering down the track eventually closing the gap. In the end Whiskery gained enough speed to overcome Osmand and win the race by a neck, Jock coming in second. The Major turned to Kiddie hugging her and announcing excitedly, "Kiddie, both of your horses won!"

They made their way to the winner's circle, the Major flashing his press badge to get them as close as possible. Kiddie felt like Whiskery knew he had done well as he stood to receive a most impressive garland of roses. After that the Major took Kiddie back to the betting tables, collecting the money from her wins. He proudly turned to Kiddie and handed it all to her, a significant amount of cash as both her horses had won. Kiddie kissed the Major on the cheek when he told her she should go buy something pretty for herself. Stuffing it into her purse she said, "Don't think I won't Major!"

Too soon Kiddie and the Major were in the hotel lobby, their bags packed, checking out, and ready to catch their trains in a few hours. The Major took Kiddie shopping after breakfast, wanting Kiddie to spend her winnings rather than travel alone with her cash. When Kiddie stopped to admire the dresses in the window of the Jenny Lind dress shop, the Major happily took Kiddie in to buy whatever dress her heart desired. She settled on a dress that was a unique shade of pale green with bubble sleeves, a flattering fitted bodice, and accordion pleated skirt. Kiddie loved how the dress looked on her. As she paid for her dress with her winnings, she asked if the shop was connected to the famed Swedish opera singer, Jenny Lind herself. Disappointingly it was a no, but they did hear the story of her visit to Louisville years ago when Miss Lind graced their small town with concerts for three nights.

Afterwards Kiddie and the Major went back to the hotel to have Hot Brown Sandwiches, Kiddie agreeing with the Major, they were a little slice of heaven for lunch. Following the Major's lead, she ordered two of them, although in the end she shoved half of the second one over to the Major to finish. Leaving their luggage behind the front desk, they went for a walk around the block, enjoying the beautiful day, knowing they would be sitting on trains soon enough. The Major had a quick eight hour trip north while Kiddie would be riding her train east for a day and a half. After Cincinnati, the Major and the team would head to Pittsburgh, then finally be home for a few weeks for the Giants to play at the Polo Grounds in New York City.

Now Kiddie sat in the dining car of the train, watching the sun set and thinking the Major was probably doing the same thing. It had been a busy couple of days and Kiddie knew she would most likely sleep well on the train tonight, before being back in New York City by early afternoon. She thought of her new Jenny Lind dress, a lovely keepsake from her first time at the Kentucky Derby and was already looking forward to when she would wear it for the Major. She had not let him see her in it, but he had agreed with the dressmaker it most definitely would look fabulous on Kiddie. He would find out soon enough and Kiddie looked forward to that, always hoping a special occasion was just around the corner.

I ris was having a flashback as she sat on Kiddie's bed helping her to go through her dresses and deciding which ones to pack. Kiddie's westbound train would be leaving Grand Central in an hour and Kiddie was trying to stay calm as she worked to get all her dresses under the zipper.

"Iris, are you sure I'm going to need all of this?" asked Kiddie doubtfully.

"Kiddie, it's Los Angeles! It's better to be prepared for anything you might need and besides, you're going to be gone for a month! I just hope you've packed enough!" Iris said helpfully.

"Ugh! This zipper! Iris come and sit on my suitcase! And then we should go. I don't want to be late for the train and not get a good spot in the dining car." Kiddie said, finally getting her bag zipped with Iris's help.

After two days of packing and many weeks of anticipation, Kiddie was finally on the train and headed west to California. The Major had suggested the idea to Kiddie when they were in Kentucky together, but she had been hesitant to go. The Major was on the road with the Giants and Kiddie was grateful to accept Iris's offer to take her to the train station. Her luggage was a beast, but very much necessary to navigate the social scene in Los Angeles. Kiddie was looking forward to seeing her parents and Freddy in just a mere four days of travel. The Major had mapped her route out for her over the phone, telling her she would go through several major cities along the way, including St. Louis. Kiddie lugged her suitcase to her assigned sleeping quarters, surprised to see she had a full bed instead of a twin. She asked the man to check it again, but he assured her she was in the right place. Maybe the Major thought she needed the extra space since she would be sleeping there for more than a couple of nights. As usual, Kiddie left the arrangements up to the Major, trusting his expertise in traveling.

As Kiddie sat at a table in the dining car, staring out the window, the scenery was mostly a blur as her mind took her elsewhere. She thought back to her birthday, almost two months ago, when the Major had surprised her with a train ticket to go to California. He had been out of town with the team, but had hidden her ticket somewhere until Kiddie's birthday had arrived and he had told her where to look. It had been almost three weeks before he was home and she could thank him properly. The Major knew Kiddie missed her family terribly, but wasn't sure if Kiddie would make the trip to visit them until the Major had left her no choice. Now here she sat, only a couple of hours into her trip. Her train had left Grand Central at 3:40 on a Monday and would arrive in LA early Friday morning. Kiddie was a little nervous about traveling so far from home alone, but she was very excited to see California for herself.

While she was busy packing, Iris had made her peanut butter and jelly sandwiches. Kiddie took one from her purse to eat now with her glass of milk and fruit plate sitting in front of her. She wasn't a big fan of train food, but knew she would have to eat something on the train sooner or later. Iris had also filled a flask for her with gin, making sure the lid was on tight before stuffing it down deep into her suitcase. As the sun went down and darkness prevailed outside her window, Kiddie decided it was time to head to her sleeping quarters and give her table up to someone else.

Sleeping on the train was Kiddie's favorite part, feeling secure with her door locked, the rhythm of the train rocking her right to sleep like a little baby. Having changed into her sleeping clothes, Kiddie pulled out her newest *RedBook* to read. She had found out about a month ago, she would be the cover for the September issue. She had been surprised when Edna asked her to pose with a golf club, but it turned out to be a fresh look *RedBook* was wanting. Kiddie loved her sporty look, grateful to Edna to trust that pose to her. It had been a year since she graced a cover, but the competition was fierce and Kiddie tried not to take it personally. She was hoping to find the magazine in California so she could share it with her family in person. It would be a month before she could show the Major, but Kiddie knew he would find a newspaper stand somewhere and see it for himself before she was home.

Kiddie would be home in a month on September 1st. She would get back late, but it was important to her to be back by then as it would be their five year anniversary. The Major would actually be home and they would go out to celebrate their anniversary and their birthdays as he had been out of town for both this year. As Kiddie closed her magazine and reached up to turn her light off, she lay in the dark thinking of all the things she had to be thankful for. Kiddie had made a resolution this year to focus on her cup half full rather than empty. Kiddie definitely missed her family and the Major when he was away, but she had learned she could be okay taking care of herself, and she was most thankful for that.

Although Kiddie had learned how to be more independent in lots of different ways, she was still very much in love with the Major. Five years ago neither one of them had realized how much time the Major's writing career would demand of him, but they continued to work to find a balance between that and their marriage. Somewhere along the way Kiddie had realized she didn't need the Major as much as she used to and she assumed that came with getting older and growing up. The Major was very good at making Kiddie feel loved, but he also loved being out schmoozing with the other writers and building relationships with the season's latest sports stars. While he loved to hang out at The Tavern with the boys, they also had their own favorites to go to such as Puncheon, The Plaza, and the Biltmore Hotel. Occasionally they would get out of their routines and see a show or go to the Palais-Royal to hear Paul Whiteman's orchestra. As Kiddie fell asleep she was happy to focus on what she had and today that was a train ticket to California. Her mother and Freddy were always telling her stories and she couldn't wait to feel the energy of LA and see the palm trees for herself. She could only hope the ride would go by quickly.

Kiddie was through the first day of her train ride, staying busy by reading, walking the train, and staring out the window when she didn't know what else to do. They would be stopping soon at Union Station in St. Louis. Kiddie thought it ironic that the Major might actually be at the station at the same time, headed north to Cincinnati for the Giants next series. The train would be stopped for thirty minutes while passengers got on and off the train depending on their itinerary. Kiddie wished she was brave enough to get off the train and see the station for herself. The Major often bragged that Grand Central had nothing on Union Station, that St. Louis could keep up with New York any day of the week. Kiddie had her doubts, but she knew the Major was a proud Missourian, even if he loved to call New York home these days. Instead she stayed at her table in the dining car, watching outside her window, part of her expecting to see the Major, even if it was more wishful thinking than a possibility.

The thirty minute stop passed by quickly and before long Kiddie was looking over the dinner menu, acknowledging her hunger pains needed to be attended to. The trouble was the menu liked to offer dishes Kiddie had eaten in some of the best restaurants, and it became a challenge for the train chefs to meet her high expectations. She realized someone was standing at her table and presuming it was her waiter, looked up to ask how difficult it would be to get just a sandwich. Instead someone was asking her if he could join her at her table.

"Excuse me miss, but could I join you for dinner tonight? The dining car seems to be quite full this evening." The man was smiling from ear to ear, clearly confident she would say yes.

Kiddie jumped up, all but knocking her chair over in her haste. "Major! What are you doing here?! You're supposed to be headed north!" Kiddie exclaimed. She jumped into the Major's arms, happy to feel his embrace and then his lips on her hair, talking into her ear.

"Surprise Kiddie! I've arranged a private party for two in our sleeping car if you care to join me?" Kiddie wasn't sure what was going on, but she was quick to desert her menu and follow the Major. She realized he was heading to her sleeping quarters, and her curiosity grew as he seemed to have a key to her little door. He opened it for her and followed her into the room, barely closing and locking the door before he pulled her to him and kissed her properly.

Coming up for air, Kiddie asked, "Major what is going on? How are you here right now?"

"Kiddie my love, I am officially on vacation as of four something this afternoon. I told my boss I haven't had a proper vacation in five years and I was way overdue for one. I'm going with you to California and I have a surprise planned for our anniversary. I know it's still a month away, but the timing was perfect so I asked myself, why not?"

Kiddie was delighted to make this adjustment to her plans. The Major never ceased to amaze her. "What kind of surprise Major?" Kiddie asked.

The Major grinned at Kiddie. "Did your stomach already forget about dinner?" he asked, pulling out a sack. As soon as he opened the sack, Kiddie could smell something delicious.

"Major what is that smell?" Kiddie asked eagerly.

"That Kiddie, is the smell of a Gioia's hot salami sandwich. Someone was going to get sandwiches for the boys on the team and I jumped in and ordered a couple for us." The Major set out lots of napkins before he unwrapped their sandwiches.

"They're a little messy Kiddie, but well worth the effort I promise." Kiddie was happy to take her sandwich from the Major. She took a big bite, her eyes rolling as the flavors of meats, cheese, veggies, and some kind of sauce descended on her taste buds. The warm garlic cheese bread was soft and fresh, but just enough to contain most of the sandwich. The thick and hearty sandwich was just what Kiddie needed after keeping her meals light since she got on the train.

"It's been a while since I had a sandwich this good Major. It reminds me of the cuban sandwiches we had at the Columbia place in Tampa a couple of years ago. So much flavor!" Kiddie was in heaven, her mouth and stomach most appreciative of the Major's efforts.

Suddenly the Major paused. "Kiddie I almost forgot the most important part!" After digging deep in his suitcase, the Major turned to her triumphantly with a bottle of champagne. "This is for later, when we're all snuggled under the covers Mrs. Corum." he said with a wicked happy smile on his face.

Kiddie laughed before going to kiss the Major on the cheek. "You do think of everything!"

The Major took a mock bow and then added modestly. "I do what I can."

It was getting late as hours later Kiddie and the Major sat enjoying a cocktail at their table in the very quiet dining car. The candle glowed between them, the flowers fresh and colorful on the white linen, their eyes on each other, their conversation quiet but excited. The Major was in the middle of telling Kiddie about his anniversary surprise he had planned.

"Kiddie you are going to love Catalina Island, I promise. From everything Bill Wrigley has told me, it sounds like just the romantic beach getaway we should have on our five year anniversary."

The Major explained how he had been in Chicago back in June for a series between the Giants and the Cubs. After one of the games, they both ended up at the same club. Mr. Wrigley recognized the Major as they stood beside each other, both of them waiting for the bartender's attention. Feeling generous about the Cub's third win in a row over the Giants, Mr. Wrigley offered to buy the Major a drink.

"One thing led to another Kiddie and before I knew it he was telling me all about Catalina Island and his vision to create a resort town even Hollywood can't resist." Kiddie smiled as the Major talked about all the things to do on the island, seeming to think she needed convincing. Kiddie couldn't be happier to celebrate their five year anniversary on the Island, reminiscent of spending their honeymoon in Bermuda.

Watching Kiddie, the Major picked up her hand and asked. "What do you think Kiddie? Does this sound like the perfect anniversary to you?"

Kiddie finished her drink and leaned across the table. "I think Major, that even after five years you never cease to amaze me. I can't wait to see Catalina Island with you!"

The Major kissed Kiddie's hand, then finished his drink. "Kiddie are we ready for bed? It's been a long day and I'm exhausted."

Kiddie downed the rest of her drink and then smiled suggestively at the Major, "I am ready for bed Major, but I'm not that tired. I hope you can keep up in your exhaustion." Kiddie had him by the hand, leading the Major back to their sleeping quarters.

"I'll do my best my love, I'll do my best." the Major replied.

K iddie and the Major were sitting poolside in Santa Monica, enjoying a beautiful day with an ocean view. Thanks to Kiddie's mother, they were currently guests of Marion Davies and enjoying the many amenities of her massive beach house. Kiddie was familiar with the starlet, a Brooklyn native, performing first with the Ziegfeld Follies before being cast into several productions on Broadway. Having acquired both fame and fortune, she had moved herself and her company, Cosmopolitan Productions, to Hollywood with Mr. William Randolph Hearst acting as her current manager. The Major had mentioned to Kiddie's mother it was a small world as Mr. Hearst was the Major's boss, owner of *The New York Evening Journal* for whom he wrote his daily sports column for.

Kiddie's mother had shared she doubted Ms. Davies really needed a manager as she seemed to be a visionary and powerhouse to be reckoned with, not only in acting, but in production as well. Kiddie's mother was working as Ms. Davies executive assistant and was privy to the numerous projects Ms. Davies was working on as well as a recurring guest at the lavish parties Ms. Davies was becoming famous for throwing at her beach house. Kiddie was excited for them to be her guests tonight as she had insisted on throwing a small dinner party in honor of Kiddie and the Major's first visit to LA and their impending five year anniversary. They had been given a room, where Kiddie's Jenny Lind dress hung in anticipation.

It was hard for Kiddie to have her mother so far from home, but she had to admit her mother seemed happy, enjoying her work as well as the California weather. Kiddie's father was busy making his own connections to the stars, becoming a well renowned plastic surgeon. Even

Freddy seemed to be getting in on the action and had shared his own vision of an expedition to New Guinea to make a film. He had renamed himself Commander Kolle in an attempt to give validity to his vision while seeking out funds for his expedition from a variety of sources. It was not lost on Kiddie or the Major, her family had a very different lifestyle here as compared to that of New York City.

Hours later Kiddie stood in front of the mirror, checking herself in her new green dress before turning to the Major and straightening his tie. The Major assured Kiddie she was stunning as her short dark curls and creamy white shoulders were showcased by the unique light green of the dress. Kiddie brought her pearls, wearing both strands to make a statement. The fitted bodice highlighted Kiddie's slim figure before dropping off into an elegant swirl of satin at the back. She went all out with her makeup, satisfied with her Clara Bow lip line. Kiddie did not want to be overdressed making them seem like they were trying too hard, but her mother assured there was no such thing in Hollywood. Ms. Davies had mentioned to Kiddie it would be a small dinner party of only twenty to thirty guests, depending on who managed to make the drive out to Santa Monica. Both Kiddie's father and Freddy were expected to be there and Kiddie looked forward to seeing them all dressed up as well.

Kiddie was thankful they would all be staying the night as guests in Ms. Davies home and had shared her appreciation to Ms. Davies for her generous hospitality. Ms. Davies told Kiddie it was the least she could do given the enormous amount of help her mother provided her on a daily basis. Kiddie's mother beamed at the compliment and it occurred to Kiddie that her mother no longer sat at home isolating herself from the world in the name of writing. The energy of LA was contagious and Kiddie felt almost giddy with excitement as she and the Major walked down the red velvet staircase to join the party. The Major could feel Kiddie's nervous energy, and held onto her hand in the crook of his arm as they descended.

Ms. Davies happened to be passing by the staircase as they descended and stopped to acknowledge what a striking couple they made. Kiddie stepped off the stairs, grateful she hadn't tripped over her dress, although Ms. Davie's positive energy and grace immediately put Kiddie at ease.

Kiddie did not recognize anyone as particularly famous around the long dining room table, but it felt good to be at a dinner party of such glamorous proportions. She and the Major sat towards the middle of the table, Ms. Davies close by, Kiddie's family across from them. As she enjoyed the evening of good food and interesting conversations, Kiddie was happy she was well read and could hold her own in a conversation. At one point she caught her father's eye as they discussed how President Coolidge faced the task of balancing economic frugality with the prosperity many Americans were enjoying. Kiddie was reminded of the political conversations the two of them often had over dinner when Kiddie was preparing to vote for the first time. Nevertheless, Kiddie was thankful when the conversation became lighter, discussing first lady Grace Coolidge's pet racoon, Rebecca.

Before Kiddie knew it, they all retired to their respective rooms, the promise of a breakfast buffet early in the morning. Kiddie and the Major would need to be getting on the steamer Catalina to depart at ten am, so the earlier the better. As Kiddie snuggled up to the Major, she relished in the happiness she felt. It had been a fabulous night blending good food, interesting people, glamorous surroundings, and her family. Kiddie wished more than anything Iris and Bernie could have been there and she smiled to herself thinking about the stories she would have to tell her when she was back home in New York City. For now, home seemed far away, and that suited Kiddie just fine.

Kiddie stood at the rail of the Catalina steamer, wondering if that was really land she could finally see on the horizon or her eyes were playing tricks on her. Deciding they finally were coming up on Catalina Island, Kiddie went to fetch the Major. It had taken the steamer a little more than two hours to travel the twenty two miles from the coast of Long Beach, but as the island grew in size, so did Kiddie's excitement. She was reminded of their trip to Bermuda for their honeymoon almost five years ago, and she squeezed the Major's arm in anticipation. As the island became more and more of a reality, Kiddie took in the curve of the coastline, the cluster of hotels and shops, the sailboats bobbing up and down in the beautiful water, and the mountains that loomed over it all. It looked very picturesque and Kiddie could not wait to spend the next four days here.

Having departed from the steamer, Kiddie and the Major stood with their luggage waiting for transportation to their hotel, the Hotel St. Catherine. Mr. Wrigley had promised the Major it was a popular destination for Hollywood and you were more than likely to run into someone famous. They didn't have long to wait before a bus of sorts pulled up. The driver greeted them cheerfully, taking their luggage and putting it on the back of their so called transportation to their hotel. They quickly learned there were few cars allowed on the island, leaving boats, horses, bikes, walking, and pure ingenuity to get around as you needed. Clearly the latter came into play as they took their seats on an open air contraption the driver called a bus.

It was a bumpy ride to the hotel, but all that disappeared as they came upon the large rambling white structure they would call home for the next four days. The four story hotel sat on the beach, appearing to have a private beach. The hotel's white structure with a red tiled roof made for a dramatic contrast to the mountains behind it, the lush foliage and palm trees welcoming and promising of things to come. The Major was getting them all checked in as Kiddie peeked around corners, discovering the hotel's amenities. Kiddie was happy to see a large pool and even bigger dining room, the white linens covering tables lined up tightly in rows, making Kiddie wonder if room service was available.

The Major had a big smile on his face as he came to join Kiddie. "It appears my new friend Mr. Wrigley has comped our room for us!" The Major held up a card that read, "Happy anniversary to you both and please enjoy your stay on our island of romance! Signed Bill Wrigley. How about that Kiddie?" the Major asked happily.

"Major, how generous of him! First Ms. Davies and now Mr. Wrigley. How lucky can one couple be?" Kiddie asked, most impressed.

They unpacked their things before going to stand on their balcony to admire their ocean view. Kiddie loved how blue the water was, almost a turquoise, graced with a mix of palm trees and mountains. "Kiddie, what do you want to do first? There are lots of things to see and do or we can just be lazy and lay on the beach. Your choice my love." the Major said.

"It's a beautiful day Major, but I'm feeling famished and lazy. Do you think we could get sandwiches in the dining room and take them to the beach?" Kiddie answered.

"Only one way to find out, but I'm sure it's not a problem."

In the next hour Kiddie and the Major changed into their beach-wear, and ordered food to go. They walked down the wooden board-walk away from the front of the hotel, not wanting to be observed by any of the hotel guests from their balconies. Now they sat on the blanket Kiddie had wisely packed enjoying dill pickles, chilled cucumbers, hot rolls with sugar cured ham, and the hotel's special baked beans. The Major somehow managed to secure a bottle of wine which they were happy to sip on as they lazed about, enjoying the waves crashing up to the beach a safe distance away from them. Kiddie's stomach and mind were happy and full as she laid her head in the Major's lap. He had stra-tegically found a large rock to lay out their blanket by, propping himself against it.

"What are you thinking about Kiddie?" the Major asked.

"I'm thinking my stomach is going to be happy to eat our leftovers for dinner later because my brain is telling me not to move anytime soon." Kiddie said lazily.

The Major laughed and said, "That's a plan I can get on board with. We have plenty of time to explore the island over the next few days."

Kiddie and the Major spent the afternoon lazing on the beach, talking about this and that, but mostly just enjoying the day and their gorgeous surroundings. At one point Kiddie had braved getting in the ocean, the water cold and the bottom rocky, different than what she was used to in Florida. As she came out of the water, she threatened to get the Major wet, and laughed when he told her there would be consequences. Taking her chances, Kiddie dropped into the Major's lap, hugging him close to her with her wet suit. As promised, the Major rolled Kiddie off of him, pinning her to the ground while he took his revenge. Kiddie was happy to pay the price, the cold water and rocks under feet very much worth it.

Kiddie and the Major did lots of tourist things, taking advantage of all the island had to offer. They walked the numerous wooden stairs to the top of the impressive rock formation affectionately called Sugarloaf. They took the glass bottom boat ride, enjoying the marine life below, and were graced with the presence of a blue whale. The Major took Kiddie to Catalina Pottery and together they picked out a beautiful blue jar made from the clay of the island.

One afternoon Kiddie humored the Major, watching him play nine holes of golf at the Catalina Country Club, more than happy to take in the magnificent views of Avalon Bay. Kiddie got excited when she suddenly noticed the herd of buffalo grazing up the mountain. The Major told her the story of the herd left on the island after they had been brought over to be filmed in a movie. Of course the Major could not leave without paying his respects to the baseball diamond next to the golf course, the place where Mr. Wrigley's Chicago Cubs were lucky enough to spend spring training. The Major also wanted to see Isthmus Cove, the place where the Great Catalina Channel Swim had taken place in January. Of the one hundred and two swimmers entered, only one had been strong enough to make it all the way across, in the process winning twenty-five thousand dollars for his efforts.

It was their last day as Kiddie stood packing, folding clothes to put into her suitcase laying open on the bed. Coming to stand behind her, the Major recognized Kiddie's dismay as he wrapped his arms around her before saying, "Kiddie don't forget you still have time here in California with your family. Then I'll be waiting for you to come home and celebrate our anniversary again."

Kiddie turned to the Major with a smile. "You're right. Paradise can't last forever. It will be good to spend time with my family and see more of LA. I wish you could stay longer, but I'm happy we had all this time together. You really need to not wait another five years for a vacation Major."

"I'll try my love, but you know how my schedule gets." the Major said.

Kiddie answered back with a sigh, "Oh yes, I do know how it gets."

The Major was leaving the paper early today to spend some time with Kiddie. Since their anniversary, the Major's schedule had been one big sports event after another. Being *The New York Evening Journal's* lead columnist, kept the Major very busy, although he had to admit it was an exciting time to be a sports reporter.

In mid-September the Major had a front row seat to one of the biggest boxing matches in quite some time. He was in Chicago, as Soldier Field hosted the major heavyweight rematch between champion Gene Tunney and former champion, Jack Dempsey. After ten rounds, the fight had finished in a controversial "long count," as the officiating ref had delayed his count long enough to give Tunney enough extra time to recover and come to his feet. Fans had been outraged and the Major had to write the way he saw it, while trying not to add fuel to the fire.

Only a week later Babe Ruth broke his own record of 1921, by hitting his sixtieth home run for the season. Once again the Major had a front row seat as the New York Yankees were in Yankee Stadium playing against the Washington Senators. The Yankees had clinched their division putting them in the World Series against the Pittsburgh Pirates. In an unprecedented series, the Yankees had swept the Pirates in four games, the combination of outstanding players such as Babe Ruth and Lou Gehrig, more than the Pirates could handle. The Yankees won their second championship and would be a force to be reckoned with next spring.

The Major had finished the Giant's baseball season before quickly moving into their football season. It paid off though as in the end the Giants won their first NFL championship in early December, losing only to the Cleveland Bulldog's for the season.

Now the Major was headed home to surprise Kiddie with an early Christmas present. The Major had learned of a new place in Manhattan called the Russian Tea Room. Apparently it was already becoming popular with the theater crowd and even ballerinas as their fine cuisine and elegance were more than they could resist. The art deco Russo-Continental restaurant seemed to be a perfect fit for his girl Kiddie. The Major picked up his pace, hopeful Kiddie wasn't out, either shopping or with Iris. He looked forward to surprising her, always his way to make up for all the times he felt he neglected her in the name of a story.

It was Christmastime in the city, Kiddie's favorite time of year in New York. Once they had been to the Macy's Day Parade on Thanksgiving, there was no turning back. This year Lelo was a little bigger and had been mesmerized by the floats, the bands, and even the parade's first helium balloon, Felix the Cat. Santa Claus's arrival in Herald Square was exciting for Lelo and even Kiddie, who relished in the sparkle and shine New York City brought to the holiday season. Kiddie loved to window shop from fourteenth street to fifth avenue, enjoying the glamourous windows at Saks Fifth Avenue, Bergdorf's, and of course Macy's.

Today Kiddie stood for the hundredth time at the Macy's window admiring the wool red coat with the fur trim around the collar and cuffs at the sleeves. Kiddie smiled thinking about herself in the coat, out on the town with the Major, turning heads wherever they went. Kiddie loved all the holiday windows, but lately Kiddie only noticed the coat. Kiddie had checked the price weeks ago and knew it was out of her reach, but you couldn't blame a girl for wishing. She didn't realize that across the street a certain someone stood watching her for a minute before crossing the street to stand beside her.

"See something you like Kiddie?" he asked.

"Major you startled me!" Recovering quickly Kiddie added lightly, "I'm just admiring Macy's holiday windows. I do love all the glamour of Christmastime in New York! What are you doing out and about so early from work?"

The Major reached over to kiss Kiddie on the cheek before he answered her. "I thought I would come home early, and surprise you, but here you are." The Major checked his watch. "It's too early for dinner. Shall we go and have drinks somewhere? Or do you need to keep shopping?"

"I would love to join you Major!" She put her free hand in his arm, settling her few bags on her other arm. She had done some shopping earlier, finding a nice dress for her mother and a kewpie doll for Lelo for Christmas. The stores were a bustle of activity, but Kiddie didn't mind. Christmas was still a few weeks away and Kiddie was soaking up every little detail of the season.

As they walked along, the Major turned to Kiddie with a question. "My love, what do you want for Christmas? Santa and I've talked and we agree you've been a very good girl this year. What does your heart desire for Christmas?"

Kiddie deferred the question, turning it on the Major. "Me? I'm trying to decide what to get you! What do you want for Christmas Major?"

Kiddie struggled with this very question every gift giving occasion. She wondered if all men were this hard to buy for, or just the Major. The truth was, the Major wasn't about having material things and if he really found something he wanted, he would buy it. Kiddie found it frustrating, especially at this time of year, when she wanted the Major to feel the magic of Christmas too.

As Kiddie could have guessed, the Major kissed her hand and answered back, "Kiddie, all I need for Christmas is you!"

Kiddie thought about the coat in the window for a minute and then just as quickly dismissed it. "Fine Major, if you really want to know what I want for Christmas, I would love for us to host a party on Christmas Eve! With all the trimmings. What do you think about that?" Kiddie asked.

"That sounds more like a gift for our guests Kiddie." the Major said doubtfully.

"What can I say Major, making others happy makes me happy." Kiddie said with a smile. "Isn't that what Christmas is all about?"

The Major looked at Kiddie then said to her. "Touche Kiddie, touche! Let's do it! You tell me what we need and I will be happy to help!"

Kiddie was excited the Major said yes so quickly. "The first question is who do you want to invite? Family of course, but are there any friends you would like to invite?"

The Major looked thoughtful, contemplating her question. "I assume most people will be with family, but if not, we should definitely invite them."

Kiddie smiled again at the Major. "So the usual suspects and we'll see who shows up? Of course we'll need a tree. Are you okay with that?"

The Major looked startled by this news for just a second, but quickly recovered. "Of course we'll need a tree Kiddie! I would love to do that with you my love."

"Really Major? Thank you! It will be so fun! And just wait until I snuggle up with you by the tree! It will be worth the effort, I promise." It was Kiddie's turn to kiss the Major, reaching up for his cheek.

"Things to look forward to Kiddie." the Major said as he opened the door to their apartment.

As they walked in Kiddie turned to ask the Major, if she should take time to change. "Dress like you're out on the town, but not out to the ball Kiddie." Kiddie laughed at this description before disappearing into their bedroom to choose a dress. She emerged in an easy ten minutes in one of her favorite green dresses for this time of year. As always she had her pearls on. She headed to the bathroom to touch up her makeup, and redo her lip line, spray some perfume, and then she was ready in no time. The Major stood holding her fur coat out to her and as Kiddie settled into it, she felt excited to be out unexpectedly with the Major.

In no time their cab deposited Kiddie and the Major outside the Russian Tea Room, next to Carnegie Hall. Kiddie was not familiar with the place, and she tried not to let her jaw drop, immediately taken with Tea Room's art deco elegance, the red, green, and gold a perfect holiday combination for Christmastime. They were quickly seated in an intimate banquet, the red leather pairing nicely with the long white tablecloth. The luxurious gold framed mirror behind them made the lights bounce off the gold ceiling and sparkle and shine down on them.

The Major informed Kiddie that a group of Russians had opened the tea room and you were more than likely to see a ballerina during your visit. He also told her that the Russians were known for their vodka, and even hot chocolate, besides a divine cuisine. As Kiddie and the Major perused the menu, they were grateful for the descriptions of the food, many of the names unfamiliar to either of them. Kiddie found it pure entertainment as the menu was a mix of sweets, main dishes, soups, and drinks. In the end they settled on starting with Zakuska, hors d'oeuvres à la Russe. Eventually the Major settled on Bitochki, which translated to chopped chicken and veal patties in a Stroganoff sauce. Kiddie decided to go with Kulebiaka, a chicken loaf baked in a pastry shell with rice, eggs, and mushrooms topped with a cream sauce.

As Kiddie and the Major sipped on their cocktails, a generous pour of vodka as the base, they started planning their Christmas Eve party. Kiddie's parents should be arriving the day before and she wondered out loud to the Major if they should invite his family to come. The Major was touched, knowing this wasn't easy for Kiddie, but told her his mother would never leave his father home to fend for himself on Christmas. The Major was happy to have the afternoon with Kiddie and experience something new. He would make sure their Christmas was memorable, making the most of their time this holiday season.

In the five years they had been married, Kiddie and the Major had never had a tree at their apartment, happy to leave that to other family members to take on. Since Kiddie's family had moved across the country, Kiddie missed the holiday cheer of a well decorated tree and little knick knacks sitting around here and there. When they moved, Kiddie's mother had given Kiddie her favorite angel. Her mother had brought Kiddie to tears, telling her the angel would always watch over her until they were home for Christmas. Kiddie was happy to get it out on Thanksgiving night, celebrating it was Christmastime and there were lots of things to look forward to.

Now it was the Sunday before Christmas and Kiddie and the Major were out shopping for their tree. The invites had been sent and per usual, people planned to show up. They had agreed over a cocktail at The Plaza one night, it made both of them happy and proud to know people anticipated a Corum party. They were finding plenty of places along the streets of Manhattan to buy a tree. Kiddie had already been to Macy's to buy her General Electric lights for the tree, much safer than the candles she could remember her family having when she was growing up. She bought glass ornaments, candy canes, and tinsel for the tree as well. She was happy to also have a dozen or so ornaments her mother had left her when they packed up the house to move to California.

Now Kiddie, but mostly the Major were struggling to get their tree home. Kiddie was thankful she had presented this as her present, because bringing a tree home was a real task and one Kiddie wasn't sure the Major was up for. Of course Kiddie picked out the roundest, fattest tree they could find on the small city lot they stopped at. Kiddie was very much entertained as she watched the Major wrestle the tree into the green cast iron tree stand, the Merry Christmas in red lettering seeming to all but mock the Major. She was doing her part to keep the tree standing up straight, as the Major secured the bolts to make sure it would stay upright for the next week.

Finally the tree was standing tall in its stand and covered in lights, as Kiddie added the final decorations. The Major was settled on the couch, content to watch Kiddie, a glass of wine out for each of them. The radio was on, their favorite station gracing them with their favorite Christmas songs. It didn't take Kiddie long to add the ornaments, the candy canes, and tinsel before settling onto the couch beside the Major to admire the tree

As they sat snuggling on the couch, enjoying their tree, Kiddie was overwhelmed with emotion as *"Oh Holy NIght"* came on the radio. Neither of them spoke, taking in the words of the song, the tree suddenly a symbol of the hope and peace the season wished to bestow upon those who believed and even those who didn't.

As the song finished, the Major said quietly, "Kiddie it's the most beautiful tree I've seen in a very long time."

Kiddie kissed the Major on the cheek, saying softly, "It really is Major."

Knowing it was very late and their bottle of wine empty long ago, Kiddie and the Major finally unplugged their tree and went to bed. As they snuggled under the covers, warming their bed, Kiddie was happy to have had this day with the Major. Kiddie discovered years ago nothing made the Major more appealing than when he invested his time and energy into her happiness, and today had definitely been that kind of day. Now as he went to kiss her goodnight, Kiddie held him to a long, deep kiss. Reaching for him under the covers, Kiddie decided the Major had earned himself an early Christmas present, which the Major was most happy to accept.

F inally it was Christmas Eve and Kiddie was running around trying not to be a crazy person. The house was immaculate and festive, the tree shining in the corner of their living room, candles waiting to be lit around the apartment. The radio was already on, the music a mix of jazzy holiday songs and traditional carols. The Major was getting dressed in the bedroom, giving Kiddie the bathroom to do as she needed. As she finished her lip line and checked her smokey eye one last time, she couldn't help but admire how pretty her dress was. The dress was made of satin in a deep, true holiday red, with a v-neckline in the front and narrow straps meeting halfway down her back to cinch in an oversized satin bow

As Kiddie emerged from the bathroom, she was surprised to see the Major sitting on the couch, his eyes fixed on her. He immediately got up, coming to her and handing her a glass of champagne. "Kiddie you look stunning as always." He kissed her on the cheek, then gave a low whistle as she turned for him to admire the view from the back. "Kiddie I don't know if my friends can handle you in this dress."

Kiddie turned to put her arms around the Major, reaching up to kiss him on the lips. "Just know at the end of the night, it will be you Major who gets to handle all this. Merry Christmas." The Major pulled Kiddie to him, relishing in the taste of her on his lips, the smell of her in his nose, the feel of her hips under his hands.

It was the doorbell ringing that disrupted the moment, but as Kiddie went to answer the door, the Major said after her, "I'm going to hold you to that!"

Kiddie turned and smiled at him, "I'm counting on it Major!."

It was Kiddie's parents who stood in the doorway, Freddy and Dot not far behind them. Kiddie was happy to greet them all with big hugs and welcome them into their home. Kiddie's mother went straight to the tree, surprised to see it. "Kiddie you got a tree!"

"Of course Mother, what's a Christmas Eve party without a tree?"

"Oh Kiddie, it's beautiful just like you my darling!" Kiddie hugged her mother again, happy to have her home. They went to join the men hovering in the kitchen, preparing cocktails.

It wasn't long before they had a houseful of family and friends, the radio blaring, the cocktails flowing. As Kiddie stood talking with some of her modeling friends, she took in all the people she held most dear to her under one roof in the name of Christmas. The tree sparkled, every-one looked divine, and the food was delicious, even if Kiddie said so herself. She stood taking it all in until her eyes rested on the Major. She watched him as he stood chatting with her father and a couple of friends from the paper, his dark hair just above his bow tie he had put on for the evening's festivities. Kiddie was content to stand and watch him, until he suddenly turned to her. She smiled as he raised his glass to her, but touched his lips with his fingers. Kiddie almost blushed as her friends caught on to what was happening, their laughter contagious.

Suddenly *Jingle Bells* came on the radio and her friends grabbed her to go dance, the Charleston in full swing before she knew what was happening. Kiddie was delighted when the Major came to dance with her as *Winter Wonderland* came on the radio next. The party was in full swing now, and Kiddie took the Major by the hand to follow her, deciding it was time to give her present to the Major. Reaching under the tree, she pulled out a small to medium sized gift, a bright red bow topping the paper.

"Merry Christmas Major. I know tomorrow is Christmas, but you might want to use it tonight." Kiddie said with a nervous smile.

"Kiddie I told you you're all I need for Christmas!" the Major protested.

"I know, I know, but just open it!" Kiddie said with a laugh.

As the Major was unwrapping it, Kiddie couldn't help but explain herself. "Major I thought you could use it tonight, but maybe also with your job."

The Major was intrigued as he unwrapped a Kodak camera. "I know how you like gadgets, so I hope you like this one!" Kiddie went on.

"Kiddie I love it!" said the Major, turning to Kiddie and pulling her in close to kiss her. Never one to miss out on anything, Iris had wandered over.

"What's going on kids?" she asked with a slight slur.

"Iris put your drink down and you can be the first one to take a picture on my new camera!" the Major announced.

"A camera? I love to have my picture taken! But sure, I can take a picture too." Iris said.

Kiddie's mother wandered over while the Major loaded the film and the flash, taking his time to just glance at the directions before putting everything where it belonged in the camera. Satisfied the camera was properly loaded, he decided to hand the camera to Kiddie's mother to take the first picture.

Standing in front of the tree, the Major put his arms around Kiddie, waiting for her mother to take their picture. Not wanting to deal with a pouty Iris, he ushered Iris and her mother to go stand by Kiddie too while he took their picture. The girls smiled at him, dressed beautifully for Christmas Eve, the tree a forever symbol to mark the occasion. After Iris and her mother had wandered away the Major went to Kiddie. Taking her face in both hands, he looked her in the eyes to tell her "Thank you Kiddie. You really know how to make it feel like Christmas." before kissing her. Kiddie smiled at him, knowing there was more to come.

The rest of the evening became a blur of drinks, holiday music, and dancing, for sure a Christmas Eve to remember. Kiddie wasn't even sure what time the last guest left, but she knew it was well after midnight. As the Major started to clean up dishes and put food away, Kiddie stopped him.

"Major this can wait until tomorrow. I have one more surprise for you." Kiddie went to fetch a small, heavy package still sitting under the tree. She handed it to the Major. "I hope you like it, Major. I thought you could put it in your office." Kiddie said, still a little worried about her choice for the Major.

"Kiddie you already got me a camera. That was plenty." the Major said, but he obliged Kiddie and tore the paper off. Opening the box he found a Limited Edition Babe Ruth bank commemorating his sixty home runs.

Kiddie could see the Major was surprised and even more so when she added, "Turn it over Major. Read what it says." Kiddie was most excited that she had found a way to get Babe Ruth to actually sign it for the Major.

"To the Major, who always bats a thousand percent with his stories." Signed Babe Ruth, 1927. As the Major sat there just holding it, Kiddie still wasn't sure if he liked it or not.

Finally he stood up and went to Kiddie. "Kiddie that is the most thoughtful gift anyone has ever given me. Thank you my love!" The Major pulled her in close for a long hug.

Before Kiddie knew it she was telling him the story of how she found the bank shopping one day and had reached out to some of his friends to help her get in touch with Mr. Ruth. Once she had explained who the bank was for, Mr. Ruth had been more than happy to sign it for the Major. "Are you sure you like it Major?"

"Of course Kiddie, how could I not!" he said as he went to pull a rather large package from behind the tree, the green paper blending in with the tree to the point Kiddie had not even noticed it. The Major led Kiddie to the couch and handed it to her. "Merry Christmas my love!"

Kiddie was surprised but asked excitedly, "Major you didn't need to get me anything, but what is it?"

He laughed and answered, "Open it and find out!"

As Kiddie tore the wrapping paper off she was quick to notice the Macy's box. Wondering what it could possibly be, she took the lid off carefully. She inhaled deeply when she saw what lay in the tissue paper. She looked up at the Major, "Major, how did you know?!"

The Major stood taking in her excitement, "I have my ways, my love."

It was the red wool coat with the fur collar and cuffs Kiddie had longed for since Thanksgiving. She let the box drop to the floor as she lifted the coat out, squealing with delight as she unbuttoned it and put it on over her dress. Kiddie went to hug the Major, then kissed him on the lips. "Thank you Major! I love it! And you!" she said excitedly.

The Major laughed, telling her "Merry Christmas Kiddie." As Kiddie went to hang her coat up, the Major paused in unplugging the tree as "I Told Santa Claus to Bring Me You" came on the radio. The Major went to Kiddie, pulling her close to dance one last song. With his face close to hers, his hands on her just below the bow on her back, the Major moved Kiddie around their living room slowly. As the song ended the Major unplugged the tree before Kiddie led him to the bedroom. It was already quite the Christmas and Kiddie was most definitely in a giving mood. Closing the door behind them, Kiddie went to kiss the Major, murmuring "Merry Christmas Major."

CHAPTER NINE

=1928=

*"ALL OUR DREAMS CAN COME TRUE, IF WE
HAVE THE COURAGE TO PURSUE THEM."*
—WALT DISNEY

It was late in the month of January, late in the morning, and Kiddie was late. The Major had long left for the office, leaving her to motivate herself to rise and shine when she was ready. Kiddie hadn't felt like herself for a while now, but that wasn't unusual for her. January was her least favorite month of the year, the winter blahs a real thing. For the past week, Kiddie had started her day the same, going to the bathroom to see if her period had started. With every passing day and nothing to find, Kiddie's anxiety grew a little more. Kiddie knew her body and her cycle well and had felt safe throughout the holidays, but Kiddie also knew nothing was one hundred percent except for abstinence and who wanted to be a scrooge at Christmas? Now as she lay in bed, she contemplated all the what if's.

What if she was pregnant? What if she wasn't ready to be a mother? What if the Major wasn't ready to be a father? Kiddie felt fairly certain that the Major would be elated if she were pregnant, even though they never talked about having children. Being the man he was, Kiddie knew he was waiting for her to be ready and that she would let him know when that time came. For today, Kiddie wished doctors would create a pregnancy test that didn't involve killing lab rats. It was the not knowing one way or another that haunted Kiddie the most. If she wasn't pregnant, she could get on with her day. But if she was pregnant, that changed a lot of things, things Kiddie wasn't ready to change. What if they had a baby, would the Major be home more? What if she was stuck at home by herself with a baby? What if she loved being a mother and she found a new sense of purpose? So many ways she could imagine writing this story.

What if she wasn't pregnant at all, but there was something medically wrong with her? What if her fatigue, her food aversions, her bloating, her moodiness were symptomatic of a different health issue? Christmastime was such a high for Kiddie, that she always struggled to get back into a somewhat interesting routine in January. Kiddie didn't like that their apartment seemed bare, that her family was back in California, or the cold and dreary weather. The Major had taken his usual trip home to Missouri to see his family, but he had been back a week now, and still Kiddie felt blah.

Kiddie knew she did herself no good lying there, wallowing in her what ifs. Pulling up her big girl pants, Kiddie started a mental to do list to take advantage of the beautiful winter day she knew was waiting for her. First she would get dressed and go for a long walk around Central Park. She thought about Dot, knowing she was missing Freddy too and she would see if Dot would meet her for lunch. Then she would go to the market and buy food to make a home cooked meal for the Major tonight. Three good reasons to crawl out of bed and get her day started. Feeling good about her plan, Kiddie hauled herself out of bed and went to the bathroom, ready to start her day one way or another.

A few weeks later, the Major came home to find Kiddie napping on the couch. The Major was very in tune with his wife and recognized something was different, even going so far as to wonder if she could be pregnant. The thought of this possibility both excited and scared the Major. As he stood watching her sleep on the couch, it occurred to him Kiddie looked almost childlike with her covers pulled up to her chin.

He left the office early, determined to have some time at home and get Kiddie to share what was going on.

Turning on a light in the darkening apartment, the Major went to sit beside Kiddie on the couch, picking up her feet to put them in his lap. It had been weeks since the Major had been able to touch Kiddie, and he was happy to share this small intimacy with her, even if she was asleep. The Major sat reading the paper until Kiddie finally started to stir.

"Good evening my sleeping beauty." the Major said softly.

Kiddie took a minute to get her bearings, before acknowledging the Major. "Hi. Major are you home early? What time is it?" Kiddie asked.

"I am home early and it's almost six o'clock." the Major answered with a smile.

"You should have woken me Major! And why are you home early?" Kiddie asked as she struggled to sit up.

"I'm home because I think my best girl needs me." the Major opened the can of worms, jumping in right away.

Kiddie studied him for a minute before answering softly, "I do need you Major, always."

"I'm serious Kiddie. What's going on with you these days? I want to be here for you, but you have to tell me what's going on." the Major persisted.

It was enough to cause Kiddie to tear up, not able to keep it to herself anymore. "Major, I think I'm pregnant!" she wailed softly.

"I see. I take it you're not happy about that?" the Major asked. He treaded lightly, not wanting to show his hand either way.

Kiddie studied him for a reaction before jumping in herself. "Major, I'm scared. I don't know if I'm ready to be a mother yet! I don't know if I'm ready to be responsible for another human being, especially one that's tiny and helpless!"

"Kiddie I'll be here to help you! We will do it together!" the Major tried to reassure her, but she threw out the brutal truth, making him flinch.

"Will you Major? I guess if it's not during the baseball season or the World Series or some big boxing match you might be here to help. And when I go into labor, will you actually be here or only a day or two away by train?" Kiddie finally shared all her deepest fears, not the least bit worried about sparing the Major's feelings.

His voice was quiet when he finally answered her back. "That's fair Kiddie. I know I'm gone a lot, but if you were pregnant, things would change. And I promise I will be here when you go into labor."

Kiddie wasn't surprised by the Major's answer. She wanted to believe him and knew he believed his words, but reality and wishful thinking were two different things, hard things for Kiddie.

Kiddie answered back sadly, "It's good to know you'll make those changes for your child Major. Too bad you can't do it for me." Then she got off the couch and went to their bedroom, closing the door behind her.

The Major was startled by her words, but had to acknowledge he already knew Kiddie wished he was home more. The Major went to pour himself a drink and then sat at the kitchen table, contemplating what Kiddie had just said. He always thought it was up to Kiddie to make the decision, but he realized he had as much to do with them having a baby, as Kiddie did. It was one thing not to be around for Kiddie, but another thing not to be around for his child. After some time and another drink, the Major had made some hard decisions and finally went to talk to Kiddie.

He found her curled up in a ball, holding his pillow and weeping into it softly. It hurt his heart to see her like that and he laid on the bed beside her, wanting to say whatever he could to make her feel better.

"Kiddie, I'm going to go to my boss and ask not to travel with the team so much this year. I'm writing a daily column, and I have plenty to keep me busy here in New York City. I'm always going to have to travel for my job, Kiddie, but I promise, come hell or high water, I will not miss the birth of our child. I'll be here for you and for him."

Kiddie smiled ever so slightly hearing the Major say him. Somehow when she thought about a baby, it was always a boy, but maybe that was because Iris already had a girl. "Don't make promises you can't keep Major."

The Major was stunned that she didn't believe him. "Kiddie, I promise you! You need to believe me!"

Kiddie tried to stare him down, daring him to cave, but the Major held her gaze, his look earnest and almost desperate for her to believe him. Finally she caved first, whispering, "Ok Major. I believe you." Only then did she let him pull her into his arms and hold her.

Eventually they went to the kitchen to scrounge up leftovers for dinner, although the Major was more than willing to go get Kiddie whatever sounded good to her. Kiddie settled on leftover Coq Au Vin, heating it up on the stove in no time, even if there were no mashed potatoes to go with it. They sat at the table, talking until Kiddie yawned and the Major ushered her off to bed. Kiddie let the Major fuss over her, wondering if there would be more of this to come, definitely enjoying it for tonight. Kiddie had been worrying about this alone for a while now and it felt good to finally share it with the Major.

They laid in bed together, the Major holding Kiddie until she fell asleep, unaware when he got out of bed. He went to the kitchen to pour himself another stiff one, then went to sit on the couch, listening to the radio. It was his turn to face all the what ifs Kiddie had been juggling for almost a month now. What if Kiddie really was pregnant? What if he was going to be a father? What if there was a baby boy on the way to teach everything he knew and loved about sports? What if his boss denied his request to work more from the city this year? And his scariest thought, what if he was out of town when Kiddie went into labor? The Major realized Kiddie had most likely faced this same roller coaster of her own, and he felt bad it had taken him so long to call her on it. He knew Kiddie was a strong woman, stronger than she realized, but that didn't mean she should have to be strong alone. The Major finished his drink and went to bed, gently pulling his sleeping wife to him, kissing her goodnight on the top of her head. His last thought was knowing he had to do better by Kiddie and quite possibly his baby to be. Only time would tell.

Only a few days later the Major came home from work and found Kiddie in bed, curled up in a tight ball, crying into his pillow again. The Major rushed to Kiddie's side, asking her what was wrong.

"We don't have to worry any more Major, I'm not pregnant!" Kiddie said fiercely. Kiddie told the Major she started cramping early in the afternoon, the heavy bleeding not far behind. She lay with a pillow scrunched under her, trying to alleviate the pain. Kiddie was surprised her heart hurt a little, realizing now she had started to accept the possibility of a baby on the way with each passing day. There was a sense of relief, but also of sadness, now that she knew she wasn't pregnant. She could only assume this was what an early miscarriage felt like.

The Major tried to do what he could to help Kiddie feel better, hovering over her, having nothing better to do than to turn on the radio for a distraction and bring her a glass of wine for some relief. The Major shared in Kiddie's disappointment although neither of them chose to share it with the other.

Kiddie woke the next day, still bleeding, but her cramping less painful. The Major was reluctant to go to work until she finally convinced him she just needed to rest and she would be fine until he got home.

It was the end of a long week before Kiddie felt recovered, embracing that things wouldn't be changing just yet. The Major came home from work to find Kiddie dressed up and ready to go out to dinner. The Major had not seen Kiddie this energetic since Christmas, her happiness making her shine from the inside out. He cheerfully called a cab to head out to the Palais Royal for a night out on the town. The bright lights and jazzy tunes of Paul Whitman's orchestra were just what Kiddie needed and they dined and danced the whole night through, the champagne flowing freely.

Now the Major lay in bed, wishful for nights that ended more intimately than a good night kiss. He felt like they were back to dating, the heat turned on, but a low flame burning. The Major knew Kiddie had been through something both emotionally and physically and he would have to be patient, letting her make the first move. Although on a much smaller scale, the Major felt like he had been through something too. He had a meeting in the morning to talk with his boss about his schedule, wanting to follow through on his promise to Kiddie. He realized he was ready to be a father, and he worried if it would be hard for Kiddie to get pregnant when she was ready. Usually when bunnies made out like they did, there were always little bunnies sooner or later.

The Major realized he needed to put in the time to make sure Kiddie knew she was his number one priority. He was very good with the fluff stuff, but the day to day nuts and bolts were what he needed to work on to keep their relationship strong. The Major kissed Kiddie on her shoulder, smiling at her soft snoring, a sure sign of a good night. Then he rolled over, determined to go to sleep, knowing his meeting would be bright and early in the morning. He could only hope he would have good news for Kiddie soon.

It was Sunday morning and Kiddie lay in bed, waiting happily for the Major to bring her breakfast. She could smell the bacon and eggs, the thought of the Major cooking in the kitchen making her smile in anticipation. The Winter Olympics were about to wrap up and the Major had saved the papers all week so he and Kiddie could sit in bed and read them together after they ate breakfast. With the Major's job, he knew how history was being written for this year's winter games in Switzerland. The Major kept it to himself, knowing with the week Kiddie was having, the Olympics had been furthest from her mind, and at times, his too.

Kiddie pulled herself up to a sitting position as the Major came in with breakfast on a tray. "Good morning my love!" the Major greeted her, adding a kiss on the cheek.

"Major thank you for breakfast and saving the papers for me this week! Tell me, am I going to be happy for my girl Sonja Henie?" Kiddie asked, eager to focus on the Olympics and back to living her life.

She felt like she had been running a race of her own lately, the last one to finish because she couldn't seem to get anywhere. After their night out on the town, she felt like she was finally moving forward again, ready to embrace life.

After devouring her bacon and eggs with a cup of hot coffee, Kiddie read through the papers quickly as the Major handed them to her to read in chronological order. He had kept only the best parts, the parts he knew Kiddie would love to read about most. Since the Winter games of 1924, Kiddie had become a huge Sonja Henie fan and he had saved everything he could about her for Kiddie. Now sixteen, Sonja had come a long way in four years, becoming the youngest Olympic champion in her ruffled short skating dress and her white boots. She had skated to Tchaikovsky's "Swan Lake" and Kiddie could imagine how beautiful it must have been to watch her skate.

Kiddie was impressed to learn that out of twenty five nations, the United States had finished after Norway in the medal count, Sweden finishing in third place for medals. Any sporting event loves a little drama and the Major had written about Irving Jaffee being cheated from a gold medal after the thawing ice had cancelled the ten thousand metre speed skating race half way through. The big highlight for the Major had been the very close bobsleigh race, the USA2 team just beating the USA1 team, both of them bringing home medals for their efforts. Stacking all the papers neatly in a pile, the Major went to move them to the floor.

Turning to face Kiddie he told her with a big smile. "Kiddie I have some good news for both of us."

Kiddie gave the Major her full attention, looking at him expectantly. "What is it Major?" she asked.

"I had a meeting with my boss on Friday and he has agreed I don't need to travel with the Giants so much this season. I will join them later in their spring training and mostly travel for the big games. Especially with the summer olympics coming up, he wants me home to comb through all those events too. How does that sound my love?" the Major asked, beaming.

Kiddie's expression said it all, but the Major was even happier when she pulled him to her to kiss him on the lips. Her voice was husky as she looked in his eyes and said, "That sounds wonderful Major. Thank you!"

The Major kissed Kiddie back, "You're welcome Kiddie. I love you and I know it will be good for us." he said, his dark eyes glowing.

Kiddie put her finger on the Major's lips, her eyes soft. "I love you too Major." The Major pulled Kiddie into him even tighter, kissing her long and deep. He was elated when Kiddie slid back under the sheets, pulling him back down with her. It had been a while since Christmas and they took their sweet time, enjoying their Sunday morning in bed, and each other.

Kiddie and the Major sat in the back of Bernie's car, Iris beside him. The girls were chatting excitedly, ignoring that they had a five to six hour drive ahead of them, and they should pace themselves. The couples were headed to Stowe, Vermont to experience their first Winter Carnival. Bernie had brought it to their attention last week, his cousin Roland a motivating force in getting them there. Roland was becoming known as an outdoor winter enthusiast and encouraged city people to get out and enjoy the snow once in a while. Bernie had been convincing in his promise of a good time and so here they all sat in the car, headed north for the weekend. He encouraged the girls to pack warm and be practical, given the majority of their time would be spent outdoors. The girls didn't mind as their husbands graced them both with warm fur coats and they were happy to wear a pair of pants in the name of staying fashionably warm.

The first Winter Carnival had been held in 1921, created by Craig Burt to help alleviate the winter blues as well as bring some economic relief to the area. Activities for the weekend included ski-jumping, toboggan runs, skating, and even a Carnival Ball on Saturday night. Kiddie and Iris made Bernie promise prohibition would not cramp their style, but in the end they brought their own libations just in case. After spending so much time reading about the winter Olympics, Kiddie was excited to embrace winter for a change.

They arrived in Stowe just as the sun was setting, the lights of the small cozy town just starting to twinkle. Kiddie and Iris were immediately taken with the charm of the snowy rural area, making a note that lots of people were out and about despite the cold weather. Bernie had booked them rooms at the Green Mountain Inn on Main Street. During the drive he told them the Inn claimed to be haunted by horseman Boots Berry, a local hero twice over. Legend had it that the ghost of Boots liked to tap dance on the roof of the Inn when there were blizzard like conditions, having saved a little girl from the roof during a fierce snow storm. After carrying the little girl to safety, Boots had sadly slipped to his own death. The Inn's other claim to fame was that before he was president, Chester Arthur had acted in a theatrical production at the Inn.

The girls stood over their luggage now, chatting patiently while the boys checked them in. Their rooms were next to each other, sitting on the back of the Inn, the mountains rising up in the dark out their windows. The clerk at the desk let them know cheerfully that there was no snow forecasted for the weekend, so most likely Boots wouldn't be bothering anyone with his tap dancing anytime soon. They gave themselves thirty minutes to unpack and then meet in the dining room for dinner.

As the Major set down their suitcases, Kiddie went to put her arms around the Major's neck. "Thank you Major, for taking this trip with us."

The Major kissed her before answering back, "You're welcome my love. It's good for us to go new places together and we always seem to have a good time with Iris and Bernie."

"It's our first road trip for the four of us Major. I appreciate you braving the elements and the possibility things may get out of hand." Kiddie said half teasing, but half serious too.

The Major laughed as he went to stretch out on the bed. Kiddie finished unpacking, hanging their clothes on the hangers provided. Kiddie checked her watch and then joined the Major, happy to have ten minutes to snuggle up to the Major before meeting Iris and Bernie. She took in the room as she lay there, the fireplace simple yet elegant, definitely the centerpiece of the room. The bed was comfortable and plenty big enough for the two of them. The bathroom was as expected, although Kiddie did notice they had a shower head available with the tub. For an inn built in the last century, Kiddie was impressed to see this update. It wasn't long before they were walking the long hallway to the dining room to find Iris and Bernie.

They were all happy to settle into a home cooked meal, choosing tenderloin steaks with baked potatoes and salads all the way around. To Kiddie's delight, their server brought a complimentary basket of hot buttered rolls. During dinner Bernie filled them in on their agenda for tomorrow. He was telling them he had signed them up with a guide to climb Mount Mansfield, the highest peak in all of Vermont. When they got to the top, there would be ski's waiting for them to get them back down the mountain. Suddenly Bernie burst out laughing, "You should see your faces! You all look mortified, but I can't tell which part scares you more! The climbing up or the skiing down!"

They all exchanged glances of relief, as Iris took it upon herself to be the one to scold Bernie. "Bernie! That's not funny! We came here to have fun, not kill ourselves trying!"

Bernie waved his hands about dramatically. "Ok, ok, my apologies people! But I do have a treat for you. My cousin Roland has a small group of friends he's taking to the top. Even if we just climb for twenty minutes, it will be a show to watch them ski down and hit the jumps. After that we can take toboggans back down. It's an easy run even for city people like you!" Bernie assured them.

"We can rent skates, there will be ice sculptures to see, and I have arranged a sleigh ride for us late in the afternoon, as the sun sets on the snow. It will be magical, I promise!" Bernie was smiling from ear to ear, quite pleased with himself and the day ahead of them tomorrow.

"Bernie that sounds like a great day! Thank you!" Kiddie said happily.

Iris and the Major nodded their agreement.

As the server brought their bill, the Major quickly picked it up. "Please, it's the least I can do." he said.

As they walked out of the dining room, Iris turned to them expectantly. It was just after nine, plenty early for this group. "What do you want to do now? We could go get our coats and go for a walk or you could come to our room and we could play a game?"

Kiddie turned to the Major, "I'm good with whatever you want to do Major."

The Major wasn't sure which way Kiddie wanted him to go, but knowing her, she was probably happy to do either. "Let's get our coats! I could stand to work off some of my dinner." the Major said.

Within a short amount of time they were outside, bundled up and ready to see the small town. There were twinkling lights everywhere, making the snow sparkle and somehow feel cozy. It was a cold, but beautiful night as the two couples walked along the sidewalk taking it all in. Mount Mansfield towered over them all in the darkness, the dark shadow impressive and intimidating at the same time. It wasn't long before someone had thrown a snowball and the two couples took shelter from each other, the girls screaming and laughing as the boys pitched their snowballs hard and fast at each other. Finally the Major called "truce!" as he pushed Kiddie out in front of him, his arms around her waist holding her close even as he sacrificed her to Iris and Bernie.

The two couples were cold, but happy as they wandered back into the inn. There was a roaring fire in the massive stone fireplace which the girls were immediately drawn to. The boys went back to the dining room and got each of them a steaming mug of hot chocolate. The Major indulged himself and came back with a piece of pineapple upside down cake, knowing he would have to share it with Kiddie.

It was getting late and Bernie had promised a fun, busy day tomorrow. Kiddie and the Major said goodnight to Iris and Bernie, walking back to their room hand in hand. As the Major closed the door behind them, he grabbed Kiddie's hand and pulled her to him before kissing her.

"I've been wanting to do that all night Kiddie." he said in her ear. The Major noticed Kidde seemed to be glowing, even dressed so casually for the night. It was evident that she was one happy, relaxed wife and he was thankful he agreed to come, feeling fairly certain that he contributed to some of that happiness. It had been an extra long winter this year from New Year's Eve to almost the end of February and Washington's birthday wasn't the only thing the Major would be celebrating this weekend.

T he next day was frigid, but sunny, the snow calling them to come out and play. They went to the dining room to fill up on heaping

stacks of flapjacks with thick slices of bacon and hot coffee for breakfast. It wasn't long before Bernie's cousin Roland came by to see them,
shaking hands with the Major and greeting the girls with a casual wave.
He declined to join them, but said he would see them at the bottom of
Mount Mansfield before lunch. They excitedly wished him luck, looking forward to watching him and his friends come down the mountain.
He let Bernie know he had left gear for them warming by the fireplace.
Bernie dismissed their concerned looks with a laugh, letting them know
he just meant boots and ski jackets.

As they walked to the trailhead to climb Mount Mansfield, they
were surprised to see lots of people had the same idea. Bernie explained
the ski jumping was a big draw for the carnival, some of them wishing
it was them, and others just out to enjoy the snow and show. They plod-
ded along up the mountain, focused on the narrow path and trying to
keep their hard breathing to a minimum. Kiddie enjoyed working out,
but this was new to her and she could feel her body begging her to be
done. Once in a while Bernie would stop, giving them a minute to catch
their breath. After a long thirty minutes, they finally came to the spectator area. As they staked out their spot in the crowd, Bernie turned to
them with a big grin.

"Not bad for city folks! You did better than I thought you would
climbing that mountain. Roland says someday there will be a better way
to get up the mountain, but for today all they have is sheer will power."

Kiddie looked up the mountain, realizing they had only come up
maybe a quarter of the way. She understood how the steep mountain
would be a beast to climb, but knew some people thrived on a challenge
like that. As they huddled together like penguins in the cold, they were
thankful for the clunky snow boots and warm jackets Roland had left for
them. As a ripple went through the crowd, Kiddie realized someone was
coming down the mountain, seeming to fly in slow motion. They were
half way down the mountain before they hit the first jump. The crowd
held their breath as the skier leaned into it, his body almost flat against
the blue sky, then giving him a round of applause as he landed with
grace on the slope, continuing his run to the next jump. They watched

as each skier made their run to jump off the ramp, their flight a marvel to the people in the crowd, before landing with their knees slightly bent, one foot in front of the other. Kiddie had read about ski jumping during the Olympics of 1924 and even a week ago for the most recent winter olympics. She admitted it was impressive to be there watching it in person. Kiddie turned to look at the Major and could see he was equally impressed. As a sports writer, this story was writing itself as skier after skier took flight off the ramp. Kiddie grabbed his hand and squeezed it, a big smile on her face. He smiled back at her, happy to share this with her.

A couple of hours later they sat at a long table in the Green Mountain Inn dining room. They had a large group for lunch as Roland invited some of his friends to join the four of them. Kiddie felt like she was at camp, everyone sharing about their adventures over hot soup and sandwiches. They thanked Roland for finding winter gear for them to borrow, but mostly made a big deal over the skier's jumps. It felt special to have them join their table for lunch and the Major even took their picture with his Christmas camera. He told them they would be reading about themselves in the paper as he thought it would make a great story for his daily sports column. Roland was appreciative, telling the Major the only way for the sport to grow was to educate the public and find investors willing to spend money to create faster and easier ways to get up the mountains. As they finished their late lunch, Bernie reminded them their sleigh ride was only a few hours away followed by dinner and then getting dressed for the ball. For now they retired to their rooms, ready for a nap.

Kiddie stood in the mirror checking herself one more time. Her long iced blue gown looked divine on her, embellished by her strands of pearls and dark curls resting on her shoulders. As usual she added her smokey eye and Clara Bow lip as the last piece to her glamorous look. The Major looked equally as good, handsome in his suit and bow tie. They were five minutes away from meeting Iris and Bernie before heading to the Winter Carnival Ball.

The girls were thankful to put on their fur coats over their dresses, having discovered there would be sleigh rides from the various inns in the area to the ball. Kiddie and the Major snuggled in the back seat, pulling the wool blanket up over them too. The full moon shone high in the sky above them, the air cold and crisp. Kiddie loved their sleigh ride earlier in the day, a festive way to see the town, the horse's bells jingling as the sleigh moved over the snow packed roads. Now Kiddie rested her head on the Major's shoulder, anticipating the ball, a perfect ending to their perfect day. The Major kissed the top of Kiddie's head, acknowledging her happiness without either of them speaking. He was looking forward to the ball, enjoying his view, and a chance to make some memories with Kiddie.

K iddie gave an annoyed sigh as she sat at their table waiting for the Major. She and the Major were once again in Louisville for the Kentucky Derby, but the Major added a twist this year, his mother part of the plan. The Major had not shared she would be joining them until they were well on their way, knowing Kiddie would have no choice but to accept the news. She did so begrudgingly, the first to acknowledge the Major was right, she would have stayed home. Currently the Major was fetching his mother from her room, to escort her to the Dinner Dance, one of the things the Brown Hotel had become famous for. Kiddie signaled the waiter for another cocktail, delighted to see a familiar face as Damon Runyon was making his way over to her.

"Wow Kiddie!" Runyon said to her as he bent to kiss her on the cheek. "Has the Major lost his mind leaving you unattended?" he asked. As usual Kiddie was stunning in her long gown, the light blue covering her curves graciously and bringing out her dark eyes and curls.

"Close," said Kiddie. "He has gone to fetch his mother as she has joined us for the Derby this year."

"I see." Runyon said with a chuckle as he pulled out a chair to sit across from her. As the waiter sat Kiddie's drink down in front of her, Runyon signaled for him to bring another one. "I'll have whatever she's drinking."

The two of them made small talk, enjoying the music, Kiddie working not to drink her cocktail too quickly, wanting to make sure she
stayed in control of herself in front of the Major's mother. They finally
appeared, the Major greeting Runyon warmly before introducing him
to his mother.

"Thanks for keeping my best girl company for me Runyon," the
Major added after introductions, reaching over to kiss Kiddie on the
cheek, his silent apology for taking so long.

"Actually, Major, we were just about to go dance! You don't mind do
you?" Kiddie asked. She ignored Runyon's eyebrow shoot up, focused
on the Major.

The Major looked at Runyon, "He's trustworthy enough, why not."

Kiddie stood up taking Runyon by the hand to lead him to the
dance floor, the jazzy tune requiring them to pull out their best dance
moves. Kiddie moved across the dance floor, commanding the room,
Runyon doing his best to keep up.

"What's all this about Mrs. Corum? Trying to make the Major jealous?" he all but shouted to her over the music, noticing her discreetly
checking to see if the Major was watching them.

"Whatever do you mean Mr. Runyon? I'm here to dance and have
fun, aren't you?" Kiddie said with a smile.

Runyon gave her a slight nod, adding "Touche!" with it. After a couple of songs dancing the Charleston, they were both ready for a break.
Runyon made a show of kissing her hand before he clapped the Major
on the back and departed back to his own table.

K idde was thankful dinner was soon served, a distraction of a different sort to keep conversation to a minimum. Between forkfuls
of potatoes and steak, they made small talk about everything from the
weather to how the Major thought the St. Louis Cardinals season would
shape up. Kiddie feigned interest in every detail, making her comments
as needed to respectfully be part of the conversation. Being around the
Major's mother always made Kiddie uncomfortable as she believed his
mother did not care for her or their marriage. Kiddie wasn't sure how,

but she always felt like she somehow wasn't good enough for the Major. Kiddie was patient, but when *"Someone to Watch Over Me"* started to play, she turned to the Major asking him to dance with her. Kiddie didn't worry about the Major's mother being in the middle of a story, she wanted to dance, interrupting as politely as she could. The Major put his hand on Kiddie's, looking at her with a smile, but clearly hesitant to interrupt his mother.

Kiddie smiled back at him, "No worries, I'm sure there's someone else here needing a dance partner. You two carry on, by all means." She got up from the table quickly, intending to head to the bathroom, ignoring the Major's hand on her arm.

She stopped in her tracks for a split second when she heard the Major's mother say, "Bill, is she always this needy? She should be taking care of you!" The dance floor was crowded as Kiddie pushed into it, wanting to be out of the Major's line of vision. She found herself at the bar, ordering another cocktail and downing it way too quickly.

Disappointed the song was over, Kiddie put her glass down on the bar and turned to go to their room, all but colliding with the Major. Without saying anything to her, he took her firmly by the arm and led her to the dance floor. Kiddie was tempted to yank her arm from his grasp, but thought better than making a scene. As the orchestra moved into the next song, the Major kept Kiddie close to him, his grasp still firm, knowing she might try to walk away. As they swayed past their table, Kiddie noticed the Major's mother was gone.

"Major it appears your Mother is on the loose. Are you sure you don't need to go see about her?" Kiddie asked.

The Major leaned into Kiddie's ear and said, "She went to bed Kiddie. Now relax and dance with me." Kiddie looked startled for a second, before turning to look up at the Major. She was even more startled when the band finished their song only to move into *"Someone to Watch Over Me"* again. Kiddie wasn't sure how, but she assumed the Major was somehow responsible for it, and she finally settled into him, enjoying their dance.

When the song finished, the Major guided Kiddie out, clearly headed to their room. Kiddie didn't argue, letting him guide her down the long hallway to their door. Kiddie tried to make a beeline for the bathroom as the Major let her in, but he grabbed her arm and pulled her close.

"Not so fast Kiddie. You wanted my attention and now you have it." the Major said, his arm holding her close to him.

Kiddie tried to push him away, saying irritably, "Lucky for me! Is that because your mother went to bed Major?"

The Major laughed at Kiddie's suggestion, making her even madder. Releasing his hold, the Major took Kiddie's hand and led her to their bed, pulling her down to sit beside him.

"Alright Kiddie, say what's on your mind." the Major said.

"I heard what she said about me, Major. That I'm so needy. I'm so needy? She has no idea how much I take care of myself! If she had said I'm so ugly I would know she was just being mean, clearly! But to say needy! That's the thing I'm always working hard not to be!" Kiddie's face was flush, her eyes flashing at the Major with a mix of hurt and anger.

Feeling like she made her point, she let the Major say his piece. "You're right Kiddie. You are one of the most independent women I know. That wasn't fair of her to say that and I told her so, hence she left to go to bed." The Major was watching Kiddie, letting his words sink in.

He could see her visibly relax some as he continued. "Kiddie, I told my mother you're my wife and I love you, but like I told her, I will never choose between the two of you. I know you were being patient with both of us tonight and I appreciate it. She's my mother and very important to me, but you're my wife and I told her I would not have her speak rudely about you. If you hadn't gone off in a huff, you would have heard me tell her that for yourself. Are we good now? Now can I kiss you?"

The Major was running his finger down Kiddie's arm, giving her a shiver of anticipation.

Kiddie stood up, inserting herself between the Major's legs, wrapping her arms around his neck. "Yes please Major, kiss me." The Major was happy to oblige.

Kiddie was thankful it wasn't her first Derby, feeling like she knew what to expect for the day, particularly how to handle the rain the Major had promised was sure to come. Now the three of them stood under the grandstands, out of the rain, thankful for the concrete cover. They still had an hour until the bugle would signal "riders up," initiating the beginning of the race. The ladies struggled to keep up with the Major as he walked briskly through the crowd, his destination uncertain to either of them. Kiddie assumed they would be sitting in the same area as last year, but she couldn't be sure. He finally turned to them with a smile.

"Alright ladies, ready to place your bets?" The Major asked, the two women exchanging glances before Kiddie answered him.

"Major you have to tell us who is favored to win. How many horses are even running?" Kiddie asked.

The Major explained there was a record number of horses running this year, a total of twenty-two horses. Looking over the list of names such as Toro and Misstep, Kiddie didn't feel drawn to any name in particular. In the end Kiddie bet on Reigh Count to win, explaining to the Major she liked that the owner was a woman, Mrs. Fannie Hertz of Chicago. Surprising Kiddie and the Major, his mother agreed with Kiddie and decided to make the same bet.

The rain was done and their bets placed, as they headed to their seats in the grandstand. The crowd of eighty thousand horse fans was undaunted by the muddy track, although Kiddie noticed there were fewer fans in the pit area this year.

As the horses paraded to the starting gate, Kiddie watched the Major, his anticipation and excitement making her smile. Kiddie noticed the Major's mother watching him as well, her pride in her son evident. Kiddie supposed it must be hard to have her son so far from home, and she could almost understand how she would be resentful of Kiddie.

Suddenly the horses were off, the three days of rain making the dirt track a slow muddy mess. They joined the crowd in cheering on their favorite horse, clapping madly, focused on the horses as they rounded the final curve of the track. Kiddie was delighted to see Reigh Count pull ahead of Misstep in the end, seeming to win easily by three lengths. Kiddie hugged the Major, announcing to his mother their horse had won.

They followed the Major down to the winner's circle, the mud and lack of a press pass allowing them to only go so far. They watched as the jockey, Chick Lang, one of the best in the business, steadied Reigh Count to accept his garland of roses, then posed them both for a picture. Despite the weather, it had been an exciting race and Kiddie was happy to be there.

It was too early the next morning when Kiddie found herself kissing the Major good-bye. Kiddie felt a pang of jealousy as he boarded the westbound train with his mother, since the Giants continued in a series with the St. Louis Cardinals. Having a few hours to wait before boarding her eastbound train alone, she went to buy a coffee and find a quiet place to sit. She and the Major had gone to a late after derby party last night, and she could feel her hangover starting to kick in. Much to Kiddie's delight, the Major's mother declined to attend claiming she needed her beauty sleep. That had suited Kiddie just fine and she and the Major made the most of the party hosted by Mr. Matt Winn. Thanks to the Major, Kiddie knew all about the importance of Mr. Winn as it related to the Kentucky Derby. She knew he was instrumental in making the Derby the race of all races, creating an event that drew thousands of people from high society to the farmland. Kiddie loved that he had used a filly named Regret, the first filly to win the Derby, to help make a name for the horse race.

As they walked the crowd, Kiddie had been impressed with how many people greeted the Major by name, making her realize he was finally getting the recognition he deserved. She was happy to see Damon Runyon there as well, at least one friendly face in the crowd. Kiddie and the Major were both pleasantly surprised when Matt Winn came up to introduce himself, happy to meet the man who had coined the phrase "run for the roses." Kiddie could tell the Major was impressed to meet him, telling her later Mr. Winn had seen every Kentucky Derby since 1875. They drank and danced their way through until the wee hours of the morning, when the Major finally called it time for bed. They were happy to snuggle together, enjoying the few hours left before the Major would need to get ready to catch his train.

Now as Kiddie sipped her coffee and watched people move about the station, she reminded herself the Major would be home in a few days. The Giants would start a series with the Brooklyn Robins and the Major would actually be home for a couple of weeks before heading to Boston and then Philly for just a few days. Kiddie was happy to have the Major home more, his boss following through on his promise for the Major to work from his New York office whenever possible. As Kiddie heard the first call for her train, she collected her things and went to board, ready to head home.

It was the wee hours of a morning late in July as the Major sat at the bar sipping his last bourbon. There had been quite a crowd of sports writers at the Tavern tonight, all pumped up for the big fight between Gene Tunney and New Zealand boxer Tom Heeney. Some of his peers had given the Major a hard time about being so bold as to put in print a few weeks earlier, that it would be Tunney's last fight, his retirement imminent. The Major knew that Tunney should easily be able to defend his heavyweight champion title, and with a purse that would make him rich, why not take the win and retire? The Major paid his bill and headed home.

The next day was a hot afternoon as the two men prepared to square off at Yankee Stadium. The Major wondered if the nearly fifty thousand fans constituted a decent crowd or not and he assumed the majority of them were there to cheer on Tunney. He felt nervous for Tunney, but he shouldn't have worried. After a brutal eleven rounds, the fight was called to save Heeney from even more devastating injuries. Despite the New Zealander's courage to keep getting up, the refs decided Tunney's relentless blows were more than any man should continue to endure. The Major was happy to see Tunney win, and would now wait patiently for him to announce his retirement, an opportunity for the Major to look good. The Major didn't have to wait long, and was happy for Tunney, and that he had taken an opportunity to appear to be in the know.

While the Major continued to follow and report on the Giants, there were numerous annual events that required his attention now as well. Some of these established events included other horse races such as the Preakness and the Belmont Stakes. The Major was finding every sport has its own prestigious event to cover now from the Stanley Cup to the Boston Marathon to the Tour de France. For the first time in history, a tennis match had been televised just a few days ago, a game changer for sure in the world of sports. In addition, the Summer Olympics were to begin in Amsterdam in just a few days.

The world of baseball itself was changing and the Major was expected to be in the middle of it, reporting stories to draw sports fans and the sale of his newspaper, *The New York Evening Journal.* With baseball stars like Babe Ruth, Ty Cobb, and Lou Gehrig standing at home plate, there was plenty to write about outside of the Giants season. The Major had spent only the last two weeks of spring training with his team in Augusta, Georgia, but was happy to see the Giants start off their season strong, winning over the Boston Braves. The Giants were playing at home while the Summer Olympics took place, leaving the Major writing double stories.

It was busy and exciting and tiring all at the same time, but the Major could see a shift in his career, feeling like he was on the cusp of being a really big name in sports journalism. Of course, he was hardly the only one out there and that was what kept him hungry most of all. Even though he was in New York more often, there were lots of nights he was out working, schmoozing other writers, athletes, and team owners trying to insure he had the first scoop. He knew Kiddie thought he was out, just drinking with the boys, but there was a lot more to it than that. The Major knew it was finally going to be his time, and he didn't want to be in bed sleeping when it came.

K iddie woke with a start, not sure where she was. She reached for the Major, relieved to find him sleeping beside her. As she took in the dark room around her, she realized she was in the Major's childhood home. They had come home to Missouri, arriving by train just yesterday afternoon. After all these years, Kiddie finally had a chance to put faces with names and see Missouri for herself. Kiddie was happy to meet the Major's brother and his father, finding them both to be a quieter, more reserved version of the Major. The dinner conversation covered everything from sports to politics to world events. There was a lot to talk about in politics as the country had just elected republican Herbert Hoover as the new president a few weeks ago. Since he had defeated the current New York governor, a democrat, it had been big news throughout New York. Kiddie enjoyed the conversation, reminding her of Sunday dinners with her own family. The food had been delicious and the Major's mother an impeccable hostess.

Now as Kiddie lay in the dark, listening to the Major's soft snores, she felt relieved things were going better than she had anticipated. The Major had offered for her to come home with him many times, but Kiddie had always declined, feeling like his mother would not approve, needing the time with her son to herself. This time the Major had insisted Kiddie come as they would take in his alma mater's homecoming. The University of Missouri was proud to boast they had started the tradition of homecoming back in 1911 when then head coach, Chester Brewster had invited alums to come back home and root on the Tigers in their game against the Kansas Jayhawks. Kiddie and the Major would be getting an early start in the morning, making the trek from Boonville to Columbia to start their homecoming festivities.

On their way, the Major told Kiddie they had a full day ahead of them, starting with the Homecoming Parade. Alums were invited to walk in the parade, but the Major assured Kiddie he would be happy to watch with her. After the parade they would head to Booches for an early lunch. Booches was the place where the Major loved to get a burger and play pool when he attended the University of Missouri. Their afternoon would be spent at the fairly new Memorial Stadium, where they hoped to cheer on the Tigers to a victory over the Kansas Jayhawks, their biggest rival in the Big 6 Conference. The Major had reserved a room for them at the newly built Tiger Hotel, ready to embrace whatever other homecoming festivities popped up after the game.

It was a chilly, but sunny day for the last Saturday in November, as Kiddie and the Major sat in the bleachers and cheered on the Tigers to a win over the Jayhawks. The Tigers defense allowed only two field goals, while their offense put twenty-five points on the scoreboard. The Major was happy to see the win, and Kiddie enjoyed watching the football game with him, reminding her of their first fall together as they got to know each other cheering on the Columbia Lions at their football games.

After the game the Major walked Kiddie around campus, clearly proud of his alma mater. He showed her the buildings where he had taken his journalism classes, and first began to learn his craft. The sun was just starting to set as they walked to the columns, a campus landmark standing guard over Jesse Hall. The Major pulled Kiddie into the shadow of a column, pulling her to him for a long kiss. Kiddie was startled, but happy to return his kiss.

"Thank you Kiddie for coming home with me. It means a lot to me and to share all this with you today has been special. It's good for a man to remember where he started from." The Major said to Kiddie.

Kiddie was touched, but also surprised to see this sentimental side of the Major. "You're welcome Major. I'm happy to share this with you too."

"There's one more place on campus I have to see Kiddie and then we can head to our hotel." the Major said, already walking along the quadrangle, Kiddie's hand in his as he headed to the east side of campus. Kiddie was impressed by the size of the house they stood in front of, the Major seeming hesitant to go in. Finally he turned to Kiddie and explained it was his old fraternity house of Sigma Nu. While they stood there, a man walked up and slapped him on the back, clearly happy to see him.

"Is that really you Corum?" he asked. "What's a big New York sports writer like you doing here in Columbia, Missouri?"

The Major seemed taken aback for just a second, until he realized he knew the man. Before Kiddie knew it they were shaking hands and the Major was introducing him as one of his former fraternity brothers.

"Why are you two standing out here? Let's go in and let those boys show us a good time!" As they followed him in, the Major turned to Kiddie, telling her it would be just a minute and then they would head to the Tiger Hotel.

As the two men entered the large house, someone shouted, "Alumni on deck!"

Immediately they were surrounded by six to seven students, each of them introducing themselves respectfully to the Major and his friend. As the Major went to shake hands with the last boy, he asked excitedly if he was a sports writer. It appeared the Major had a fan in the house, the icing on the Major's day for sure. Kiddie laughed when the Major's friend rolled his eyes over it, asking her if this was what it was like to take him anywhere these days.

Before they knew it someone brought them cold beverages, the Major happy to have a bottle of Anheuser Busch in his hand. The boys led them out to the back of the house where they had a pig roasting down in a pit, the fire making it seem less chilly for the end of November. One of the boys pulled up chairs around the fire, inviting Kiddie to sit down and make herself comfortable. As she turned to thank him with a big smile, he tipped his hat to her with a "ma'am." The Major's eyes danced as Kiddie turned to him mortified to be called ma'am. Sitting down in the chair next to her, the Major took her hand and squeezed it.

Despite being called ma'am, Kiddie was impressed with the hospitality of the boys, the dinner delicious and the beers plentiful. Later than sooner, one of the boys was driving them to their hotel, more than happy to spend time with someone he aspired to be. Kiddie smiled as the Major told him to reach out to him at *The New York Evening Journal* when he had a degree and was looking for a job.

As the car drove off, the Major paused to admire the new hotel. He had read it was the tallest building now between Kansas City and St. Louis, strategically built close to campus. The Major pointed to the eight foot tall letters atop the hotel, commenting to Kiddie the Tiger Hotel would become a Columbia landmark in no time. Kiddie was impressed as they walked in, the velvet carpet plush and welcoming as they walked up the lobby steps to check-in. They were impressed to see the hotel had an elevator, which they were thankful for when they learned they were on the top floor. As soon as they entered their room, the Major went to look out their window. He was delighted to see their view included Jesse Hall all lit up, the moon shining down on the columns. Putting her coat on the chair, Kiddie went to stand beside the Major, enjoying the view with him.

"I'm happy you had such a good day Major and that I was here to share it with you. Thank you for insisting that I come." Kiddie said, her arms around his waist. The Major disengaged from Kiddie, pulling two bottles out of his coat pockets with a big smile.

Kiddie laughed and said, "Major you didn't! But I'll take one of those!"

They sat in bed together, drinking the last of their beer, and talking about their day. Kiddie finished her beer, putting the bottle on the nightstand beside the bed, before snuggling up to the Major.

The Major did the same before turning Kiddie to kiss her. "Well Mrs. Corum, you've seen where it all began. I consider myself a New Yorker now, but it does feel good to come home once in a while."

"It feels good to be here with you Major. I know something else that feels good." Kiddie said invitingly. The Major smiled in anticipation as Kiddie leaned over and whispered in his ear.

"You're in Missouri Kiddie, you're going to have to show me." the Major said teasingly. She was happy to do so, proud of her Missouri alum.

K iddie and the Major lay in bed having a debate. They had finished a big Sunday dinner with the family and were scheduled to catch the train back to New York City tomorrow afternoon. Tonight the Major's mother had made her first challenging comment towards the end of dinner. Kiddie had been thanking her for the delicious meal, appreciative of all the food she had gone to so much effort to cook. It had been a long time since Kiddie got to enjoy a Sunday dinner and she had enjoyed herself.

Kiddie had been caught off guard when the Major's mother said, "This is nothing compared to our Thanksgiving. It really is a shame you can't stay long enough to be here." Kiddie had glanced at the Major to see if he had heard it, but neither of them responded back.

As Kiddie and the Major were getting ready for bed later, she told the Major his mother most likely blamed her for them not staying when the truth was, it was the Major with the busy schedule. Kiddie let him know the decision was all his to make, although he seemed torn as to what to do. Kiddie knew it would be annoying to change their train tickets, but not impossible. She knew Iris was expecting her for Thanksgiving dinner, but she would have a houseful of guests either way. She could always wish her a Happy Thanksgiving by phone, just as she planned to do with her parents.

Kiddie stood in front of the Major as he sat on the bed, sharing in his quandary of what to do. She would miss seeing the Macy's parade and spending Thanksgiving with Iris, but she also knew it could be a long time before this opportunity presented itself again. Kiddie reminded the Major he turned in stories from lots of different cities, so why should this be any different. The Major was studying Kiddie, wanting to make sure she was really okay with staying. With a big sigh, the Major pulled Kiddie to him, kissing her lightly on the cheek.

"Okay Kiddie, if I can get our train tickets changed in the morning, we will stay. I feel like you should be the one to tell my mother, since really you're the reason we're staying." the Major said with a smile.

Kiddie laughed. "She would still think you had twisted my arm Major. But, I do think it's the right thing to do." Kiddie said.

"Should we go tell her now? I hate for her to have us halfway out the door, with a surprise, we're staying!" the Major asked, but Kiddie shook her head.

"I'm going to bed. You go tell her and bask in the glow." Kiddie kissed the Major on the lips and then went to pull back her covers. "I'll just read for a bit."

The Major watched as Kiddie crawled into bed, making herself cozy under the quilt. There was something about the bed that reminded

Kiddie of staying at her grandmother's and it felt more than just comfy to her. Sitting in the big bed with her book in her hands, Kiddie realized with a pang of sadness it felt like home, a place she hadn't been in a long time.

The lights on the tree glowed over the presents beneath it, the radio playing Christmas songs, the champagne and gin ready to be mixed into a holiday cocktail. The family buffet sparkled in candlelight, the glass dishes full of the usual nuts, olives, and pickles. Platters of ham, cheeses, rolls, and Christmas cookies were lined up invitingly on the dining room table. As Kiddie stood surveying the apartment for a last double check, she heard the Major's key turn in the door.

As Kiddie went to open it for him, she was surprised to see her mother standing beside him. "Mother, what on earth are you doing with the Major?!" she asked.

"Kiddie is that anyway to greet your mother? Or your husband for that matter?" she responded with a smile.

The Major was amused watching this exchange going on between the two of them. He went to kiss Kiddie on the cheek before jumping into their conversation. "She was just getting out of a cab as I walked up my love."

"Yes, I thought I would come early and help you get everything set up, but it looks like you clearly have everything under control." Kiddie's mother kissed Kiddie on the cheek and gave her a big hug with, "Merry Christmas, darling!"

Having recovered from her surprise, Kiddie hugged her mom back fiercely. "Merry Christmas Mother! It is nice you're here early. I just need to finish getting ready. Major can you. . ." Kiddie laughed as he handed each of them a cocktail, raising his own glass in a toast.

"Cheers and Merry Christmas ladies! Kiddie do you have my camera out? I want to make sure we take pictures tonight." the Major was looking around the room, finally seeing it sitting on top of the radio.

Kiddie put her arm around her mother as the Major took their picture by the tree. Kiddie suddenly remembered she needed to finish her makeup, calling to them both she would be out in a jiffy before closing the bathroom door behind her.

It was way past midnight as Kiddie and the Major climbed into bed. Their apartment was a disaster of used cups, dried food on plates, and wrapping paper, but Kiddie didn't care. Their Christmas Eve had been full of family and laughter, dancing and cocktails, a perfect night in Kiddie's eyes. She and Iris had been surprised when their father had turned the radio down to make a toast. Not one for public speaking, he kept it short and sweet, but his sentiment was enough to bring a tear to more than one eye. It warmed Kiddie's heart to see her father embrace the holiday spirit, dancing with her mother and enjoying his cocktails. Kiddie watched in amusement when Iris had cornered Freddy, asking him when he was going to give Dot the relationship she deserved. He tried to stand his ground, reminding her he would soon be gone for two years for his expedition to New Guinea. Iris dismissed it as a poor excuse, not really believing he would go. Now as Kiddie and the Major snuggled in bed, talking about the highlights of the evening, they still had the tree lit and the radio softly playing Christmas music

"It was a wonderful party my love. Did you enjoy yourself?" asked the Major, running his finger along her arm.

"I did Major. I love Christmas so much!" Kiddie said happily.

The Major turned to face Kiddie. "Not to worry. You have presents waiting for you in a few short hours and then a new year to look forward to."

"That reminds me! Have you looked under the tree Major? Your mother stowed some away in my luggage before we left at Thanksgiving. There's even a little one for me!" Kiddie sighed dramatically. "It seems fair since I have been such a good girl this year! Wouldn't you say Major?"

The Major's eyes were dancing. "Hmm, I'm not really interested in good girls, but you do what you need to do for your presents."

Kiddie felt a shiver of anticipation. "Really Major? I was hoping you were going to tell me I'm the best present any man would be lucky enough to have." Kiddie's eyes were dark as she pulled out a piece of mistletoe.

"You know the rule Major, kiss me and make it good." Kiddie said playfully.

The Major pulled Kiddie close and said, "You are the best present I could ever ask for my love. Merry Christmas Kiddie." Then he kissed her long and deep.

"Merry Christmas Major." Kiddie said before pulling him back to her and tossing her mistletoe.

CHAPTER TEN
=1929=

"TO CHEERFUL YESTERDAYS AND CONDENT TOMORROWS."
—BILL CORUM

K iddie's head was pounding as she moved gingerly to turn to her other side. She put her hand out without opening her eyes, feeling for the Major, a slight smile curving her mouth as she made contact with his back side. Their room was dark, but she could tell it was daylight out. She remembered the freezing rain falling on them as they exited their cab, welcoming in the new year until the wee hours of the morning. The Major took her out for dinner before meeting Iris and Bernie at Jack and Charlie's for drinks. As the evening went on, their group grew into a large rowdy collection of friends, Jack and Charlie both there to join them in one round of drinks after another. Jack had confirmed the rumor the Major offered that they would be moving their business by the end of the year to make room for the construction of Rockefeller Center. They would be offered a nice financial stipend for their trouble and already had their eye on a property at 21 West 52nd Street.

By the end of the night everyone agreed the new name should be 21 Club. Kiddie gave up trying to keep up with all their name changes over the years and let them know wherever they served her cocktails, she would lovingly refer to it as Jack and Charlie's. Although Puncheon had a much more exclusive clientele than The RedHead ever did, the real party had started after the club closed, a very exclusive group of fifteen to twenty friends left trying to outdrink each other. The Major of course always won, his jovial personality unphased by the strongest of drinks. When they finally brought their evening to a close, the Major had paid their tab and Iris and Bernie's too. He had given them dibs on the first cab, insisting Bernie should not be driving over the Brooklyn bridge tonight. When Kiddie and the Major finally made it home, they were happy to crawl under the covers and call it a night.

Now Kiddie forced herself to get up and go get a glass of water, but upon opening the icebox settled on a glass of milk instead. She'd had enough hangovers to know a glass of milk and a couple of Bayer aspirin would make her good as new. Of course she would need a minimum of another three to four hours of sleep to really feel better. Before getting back into bed, she peeked out the bedroom window, admiring the icy winterland before her. Checking the clock for the time, she realized the electricity was out, but she wasn't surprised. It was a perfect morning to spend in bed and Kiddie couldn't ask for a better way to start the new year. As she got back into bed, the Major rolled over and pulled her to him, his eyes still closed.

Not sure if he was asleep or not, Kiddie said softly, "Happy New Year Major."

They had finally made it out of bed around noon and were out walking the icy streets in search of burgers and fries, a sure cure for any heavy drinking. Their electricity had been restored sometime while they lay sleeping and Kiddie had been grateful for the cup of hot coffee the Major had brought to her in bed. Bundled up in her fur coat, her cheeks were rosy from the cold air, as the Major held the door open for her to go into P.J. Clarke's. Kiddie and the Major were regulars there and were greeted as such as they walked in. They knew the Clarke family well, the Major always trying to have a witty comeback for Paddy Clarke's well known line, *"Prohibition is like a bad cold; it will go away."* Kiddie had her doubts, but was happy to sit at the bar and enjoy her cheeseburger and fries, alcohol the furthest thing from her mind for now.

One of their favorite things about sitting at the bar, was that someone always had the radio on. If it wasn't music, it was a sports event and now the Major was happy to hear the Rose Bowl from Pasadena, California. Although the Major missed the first quarter, someone at the bar was happy to fill him in on what had happened so far between the Georgia Tech Yellow Jackets and the California Golden Bears. The Major had just ordered another beer when he stood up, holding his hand up to silence the bar. Everyone looked around at each other in disbelief as they listened to the announcer get fired up over the latest play.

In a fumble by the Golden Bears, Roy Riegels had recovered the ball, but carried it sixty-five yards the wrong direction, mistakenly trying to score a touchdown in the Georgia Tech end zone. The bar sat dumbfounded as the announcer shouted excitedly that Reigel's own teammate tackled him just short of a touchdown. Trying to recover, the Bears chose to punt, but the kick was blocked giving Georgia Tech a safety. The Major was all smiles, telling Kiddie it was the stuff that made sports writer's dreams come true. Kiddie felt bad for Riegels who felt so distraught he had to be talked into coming back after half time. Remarkably he regained his composure enough to block a Georgia Tech punt in the second half, but in the end Georgia Tech won the game with a final score of 8-7. Kiddie made the Major promise he would write his story, giving Riegels the grace he clearly needed. The Major promised, telling Kiddie that one play didn't compromise Riegels as a talented football player.

Kiddie hurried to the office with the Major, watching quietly as he quickly typed up his story trying to beat the clock and get it in *The New York Evening Journal's* first paper of the new year. The Major was still riding the high of such a story as they left his office, offering to take Kiddie anywhere she wanted for dinner. As usual, Kiddie deferred to the Cascades at the Biltmore Hotel, her favorite go to for any occasion. The Major readily agreed, announcing it was the perfect spot for them to welcome in a new year.

As Kiddie and the Major enjoyed their prime rib dinner, the Major surprised Kiddie with a suggestion. "Kiddie what do you think about spending some time in California with your family later in January? I know how much winter bothers you, the sunshine and palm trees might be just what you need."

Kiddie sat her fork and knife down, looking at the Major quizzically. "Are you sure about this Major? For how long? The train ride alone would take me nine to ten days going out there and back."

The Major met her gaze with a smile. "I'm going to delay going to Missouri since we were just there, so I could ride the train for the first half with you. And you could see if Iris wants to go with you. You know she's been dying to go. It's something to think about, wouldn't you say?"

Kiddie wasn't sure how to take the Major's offer. She knew last winter had been rough, but there had been extenuating circumstances. "I feel like I should spend at least ten days out there, if I'm going to spend ten days traveling. That means I would be gone for three weeks, Major."

The Major patted Kiddie's hand on the table. "And I will miss you my love, but I will be in Missouri for a week of that myself. Would you want to ask Iris to join you?"

Kiddie picked up her knife and fork, resuming eating her dinner while thinking this possibility through. "I suppose I could ask. I wonder if she would want to bring Lelo?" Even as she said it, Kiddie was doubtful Lelo would come, but it could be fun to do a sister trip. Having the five of them together in sunny L.A. while New York suffered through the wintry weather did sound lovely to Kiddie.

"Thank you Major for suggesting it. I'll call Iris tomorrow and see what she thinks. When were you thinking about going to Missouri?" The Major dismissed her question, telling her they could figure that out after she talked to Iris. Kiddie raised her glass to the Major, clinking happily with his. Kiddie had a great day with the Major, getting the new year off to a good start and for that, Kiddie was most grateful.

K iddie and Iris stood on the train platform at La Grande Station, both of them searching for Freddy's face in the crowd. They had their doubts he would be on time, but they were happy just the same to finally be off the train and in warm sunny LA for the next week. Iris wasted no time finding someone to help them with their luggage, and now she sat down on her trunk, sighing dramatically. Shedding her fur coat, Kiddie joined her, embracing the warm sunshine on her face. It was almost late January when they left New York City, the Major accompanying them as far as St. Louis. They were due back in New York City just in time for Valentine's Day. It seemed like a long time, but Kiddie had no doubt the time would fly by.

"Iris! Kiddie!" The girls turned simultaneously toward the person calling their name. Kiddie stood up first, going to greet Freddy with a big hug, Iris not far behind, both of them happy to see their big brother. Freddy maneuvered their trunk, leaving the two of them to follow him with the rest. He explained he had parked in a precarious location, hoping the city didn't have time to get a tow truck there while he collected the two of them. Iris sat in the front chatting nonstop with Freddy while Kiddie admired the palm trees and mountains from her car window. She took a deep breath, breathing out the long train trip to embrace beautiful LA.

The girls were staying at the Los Angeles Biltmore Hotel, assuming it would be the west coast equal to their own beloved New York version. The hotel was massive, a city block of concrete and glass, an opulent icon in downtown Los Angeles. Kiddie had read that the Italian genius Giovanni Battista Smeraldi designed the hotel, his most notable works before that, the Vatican and the White House. The girls were not disappointed as they walked into the hotel, taking in the feel of the Renaissance, the lobby reminiscent of a Spanish cathedral. Freddy gave the girls a minute to take in the three stories of travertine walls, the paint enhanced with twenty-four carat gold, and elaborate carvings. The girls smiled at each other as Freddy murmured in their ear, "Wait until you see the speakeasy in this place."

The girls were finally all checked in, waiting at the elevator to go to their room. Having secured their luggage with a bellhop, Freddy gave them an hour to unpack and freshen up and then he would be back for them to go and have lunch with their parents. As they heard the familiar ding of the elevator, Kiddie and Iris prepared to step on as the doors slid open. They were both more than surprised to see Gloria Swanson step out, giving a nod to the two of them as she passed them by. It was Kiddie who pushed Iris forward, both of them playing it cool, but smiling from ear to ear.

As they entered their room, they were first delighted to see their luggage already sitting there, and second to take in the glamorous room they would call home for the next week. For just half a minute Kiddie wondered if they could really afford the room, happy to be sharing the bill with Iris. Seeing the phone sitting on the small ornate table between the two beds, Kiddie hurried to call the Major. She couldn't wait to talk to him and thank him for sending her on what was sure to be a lovely trip.

It was a fast few hours later that Kiddie sat with her family having lunch in the well known Musso and Frank Grill on Hollywood Boulevard. It was a Thursday and Kiddie's whole family was enjoying the daily special of home-made chicken pot pie. While Kiddie feasted on her delicious pie, she was happy to have her family together, their conversation lively as usual. Her father was first to talk politics, looking forward to Herbert Hoover's inauguration scheduled for early March. Iris quickly changed the subject, asking Freddy excitedly what they should do first. Their mother let them know they were invited to stay two to three days with Marion Davies as guests at her beach house, giving them some time to soak up the beach in Santa Monica. Kiddie told Iris it would be the perfect way to end their trip, before heading home to New York.

As their father paid their bill, Kiddie noticed a bookstore across the street. Grabbing her mother's arm, Kiddie asked her excitedly to go book shopping with her. Kiddie's family left scholarly reading to their father, but the entire family loved to read and collect books. The bookstore was large and Kiddie embraced the smell of new leather as they walked in. There were chairs strategically placed around the perimeter of the numerous shelves, inviting patrons to read a page or two before making their purchase. Kiddie wasn't even sure where to start, and Iris laughed when Freddy led Kiddie to a section marked "cookbooks."

Kiddie was slightly amused, but hurried off with Iris to see how extensive their collection of books by F. Scott Fitzgerald was. In the end she bought *This Side of Paradise* by Fitzgerald to add to her collection, as well as *To the Lighthouse* by Virginia Woolf. She thought about getting a book for the Major, but knowing he liked to write much more than he liked to read, decided against it.

Climbing into the middle of the backseat, Kiddie asked Freddy if he could drive them around the Beverly Hills area. Kiddie had read the area was established as one of the wealthier neighborhoods in the LA area. Having grown up in Prospect Park in Brooklyn, Kiddie was quite familiar with big houses, but now she was curious to see the west coast version. Iris agreed with her, urging Freddy on, which he did with a roll of his eyes, but a smile on his face. It had been awhile since his sisters bossed him around.

The Kolle family found themselves having dinner at the dining room in their parent's hotel, eventually dropping Kiddie and Iris back at their own hotel. Kiddie was surprised her parents were still living in an apartment hotel, instead of finding a house to rent somewhere. Her mother had told her it was nice to have the freedom to not worry about cooking or cleaning, able to eat in their suite or be sociable and go to the hotel's dining room. Kiddie couldn't help but hope it was also an indicator they planned to move back to New York City at some point, able to check out at any time.

As they came into the Biltmore Lobby, Iris grabbed Kiddie's arm as she headed to the elevator. "Kiddie, we are headed to the Gold Room! We won't be needing the elevator just yet!" Kiddie paused to check her watch.

"Iris, it's much too early. Besides, we need to change. We can't go like this!" Kiddie said knowingly.

"You're right! Tomorrow we shop, but I have something that will work perfect for tonight!" The girls rode the elevator up, excited to change and perhaps to rub elbows with a famous hollywood actor.

An hour later they stood just inside the Gold Room, taking it all in. They could see there were two levels to the room, the ballroom glowing in all the lavish red and gold on display. Looking up to appreciate the ornate sparkle of the chandeliers, Kiddie drew in a sharp breath upon seeing the stunning ceiling, the honeycombed shaped plaster seemingly made out of gold. Kiddie was happy they were dressed to the nines, each of them stunning in their dresses. Iris was wearing a black dress that dipped into a V in the back, with a halter neckline that gathered into a ruched bodice accentuating her curves. Kiddie was dressed in green, her draped cowl neckline suggestively low, but still respectful, before the silk fell into a long skirt. They both wore pearls, their go to jewelry their mother instilled in them years ago.

The girls took their time, getting a lay of the room, and were grateful when a server walked up to them asking if he could get them anything. Iris quickly responded with "Two glasses of champagne please!"

He was back within minutes, bubbles rising deliciously to the top of their coupe glasses. Iris turned to Kiddie with a big smile, clinking her glass after toasting to her.

"To sisters and to mine in particular!" Iris said, making Kiddie smile. The two of them went out drinking on the town quite often, but this was different and Kiddie was happy to see Iris appreciate it too.

After walking around the room, they came across an empty table. Assuming it was free for the asking, they pulled out the ornate chairs and sat down. A lively orchestra was busy playing, yet it seemed like background music as no one seemed to be dancing. Kiddie and Iris didn't mind though, happy to sit and people watch.

"Kiddie, if anyone asks us to dance, we have to agree to say no. Unless there are two handsome fellows, and then I say, why not?!" Iris said to Kiddie with a playful smile.

Kiddie raised her eyebrow at Iris, sipping her champagne without saying anything. Long ago, after they both had wedding rings on their fingers, they made a pact to not dance with any of the handsome devils that might hit on them when out on the town in New York. They had managed to stick to their pact all this time, and Kiddie couldn't imagine tonight would need to be any different. As Iris signaled for another round of champagne, Kiddie wondered what the Major was drinking right now, and with whom. She felt pretty confident he was at The Tavern, drinking with the boys, trying to work up a new sports story. At least tonight she wouldn't be wondering and waiting for him to come home.

Many glasses of champagne later, Kiddie and Iris were struggling to get their key in the door, shushing each other to be quiet. Clearly important people stayed at the Biltmore and they did not want to be the ones waking up Miss Gloria Swanson, or anyone else for that matter. As they finally got the key to work, they both burst out laughing as soon as they closed the door. Iris was stepping out of her dress, making a beeline for her bed before Kiddie could even get to the bathroom. She thought Iris would be asleep by the time she was ready for bed, Kiddie needing her nighttime routine regardless of how many glasses of champagne she had to drink.

When she finally crawled into bed, Kiddie was surprised to hear Iris say softly, her eyes closed, "Thank you Kiddie for asking me to come to California with you. I haven't had this much fun in a long time."

Kiddie froze for a moment, not sure what to say. She was reminded of all the times Iris would be in her bed, waiting for her to come home from her date with the Major. Those nights were so far away and yet in some ways, they seemed like just yesterday.

Kiddie smiled at Iris fondly. "You're welcome Iris." Kiddie said, turning out the light and falling into her own champagne induced dreams.

K iddie and Iris sat in their chairs, enjoying the ocean view, the sunshine warm on their winter white skin. It was their last full day in sunny LA and they felt just short of guilty as their mother was somewhere deep in the big house assisting Ms. Davies in her latest cinematic endeavor. Just yesterday, on the beautiful drive out to Santa Monica, Ms. Davies had informed the girls she had accepted a screenplay from their mother. Being way too modest, their mother dismissed it as not a big deal. Surprised, the girls demanded to know if Freddy or their father knew yet. She shook her head no, whereas Ms. Davies laughed and announced they would celebrate with a nice dinner on the Veranda tonight. True to her word, Ms. Davies sent a car for the men, inviting a few others that worked with their mother and herself, to join a celebratory dinner for the evening. As the girls walked out onto the veranda for dinner, they were quite taken with the tablescape, the crystal glasses sparkling in the candlelight, the sun setting on the ocean breathtaking. Kiddie was proud of her mother as Ms. Davies raised her glass to toast her and the way she could weave words into magic.

Sometime during dinner, someone had gone out to the beach and built a bonfire. After dinner, the family was happy to migrate to the beach, Iris and Kiddie leaving their heels on the veranda. Chairs had been set up around the fire and Kiddie's family settled into them, happy to embrace the view and listen to the ocean waves crash on the shore in the darkness. It was a beautiful night and Kiddie was sad their time in LA was soon to come to a close. As if sensing her mood, her father reached for her hand and squeezed it.

"I'm so happy we've had this time together. Thank you girls for making that dreadful train ride to come see us. It's been wonderful." her father announced.

Iris quite agreed with her father, chiming in, "Yes, this was a fabulous idea the Major had! Kiddie be sure and thank him properly." Even in the darkness, Kiddie could see Iris's wicked smile. Kiddie laughed, but quite agreed with them both.

"Kiddie, it seems the Major is making quite a name for himself at the *Evening Journal*. I'm proud of you both." her father said with a smile. Seeing her surprise, he added, "I read his paper everyday Kiddie."

"Oh I have no doubt, Father. No one reads more than you do." Kiddie said.

"What your Father means Kiddie is that the Major's accomplishment is something you've done together. For that, he's proud of you both." her mother clarified.

"I'm not sure what I have to do with the Major's column." Kiddie said doubtfully.

Kiddie's parents exchanged looks before her father explained. "Kiddie, no man is successful without a good wife to support him, push him, inspire him, and love him. The Major has that success because you do that for him, therefore, his success is your success." Kiddie noticed her father was holding her mother's hand and she smiled as he bent to kiss her mother's hand.

"And Mother's success is your success too Father?" Kiddie asked.

Her father looked startled for a moment, but recovered quickly. "Touche' Kiddie. Luckily for me!" he responded.

Iris had quite enough of such serious talk and turned to punch her brother in the arm. "See Freddy, if you could give Dot the relationship she deserves, you would have already sailed to New Guinea and be back by now!" she said teasingly. Freddy rubbed his arm and turned to Iris with a smile,

"Patience Iris, patience. Someday it will make me the happiest man in the world to marry Dot." Iris was smiling broadly and reached over to clink her glass to Freddy's.

"I'll drink to that!" she said triumphantly.

Now Kiddie's father had his glass in the air. "A toast to all my children. I'm proud of each of you and I love you! Prost!" Kiddie's father said, letting his German take over.

"Prost!" they all said in unison.

It wasn't much longer before her parents were turning in and Kiddie stood up to hug and kiss them both goodnight. Freddy had gone with them, walking them back up to the house, claiming he never could keep up with the night owls his sisters were. Kiddie was thankful for the darkness, the fire starting to fizzle out. She could feel herself becoming melancholy, thinking about her father's words and the thought of going home soon.

"Iris, what do you think of what Father said? Do you agree our husbands accomplishments are also ours?" Kiddie asked.

"Kiddie you are always such a deep thinker. Of course it's true! A happy man is productive, makes things happen, takes care of his family. Just like happy women are the prettiest, shining from the inside out." Iris said matter of factly.

Kiddie laughed. "Hmmm I suppose." Kiddie said, finishing her drink.

Iris did the same before turning to Kiddie with some impatience. "Kiddie, if being Mrs. Bill Corum isn't enough for you, go get your own job! New York City is full of art galleries, big and small. You have the credentials, the smarts, the looks. It's up to you to figure out how to make it work for you. Isn't that what our husbands are doing? There's no reason why you can't do it too!" Having said her piece, Iris stood up holding her hand out to Kiddie. "Now it's time for bed Kiddie. I can't wait to settle into that cozy bed. They sure know how to live it up out here in LA."

Kiddie laughed, using Iris to pull her out of her beach chair. Together they walked up to the house, arm in arm. Kiddie looked at Iris with a big smile, surprised by what she had said, but knowing it was true.

It was their last day and Kiddie sat on the beach reflecting on last night. Kiddie was always proud of her mother, but sometimes wished she had just even half of her talent. Kiddie enjoyed modeling for Edna and Brownie, but she and Iris agreed long gone were the days of Edna painting them into magazine covers. Photography was taking over, changing the needs and the look of a magazine cover. Kiddie occasionally still got a call from Brownie, but she knew those days were numbered too. As they moved through 1929, Kiddie felt some regret for the end of an era, not just a decade. Kiddie admitted to herself a pang of jealousy as her career was fizzling out, the Major's seemed to be getting stronger and stronger. She could agree with her father, his accomplishments should feel like her accomplishments, but that didn't keep her busy during the day.

She was happy for the Major, and proud of him too, but she continued to worry how his success might affect their marriage. She knew from the outside looking in, Kiddie and the Major seemed to be all champagne and roses, but from the inside out, it was lonely, sometimes more than it was magical. Sipping on her cocktail, Kiddie supposed one couldn't have the highest highs without the lowest lows. She knew for sure it was better to have the highs and lows than a life of mediocrity. In the end it wasn't really for Kiddie to say as the Major was her true love, and she would be stuck on him always, thankful for their highs, as they outweighed the lows.

"Kiddie are you alright?" Iris demanded to know. "Whatever are you thinking about?"

In a flash, Kiddie dismissed her reverie, turning to Iris with a quick smile. "I'm wondering if it will be rude to ask for another round of drinks. Why, what are you thinking about Iris?" Kiddie tried to be flip, knowing Iris was the only one to know her better than the Major. She held Iris's gaze, daring her to push any further, knowing Iris had her own demons in the closet.

Iris returned Kiddie's smile with, "Actually Kiddie. I was wondering the same thing. Who do you think we should ask?"

K iddie was happy to be in her own bed, her head resting on the Major's shoulder, her arm across his chest. It had been late afternoon when Bernie and the Major had met the girls at the train station together, Bernie having graciously offered to get Kiddie and all her luggage home too. The Major had given Kiddie some time to unpack and settle in, running to P.J. Clarke's to get burgers and fries to bring home for dinner. Kiddie was not a fan of train food and scarfed her burger and fries down in no time. Afterwards they opened a bottle of wine and sat on the couch, listening to the radio, Kiddie sharing all about her adventures in LA.

She told the Major about hiking at Griffith Park, much easier than hiking in the snow up Mount Mansfield. She told the Major how Freddy had driven them past the La Brea Tar Pits, finding it fascinating to see the men working meticulously to dig up fossils from the ice age and put them together into a variety of animals including an occasional woolly mammoth. Kiddie and her family had walked through the Natural History Museum of Los Angeles County, admiring hundreds of exhibits celebrating more than four billion years of history.

Freddy had been quite the host driving them all over LA. They had seen the big houses in Beverly Hills, admired the Hollywoodland sign, and had lunch at the Hollywood Roosevelt Hotel where the first Academy Awards had taken place not that long ago. They had been fortunate to attend an event at the Hollywood Bowl Amphitheater, enjoying Franz Schubert's *Unfinished Symphony* while dancers performed ballet. Kiddie loved to attend musical events, but sitting outside under the stars, made it a totally different event.

Kiddie stopped suddenly, realizing she was probably rambling on and boring the Major. "Major, this must be boring for you by now!"

"Not at all my love. I'm happy you could make some great memories." the Major said sincerely.

"By the way, my family sends their love and you should know my father made a point to tell me he's proud of you and the name you're making for yourself at the paper." Kiddie shared happily. "Oh and something about having a good woman help you be the best you can be."

Kiddie noticed the Major had an odd look on his face. "Ah so kind of your father to say that. And so wise to know it takes a good woman to make a man shine. Cheers to him and to you my love." The Major raised his glass of wine to hers before finishing it.

Now as Kiddie lay listening to the Major softly snoring, she thought about the Major's reaction, seemingly just short of sadness. Maybe the Major wished he had been able to join her and Iris for the trip, although that would have made it a completely different trip. Kiddie knew the Major loved her family too, and she was grateful to have created memories that would last a lifetime. She closed her eyes, seeing the beach in Santa Monica, vaguely wondering if they would ever have enough money for a beach house of their own. Kiddie could hear Iris in her head, "it doesn't hurt to dream."

K iddie lay on the top of the covers, fully dressed, her eyes red and swollen, her nose stuffy and hard to breath through. The room was growing dark as the sun was setting on a beautiful day in late April, but Kiddie didn't even notice. The inevitable evening darkness would match the darkness in her heart as she lay trying to make sense of the news she had received a few hours ago. For once Kiddie dreaded hearing the Major's key in the door. How would she even be able to face him with this news.

Hours later the Major searched for Kiddie, calling her name as he went through the small apartment turning on lights here and there. Standing in the bedroom doorway he said Kiddie's name softly, wondering if she was asleep. He became alarmed when he heard her answer back.

"Major something awful has happened." She started to sob as he pulled her to him, asking her what happened.

"Father has cancer!" Kiddie wailed into his chest. "All the experiments with radiation for his precious x-ray have caught up to him!" Kiddie added bitterly. "Freddy called this afternoon and told me the news. He said it doesn't look good, but they're coming home to New York. There's a surgeon here who thinks he can operate and save him, but we shouldn't get our hopes up. Major, I can't bear to think of losing Father!"

The Major could feel himself becoming overcome with Kiddie's emotion, agreeing with her the thought seemed impossible to fathom. "Kiddie I'm so sorry." the Major couldn't think of anything comforting to say besides that. He held Kiddie, letting her cry into his shoulder and wishing there was more that he could do.

"When are they coming home Kiddie? Is it soon?" The Major asked gently.

Kiddie finally sat up in bed, her emotion drained, the Major's presence calming her. "They need to get their affairs in order and they will come by train. Freddy will come with them to help Father and Mother as needed. Surgery is scheduled for May 10 so they will have some time before." Kiddie didn't finish her sentence.

The Major rubbed his hand over the back of head, desperate to help Kiddie through this. "Kiddie what can I do to help? What can I get you my love?"

Kiddie could see her heartbreak reflected in the Major's eyes. She took both his hands in hers. "Major, all we can do is hope and pray for the best. We have no other choice." Kiddie said sadly.

The Major pulled Kiddie to him, telling her that's what they would do, hope and pray everyday. Talking to herself as much as to the Major, Kiddie mumbled, "Thank God Iris and I had our time with them this winter. If it wasn't for you Major, I would never have thought to go out there. Thank you for sending us."

The Major squeezed Kiddie and said over her head, "Please don't thank me Kiddie. I wish I could do more, but I knew it would be important for you to have that time together."

Kiddie pulled away from the Major, looking into his face. "What do you mean by that Major? Are you saying you sent us out there because you knew my Father was sick?" Kiddie could feel her heart beating faster in her chest, her outrage coming from deep in her stomach out her mouth.

She jumped off the bed like the Major was a snake that had just bitten her. "Why in the hell would you not tell me he was sick, Major? How did you think you should keep this to yourself? And who the hell told you?" Kiddie all but screamed the last question at the Major. Kiddie went and stood by the bedroom door, not giving him a chance to answer her questions. "Get out! Get out NOW Major!"

The Major stayed where he was, his voice steely quiet as he calmly answered her questions. He had been dreading this day since Christmas Eve when Kiddie's mother had come to see him.

"Kiddie, your mother came to see me at the office when they were home for Christmas. They wanted me to know, hoping I would send you and Iris out there while your father was still feeling well enough to enjoy your time together. I didn't tell you because I respected your Father's wishes."

Kiddie was shaking with anger. "You're my husband! You're supposed to put me first! How could you Major?"

The Major got off the bed and stood in front of Kiddie. "Kiddie this has weighed on my mind since your Mother told me, but I had to respect his wishes. If you had known when you went out there, it would have been a whole different trip. A much harder trip for all of you. Your father didn't need another caregiver, he needed time with his family, happy times. You and Iris gave him that."

Suddenly certain little images flashed before Kiddie, Freddy helping their father out of the car, escorting them up from the beach, walking down the stairs at the Hollywood Bowl, his hand always on their father's arm. Kiddie looked up at the Major incredulous.

"He knew, didn't he. Freddy knew this whole time?!" Kiddie felt like she was going to throw up.

"Kiddie he sees them almost every day and he could tell. He's actually the one who urged your Father to see a doctor. If you had known earlier, how would that have helped?" The Major was spilling it now, having stayed in touch with Freddy over the past couple of months.

"Iris and I deserved to know! We aren't children Major and we deserved to make the decision of how to handle it for ourselves!" Kiddie was all but screaming at him, tears streaming down her face. "We would have had more time with him, I need more time with him, Major!"

The Major moved closer to her, but didn't touch her just yet. "Kiddie you had a wonderful trip in February and he has been in and out of the hospital ever since. He needed time to figure out what was wrong, how he can save himself, time to focus on himself. He doesn't have the strength right now to take care of you and himself so he didn't want you to know. I'm sorry Kiddie, but I had to respect his wishes. We all did."

It was true. The Major wasn't the only one who had known about her father being ill and none of them had thought she should know. Kiddie was reminded of the pandemic, when her father had kept them all home from school, needing to focus on fighting the pandemic rather than worry about them and their safety. Kiddie looked at the Major, whispering, "Major I'm scared."

Then the Major pulled her into his arms, holding on to her tightly. "I know Kiddie, so is he. But we are going to hope and pray everyday. We're going to be strong for him and ourselves, because that's what he needs us to do."

Kiddie sobbed into the Major's shoulder, her heartbreak over-coming her anger. They stood at their bedroom door, maybe minutes, maybe an hour, the Major not even sure. Finally Kiddie asked the Major for a glass of water and some aspirin, her head pounding. The Major was more than happy to finally have something to do. He led Kiddie to the couch, hurrying to get her a glass of water and two aspirin.

Handing them to her, he said, "Kiddie you should probably eat something too. Do you want me to go get burgers? Sandwiches at the bakery?"

Kiddie finished her glass of water, feeling completely dehydrated. "A burger sounds good Major, thank you." Kiddie doubted she would be able to eat, but she knew she should try. The Major brought her a pile of magazines and covered her with the blanket from the back of the couch.

"Major, I'm not sick. I'll be fine. I promise." Kiddie said quietly.

"I'll be quick Kiddie." the Major said as he walked out the door.

While she waited for the Major to return, Kiddie went to wash her face and change into her pajamas. As she pulled her silk robe around her, she was reminded of their day shopping in Beverly Hills. Kiddie had wanted just one souvenir and bought the robe for herself and then impulsively got a matching one for the Major too. Kiddie had given the Major his for Valentine's day, telling him they could wear them on Sunday mornings, their one time during the week to lounge about. As Kiddie went to pay for them, her father suddenly appeared, paying the bill for her. She had kissed him on the cheek, thanking him, teasing him not to tell the Major his present came from him rather than her. Her father waved her off, telling her it was a collaborative effort from them both. As tears started to fill her eyes again, Kiddie brushed them away and went in search of a bottle of wine. She was going to have to find a way to deal with this news, and wine seemed as good a place to start as any.

Kiddie thought about the Major, grateful he would be there for her to lean on. She was still mad at all of them for not telling her, but when she saw her family again, there wouldn't be time to waste on useless emotion. Kiddie smiled slightly, thinking that sounded like something her father would say. As more tears started to flow, Kiddie realized no matter what happened in surgery, her father would always be a part of her. Having opened the wine, Kiddie went to get two glasses, getting a jump start on the Major. She was just taking her first sip as he walked in with the burgers and fries. As the delicious smell filled the apartment, Kiddie embraced the normalcy of it.

K iddie stood by her father's bedside watching him sleep. He had been admitted to St. Luke's as soon as they stepped off the train. It had been a long difficult ride for the three of them, Kiddie and Iris meeting them at the train station with Bernie. Kiddie had been shocked to see how much her father's appearance had changed in the three short months since their trip to LA. For the first time, she had an inkling of what her mother and brother were going through as her father's caregivers. There had been hugs all around, Iris doing her best to keep their conversations quick and lively for the sake of everyone.

Tomorrow was her father's surgery and Kiddie had shooed everyone off, needing some time with her father to herself. She didn't mind that he was sleeping, she just needed to be with him, sitting beside him holding his hand. Kiddie realized the room was growing dark as the nurse and her mother came in. The nurse reminded them softly he would need his rest for tomorrow. Kiddie was grateful her mother would stay with him through the night.

Kiddie put his hand to her cheek and then kissed it, standing up to kiss him on the cheek and whisper "I love you Father." She hugged her mother and told her the same thing.

Kiddie was proud of herself for keeping her tears under control until she was out the door. She stood for a moment regaining her composure, then looked up to see the Major standing down the hall a bit, watching her, his hat in his hand. Kiddie went to him, letting him put his arm around her and guide her out of the hospital into a cab. "Hope and pray Kiddie, hope and pray," the Major said as he kissed her hand in the back of the cab. She leaned her head on his shoulder, and said, "Yes, Major, it's all we can do now."

K iddie went to Iris's kitchen to put on another pot of coffee. She wondered how long people would keep coming to the house, the kitchen overflowing with food cooked with sympathy and love. Kiddie thought the Fairchild Chapel had been overflowing with friends and family mourning the loss of her father this afternoon, but this parade to Iris's house seemed endless. Kiddie supposed they should be grateful for the distraction, the love, but she needed a minute to herself for grieving before she could start to move forward. The Major was suddenly beside her asking what he could do to help. The Major had been keeping his eye on her, ready to help in any way he could and Kiddie had been more than grateful to lean on him.

"I'm thinking one more pot of coffee Major and we're done for the day." Kiddie said tiredly.

She went to run the water hot to wash the stack of dishes in the sink, mostly coffee cups and small plates. Feeling the Major beside her, Kiddie turned to him with a smile and said, "It's fine Major. It gives me something to do. Grab a towel if you like and you can dry. It's that long rectangular piece of fabric on the back of the chair." Kiddie teased him.

The Major smiled, flicking it at Kiddie after picking up the towel. Taking a plate from Kiddie he said, "I'll have you know I perfected my drying skills at age nine, as my Grandmother America always assigned me that duty after her big Sunday dinners."

Kiddie smiled at the Major. "There is just no end to your talents is there Major?"

Suddenly Iris came through the door, pausing in surprise to see the two of them doing dishes. "So this is where you're hiding Kiddie! I don't blame you. I took an extra long time getting Lelo down for bed, although of course Bernie could have done it."

It was Kiddie's turn to pause in surprise as Iris picked up another towel and joined the Major in drying the dishes Kiddie was piling up on him. "What? I need something to do too!"

All three of them turned as the door swung open again, this time Freddy coming through. He rubbed his eyes feigning disbelief, "Am I in the right house?" he asked lightly, teasing them all.

"You are and just in time to take a fresh stack of plates out to the table. But when those plates are gone, we're turning the lights out and locking the doors!" Kiddie said forcefully. Freddy met the Major's gaze over Kiddie's head and didn't argue.

"Works for me." was all he said, as he did as he was told.

As Freddy walked out, Kiddie's mother walked in. Without saying anything, she went to pull a chair out and sat down. Kiddie dried her hands and went to her. She could see she was exhausted.

"Mother, are you okay?" Kiddie asked, putting her hand on her shoulder.

"No Kiddie I'm not! I'm overwhelmed by all the people. I'm missing your Father, and I haven't eaten all day!" Seeing Kiddie's look of concern, her mother took her hand. "But I will be okay Kiddie. The Kolle women are strong, aren't we Major?!"

The Major put down his towel and brought Kiddie's mother a cup of fresh coffee. "Oh most definitely you are." he agreed with a smile. "Now what would you like to eat? As you can see there's a plethora of food to choose from!" He said waving his hand around the large kitchen.

"Major, can you surprise me? I don't even know what sounds good!"

Kiddie tried to step in, "I can do it Major." Seeing him wave her off, she responded with, "You will do anything to get out of doing dishes Major!"

Kiddie's mother laughed, the response she was hoping for, adding "Won't we all Kiddie, won't we all!"

It had been three weeks since Kiddie's father had passed away, the outcome of his surgery not successful. Kiddie's birthday was a few days away and the Major had promised he would be home. Kiddie originally thought she would be in California with her mother, more than eager to take care of her and help her through this difficult time. A few days after the funeral, Kiddie's mother had called a family meeting. It had been emotional for all of them, but Kiddie's mother had let them all know she would need to figure out her next chapter for herself. She had a job she loved in California and as of today, she couldn't see why she shouldn't continue with it. She loved them all, but she didn't need anyone to take care of her. Iris and Kiddie had let her go, thankful that Freddy would be there to keep an eye on her. There had been more tears to go with fierce hugs at the train station, leaving Kiddie and Iris to stand together in their sorrow.

The first night the Major had been on the road, he called Kiddie three times throughout the day. She felt like her mother, telling the Major she would be fine on her own. In the end she had been grateful when Iris showed up with food and wine for dinner. They had stuffed themselves full of their favorite comfort foods topped off with a flourless chocolate cake and lots of red wine. They sat in the robes Kiddie's father had bought, Iris having to double wrap the belt to make the Major's robe fit her. They played records and reminisced and cried and laughed together, toasting to their father more than once.

As the Major promised, he was home for Kiddie's birthday, taking her out to dinner before heading to Jack and Charlie's for drinks with friends. It was the first time Kiddie had been out since her father's passing, but she assured the Major she was ready. Kiddie followed her mother's example of moving forward and getting on with the business of living. Kiddie and the Major made the most of her birthday, moving their celebration to a private party somewhere in the wee hours of the morning. The Major would be leaving in just a few hours, taking the train to St. Louis for a series between the Cardinals and the Giants. He would follow the Giants to Cincinnati and then Pittsburgh before coming home. Knowing it would be a while until they saw each other again, Kiddie and the Major made the most of their time together, the Major happy to give his birthday girl anything she wanted.

A few days later, Kiddie hurried to unlock the door as she could hear the phone ringing. She assumed it was the Major, knowing the series with the Cardinals would end today, putting him back on a train, this one headed to Cincinnati. She finally got to the phone, answering with a breathless "Hello!" When no one answered, Kiddie almost hung up thinking she had missed the caller. Having heard her name, Kiddie put the phone back to her ear. "Hello?" she said again.

"Kiddie, it's me." the other end said. The voice was speaking softly, but she was certain it was the Major.

"Major is that you? I can hardly hear you." Kiddie said.

The Major cleared his throat, "Is this better Kiddie?" he asked.

"Major it is you! How did the Cardinals do against the Giants?" Kiddie asked. She knew the Major always came out with a win in that series, happy for either team.

"Kiddie, I'm in Boonville. My father passed away a few hours ago."

Kiddie's hand froze on the phone receiver. "What did you say, Major?"

"He was rushed to the hospital, but it's so far away, there was nothing they could do. They think he had a heart attack, but can't be sure. I got here as fast as I could. It helped I was already in Missouri." The Major was rambling, unable to stop. "I'm so sorry to bother your day Kiddie, but I wanted you to know. We don't know anything about arrangements yet."

The Major finally ran out of things to say, giving Kiddie a chance to talk.

She didn't even know where to start. "Oh Major I am so sorry! How is your mother? What can I do to help? I'll be on the next train to Missouri!" It was Kiddie's turn to ramble, wishing more than anything she could hug the Major.

"Kiddie you don't have to come. I know you've been through a lot in the last month. You don't have to come. Mother is in shock, but I guess we all are. She's strong, like you Kiddie." Kiddie could hear the quivering in the Major's voice, causing her to tear up.

"Yes, she is strong, Major. And I will be there. I'll call you back when I know details about my train. I'll be there as soon as I can. I love you Major." Kiddie said, trying to keep her emotions together.

"I love you Kiddie. And Kiddie," the Major paused. "thank you for coming."

With that he was gone.

As Kiddie put the phone down, she didn't know what to do first. She was stunned by this news. How could it be true? How could both of their father's die within four short weeks of each other. Then she was mad, so mad! Kiddie started pacing around the apartment, looking for something, anything to throw. Finally she stopped and screamed to no one in particular, "How the hell does this happen!?"

Kiddie went to the couch and picked up a pillow to throw. It didn't make her feel better so she picked up another, screaming into it until she couldn't any longer. Getting control of herself, she went to the phone to call Iris. Somehow she kept her voice calm, her emotions shut down. Kiddie was thankful Iris offered to come right away. She could help her pack and then take her to the train station when the time came. When Iris arrived, Kiddie let her hug her, but kept her emotions in check. Kiddie turned to Iris, "I need to get to Missouri now. I don't know how to do it, the Major always handles my travel arrangements, but I need to get to Missouri now."

"Kiddie I can take care of your train ticket. Go and get packed and then I'll take you to the station." Iris told her. Kiddie was grateful to let her be in charge, going to dig out her suitcase. She opened it on the bed and started taking out all the black dresses she owned. When she came to the one she had worn just a few weeks ago, she started to sob. Iris found her sitting on the floor, the dress in her lap. Iris helped Kiddie to get up, taking her by the shoulders, speaking to her like she was a child.

"Kiddie I need you to focus on packing. We need to leave for the station in thirty minutes so you need to be packed and ready to go in thirty minutes." Iris searched Kiddie's face, looking for confirmation she understood.

Kiddie smoothed back her hair, smiling weakly at Iris. "Thank you Iris. I'll be ready in thirty minutes, I promise." Looking down at the dress in her hand, her eyes started to fill with tears. "I just don't know if I can wear this dress again Iris. It's too soon. How did this happen?" Kiddie said sadly.

"You're right Kiddie. It is too soon to wear this dress again. We'll find a different one." Iris took the dress from Kiddie and hung it up at the back of the closet. She sent Kiddie to the bathroom to pack her toiletries, while she found suitable dresses for Kiddie to wear while she was in Missouri. Thanks to Iris, Kiddie was packed and ready to go in thirty minutes. Knowing how Kiddie disliked train food, Iris made Kiddie some peanut butter sandwiches and stuck them in her purse. It broke Iris's heart to put Kiddie on the train, but she knew that Kiddie needed to be with the Major as much as he needed her to be there with him. When she got home she called the number Kiddie had given her and let him know Kiddie would arrive in Boonville tomorrow night around eight. Having given him Kiddie's information, Iris paused before sharing her most heartfelt condolences with the Major. Sadly Iris hung up the phone, wishing more than anything she could give the Major a hug.

Kiddie had been on the train for a couple of hours now. As she watched the sun set, she had regained her composure, finding comfort in the rhythm of the train. It wasn't like Kiddie knew the Major's dad well and she was thankful they had gone home last fall so she had at least met him. It was the Major who Kiddie's heart was breaking for. When Kiddie lost her father, the Major had never once faltered, always strong besider her. Kiddie knew the Major loved her father, his father away from home. The Major spent a lot of time with Kiddie's family and she knew it hurt him deeply to lose him. Kiddie couldn't imagine how much he must be hurting to lose his own father on top of it, their wounds still fresh, barely a month old. Kiddie could not wait to be with the Major, although now she felt his frustration of not being able to do anything to make the situation better. More than anything Kiddie wanted the Major to lean on her and let her be strong for him, just as he had done for her.

K iddie could see the Major walking toward her train, waiting for it to stop, searching the windows for her face. Seeing him anywhere always brought a smile to her, but seeing the grimness in his face caused her to pause her relief to see him. She wanted to run to him and throw her arms around him, telling him how sorry she was, but she kept her emotions in check knowing that's what the Major needed most. The

Major bent to kiss her on the cheek, taking her luggage from her. She followed behind him to the car, wishing she could be like Iris and start a distracting lively conversation. He opened the car door for her, pausing long enough to say, "I'm glad you're here Kiddie." before closing it on her gently.

They made small talk like they were strangers, talking about the weather, how the Cardinals were doing, and finally how was her ride. Kiddie didn't know whether to be relieved or nervous when they pulled into the driveway of his family home. As the Major grabbed Kiddie's bag, his brother came out to greet her, asking if the Major needed any help. He greeted Kiddie stoically, accepting her impulsive hug and sharing his condolences with Kiddie for her own father. As Kiddie walked up the porch steps she automatically thanked him, suddenly concerned this could be a recurring theme. It hadn't occurred to her they would all know about her father, and she wanted to tell them she wasn't here for him, she was here for them.

The Major set Kiddie's luggage down at the bottom of the stairs. "I know how you hate train food Kiddie. I'm sure you must be starving." The Major was walking her to the kitchen as he said it, not really giving her a choice in the matter. They found his mother at the sink, her sister Maddie standing beside her, the two of them talking quietly. They paused their conversation upon seeing the Major with Kiddie in the doorway.

Maddie came to her immediately, giving her a hug. The Major's mother made a big show out of wiping her hands before she came to stand in front of Kiddie. Kiddie recognized her face, the same look her mother had much too recently, the exhaustion and loss evident in every line on her face. Kiddie took her hands and held them.

"I am so sorry for your loss Viva. Please let me know if there's anything I can do to help." Kiddie said it tentatively, but sincerely, not sure which way the Major's mother would go.

To her relief, his mother squeezed her hands. "Thank you Kiddie for coming. It means a lot to us all. We know that you know how much this hurts."

The Major cleared his throat, "Mother I'm sure Kiddie hasn't eaten since this morning. Do we have a plate we can fix for her?"

Her mother turned her attention to him, and then moved to get her a plate, quickly pulling a plethora of food out of the ice box. Kiddie knew it would be rude to decline to fix a plate and she turned to look at the Major, silently wishing for him to join her. "Seems to me like you could both eat," his mother announced gently, handing him his own plate.

Before long there was a group of family sitting around the table, each of them with their own plate of food, some with more piled on than others. Kiddie had been famished, Iris's peanut butter sandwich for breakfast long gone. Kiddie sat eating and listening while they took turns telling stories about the Major's father. The conversation moved along, someone always jumping in with another story, no one wanting to feel the pain of a lull in the conversation. Kiddie was most grateful when the Major stood up and carried her plate and his to the sink.

"I'm sure Kiddie's exhausted Mother, so we'll be turning in now." The Major went to kiss his mother on the cheek as Kiddie thanked her for the delicious dinner and followed him up the stairs. She was surprised to see it was already after midnight by the bedside clock. Silently they both got ready for bed, the Major crawling under the covers first. Kiddie could tell the Major didn't want to talk, but still she needed to feel his arms around her.

"Hold me Major, please." Kiddie asked softly. She could feel the Major stiffen just slightly.

"Kiddie it's late, I'm sure you're exhausted." the Major said.

Kiddie half sat up in bed. "You're right Major, I'm sure we both are. But either you're going to hold me or I'm going to hold you, your choice."

The Major didn't even look her in the face, but instead rolled over to his side and buried his head in her chest. Kiddie knew the tears were coming and she kissed him on the top of his head, her arms around him tightly. "I'm so sorry Major, I'm so sorry." She didn't know what else to say or do, but to hold him, and hold him tight.

K iddie and the Major were at the train station once again. This time he was putting her on the train headed home to New York. It had been a somber couple of days, but with the funeral done, it was time for the Major to help his mother through the aftermath of taking care of his father's affairs and her financial security. Kiddie knew all about this, having had a conversation with her own mother and siblings not that long ago. The Major promised he would be home soon, both of them grateful the Major's mother would have his brother to lean on. As the whistle made its final call, the Major took her face in his hands and pulled it close to his.

"Thank you for coming, Kiddie. I'll be home soon, I promise." Then he had kissed her lightly on the mouth, leaving her to turn and board the train. As Kiddie got to the top step, she turned to give the Major a final wave. She called out to him from the stairs, "I love you Major." Finally he smiled, calling "I love you" back to her. She blew a kiss to him before disappearing into the train completely.

As the Major left the train station, he drove to the river instead of straight home. He got out of the car and went to sit on top of a large boulder, both amazed and comforted to know it was still there after all these years. He sat looking down on the river, grateful to let himself be distracted by a barge pushing a large load downstream. The sun was setting and the pink and yellow light looked beautiful on the water. The Major thought about Kiddie, already missing her beside him, her presence giving him the strength he needed. He was grateful he and Kiddie had each other to lean on, but he worried about his mother. Actually he worried about both of their mothers, wondering what it would take for them to be okay and able to move forward. Like with anything, he knew only time would tell.

T he Major was tired. It had been a long brutal summer, a blur of mediocre sports stories, phone calls with his mother, and too many late nights at The Tavern. Kiddie had tried to get him to open up, share his pain and worries of losing his father and hers, but like a fool, he pushed her away. He was having war dreams again, back in France fighting for his life and his friends around him. He hoped if he drank enough and stayed up long enough, he would be too exhausted to have dreams at all. The Major found this the most disturbing thought of all. If a man didn't have his ambitions, his dreams, what moved him forward? The Major hated to admit it, but he was derailing his own dreams and even worse, losing Kiddie.

The smartest thing he ever did was to enroll at Columbia University after the war. His days at the University of Missouri had been carefree, but also such a time for growth. After the war, he had craved that and enrolling at Columbia had seemed like an obvious choice. He had never dreamed it would turn him into a New Yorker, let alone bring him Kiddie. The Major knew he needed to make things right with Kiddie. He hated himself for adding to her pain and wanted to take her away somewhere, just the two of them, giving them time to heal together. He needed a vacation, but it was hard in the summer with the sports world one story after another. Knowing he would not survive without Kiddie, he decided the paper would survive for a week without him. Looking into the bottom of his bourbon, the Major made a decision it was time to let go, to move on, and find his way back to Kiddie.

The Major finished his drink, paid his tab, and headed into the warm summer night, deciding to walk home. Half way home, he regretted not getting a cab, his intoxication making his walk more of a challenge than it needed to be. He was crossing the street to Morning Glory, when suddenly lights were in his face, a horn blaring, brakes screeching to an abrupt stop. The Major turned in surprise, realizing he had stepped out in front of a car.

"Watch where ya goin boozehound!" the driver yelled angrily to the Major.

The Major hurried over to the sidewalk, waving apologetically to the driver, who was long gone and probably under some influence as well. The Major was shaking as he unlocked the door and went into their apartment.

He went to the couch, sitting down heavily. He could still fill the car's grill pressed against his leg, the horn blaring in his ears, the lights blinding him.

The Major was dumbfounded as he realized he had almost been hit by a car, possibly severely injured or even killed. As the realization sank in, the Major rushed to the bathroom thinking he was going to throw up. He sat down on the bathroom floor, wishing he could, purging all the alcohol in his body, purging all the guilt in his head, purging all the sadness in his heart. The Major was a firm believer in the afterlife and now sitting there in his drunken state, he wondered which of his angels had sent the car as a wake up call. Or had an angel stopped the car and saved him, giving him a chance to save himself. The Major was overcome by it all and started to weep. It was in this state that Kiddie found him.

Seeing him on the bathroom floor, it wasn't a surprise to Kiddie the Major had come home drunk again. She could feel her anger rising up, until she realized something was wrong with the Major. She went to him, bending over him, asking him what it was. When the Major looked up at her, she realized he was crying. Feeling scared, Kiddie sat down beside him, afraid to hear his answer when she asked what was wrong.

"Kiddie I'm so sorry I've been a damn fool! I've let you down at one of the hardest times of your life and I'm sorry! I need you Kiddie, if you'll still have me?" the Major looked so heartbroken, so earnest in his apology.

Kiddie was hesitant to let go of all her anger, her annoyance, her disappointment, her hurt he had dealt her over the past couple of months, but seeing him like that, she could not turn him away.

"Major let's get you to the couch. And maybe a cup of coffee?" Kiddie said as she helped him to his feet.

The Major leaned against the vanity for balance and pulled Kiddie to him. "I mean it Kiddie. I'm done being a boozehound. I'm going to do better by you. I love you Kiddie. Do you still love me Kiddie, can you forgive me?"

Kiddie wasn't sure where this change in heart was coming from, but Kiddie was grateful. She understood why the Major was pushing her away, but it didn't make it any less painful.

"Yes Major, I forgive you. And I love you, always Major."

The Major leaned on her as they walked to the couch together. "Major, are you hurt? What happened to you?"

As the Major shared his story, a near miss so close to home, Kiddie's face became grim. She felt a mixture of relief and anger at the same time. This was what kept her awake at night, worrying something stupidly tragic would happen to the Major.

"I'm going to make you some coffee Major." Kiddie got up abruptly, not wanting him to see her anger. He was in no state to have a fair fight with her tonight, and besides they were both too tired to fight,

The Major came to stand behind her, knowing she was mad. "Kiddie, I promise that's never going to happen again. I'm going to get myself together and start being the man my father raised me to be, the man your father expects me to be." last the Major added softly, "The man you need me to be."

Kiddie stopped what she was doing and turned to the Major. "I'm holding you to that Major. I can't take it anymore. You have to let me in, let me help you through this. We need to help each other through this."

The Major pulled her to him, "I promise Kiddie, I won't let you down."

Kiddie kissed him on the cheek, turning to pick up his coffee. "Here Major. Drink this and then we have to get some sleep."

The Major chugged it down, grimacing slightly, before following Kiddie into the bedroom. He climbed into bed, asleep faster than she could plump her pillows. Kiddie lay on her side watching him sleep. She could only hope the Major remembered this in the morning, and that he would be true to his word. She leaned over to kiss him on the cheek, before pulling her covers up around her chin, ready to sleep too.

K iddie woke up to find the Major gone. He had left her a note saying he had gone to the office early so he could be home early to take her out to dinner. Kiddie wasn't sure if this was because of last night or just a plan he had this morning that would somehow fall by the wayside over the course of the day. As Kiddie threw the note down on the table, she realized the Major had written more on the back. She picked it back up to read "I love you Kiddie." A slight smile crossed her face. Maybe he did remember.

Kiddie was just coming in from a tennis match with Iris, trying to hurry as she could hear the phone ringing.

"Hello!" she said out of breath, hoping she had got to the phone in time.

"Hello Kiddie! Did I catch you at a bad time?" It was the Major.

"Oh hello Major. I just got home from my tennis match with Iris. How's your day going?" She was preparing herself for his reason he wouldn't be home early after all, lately the master at crafting reasonable excuses.

"It's fine. I wanted to see where you would like to go for dinner tonight my love." When Kiddie didn't answer back, the Major said softly, "I remember everything Kiddie and more importantly, I meant every word."

Unexpectedly Kiddie found herself choked up, unable to get her words out. She couldn't remember the last time the Major had called her his love. "Let's figure it out when you get home Major. Does that work?" she finally answered back.

"Whatever makes you happy Kiddie." and he was gone.

As Kiddie hung up the phone, she was suddenly filled with nervous excitement. What she really wanted to do was have a nice dinner at home with the Major. She grabbed her purse and went back out, hurrying down the street, making a mental list of where she would need to stop and to get what. Kiddie checked her watch, finding it was early afternoon, and giving her plenty of time to get her to-do list done. It felt good to have something to look forward to, and Kiddie pushed her cautionary voice to the back of her mind. She was going to choose to believe the Major would be home, and they would have a lovely evening together, knowing they were way overdue,

Kiddie was just lighting the last candle as the Major came in. She had the table set for two, a glass of wine poured for each of them. Her Coq au vin was simmering in the oven, but she had an olive, cheese, and bread plate ready to share. The apartment looked cozy in the candlelight, their favorite radio station on. Kiddie was dressed in one of her favorite pink dresses, not over the top, but the Major would know she had put some thought into it. She went to the door, a big smile on her face that he had made it home.

"Welcome home Major. How was your day?" Kiddie said with a kiss to his cheek.

As the Major hung up his hat, his glance swept the apartment. "I take it we're doing dinner at home tonight? It smells divine Kiddie."

He went to take his glass of wine from Kiddie she was offering him, his eyes lighting up on the cheese plate.

"I thought we could use a night at home, just the two of us Major." Kiddie said, meeting his eyes over the rim of her wine glass.

"I'll drink to that!" the Major said, clinking his glass to Kiddie's. "This cheese plate looks good. I'm starving!"

Having fixed themselves small plates and refilled their wine, Kiddie and the Major went to sit on the couch. The Major turned to Kiddie to say, "Kiddie I have a surprise for you!"

Before she could think better of it, Kiddie said, "Besides that you're actually home for dinner tonight?" Kiddie felt bad as soon as she said it, watching the Major flinch. "I'm sorry Major. I didn't mean to say that. What's your surprise?" Kiddie asked expectantly, putting her hand over his on the couch.

The Major was quiet for a minute, then picked up Kiddie's hand and kissed it. "I deserved that Kiddie. I'm sorry for all that, but I have a surprise I hope will help make up for it."

The Major went on to explain he had made reservations for them in Florida for the next week. They would be celebrating their anniversary at the Biltmore Hotel in Coral Gables, his friend Babe Ruth highly recommending it as a glamourous, romantic getaway for two. The Major planned to take a week off from work after covering a series with the

Pittsburgh Pirates. They would be catching the train at Grand Central early in the week, arriving before dinner on Wednesday evening. They would have five nights to relax and enjoy themselves before taking the train home next Monday.

Kiddie was overcome, all her grief, frustration, worry, and anger catching her off guard at that moment. She focused on her wedding ring, wanting to compose herself before she said anything.

She finally looked into the Major's face, her voice husky with emotion. "Thank you Major. That sounds like a lovely anniversary and something we definitely both need."

The Major could see all the emotion in Kiddie's face and he pulled her to him. "Kiddie I'm so sorry. We are going to get through this. I promise to do better for you and for us."

Kiddie laid her head on the Major's shoulder momentarily, wiping her tears away. Pulling back to look at him she said, "Major we have to talk this out. We can't move forward and heal, until we've grieved. You have to trust me with your feelings."

It was the Major's turn to distract while he gathered himself, refilling both of their wine glasses. He knew Kiddie was right, but he didn't even know where to start.

"I'll go first Major. Tell me how in the hell it's fair for both of us to lose our fathers at the same time?! How does that happen?!"

The Major was startled by Kiddie's question, her hurt and anger apparent.

"You're right Kiddie. I miss them both, but then that feels crazy because it's not like we saw them all the time. I think about them everyday."

Kiddie was relieved to see the Major open up. "So do I and our mothers. I feel so bad that my mother's trying to figure life out without my father. I feel like I should call her everyday and check on her, but then I know she gets annoyed I'm calling, so I feel like I need an excuse to call her. I just don't want her to feel alone though. I can't bear it!"

The Major looked at Kiddie. "Or your mother calls you so much you feel guilty you're not there taking care of her. I feel like I should be doing more for her, but I can't. And I feel guilty I'm not taking care of you either Kiddie!"

"Or yourself, Major." Kiddie said softly. Kiddie moved to lay her head back on the Major. "Major, we deserve to take care of each other and find our happiness again. We can't be responsible for their happiness, we have to let them find it again for themselves."

Kiddie sat up suddenly, looking at the Major with a funny expression. "What is it my love?" the Major asked.

"I sound like my father. He told me that the first time you went away. When you went to Montana for that fight and I was so sad. He told me that I couldn't hold you responsible for my happiness, but I had to make it for myself. Oh Major!" Kiddie started crying. "He's gone, but he's still here, with me in my head and my heart."

The Major held Kiddie, offering his handkerchief to wipe her tears. "You're Father was a wise man." Watching Kiddie open his handkerchief, he added, "It's clean, I promise."

He was trying to lighten their mood, but Kiddie could see the emotion on the Major's face, his face full of grief. "Tell me Major." Kiddie said softly, moving away from him so she could look him in the face.

The Major was trying to compose himself, full of so much emotion he needed to let go. "Kiddie I never told my father I loved him, how important he was to me. I never thanked him for all he taught me. He helped make me the man I am today, but then he was gone, just like that!"

Kiddie understood what the Major was saying. With her father they knew it was coming, they had time to prepare and say their good-byes. With the Major, it had been so abrupt, his father was already gone when he got home to him.

Kiddie's heart went out to the Major. "He knew you loved him Major. He was so proud of you. He knew you're doing what you were born to do and he understood why you're so far from home."

The Major laid his head in her lap, and cried for the first time since Kiddie had arrived in Boonville that night. She knew he wanted to be a rock for his mother and he believed that meant shutting down his own emotions. In his mind, the only way he could do that was to avoid Kiddie, staying out late and drinking too much. This conversation should have happened weeks ago, but Kiddie knew she had to wait for the Major to come to her on his own terms. She couldn't be the only one grieving.

Kiddie kissed the top of the Major's head. "I love you Major. Maybe someday we'll have our own son, and we can name him after both of our fathers." Kiddie said it, not even realizing she was going to, the idea catching her off guard as much as the Major.

The Major sat up, somewhat shocked by what Kiddie had just said. "Kiddie, I would love that very much."

Kiddie recovered quickly, moving the conversation back to safer ground. "I'm happy to go to Florida with you Major. I think this trip is just what we need."

The Major smiled at Kiddie, picking up her hand to kiss it. "I'm happy it makes you happy Kiddie. I know we need time to be together."

"And dinner. I think it's more than ready. Shall we eat Major? And then start packing!" Kiddie said, trying to find a way for them to move on.

The Major stood up with Kiddie, pulling her to him and holding her tightly in an embrace. "Yes to dinner, yes to packing, yes to our happiness Kiddie!" He kissed her on the top of her head and then he followed her to the kitchen, ready for dinner and more than ready to move forward.

Kiddie was happy to sit by the hotel's enormous pool, the magnitude of it not lost on her. They arrived yesterday to the magnificent Biltmore Hotel in Coral Gables, the sixteen story center tower calling to her like a beacon. The elegance and luxuriousness of the hotel had impressed Kiddie from the moment she and the Major stepped into the lobby. Similar to her sister hotels in New York City and Los Angeles, the hotel was an elaborate blend of travertine floors, marbled columns, ornate chandeliers, and arched hallways. Kiddie caught a glimpse of the lavish gardens surrounding the courtyards, determined she and the Major would find an afternoon to walk them.

The Major told Kiddie the hotel was only a couple of years old, and even Coral Gables itself was the fairly recent vision of George Merrick, eagerly taking advantage of Florida's land boom. Kiddie appreciated his dedication to the Mediterranean Revival Style of the buildings, easily explored and admired from one of the trolleys that ran the two miles of downtown. Merrick liked to boast that any business in Coral Gables was less than a two-block walk. The small tourist town boasted a few attractions such as the Ventian Pool, the Coral Gables Congregational Church, and the University of Miami. Kiddie had been happy to catch a glimpse of the small city's highlights during the cab ride to their hotel.

Arriving in the early evening, Kiddie and the Major took it easy their first night. They had freshened up from their travel on the train and gone to enjoy dinner in the hotel dining room. The tables sat around a large dance floor, the orchestra starting just as Kiddie and the Major were about to head to their room. They had ordered another glass of wine and stayed long enough to dance to a song or two. Kiddie had been touched when she saw the Major go to request the band to play *Someone to Watch Over Me*. She had rested her head on his shoulder, the two of them swaying around the dance floor, hopeful their week in Coral Gables would be the romantic getaway they both needed.

Now she and the Major sat by the hotel's half acre pool, surrounded by Roman statues, palm trees, and other beautiful people who had flocked to Coral Gables to take a break from the realities of life. It was a warm day, even for the end of August, the sun shining down on them. Kiddie was happy to sit and do nothing but relax by the pool, the Major in the chair beside her. She knew that was much harder for him to do and was happy to let him be the drink runner, not concerned with where or how he managed to procure them. They lazed away their afternoon before finally heading in to get dressed for dinner.

They were eating in the dining room again, but after dinner they planned to visit the Everglades Suite, the Major having it on good authority it was the hotel's speakeasy. Kiddie had brought her green dress from the Jenny Lind dress shop in Kentucky, ready to see people and be seen. Her green dress was stunning with Kiddie's dark hair and eyes, and she anticipated the Major's reaction to be worth her effort with hair and makeup.

It was only a few hours later, she and the Major stood in the Everglades Suite, enjoying their favorite cocktails and taking it all in. The room was two stories, anchored by a stone fireplace, velvet chairs and couches scattered here and there to offer private conversations or a rowdy group. Kiddie was sipping from her French 75 when her eyes lighted on someone in particular. She nudged the Major, using her eyes to direct his attention.

"Well I'll be damn!" the Major responded, meeting Kiddie's gaze with a smile. "I heard he runs this room, but you never know what's true and what's wishful thinking."

Kiddie smiled at the Major, leaning into him to say, "You do seem to always know where the action is Major."

Kiddie and the Major were even more stunned when their person of interest walked up to them. "I'm sorry to intrude, but are you not Bill Corum?" he asked respectfully.

The Major held out his hand cautiously to the man, "I am Bill Corum, good to meet you."

"I have to tell you I read your column everyday, whether I'm in New York or Chicago. Al Capone, the privilege is mine." he said, Mr. Capone's gaze sweeping over both of them.

Seeing their look of surprise, he added. "I may live in Chicago, but I like to keep up with New York too."

Kiddie smiled as the Major turned to introduce her as well. She almost blushed when Mr. Capone took her hand and kissed it. "That's a lovely dress on you Mrs. Corum. Clearly you lead a charmed life Corum." The Major nodded his head in agreement, not sure what to say. Mr. Capone raised his hand suddenly, signaling a waiter, who appeared beside them instantly.

"Please see to it their drinks are refreshed and on the house for the evening." The waiter nodded dutifully to Mr. Capone before disappearing to follow through on his request.

"What are you drinking Mrs. Corum? I'm not sure I recognize it."

"It's a French 75," Seeing his confused look Kiddie hastened to add. "It's a combination of gin, champagne, and lemon juice. The Major introduced it to me as a birthday present years ago at the RedHead." Kiddie said cooly.

"Ah the RedHead. Those were the days, were they not? Jack and Charlie know how to run a first rate business. Your drink sounds like a delicious combination, much like the two of you, I'm sure" Mr. Capone said.

Not knowing what to say to the last part, the Major merely agreed with their host. "Great chaps for sure." As the waiter appeared with a new round of cocktails, Kiddie and the Major happily switched out their drinks. Mr. Capone had magically signalled the waiter to bring him one as well.

He raised his glass to the two of them, "Cheers to you both!" before downing his drink and placing it back on the waiter's tray. Kiddie and the Major raised their glasses, watching with disappointed relief as Mr. Capone moved onto the next guest.

Kiddie and the Major enjoyed taking in all the people, the music, and the energy of the room. While Kiddie and the Major were true New Yorkers and could enjoy the nightlife with the best of them, this was a different mix of people. It had been a fun and interesting night, but they didn't want to overstay their welcome. They left hand in hand, headed to the elevators, just a little past tipsy thanks to Mr. Capone's generosity. The Major may not have paid for their drinks, but he had made their waiter's night with a generous tip.

Having made it to their room, the Major quickly undressed and climbed into bed, giving Kiddie the bathroom to do her nighttime routine. She was in bed in no time, joining the Major under the covers.

They lay in bed on their sides facing each other. "So Mrs Corum, how does it feel to meet a mobster and have him buy you drinks no less?!" the Major asked, an amused look on his face.

Kiddie laughed. "It was quite intriguing actually. Clearly he thought I was the champagne. Major did you ever think you would have a fan like that? No reason why not, anyone who reads the paper finds their way to your column sooner or later." Kiddie said proudly.

"So kind of you my love. You most definitely are the champagne and we both know it was you in that green dress that caught his attention. My column was just his way into our conversation." the Major said, giving Kiddie the credit for the exchange.

"I didn't tell you earlier, but a mobster was shot and killed there in the spring. I guess I didn't really believe it was Capone's room until I saw him there tonight." the Major said.

Kiddie's eyes were wide. "What?! Major what if something like happened tonight? Was it safe to even be there?" Kiddie asked.

"I would protect you my love, I promise." the Major said drowsily, pulling Kiddie into his arms and kissing the top of her head. They were asleep in no time, their mobster cocktails getting the best of them both.

K iddie and the Major stepped out of the Biltmore's private gondola, Kiddie grateful to be off the long narrow piece of hollowed out wood with a paddle. Kiddie didn't care if the gondolas were imported from Italy or not, they seemed precarious at times, ready to dump them into the water without hesitation. As soon as Kiddie saw Tahiti Beach, the Biltmore's private sandy playground, all was forgotten. It was magical, tall palm trees welcoming them, thatched tiki huts offering privacy as you enjoyed the sand and sun. It was late afternoon and the beach was busy with tourists, sunbathing and embracing the good life. As Kiddie and the Major walked to explore the beach and find their reserved tiki hut, they stopped on the outskirts of a small group, enjoying a musical dance number from Tahitian natives. Kiddie was delighted they hadn't missed them and joined the crowd in their enthusiastic applause when they finished their routine.

Before long Kiddie and the Major were directed to their hut, reserved until the wee hours of the morning, having been promised that's how long the well known Jay Garber Orchestra would be playing for dancing in the moonlight later tonight. They brought with them a picnic basket deluxe, full of seafood, cheeses, olives, fruit, and fresh breads to snack on. The deluxe guaranteed a bottle of champagne for two, although Kiddie was delighted to find two bottles stashed discreetly under all the food. The Major had been watching her as she went through the basket and laughed to see her enthusiasm for what she found. Looking around, Kiddie handed the Major a bottle to open, pulling out the two coupe glasses expectantly.

Kiddie was soon stretched on her towel, enjoying her champagne from one hand, the other hand resting on her stomach, her eyes closed, her face relaxed and happy. The Major himself assumed a similar position, although he was discreetly admiring Kiddie's lean curvy body in her sunbathing suit. He appreciated how the suits seemed to show a little more leg every year, grateful to whatever fashion designer was willing to take that on. It felt good to lay beside Kiddie and soak up the sunshine, symbolic of the happiness they were here to enjoy as well.

"Major," Kiddie said lazily. "Thank you for bringing us here. It's been so good to be here with you."

The Major smiled, although Kiddie had to hear it in his voice, too lazy to open her eyes when he answered back with a simple, "You're welcome my love."

K iddie and the Major sat close in the cab, their first step before catching the ferry to enjoy a day on Miami Beach. The Major's friend, Runyon had highly recommended they make the trip over, and to particularly find Joe's Restaurant to eat at. The Major explained to Kiddie that Runyon was friends with the family who owned the restaurant, particularly Jesse, apparently the star of the family who didn't seem to know a stranger. Arriving early in the afternoon, Kiddie and the Major made Joe's their first stop, planning to walk to the beach after they ate.

The Major did not hesitate to drop Runyon's name and Jesse had been more than happy to make a fuss over the two of them, giving them one of the coveted tables on the front porch, the view breathtaking. Kiddie and the Major indulged themselves on delicious chilled and cracked stone crabs served with hash brown potatoes, cole slaw, and mayonnaise. Jesse had tried to give them lunch on the house, but the Major always paid his tab, appreciative of good service and good food, and promising to give Runyon Jesse's regards. The Major was a charmer himself and Jessie's mother Jennie had packed them a picnic basket for later, full of fish sandwiches, fresh fruit, olives, and even two slices of something called key lime pie.

The Major carried their basket as he and Kiddie strolled down Biscayne street. The ocean looked different here, the nearby everglades offering a different kind of aquatic adventure. Kiddie and the Major were in search of one of the bathing casinos, in particularly the Roman Pools and Casino. It turned out Miami beach was a hubbub of activity, lounging on the beach seemingly on fewer people's minds. The pool was long and narrow, anchored on the ocean end by a very large windmill of some sort. Kiddie and the Major took it all in, walking along the strip of activity before heading to the beach, ready for a little less hustle and bustle. They found an umbrella to lay under, spreading their towels out close to each other. Kiddie wasn't surprised when the Major pulled out the pie from their gifted picnic basket.

"Kiddie you need to try this key lime pie. It's quite good. Tart and sweet at the same time," the Major said appreciatively.

Kiddie smiled at the Major, leaning over for a bite of his before committing to the effort of getting her own piece. "Oh you're right Major. That's good, but feel free to help yourself to mine too."

It was the Major's turn to smile as he handed Kiddie another bite of his pie, having learned that meant Kiddie would need her own bite every so often.

Kiddie and the Major spent the afternoon enjoying the ocean views, relaxing while they people watched, and being lazy together. They had taken in the beautiful sunset while enjoying the food Miss Jennie had packed for them just hours ago. As darkness descended, Kiddie and the Major sat snuggled together on one towel. Kiddie's head resting on the Major's shoulder, happy and reluctant to leave this place ever. Tomorrow was their last day and their anniversary. The Major told her he had it all planned out, leaving Kiddie to just enjoy their day. Kiddie was good with that, ready to embrace whatever the Major had in mind.

Hearing Kiddie's sigh, the Major asked, "Shall we pack it up, my love? We can walk back to Joe's and return the picnic basket before we catch the ferry."

"I suppose it is time to go." Kiddie agreed, standing up to start packing up their things.

Kiddie and the Major were greeted warmly as they reentered Joe's, a large rowdy crowd already on hand. They thanked the family profusely before being on their way and finally back in Coral Gables. As they entered their hotel, they had to agree it already felt like their home away from home.

I t was early evening and Kiddie was finishing up her makeup in the bathroom. She had taken her time in the hot shower, one of her favorite perks of the luxurious hotels they stayed in these days. The Major had mysteriously been gone this afternoon, making arrangements for their anniversary. It had been a lovely day, Kiddie sacrificing a few hours out of their day for the Major to play some golf. She didn't mind following him around as he hit balls both far and near and she was eventually rewarded with a cool refreshing beverage in the club house. They had walked back to their room, the Major telling Kiddie to take her time getting ready. As she finished her Clara Bow lip, she could hear low voices talking. She waited by the door, waiting for them to cease before opening the door.

As she came out, making an entrance, the Major literally stopped in his tracks. "Kiddie my love, you look gorgeous." He came and pulled her to him, kissing her firmly. Kiddie smiled as he said in her ear, "You know what that dress does to me."

Kiddie was wearing the same dress she wore on her birthday so many years ago, the night she made her commitment to the Major. She looked up into the Major's face and said, "I'm counting on it Major."

The Major admired how Kiddie filled the dress out in all the right places, even more so now. She had been just a girl the first time she had worn it for him, turning twenty and taking her destiny into her own hands. She had been gorgeous then too, but now she was all grown up, and all his for the evening.

Kiddie followed the sound of music, wandering out to their balcony, happy to find a small table for two set up for dinner. A single candle was lit, their dinner sitting under silver covers, coupe glasses of champagne already poured, the bubbles welcoming her cheerfully. The sun was just setting, adding a pink glow to their beautiful surroundings, the smell of jasmine coming up from the garden below them. The Major went to pull Kiddie's chair out for her before pulling the lids off their hot plates of steak and potatoes, a basket of bread between them. Kiddie realized it was the same dinner they had served to their guests on their wedding night.

"Major this looks so lovely! Thank you!" Kiddie said, touched he had gone to so much effort.

"You're welcome my love. Happy anniversary." the Major said, picking up his coupe. Kiddie joined him, happy to toast their seventh anniversary.

As they enjoyed their dinner, they happily shared memories of past anniversaries, starting with their honeymoon to Bermuda. It seemed so long ago in some ways, in other ways like just yesterday. Kiddie remembered the time the Major had come home on the train to surprise her, finding her on the couch, asleep and unaware. The Major reminded her of their trip to Philadelphia, one of his favorites as he had squeezed in some personal time before a series between the Phillies and the Brooklyn Robins. Of course Kiddie loved their most recent trip to Catalina Island. Baseball had always dictated what their anniversary looked like, and yet the Major always found ways to make it seem special every year.

After stuffing themselves with their delicious dinner, Kiddie asked the Major if they could go for a walk in the gardens. She knew they would be leaving in the morning and it was the one thing they hadn't done yet. The Major was happy to oblige, giving Kiddie his arm as they walked around the lush tropical plants, the sound of water from the decorative fountains, comforting like the waves on the beach.

"Kiddie, did you know this hotel has already survived a hurricane and declaring bankruptcy?" the Major asked.

"That seems like a lot for how short a time the Biltmore has been here. And don't forget the mob shooting!" Kiddie said, whispering the last part. The Major laughed and nodded.

"Touche. I thought all that made this even more the perfect place for our anniversary Kiddie." The Major had stopped her under a palm tree, turning her to face him.

"We do love the Biltmore hotels and this certainly has been the perfect place for our anniversary. Are you trying to say something Major?" Kiddie asked, looking into his face.

"This hotel reminds me of us Kiddie. It's had some serious ups and downs, but here it is, strong and beautiful, offering opportunities for people to enjoy life, to pursue their happiness."

Kiddie was touched by the Major's sentimental metaphor. "You're right Major. Our love is strong and beautiful and we do have lots of opportunities for happiness ahead of us." Kiddie said, reaching up to kiss him. The Major took Kiddie's hand, walking at a less leisurely pace as they headed back to their room.

They returned to find their dinner cleaned up, a fresh bottle of champagne waiting for them in a silver ice bucket by the bed, the radio still playing music softly. Kiddie pulled the Major out onto the balcony with her. The night was cooling off, a slight breeze ruffling Kiddie's curls, a full moon shining down on them. Kiddie pulled the Major to her, shivering from the breeze as well as the anticipation of what was sure to come. Given all they had been through, it had been months since Kiddie and the Major had been intimate and now Kiddie felt a nervous excitement just like she had all those years ago when she wore this dress for the first time.

She looked up into the Major's face expectantly. He kissed her long and deep, putting every inch of Kiddie on high alert. The Major pulled away, looking at Kiddie and taking her all in, under the moonlight. He took his finger and ran it down her V-neckline, pausing deliberately in his favorite place.

"Kiddie you are so beautiful." said softly.

Kiddie led the Major inside, to stand beside their bed, the moonlight following them. The Major pulled Kiddie's dress off her shoulders to bestow kisses on her skin before eventually finding his way back to her mouth. His eyes were glowing and Kiddie's anticipation was mounting. She needed and wanted what was to come. As if reading her mind, the Major unzipped her dress, letting it fall to the floor before he picked her up and carried her to the bed. Climbing under the covers with her, he found her lips in the dark, his own anticipation mounting. Letting go of all the hurt, Kiddie still deeply loved the Major and she was happy to show him just how much.

Kiddie and the Major sat snuggled in bed, a small candle lit, their champagne open, their coupe glasses half full. The Major's arm was around Kiddie, the two of them basking in the glow that was theirs. Kiddie gently clinked her glass to the Major's.

"Cheers to many more years, Major." Kiddie said, both of them finishing their champagne.

"Cheers to many more, my love." the Major echoing her sentiment.

Spying her dress on the floor, Kiddie turned to face the Major. "Do you remember what you told me the first night I wore that dress, Major?"

"Yes Kiddie, I do. I told you, you would be stuck with me forever. After that night I had to make you mine for the world to know and we took our vows for better or worse. I still mean all of it, my love. Do you still love me Kiddie?" the Major asked. His eyes were glowing again in the candlelight.

Kiddie's voice was husky with emotion. "I do, Major. I can't imagine being anywhere but to be stuck with you. Whatever is to be our for better or worse, I will always love you. Happy anniversary, Major." Kiddie said, sliding back down into the bed, taking the Major with her.

Pulling the covers up over them, the Major paused just long enough to say in her ear, "Happy anniversary my love, happy anniversary."

Dear Reader,

Thank you for finding your way here and for reading Kiddie & the Major. I'm hopeful you became attached to them and feel like you know them well. Now that you've read the story, there are a few things you might want to know. First, Kiddie & the Major were real people and my paternal grandparents. Because my parents divorced when I was young, I grew up knowing nothing of this side of my family. Both Kiddie and the Major died in the fifties, before I was born. Their only son, my father, also died before I had a chance to know him. This leaves a small hole in your heart, that you don't even realize existed until it begins to be filled with facts, letters, pictures, and stories about your people.

Somewhere in adulthood, my sister found a book written by Bill Corum, his autobiography titled "Off and Running." This began our journey of getting to know the other side of our family tree. Through reading his book I learned Bill, who's boss really did rename him, was a celebrated and beloved sportswriter who lived in New York City. He became friends with sports legends like Babe Ruth, Jack Dempsey, and Lou Gehrig, all of whom sent congratulatory telegrams when Kiddie and the Major finally became parents. Although he wasn't at the Derby in 1925, he coined the phrase "Run for the Roses," and later served as President of the Kentucky Derby from 1950 until his death in 1958. He served in World War I and became the youngest Major ever, hence his nickname the Major. After the war, he attended Columbia University where he met and eventually married one Miss Elaine Kolle, or Kiddie as she was called. This Columbia art student would become my grandmother and my namesake years later.

Around this same time, second cousins reached out to us, wanting to share information and reestablish family ties. Their grandmother Iris, was Kiddie's sister, and as you have read, an important part of Kiddie and the Major's story. My sister and I are grateful to them for sharing what they know. We learned Kiddie's father was a celebrated pioneer in medicine and instrumental in creating the X-ray. Kiddie's mother was a celebrated author, her first successful title, *The Blue Lawn* published in 1910. She really did work with Marion Davies and did have her writing put into production more than once. Kiddie's grandfather was the one to build Grand Prospect Hall in Brooklyn and where Iris had her wedding. We know that Kiddie and Iris were both models for magazine covers and Kiddie really did pose for Arthur William Brown, always happy to sign her work after saving it. We know the Major was very social, listing his favorite bartenders in his book. We assume Kiddie and Iris and Bernie were often out on the town as well, rubbing elbows with the best of them, making up their own rules as they went. Sadly, Kiddie and the Major's fathers really did die a month apart in 1929, a hard chapter to write as Joe and I lost our fathers a day apart.

Because no one is around to clarify much of anything, I've written this story through countless hours of research. I researched Kiddie and the Major, their families, New York City, the 1920's, speakeasies, Brooklyn, sports legends, you name it. I did this because I want this book to be as authentic to their life as possible. My cousin Glenn and I have learned, it's endless what you can find on the internet.

Through Google I found the actual 1920 football schedule of Columbia University, which I used to create Kiddie and the Major's first date. When I came across the cover of the Ziegfeld Follies show, I used it to create pure fiction of that night the Major tells Kiddie he loves her. I found more than one wedding announcement for Kiddie and the Major, who celebrated their small wedding at the Biltmore Hotel, truly a surprise to their family and friends. I know they honeymooned in Bermuda, yet what they wore and how it all took place, was left to my imagination. Through Ancestry.com my aunt found the actual manifest of the ship they sailed on to Bermuda for their honeymoon. Their honeymoon is mostly fiction, but from reading the Major's book, I know that Kiddie somehow truly did suffer a serious bike accident.

While I have tried to incorporate as much fact into this story as possible, the truth is, most of it is fiction. I don't know where, when, how Kiddie and the Major met, except that they were students on the Columbia campus at the same time. I assume they dated for almost two years before tying the knot in 1922, and yet I've totally fabricated how this took place. I know who their family members were, and I've tried to weave a web of relationships to tell their story. Their relationships aren't based on any truths I know, but more on my own personal experiences and of what I want the truth to be. I realize it may seem I'm wearing rose colored glasses at times, but like me, I like to believe their coupe glasses to be half full, rather than half empty.

When I think of Kiddie and the Major, it seems odd that these two are my grandparents. In the beginning, I felt I had nothing to show of being related to them. I've discovered their story, at its best, is a legacy to know and celebrate. At its worst, it seems often lonely, for Kiddie in particular, as they worked to make sense of all that the 1920's offered to busy, young, prominent socialites. Realizing I come from a family of writers, I decided my ownership to their legacy lay in writing their story in hopes to share it with you. I printed pictures of Kiddie and the Major, and kept them under my laptop when I would write. On nights when I was unable to sleep, I would call to their spirits to inspire me to know what to write next, although that probably sounds corny. While I've used as many truths as I could find, it is still after all, just a story, a delicate weave of historical facts and pure fiction.

Please know it's not my wish to tarnish their memories, to gossip, or to trample on their relationships and the love they had for each other. For sure this is a love story, the love between a man and a woman, a man and his craft, a love for family, and even a love for New York City. Indeed it's only a fraction of their thirty year marriage, the twenties taking four hundred pages to tell. I already know where I want to start the next part of their story, as I am nowhere near ready to leave them yet. I hope you find I've written a story that will make you smile, celebrate love and romance, and encourage your own pursuit of happiness. I hope you enjoyed my story, my first novel, my long and winding ode to my grandparents. I hope you enjoyed reading Kiddie & the Major.